*To Kay —*
*I hope you like it —*
*Jane Parault*

# Drinkers of the Wind
## An Afghan Odyssey

Jane Parault

PublishAmerica
Baltimore

First printing

ISBN: 1-4137-6081-3
PUBLISHED BY PUBLISHAMERICA, LLLP
www.publishamerica.com
Baltimore

Printed in the United States of America

*To Jim Parault*
*Whose spirit would not let me stop*

# Acknowledgments

Loving thanks to my daughters:

SUE WEBB, who worked so hard to make sure this project was completed,

MELINDA McKAY, my computer assistant and critic,

BARBIE McCONNELL, my first reader and critic.

And a special thanks to Bob Webb.

# Table of Contents

# I. Land of the Afghans

She was dressed in black: black pants, shirt, tunic, boots, black scarf covering her head. Her face was accented by emerald green eyes. Except for the horse, a pale Arabian, she blended well into the deepening dusk of the Khyber. She had made it into Afghanistan, and she could smell its danger, feel it seeping into her bones, this land of warlords and bandits, ancient conquerors, and wild horsemen. Andrea McAlister rode cautiously as the jagged black curtain of the Hindu Kush came down upon her. It had been an easy journey from Islamabad to Peshawar in the Toyota. Waiting for her just outside that city was the beautiful Arabian she decided to call Buttercup. At the border, Patrick had worked his magic; no trouble getting past the guards, but that was the least of her concerns. Andrea knew her American currency, though well hidden, would not be safe from a bandit or a desperate *mujahidin*. Kidnaping, rape, murder were all scary possibilities. Mohammad, the escort provided by Patrick to take her to Lal Pur, soon abandoned her with a parting *"Natars, Allahu Akbar!"* (don't worry, God is great!) She was left alone on the Khyber Pass.

Pushing all uncertainties out of her mind, she concentrated on guiding Buttercup to Kabul. *Follow Patrick's plan.* Confident she was making good progress, Andrea suddenly heard a sound that sent a quick chill of fear through her body, a faint rhythmic clip-clop of horses coming her way. Too late, she realized how foolish it was for her to have proceeded alone, and concealed herself behind some rocks, waiting, gun drawn. Patrick's loud boast echoed in her head, "Andrea's ready for anything; oh she's a wee lass now, but just wait till she's grown–she'll get the best of any bugger who tests her!" The sound of the pounding hoofs became louder, louder, and in the

9

darkness, Andrea could just make out the forms on those horses-soldiers! Guns shouldered, heads turbaned. For one paralyzing moment, Andrea felt the thunder of Alexander storming his way through the Hindu Kush passes to conquer all within his reach. She shook herself out of such an imagining and waited.

It took about fifteen minutes for them to pass her–thank God they didn't stop; the wait seemed forever. The black, icy night held a threat like no other she had ever encountered; the gun would have been useless. She waited a while to be sure there were no stragglers bringing up the rear, then continued, knowing this was the point of no return. If she survived the Afghan night, she could hide in one of the designated safe houses during the day. But she was determined to reach Kabul and Laura tonight. Those soldiers must have been Taliban, she thought, and again, a chilly fear crept through her; the threat now seemed real, and imminent. *Oh, Laura, why in hell did you come to this place?... It all seemed logical at the time...in the summer...*

Summer 2001–In a rare effort to connect with her mother, Andrea was staying in New York while Wenonah's paintings were being shown at a small gallery. At the exhibit, she stood behind a tall, attractive young woman intently studying a painting of a young Apache girl with her pony. The woman turned abruptly and the two almost collided. "Oh, excuse me, I didn't mean to..."

"Don't worry about it," said Andrea.

The stranger flashed a friendly smile. "Don't you just love this painting? I'm thinking of buying it if it's not too expensive."

"None of my mother's paintings are expensive enough, actually. You'd be getting a good deal." The voice had a silky, sultry quality with a trace of Country Western twang.

."Your mother's the artist? You must be very proud of her."

After a moment's hesitation, she replied, "Well, of course."

Laura Martin looked at the pretty young girl who stood before her. She was a Rubens painting come to life, though slim, with a halo-like luminescence that radiated from green eyes and strawberry blonde hair. As she spoke about her mother, an impish smile lightened the serious demeanor. According to the brochure Laura picked up as she entered the gallery, the artist was a Chiricahua Apache who lived and worked in Arizona, and the photograph on the handout showed a handsome woman with the classic features of the Indian. Fascinated by the improbable racial mix, Laura felt a strong need to know this brusque young woman who seemed uncomfortable in the role of her mother's assistant. It was one of those moments when you know something important is happening, a connection you cannot let pass by–a friendship, a true love, perhaps a story for Laura the actress. Andrea, feeling bound by her mother's request that she respond with courtesy to questions or comments, introduced herself. "I'm Andrea McAlister," and delivered her rehearsed speech about the paintings, the artist, and Apache culture.

It's a start, thought Laura, as she paid for the painting. Checking her watch, she saw it was 12:30. "Have lunch with me, Andrea McAlister!"

Andrea surprised herself when she agreed. There was something special about Laura; a genuine warmth and empathy flowed from this woman.

The pair left the pristine little gallery; out in the mad din of Manhattan's streets, Laura flagged down a taxi and their wild Middle Eastern driver sped away with sudden jerks, blaring horns, and near collisions. It was a miracle they reached the restaurant without an accident, thought Andrea–New York, what a crazy place!

The main entrance to Angelina's was blocked by construction repair.

"We'll go into the bar," said a somewhat exasperated Laura, familiar with the ongoing repairs. The bar décor featured an Italian flag, scenes of Ireland, and an array of bizarre cookie jars for sale. Andrea and Laura made their smoky way past the paunchy middle-aged regulars and a few bejeweled women ,and entered the smoke-free dining room. Laura dismissed the inauspicious beginning.

"Don't worry, it's a weird place, but the food is great and it's cheap."

She was right–Andrea's seared, lightly seasoned tuna steak was delicious and she ate every bit as Laura joked about the restaurant. "Owner John Fitzgerald, chef Angelina Fiori. Just another little oddity in the big city."

Andrea laughed. "Does anybody buy those cookie jars?"

"Angelina's mother makes them; I understand they actually do sell them!"

Laura talked about her life in New York as an actress, recounting sad and humorous stories of the theater, and the pathos behind celebrity life of the famous. As soon as she mentioned her husband John, a U.N. relief coordinator, it was plain to see this was a well loved woman. "You'll love him, everybody does! At the moment, we're waiting to find out if he's going to be sent to Africa; he wants to help the world." She laughed. "I just want him to help me. I'd rather not go overseas just now…because, well, that's a story for later."

Andrea was put at ease by Laura's warm, unassuming manner and her easy confidences. Seduced by the prospect of real friendship, she was drawn to this woman whose words flowed effortlessly about her husband, friends, parents, her first important acting role. Andrea was speechless at this stream of information, overwhelmed by an irresistible yearning to belong to Laura's world. What a relief it would be to tell the whole truth about her life instead of hiding secrets that should not belong to her. But trust was a dangerous concession she rarely granted; certainly not to this woman she had just met. So Andrea responded by entertaining her companion with a sitcom version of life on the ranch, painting flamboyant pictures complete with a cast of larger-than-life characters.

In the midst of her laughter at the wild stories, Laura asked, "What does your father do?"

Andrea gave a curt reply, "He's a doctor, teaching in Pakistan."

Yes, there is a story, thought Laura; let it go for now.

"What do you think of New York?" Andrea shrugged.

"It's different."

Laura felt her new friend cautiously reaching out, ready for escape. As they finished their coffee, Laura said, "Let me show you another side of New York; we need a shopping trip!"

"Are you kidding–I hate shopping!"

"Do you wear anything besides jeans?"

"Not if I can help it!" Laura laughed.

"Well that won't do; pants are all right, but you need something feminine, sexy, with an exciting top."

"Why?"

"You said you're a dancer; you love music–our little group hits the after-hours clubs once in a while. We dance, relax, sing a little for the crowd, and…"

"Now you're talkin'!" exclaimed Andrea. What the hell, she thought. Go for it. So she became part of the group John had dubbed the "Wannabes" and danced, played, and breathed the eclectic air of New York.

"Summertime, and the livin' is easy," sang Andrea, who always set life's significant moments to music. She felt as if she owned New York that summer, the summer without Patrick, when her life became all about fun–and freedom.

Getting ready to meet Laura one morning, Andrea applied a new shade of lipstick and took a critical look at herself in the mirror. Long minutes went by–she saw a child, hurriedly washing her face, impatient to finish and leave the mirror behind. The child disappeared, and the nineteen-year-old was seeing a strange unhappiness in her eyes, a long-avoided recognition that this trip to New York was the beginning of a breaking away from her father. There was a painful finality in her heart; she knew she was close to the end of a journey that felt much longer than her nineteen years on earth. Just one more time–she shouldn't have agreed–promised, actually–to go to him in Pakistan. Why did he need her there–another conspiracy, another enemy to be eliminated? He had never used her for those operations, knowing he couldn't yet cross that line, however well she had been indoctrinated in guerilla warfare. Andrea thought about his vague hints, analyzing Patrick's devious thought processes. Why did he need her in Pakistan? As a courier or a procurer of money? It must be a hell of a lot of money from…Who in the wild witch's brew of Pakistan had that much money? The president…the Pakistani ISI, a wealthy *mullah*? She was intrigued, but after this, no more; it would all end. She had a real friend for the first time in her life. She would no longer be part of Patrick's conspiracies.

Whatever her father had planned next for his daughter could wait–

forever, thought Laura. She knew almost nothing about Patrick McAlister, but Andrea's few unguarded comments told her he exercised a strange control over her life. A meeting with Andrea's mother was even less productive. It was surprising to find Wenonah McAlister so benign; her passion for her work and her people was obvious, but her persona was one of tranquillity bordering on passive.

"There's more to this story," Laura told John. "I hope one day she'll be free from her father."

John burst out laughing. "Oh, come on, you're under the spell of that play, Miss Drama Queen. Really, Laura, chill out. Don't obsess about Andrea; she'll find her way. After all, she's only nineteen. Her parents are still protective."

"That's not it, John. There's something weird about her father...oh, I don't know."

John finally satisfied Andrea's curiosity about Laura's play and took her to the theater one night, saying on the way, "I don't know if she'll be able to stay with it much longer."

"Why not?"

"Well, I may be sent to Africa, don't know for sure, but where I go, so goes my lovely Laura."

"From New York City to a village in Africa? Wow!" Her laughter died and her voice took on a solemn tone. "I don't think Laura belongs in an African village."

"Village? It could be Cairo for all I know; I have no idea."

"Not in Cairo, either."

"Well, I have to go where I'm sent, and I'm ready; been ready for three years, Andy."

The sudden flash of anger she directed at him was disconcerting. "Don't call me that, ever! It's Andrea!"

"Sorry." But the anger settled into a general irritability as she reached down, trying to adjust her strappy, high-heeled shoes. "Damn, these things hurt," she said, finally kicking them off. They arrived at the theater and took their seats; Andrea again removed the shoes. John laughed, thinking of how Laura had described Andrea as Gigi.

"Poor Gigi!"

"Gigi? How did..."

"Shh, Andrea, curtain's up."

The play turned out to be a talky disappointment. Andrea was ready to leave after the first act.

"My God it's boring. No offense, John, but Laura's the only good thing about it!"

John said, "I know. But, it's work; she was thrilled to get the part. She's just starting out, after all." Breaking an awkward silence, he said, "I think you're right about Africa–there are reasons–I'm going to tell Laura to stay here." Andrea was surprised by his sober statement. As the play droned on, she closed her eyes, and would have slept through the whole thing if it hadn't been for John's unwelcome jabs keeping her awake. At last, the final curtain fell.

"Thank God it's over!" she proclaimed, to disapproving and amused looks around her.

Back in their apartment, Andrea, shoes off, lounged in one of the cushy old armchairs; she couldn't avoid giving a blunt answer to Laura's question. "What did you think about the play?"

"I don't think it'll be running much longer; your performance was the only thing I liked about it. Sorry, sweetie!"

Laura, unmoved by her opinion, smiled, not joining in Andrea and John's conversation. At last she broke her silence. "Shall I tell her, John?"

"What?" asked Andrea. "Let me guess, you've won the lottery, you're starring in a movie, you've bought a house!"

"No, better than any of those things. We're going to have a baby!"

A baby! Laura couldn't help laughing at Andrea's attempt at an appropriate response and her look of polite horror. Mouth open, Andrea finally said slowly, "Holy shit... sorry!"

"Yes, girlfriend, a baby; you know, those little things that cry and keep you up at night! Oh yeah, I've heard about them!" The only babies I know about are foals or puppies, or calves! You having a baby...?"

"Andrea, they're not aliens, for God's sake! And John and I would love to have you as godmother."

"What? No way! I'm the last person you should choose. Anybody would be better than me. Ask Jen, or Krista, or..."

Laura interrupted. "Hold it–if you don't want to, we'll get someone else, but believe it or not, I think you'd turn out to be a good godmother. Someday you'll feel differently about children."

"You think so? I doubt it. Anyway, I'm probably going to be in Pakistan when the baby comes...even when I come back, I won't stay here." She paused. "I don't really belong in New York."

"Back to Arizona?" asked John.

"I don't know."

What a sad commentary on her life, thought Laura, and felt an increasing hostility towards Andrea's father. "Andrea," she said, "someday you'll find where you belong, and it won't be with your father!"

Surprised at the force of Laura's statement, Andrea replied, "Who knows?"

"I mean it, Andrea, I'm serious."

"I know. So, how far are you with this baby thing?"

Baby thing! "Well, I have about seven months to go. It really is exciting; we have so many plans. I'm going through some morning sickness right now, but..."

Andrea interrupted, having no desire to hear about problems of pregnancy. "Please don't have the baby in Africa."

John and Laura smiled at one another; in the comfortable warmth of her friends' apartment, Andrea felt an emptiness settle itself in her heart. Once again, she would be alone.

Laura called with the news just as Andrea was getting ready to leave for the gallery. "Bad news. Oh, Andrea, John has been assigned to Kabul in Afghanistan! We didn't expect this so soon. It's upsetting, we were thinking Africa–but–Afghanistan! Have you ever been there?"

"No. Wait a minute–you know I'm going to Pakistan. I doubt I could get into Afghanistan–why don't you meet me in Peshawar?"

"I don't know anything about Peshawar, is it very far from Kabul?"

"No, well, a short flight–it should be easy enough."

"I don't know, Andrea ...maybe... I'll try...you know, I really don't want to have the baby in Afghanistan."

"Maybe you'll come home before the baby's due."

"I hope so; this duty is supposed to be about six months and that's cutting it close. I wish we didn't have to go at all."

A bittersweet air of sadness overshadowed their farewell party.

Summer was over, and with it the end of a wonderful superficiality. John was happy; he was going to a place where he was needed, but hard as he tried to convince Laura to stay in New York, she refused. "Nope, I'm your sidekick through thick and thin, pardner," she said, and flashed one of her famous smiles as she joked, but it was obvious she wasn't the confident Laura this time. The two women made tentative arrangements to meet in Peshawar, barring any problems about visas; both knew the meeting might not happen. The regime in Afghanistan was repressive, the climate in Pakistan hostile.

Summer in New York had been a sweet dream, but it was over. Andrea tried to ignore the danger signals going off in her brain. She told herself that John and Laura should be all right; they would be under the protection of the U.N. The following week, she saw them off at Kennedy. "Love you both; take good care of yourselves. Good luck–I'll call you in Kabul, and we'll make plans for Peshawar," and she evaporated into the crowd, missing them already. She wished Laura wasn't pregnant.

Then came 9/11 and the world changed. The call she received a few weeks later was devastating. Her competent, mature friend was crying, incoherent. Between Laura's sobs and a very bad connection, Andrea understood just enough to know that John was dead, killed by the Taliban, and Laura was in fear for her own life.

"I'll call my father, he can help–I'm coming as soon as I can."

"Don't come, Andrea, it's too dangerous…and it's too late," Laura cried into the phone; she only wanted whatever happened to her to be documented, her call to be witnessed.

"Please get in touch with our families. I wasn't able to reach anyone else and there's not much time left. Pray for me, Andrea and…be happy." Her voice became fainter.

Andrea yelled, "Damn it, Laura, don't you dare give up! We'll get you out. Do whatever you need to do, whatever those bastards want! Hang in…"

The connection was broken. Frantic with worry, Andrea called her father. He agreed to make some calls to the U.S. Embassy in Islamabad, but there were no guarantees. Disturbed by this unwelcome development, Patrick faced a dilemma. Andrea was determined to take action of some sort–already she was on her way to Pakistan. Ever the conspirator, Patrick was far from Northern Ireland, but it was a challenge, an opportunity…His trenchant hunger for the streets of Belfast fed a simmering fire that had not quite died out. I'll take her into Afghanistan myself! The prospect of leading his daughter into danger excited him, but he was about to leave for Belfast to deal with the problem of Sean Murphy. Andrea's decision to rescue a friend in Kabul made no sense to him, considering how quickly the Taliban eliminated their opposition. Giving himself credit for her stubborn determination, he quickly made a plan, calling in favors from Pakistani agents who owed him big time.

❊

Their last conversation came to mind; now she'll be glad to know the language. "Why Pushto and Dari, Dad? I don't need another language; what will I do with Dari, for God's sake?" At a dark glance from her father, she said nothing more.

"Listen, lass, I'll soon be off to Pakistan. I've learned a couple of the languages in that area and I'll be calling you, so we'll be talking often. And when you visit, you'd do well to speak the language. So learn it, my girl."

Andrea's lack of enthusiasm did not matter. He knew years of discipline and her quick mind would not let her refuse–she knew that almost every communication between them would be in Dari, or one of the other dialects spoken in Pakistan. So what else is new, she thought.

Andrea's childhood had been a puzzling maze of contradictions; after the age of six, the indulgent love of her father underwent a gradual change. In the end, it became a tumultuous lesson in toughness and survival. Her mother retreated, fading to a gentle presence absorbed in her art. The first time Andrea was thrown from a horse and fell in the dirt crying, her father's response was a stern lecture, "Stop crying, Andrea, it won't help! Get back on that horse; always get back up, lass, whatever it is, and do it again–it's the only way to win."

Andrea found it easier to get back on the horse than to get back up from the taunts of the kids at school about her wild hair, her irritatingly superior abilities, her Indian mother, her boisterous Irish father. She learned not to cry. Patrick McAlister encouraged her passion for music and dance, and gave her affectionate hugs. The music gave her joy, but the military training gave her power. If one day she decided to delve into the labyrinth of her childhood, she would need to confront demons that waited, patient, in a dim corner of her mind. In the meantime, weakness was not an option. How could she get to Laura before….no, don't go there.

Islamabad and Peshawar were chaotic, no flights into Afghanistan for at least a week. "Remember, always be ready for a change in the plan," said Patrick, "secrecy and disguise first and foremost. On the Khyber, you will come to a village called Lal Pur; leave the horse and meet Hassein, he'll take you to Kabul in his truck. You know what to do there; follow my instructions and everything will go well. Good luck."

Her pace over the Khyber was not fast; she didn't know the terrain well enough to speed over this rutted road. Oh God, I hope I get there in time; maybe Dad already got her out somehow. Andrea realized with a start there was someone on horseback coming toward her, coming at a gallop.

He spurred the horse, Sultan, over the rough road. Night had descended upon the Khyber, and he had no time to lose. His pursuers would double back in their search for him–the killing of Khalili made him a wanted man. But he felt good, a euphoric satisfaction permeating his senses; he had killed an important commander–one more leader of their perverted cause was gone. Long experience, observation, and skill led him, unseen, to the commander's tent. Seizing an opportune moment, he slipped inside behind Khalili, grabbed him by the throat, and spun him around so he could know his killer. Eyes wide with rage and fear, the man tried to scream, but Ahmed clapped one hand over his mouth, thrusting the blade of his knife into his enemy's heart with the other, whereupon Khalili's life ended in an ignominious gurgle. He ran out, leaping upon Sultan, and galloped off into the night. It wasn't long before they were after him in force, but the Hindu Kush was his friend that night. Its mountains were home to him; he knew all its hiding places and hid as he watched the soldiers pass by. Hurry–get to the safe house. As he sped to his destination, a shot rang out close to his head, just missing him.

One rider–she waited until he was closer, took aim, and fired her gun. A small explosion sounded; still he came. Damn! She missed him. She took aim again at close range; before she could shoot he was upon her in a furious cloud of rocky dust, pulling her off her horse. Andrea had a blinding image of a man jumping to the ground, pinning her arms behind her, pulling her over to a rock, pressing her against it. She felt pain shooting through her arms and legs and a throbbing fear in her heart. Was she about to be killed?

"No, no, no!" she shouted, "let go of me, you son of a bitch!" she shouted in English.

He didn't speak, simply stared at her. Andrea looked into a face full of rage, into eyes hard and black as coals, at unruly black hair escaping from a scarf tied around his head, a hint of a beard, a mouth locked in grim disapproval. Her head scarf had come off and she saw him staring at her hair, the curls she hated. *Fight? Submit? What should I do?*

He finally shouted at her in Dari, "Who are you–what are you doing here alone? You're not Afghan–that bullet just missed me– what evil are you up to–look at me when I speak to you!"

Andrea became uncomfortably aware he was tall, muscular, lean– a handsome young man. Her words came out in a rush of imperfect Dari, "Oh, I'm looking at you all right; you're the one who's evil! Damn you! I was only defending myself! You're lucky; I don't usually miss. Now let me go; I have business to take care of in Kabul."

"No! Crazy American! You can't go to Kabul–too many Taliban. They will be coming back soon. You don't want to meet them. No, you come with me. I assure you, I'm safer than the Taliban."

"How do I know that–oh, you don't understand. I have to get my friend out of Kabul. Her husband was killed and she's in danger. I've wasted too much time with you."

"Your friend–is she American also?" His tone suggested he knew something.

"Yes, Laura Martin, her husband was with the U.N.; do you know her?"

His voice became softer. "There's no use going after her. The Taliban killed all three of the U.N. people, including your friend. There's nothing you can do for her now." His terse statement was almost a physical blow.

"No, no! I don't believe you, you're lying! How do you know?"

"I saw their bodies with their IDs and documents on them. We tried to save them, but we were too few; the Taliban's numbers were greater. We fight another time–for now we must wait. Come with me."

"No–I'll see for myself!"

As Andrea started to mount her horse, the tall Afghan restrained her. She fought him with an anger he had never seen in a woman; he suddenly struck her hard across the face. Enough of this, he thought, and he put his face close to hers.

"Look at me! Look into my eyes, American." His eyes met hers with an overpowering force and intensity. "You're in my world now, at my disposal; I'll do with you what I wish!" It took every bit of the rebel in her to meet his look with some defiance. She must keep her head in this situation. Don't antagonize him any further, be quiet.

The thought of Laura's lifeless body lying on the ground in Kabul brought bitter tears to her eyes; her mission had failed. Laura was gone, along with the baby she had so happily anticipated.

"Oh God, her baby is dead–why did she have to be in this godforsaken place!"

"What baby? I saw no baby."

There was a pause. "She was pregnant." The American girl looked defeated, uncaring about her safety.

Ahmed Sharif knew he couldn't let her go on by herself. "You ride with me. Quick now. I've no time to waste. Get on my horse."

She mounted his horse as he secured hers and mounted behind her. He felt her shaking with cold or fear as he spurred Sultan to the safe house. Abdullah would be there. The thought crossed his mind that this might be a difficult problem. Andrea was numb with shock and exhaustion–she stayed in the saddle only because the Afghan had hold of her. They kept a steady pace, and as Ahmed came to the compound and entered the house, Abdullah was waiting. The Afghan pulled the girl along, cursing to himself at having come across this wild creature who now seemed to be his responsibility. Ahmed knew his explanation of this girl did not find favor with Abdullah; he wondered if he should have left her where he found her. But he could not in good conscience have done such a thing. She was here and that was that. What to do with her he didn't know. He hoped Abdullah could deal with her; ultimately Ahmed knew it would be his own decision.

He took her to a bedroom and told her to get some sleep. Her failure to reach Laura, the shock of Laura's death, and her capture by this savage Afghan all took their toll; she would rest, then figure how to get out of this situation. Ahmed needed sleep; he would think about the problem later. He washed off the dust and dirt of battle, then entered the bedroom quietly so as not to wake her. All he wanted now was rest, but...

He couldn't avoid looking at the girl on his bed whose sleep apparently was not peaceful. The red-gold hair was wild and tangled, bed cover thrown off–a sound of pain or fright came from her lips. Guilt led him to her side, his conscience told him to cover her, yet desire whispered, she's yours for the taking. He pulled the cover up over her partially clothed body, admiring the lithe form with wariness. My God, she almost killed me; who is this wild girl? An American who spoke fairly good Dari–CIA? Her story was true enough; but what kind of American would have done what she did, and a woman at that?

Ahmed looked down at the girl on his bed, knowing he should leave the room. Abdullah had cautioned him, "Be careful, Ahmed– you will want her, but it is against Allah, and she may not be what she seems." Yes, she was what Abdullah had warned him against: a foreigner, profane, disobedient. And this girl had no qualms about trying to kill him; how could he think of wanting her? But, one of the spoils of war–why not? Ahmed was tired of the fighting, tired of war; he hungered for beauty, a woman's body to warm him, something more than a moment of sexual satisfaction, and her reaction to his news about her friend triggered an emotional response in his heart. Seeing her for the first time in the intimate setting of his room, he saw her youth, her vulnerability, her innocence. This was wrong, but there was no turning back. He stared down at her, giving in to an unwelcome but irresistible urge to comfort her; he had struck her too hard and her face was starting to show some bruising. He brushed a strand of curly hair from her eyes, lightly stroked her face and whispered, "Who are you, wild one; you don't belong in Afghanistan. You're lucky I caught you instead of the Taliban."

She opened her eyes–green eyes looking up at him startled him into the realization that she was indeed very young. "You're a child!" he exclaimed. Ahmed felt an uneasy sensation of conquest and surrender at the same time, knowing the moment for thinking sensibly had passed. The girl looked up at him, uncertain but defiant.

"Taliban?"

"No! I told you I'm not. You wouldn't have been brought here unharmed and been given my bed if I were." As he spoke, he knelt and put his lips close to hers. "No, I am Ahmed Sharif, a Panjshiri, Tajik, Northern Alliance."

She was a stranger to him, yet familiar somehow. His heart beat faster at the thought of making love to her, and anticipation flooded his veins and overwhelmed him. He felt helpless to stop the urgency of his need. His lips touched hers, softly, carefully. She did not try to stop him, choosing to let him caress her. In a slow, dreamlike trance, Andrea felt herself being swept up into a preposterous fairy tale, and a reckless sense of abandonment washed over her–*let it happen*. Ahmed slowly explored her body, kissing her, his desire growing stronger. With each breath coming faster, she looked at him, wondering if he would hurt her, trying to prepare herself to strike back if necessary. But his strong hands were gentle and his eyes seemed to tell her there was nothing to fear. Her response was cautious at first, then became eager as he continued to caress her. Ahmed felt a tenderness war and self discipline had almost erased.

"Look at me, look into my eyes; I want to have sex with you, but I do not rape women."

She was surprised by his hesitation, remembering Patrick's warnings about the Afghans: "They are dangerous, especially the Taliban. Taliban are bloodthirsty bastards; they'll cut your throat soon as look at you. The others, well, don't trust them–they're all savages." A savage? Maybe, but this was also the face of desire–impatient, demanding. She couldn't let herself be a helpless captive submitting to her fate; she must remember who she was.

"Look at me, Afghan!" she commanded.

Ahmed took his hands from her breasts and stared at her.

"I'm a virgin. If you force yourself on me, I'll kill you!" Then her voice assumed a sly, seductive timbre. "If I let you make love to me, it will be because I want you to. Don't mistake me for a trophy of your war."

Not such a child after all. The Afghan seemed amused at her defiance. "What is your age?"

"Nineteen."

"And still a virgin–surprising. If you want me to stop, say so."

This was a token nod to virtue–he had no intention of stopping, and she knew it. Eyes filled with doubt, she raised a hand to his face as though by touch she could determine his true character. Her fingers lingered on his mouth, then found their way over the brown body, examining him with a childlike curiosity. Desire overwhelmed her as she whispered, "Don't stop." She pressed against him, deciding this was exactly where she belonged at that moment. It was so foreign to her, so erotic, so unbelievable, she almost laughed. Weightless, she became a spirit dissolving into the Afghan's body.

Andrea was not naïve about men and the lives they led, particularly the men with whom she had lived since childhood, doing the hard work of ranching along with them. Her life among the tough cowboys exposed her to their violent natures, their physical vagaries, their artless, crude ideas about women. They were men who, without apology, lived as their fathers and grandfathers had for many years before them. Their well-meaning attempts to keep Andrea's life innocent were doomed to failure. She had already been indoctrinated into a man's world by her father, and was comfortable in it. The boys at the ranch were her "gentle giants." But this–this was different. This was a man who was completely enchanting her with his blazing eyes, his warm smile, and the skillful touch of hands that soon possessed every part of her body.

Ahmed tried to be as gentle as possible when he entered her, but he could no longer control his passion, quickly reaching a climax. He heard a small gasp escape her lips, a swift reaching for air after a breathtaking moment. Rolling off her, he uttered words in a strange dialect and leaned over, studying her in some amazement. Andrea had not cried out as he ended her virginity–she, at that moment, felt something akin to pain–an extraordinary agony of joy. He smiled at her, concern in the dark eyes. "Are you all right?" he asked.

"I think–I guess so," she stumbled, unsure of what she was supposed to feel, or think, or say. Rarely at a loss for words, the unanticipated wonder of her first sexual experience silenced her.

She tried to remain dispassionate, looking at her surroundings. She was in an Afghan house for the first time in her life; she looked at the room. No setting out of the *Arabian Nights*, it was plain, sparsely furnished with table and chair, mattresses, colorful carpets and coverings. This mud brick house must have been used for generations; its Eastern cooking permeated the structure, the smell of exotic herbs was imbedded in its walls and coverings. Now it was a safe house. What happened to the people who once lived here?

"Oh God, I think I'm bleeding!"

"Go into the room next door and wash–you'll be all right, it's normal."

His eyes seemed to look past her naked body into her soul. He laughed softly. "Fate has played a trick on us, my wild American."

"What?"

"How do you feel about fate, kismet?"

"I don't believe in it."

"You will." She quickly ran into a room containing a tub, bench, a large container of clean water, soap, sponges, and towels. There was a toilet, well, a hole in the floor! Andrea returned to him cleansed, still feeling the rhythm of his movements inside her. As she slipped into the bed beside him, he said, "Tell me how you feel; did the sex embarrass you?"

Reluctant to concede weakness, she replied, "A little," and turned away from his gaze.

"Look into my eyes and tell me, how did it make you feel?"

Unable to pretend a sophistication she didn't possess, Andrea blurted out, "Like a wild animal out of control, out of breath!" She paused. "I always thought….it must be an act of love, but it's not; it's just basic instinct, isn't it–like animals!" He studied her for a moment.

"Look closely, what do you see in my eyes?"

Careful, black magic at work–but she looked into the spellbinding eyes, felt them pulling her into his world, and answered. "Danger."

He laughed. "No, what you see is love. Animals we are, but love saves us, and danger–well, perhaps a little danger suits you." With a contented sigh he embraced her; he knew it would take longer than one moment of seeing love in his eyes to trust such fragile assurance.

Andrea suddenly thought of her friend. Laura. Laura was dead; how could she have forgotten? This was why she came to Afghanistan. Laura's image appeared before her, laughing. We're going to have a baby! Quietly she said, "I was too late. There was no one to help her."

"She is with Allah–her husband, their baby–with Allah."

"Allah! Well, Allah–or God–both are cruel. I lost my best friend, my only friend." For the first time, Andrea wondered why she was really here.

His look was reflective as he said calmly, "Allah is God, God is Allah–they are one."

"Whatever."

"I'm sorry you've lost your friend. Don't hate my country. Afghanistan is bleeding, broken, full of sorrow for the plague others have visited upon us!"

His hand touching her face was comforting as she held back stubborn tears she didn't want him to see. She looked closely at the face of this man whose tender gesture confused her. "Who are you, Ahmed Sharif?"

"I am the first man who made love to you, and I think I'll be the last."

Spent from all the conflict raging within her, Andrea said, "I'm Andrea McAlister, and I'm tired, and cold."

"Come close; I'll keep you warm."

She lay her head on his chest; his warm breath and body were pungent with the aroma of Middle Eastern herbs–cardamom, coriander, mint–and the brown body entwined in hers was warm and soothing. "Andrea–a beautiful child of infinite delight," he pronounced in a mocking tone, "and you belong to me."

"No," she mumbled sleepily, "don't belong to anyone." But sorrow, anger, fear, excitement, desire, doubt, fulfillment, all vanished as sleep overtook her.

He contemplated his violent, sultry-voiced young lover–there had been no vision, no dream, no warning; she had simply burst into his world like a blazing comet, scattering pieces of his life to the winds. The beautiful mass of contradictions lying in his arms mystified him. He had not asked for such a complication in his life, this girl who stumbled into the heartbreak of Afghanistan; he could not let this defiant American change his life, yet...it was as though he had always known. A sign from Allah that his life was changing, never to be the same? He sighed, content and tired as he held her, and fell asleep. In one of time's capricious moments, Andrea and Ahmed discovered their future.

# 11. Awakening

Andrea awoke to find her Afghan lover gone. What was his name–oh yes, Ahmed Sharif. She shivered with the memory of his body against hers, his arms holding her close, the ecstasy of the sex and the tenderness of his voice and manner toward her. Good God, she had almost killed him! She felt happy and excited; she wanted to dance, to sing. This is crazy, she thought, and jumped out of bed, his bed. Wow! He's my lover, this beautiful Afghan, and she burst into song "I feel pretty, oh so pretty..." There was a tap on the door just as she finished dressing, and a tall bearded Afghan entered the room. Startled at first, she then remembered him from last night.

He introduced himself in rather halting English, "I am Abdullah, Ahmed's guard. I am to see to your needs. Come, you must eat."

In an effort to gain something of an upper hand, she told him, "I speak Dari."

His stern, dignified manner made Andrea feel like a silly child, but she quickly regained her composure; she had little patience with haughtiness or disapproval. At the same time, her opinion of him did not concern Abdullah–she was only an annoyance to him, about to say something disrespectful. Instead she held her tongue, then answered him. "Yes, whatever you have will be fine."

As though I have a choice, she thought.

He served her a simple meal of rice, yogurt, and fruit, along with a glass of hot tea. No meat, thank God; that was something she'd have to be careful about. Andrea now had a burning curiosity about Ahmed and his status in the Northern Alliance. A guard, a house with three bedrooms and large living room or parlor–she wasn't sure what

28

they called it–this couldn't be the situation of an ordinary soldier. Abdullah sat in the kitchen watching her, expressionless. If his intent was to make her feel embarrassed in any way, he failed. Using her *naan* (bread) as a utensil, she finished eating and asked Abdullah, "Where is Ahmed?"

"You do not need to be concerned about that; he may be gone for two weeks or more. When he returns, he expects you to be here."

"Expects me to be here? Hell, I can't just sit here waiting for him, I have other things to do!"

Abdullah replied calmly, "You cannot leave, it is very dangerous in this region right now. The Taliban are rounding up people they consider a threat and they take special actions against women, any women who happen to displease them. Ahmed has entrusted your safety to me."

Ahmed had indeed assigned an order to Abdullah. "Keep her safe; don't let her go." In a conciliatory tone, he told her, "I have served Ahmed since he was a young boy."

It took Andrea a few minutes to digest this information and come to a decision. Her mood by now had changed somewhat. It seemed Abdullah considered her his charge and promised Ahmed to care for her, to keep her safe. An Afghan soldier made love to her, cared about her. She could see Abdullah was not pleased to be her guardian. This old Afghan wants nothing more than to have me gone; I guess he obeys Ahmed out of years of devotion. And Ahmed–he must be special in some way. The anticipation of Ahmed's return was enough to make her stay; after all, she thought, I'm waiting for…what? for my life to change! Then she remembered his words–something about infinite delight and his last words before she fell asleep. "You belong to me." A trace of fear crept into her excited anticipation.

Facing Abdullah, Andrea declared, "I'll wait here, but I want to go out, not far; I can't just sit in this house, though I could clean up some of this dust." At this remark, there was a black look from Abdullah.

"There's something really important that needs taking care of–I've got to get in touch with my father in Islamabad as soon as possible."

Ah, a father waiting to hear from her–this could be complicated. Abdullah answered, "I'll be in contact with Ahmed tonight. If you give me the number for your father, he can get a message to him quickly. About going out, I'll look into it–but you will need to wear a *burqa.*"

Abdullah appeared calm and in charge, but his mind was a turmoil of resentment, anxiety, and doubt mixed with a bit of reluctant admiration for her seeming lack of fear.

Andrea remembered Buttercup. "Where is my horse? Has he been taken care of?"

"Yes," he said, acknowledging to himself the Arabian was a beauty; whoever had chosen him knew horses.

"Thanks for that; Buttercup is a love, very obedient."

"Buttercup, that is the name of your horse?" Buttercup–how ridiculous!

Her tone was defiant as she answered, "Yes, what of it?"

Abdullah did not deign to answer. What could he make of this lovely young girl whom Ahmed took to his bed and loved–American, an unbeliever, headstrong and frivolous, with her songs and American slang. For the first of many times, Abdullah asked Allah what he had done to be punished with the care of this creature. Andrea reluctantly gave Abdullah her father's number along with the message that she was all right, but had not been able to reach her friend–friend did not survive–please see about notification, possibly funeral arrangements. She was forced to trust Abdullah.

Last night's events spun dizzying circles in her head. She had been seduced–no, she had been only too willing; how could she have allowed herself to so easily submit; was it the excitement of the moment they collided, the dark eyes that turned from fury to concern to desire, the sense of being protected and cared for? How could I be attracted to an Afghan? Attracted? I'm in love with him, oh my God! What would Patrick say; who cares? I'm so confused. I'm happy and I'm sad. Laura. Laura, oh Laura–I can't believe you're gone, it's all so wrong...I was going to rescue you; I can't believe I've fallen in love with an Afghan I don't really know, an Afghan who tried to save you. I wish I had told you how much I loved the two of you–damn it, you shouldn't have died, you should have lived and raised your child! Why didn't you listen to John and stay home! And here I am in this strange place...the Afghan made love to me as though he knew...can you hear me, Laura, tell me what to do!

If Andrea had been bewitched by the Khyber and the crying winds of the Hindu Kush at nightfall, she was awestruck by her first sight of

Afghanistan in the early morning. Standing just outside the compound wall, she breathed in the thin, pure mountain air, gazed at the clearest blue sky she had ever seen; mountain formations stood like proud sentinels protecting the valley below. Crystal air and sharply delineated edges gave the scene a picture postcard look. She called Afghanistan Godforsaken last night. This morning, from the place where she stood, it looked as though God decided this land would be his most beautiful creation. How ironic that this exquisite place held some of mankind's ugliest handiwork. Oh, but one of its most handsome people. She had not planned to be dazzled by Afghanistan's mountains; she had not come to seek adventure, to join the *mujahidin*, to help in any humanitarian effort; she had not expected to stay in a country about which she knew almost nothing. She was definitely unprepared to be enchanted by one of the savages Patrick had warned her against. She smiled–a savage? More like a sorcerer!

Andrea turned and saw Abdullah motioning her to come inside the walled compound–reality check, she thought. In the stable in one end of the compound, she found Buttercup, brushed and groomed, fed and watered. As she stroked him, he nuzzled her in contentment. "Oh, Buttercup, my love, what's in store for us now?"

Suddenly, she laughed out loud, thinking what her father would say if he could see her here, if he could see her with Ahmed! And her mother–maybe she would smile. Andrea put it out of her mind and went in the house to talk to Abdullah. "Abdullah, am I not allowed to go outside the wall?"

It was an abrupt question. He suppressed his urge to scold this girl and answered, "Outside the wall you must wear the *burqa*–it's for your own safety, also for Ahmed's security. It provides the best cover for many activities, but it is not foolproof. You must still be very careful. You were admiring our scenery; I know in your country you also have beauty such as you see here. But Afghanistan is not like America, and we don't wish it to be! Freedom as you know it does not exist here; when we win we will have more freedom, also the problems that go with it. For now you must remember this is a very dangerous place for you to be."

Let this be the lecture for the day, thought Andrea. She had to ask, "Is Ahmed an important person here?"

"He is Ahmed Khan Sharif, a commander in the Northern Alliance. We will not discuss it any further now. If you ever wish to go into the village, you must tell me so I can accompany you. Women must be escorted by a man."

Khan–a ruler, landowner, a person of importance. His speech and bearing were confirmation of the title, apparently a title he had no desire to acknowledge, at least to her.

Andrea's thoughts turned to Arizona with its deserts and mountains; a little like Afghanistan. "A very dangerous place"–that's what her mother called Arizona in her stories of their Apache ancestors' savage battles with the Spaniards and Americans in the Southwest. She decided to pay attention to Abdullah, at least for now. True to her word, Andrea swept out the house and found more than dust: An assortment of bugs lived in the house along with them. Most menacing of all was a huge spider she came upon, lurking in a crevice. *Oh my God, I need bug spray; no bug spray to be found.* Andrea was determined to exterminate the pests, especially when she found herself constantly itching and scratching the blotches forming on her arms and legs. With the bleach and strong soap powder Abdullah finally produced, she scrubbed everything, carpets, cushions, mattresses, from top to bottom, until the house was redolent of the mixture's pungent aroma. At least her little corner of the Afghan world was clean and bug-free for a while. Though he had shown no inclination to help her, Abdullah was impressed with her accomplishment. But Andrea was still in search of bug spray.

# III. A Different Light

It was a cold night when Ahmed returned; ten days at the front had won a small victory for the Alliance, but they were far from defeating the Taliban. Only when the Americans came to help would they have a real advantage. He was tired, his arm badly bruised and sore where it had been grazed by a bullet–a small thing when he thought of the two young brothers who were dead. Only fifteen and sixteen, Asaf and Abdul were good soldiers. From the time they came to join his army, Ahmed told them to go back home to their mother to help the family, but they needed their salary from army service, and as they pointed out to him, they were excellent marksmen. Besides, they said, they were eager to rid their country of the cruel Taliban and help Afghanistan be progressive, like America. Like America? Ahmed thought they probably saw too many forbidden videos. And now they were gone, along with their dreams. There was something about these two that touched his heart and brought tears to his eyes. They had an innocence, an unfailing optimism; their infectious laughter spread through the company of battle-hardened men. Against his better judgment, he grew fond of them, thinking of the boys almost as sons. Weary as he was, he felt compelled to take their bodies home to their family so they could be buried properly. As he rode to their village near Golbahar, he felt an intense anger and pain in his heart, emotions he kept locked within himself. He longed for his wild American captive.

The family was distraught upon seeing the boys' bodies, their mother bursting into the unrelenting wail of the bereaved; Mohammed, the boys' father, was grateful to have them returned so they could be buried the next day in the local cemetery. He thanked

Ahmed for his kindness, offering him food and rest. Ahmed accepted bread and fruit, explaining that he could not stay; he gave Mohammed the salary owed to the brothers plus something extra, a meager recompense for two young lives. When he arrived home, Ahmed was in need of sleep and comfort and wanted to forget the battlefield, but Abdullah was awake, eager to hear about all that had happened.

As Ahmed gave a brief report, Abdullah noted the tiredness in his eyes, the weakness in his arm. "You need rest; I hope you get it," referring, of course, to Andrea. "Ahmed, consider your position; do you understand the problem of—"

Ahmed interrupted, "Is she being difficult?"

Abdullah knew this was not the time to pursue the subject, so he just rolled his eyes and raised his hands heavenward to signify "she's impossible."

Ahmed paid no real attention to all this; he would work it out later. "Get some sleep, Abdullah, we'll talk tomorrow."

Andrea lay in a peaceful sleep when he got into bed. Ahmed looked at her–her warm body enticed him; her skin was soft and inviting. As he kissed her, she opened sleepy eyes. "Ahmed, oh I'm so glad you're back. I was beginning to think you were just a dream."

"Shhh," he whispered, "no talk, no talk." He wrapped his body around hers and made love. No words; when she started to say something, he placed a firm hand over her mouth. "I told you, do not speak!"

A tremor of fear ran through her; she sensed his anger, feeling if she were to defy him at that moment, he would strike her. It was clear any Western leanings he might have were limited. He's different tonight, she thought; something happened. Whatever the case, she couldn't turn back; it was too late, she was in love. Though training had taught her otherwise, instinct told her to trust. He kissed her and fell asleep with his arms around her.

"You're one hell of a sweet savage," she whispered, and caressed his injured arm.

Ahmed stayed at the house for six days. Abdullah wasted no time starting Andrea's Afghan education. In his dignified, ever polite way, he read from a paper the traditional duties of a woman: mattresses to be rolled or stacked against the walls, *toshaks* (long narrow cushions) kept neatly along the walls, fresh water taken from the pool or stream to be carried to the kitchen and bathroom, clothes to be washed and spread out to dry on rocks, food to be prepared in the *tandur* or on the grill outside, wheat and corn to be ground to fill the earthenware pots, sewing as needed. As Abdullah recited, with what seemed unusual pleasure, the host of duties that made up an Afghan woman's average day, Andrea gave him a look that had only one meaning. Noting with satisfaction his disapproving expression, she resisted the impulse to laugh–this was not the time to dismiss Afghan pride. Instead, she gave Abdullah a demure, apologetic look, and was rewarded by a hint of a smile on his normally impassive face. "I can do all those things except cook. Hell, I did harder work than that on the ranch, but I never cooked. We had Maria to cook."

It was a casual comment, uttered in complete self-assurance. Abdullah was disturbed by this American girl's seeming arrogance, her frequent use of profanity, but after all, she was not Muslim.

"I will teach you to cook Afghan food. Tell me about your ranch."

Abdullah listened to her story of ranch life, shaking his head at her tales about breaking horses, her laughter about falls and broken bones. He saw a strong young girl who seemed to be as tough as an Afghan, who loved horses–Buttercup indeed! Abdullah immediately renamed the splendid Arabian Zabuli, a proper Afghan name.

The two drifted into an understanding that gave Andrea some Afghan cooking skills and Abdullah help in perfecting his English. Ahmed was pleased to see cooperation, if not affection, between them, but he needed Abdullah's skills put to wider use–Andrea must learn about Afghanistan, and Abdullah was the one who could teach her. Ahmed had no thought of sharing his future plans with Andrea; it was too soon.

The cooking lessons were not going well. Neither enthusiastic nor intuitive in the kitchen, she practiced with a grudging persistence, serving them passable kebabs and various forms of *pilau* (rice.) To Andrea, it was drudgery; the joy of cooking escaped her, but she kept at it.

"Don't worry, Andrea, you'll be learning other things; then Abdullah will help with the cooking," Ahmed said, and gave her an impulsive kiss. "You will learn to be Afghan; I will be proud of you!"

Really, she thought, an alarm going off in her head. "Does that mean you'll keep me?" At the look on his face, she gave a hollow laugh. "Just kidding, sweetie, it's a joke."

"A bad joke," replied Ahmed, not sure who or what this girl was. He knew he loved her, but what a challenging gift he had been given. What potential for disaster! In the end, he knew only that he was committed; he would not turn back.

Andrea awoke abruptly; the unfamiliar sound of the *azan* echoed throughout the region, birds were chirping and singing nearby, and something...it sounded like bombs...exploded in the distance. She turned to Ahmed, who was waking to obey the call to prayer. He looked as she imagined he might have as a child: young, vulnerable. As he kissed her, Andrea thought about the night he came back: her moment of fear, his almost desperate lovemaking. What had so disturbed him that night she might never know. That one frightening moment stuck in her mind. *Oh, get up, stop thinking about it, it was nothing.* One thing she knew: Ahmed made her feel, for the first time in her life, more than an unrealized dream of her parents. She went into the bathroom; Abdullah had filled the large basin with hot water. She soaped and rinsed herself from head to toe, feeling happy and refreshed, as Ahmed went to the kitchen to perform the ritual ablution before prayer. Andrea decided today she would fix an American breakfast, an omelet with peppers–no bacon or sausage, of course; heaven forbid! Well, Allah forbids it, according to the *Qur'an*. When Ahmed and Abdullah returned from prayer, she had the omelet ready, along with *naan* and yogurt. They complimented her on the meal–sometimes a little encouragement helped–but Andrea's mind was not on her cooking.

"The night you came home from the front, you made love to me, told me to be quiet. I started to speak and you..."

"I kept you silent."

"Yes. I had the feeling that if I spoke you would have..."

"Would have what?"

"I don't know. I was almost afraid..."

"Afraid I would hurt you?"

She lowered her eyes. "I wasn't sure."

"I will tell you. I would never strike you."

"But why did I feel so much anger?"

"Because it was there! There are things I must keep to myself;

there's a lot of anger, a lot of rage in Afghanistan, a lot of injustice! You will see the anger in the streets one day. I promise I will never strike you. I love you, Andrea."

The last words flew out of his mouth unintended. He had not planned to tell her he loved her, having just come to terms with it and all it might mean in his life, yet what time would be any better? "You are the only one who will know me completely, as I will know you." He talked of the pain of losing the boys, his anger at having to fight one war after another. "I needed you that night. I've been fighting since I was fourteen, a long time. I'm tired of seeing children killed and maimed. I would never hurt you. I love you; I want you with me, though you are such a difficulty!"

I love you. She smiled upon hearing those three trite words, possibly the most dangerous in any language. At the description of her as a difficulty, she couldn't help laughing, seized by a sudden sense of Afghan absurdity. Composing herself, she told him, "I've been a difficulty all my life!" She looked into his eyes and said, "I adore you, Ahmed Khan Sharif."

Ahmed had known that from the first time he made love to her; but how could this nineteen-year-old girl really know what her declaration of love meant? He knew he had waited too long to explain the cold reality of Afghan life. I must try at least, he thought. Reluctant, he began, "It may take a long time before you understand me–I wonder if you understand yourself yet," he said, forcing himself to preserve a certain detachment. "Afghanistan may remind you of your Arizona, but they are as night and day. You are in a country that is ruled by Allah and men who judge people, especially women, harshly. At nineteen, I was sure I knew everything, though I knew little! How sure are you?"

"I'm sure I love you."

"Then you must accept my country and its ways–or would you rather go back to Arizona?"

"No! I won't go back!"

"Good–I want you to stay with me always. You'll learn–we'll both learn," he said, in his heart an anticipation mixed with joy and doubt.

Andrea was sure she wanted to be with Ahmed, and very sure she did not want to be alone in the world.

"About Abdullah. Pay no attention to his moods, but respect him,

Andrea. He is like a father to me. He will make his peace with you, and I make my own plans and decisions. You, my wild one, belong with me, and Abdullah belongs with us. He will be your teacher, your mentor, your friend, and perhaps some day more than that. He's pleased that you learn so quickly, but some things…well, experience will teach you best. The most important thing to know is that family and tribal honor come before everything else. Afghans do not endure insults or loss of honor to themselves or their family and tribe."

"Do you know that I belong to a tribe?"

"What tribe is that?"

"I'm not joking; I'm half Apache Indian, my tribe is the Chiricahua; one day you'll meet them."

Their days in what appeared to be a damaged, abandoned compound were an odd mix of military strategy and domesticity. The two men had long discussions in a dialect–Uzbek?–she didn't know. Andrea was starting to feel confined; she had not been out of the house since Ahmed had brought her here, had not seen anything of everyday Afghan life. *I feel trapped. God, I can't stand much more of this!* She was no longer doing all the chores. Her time was spent learning about Afghanistan, and Abdullah was a good teacher. He was patient, even when she spoke to him rudely in outrageous American slang. Nothing fazed him, so she gave up, becoming a model student. Her crash course in all things Afghan included history, poetry, music, culture, and Islamic law. Andrea's thoughts often strayed from the teaching, turning to memories of New York and Laura, and she found herself speaking of her lost friends to Abdullah. When she was reading a book, or making notes, or trying to master the baking of *naan* in the *tandur*, he would study her, stroking his long beard, his expression pensive.

Abdullah was an academic; he had taught at Kabul University. Beaming with enthusiasm as he told Andrea about Afghanistan's history, he brought the characters to life. She came to know Alexander and his beautiful Roxane, the tribes and nomads who conquered and ruled for a while, Genghis Khan, and Timur, his descendent, and the countless number of rulers who waged war over this beleaguered land. With only one long period of peace and prosperity, 1370 to 1505, it seemed a miracle to Andrea that the people survived such constant upheaval in their lives.

"Yes, wars will always be waged," pronounced Abdullah with a heavy sigh. "Some people welcomed the Taliban because they brought a sense of order and a return to a pure Islamic state. Of course," he said with heavy sarcasm, "Afghanistan has never been a pure Islamic state. Afghans disagree about everything!" Then, in a somewhat sinister tone, "Taliban decreed no music, no dancing, no kites, women kept hidden behind walls–no schools for them–what do you think of that!"

She knew Abdullah's sly remark was meant as a provocation to her. *He wants to hog-tie and brand me. Well, you won't, my Afghan scholar– I'm young and American, but I'm far from dumb. You're not such a big deal to me.* Andrea shrugged. "As an American, I have to say it sounds pretty stupid. But then, I don't know much about Islam."

It would not be until much later that she learned what an intricate tapestry Islam was and would feel she was in any position to debate it, but she did know men, and commented, "Men will always find a reason to wage war."

Abdullah felt some sadness at the bitterness and cynicism in her voice, and decided the history lesson was finished. He was a consummate professor, wanting Andrea's Afghan education to be as complete as possible. In truth, he loved teaching again, and knew Andrea's keen mind was a gift for any teacher.

With Afghanistan steeped in all this culture, she wondered why so much of the country was still primitive and savage: constant battles between its fierce ethnic tribes, its use as a stepping stone for those on their way to greater glories and riches, its forbidding terrain. Whatever, it was a sad story, yet....its people were warm, hospitable to a fault, and they still laughed. She thought again of the Indians who in the end were buried under the greater number of their conquerors. Andrea learned more about Abdullah, and Ahmed's relationship with him. He had been the tutor for the Sharif family since Ahmed's brother Rashid was five years old. After Fara and Haroun Sharif were murdered, Abdullah became their children's guardian, teacher, advisor, and surrogate father. They were a family again–Abdullah's brand of affection was more circumspect than their parents', but it was a genuine affection. Andrea knew she must adapt to Abdullah's role as head of the family; in Afghanistan, there was no room for protest, much less rebellion, against the family patriarch. At least

Abdullah was tolerant of this strange American.

Andrea's sleep that night was interrupted by the sound of men's voices raised in jubilant greeting: "*Salaam, salaam aleichum, Allahu Akbar!*" followed by hushed but heated discussion. Alarmed at first, Andrea realized the men were *mujahidin*, Ahmed's men. Carefully opening the door just a crack, she saw them gathered in a circle on the *toshaks*; they seemed to be excited about some success in battle, speaking in a rapid Dari. Their weapons were stacked against the wall–rifles, grenades, ammo clips. There was a smell about them, more than the dirt and dust of Afghan soil; she picked up the faint air of high explosives. The familiar acidic scent of cordite stirred Andrea's memory; all the training in the world did no good when she was virtually a prisoner in this house. After long moments of deep thought, she looked at what she considered the war council. The discussion had ended; the weary, half-starved men were sleeping the sleep of the faithful. They came and went in the night, fed by Abdullah, inspired by Ahmed, thankful for clean water that prepared them for prayers as they left in the darkness.

Andrea awoke out of a dream the next day, a dream of racing through the valley astride Buttercup and drinking a cup of fresh coffee. For a few minutes after awakening, she could still smell its aroma. Her unrest had reached fever pitch, especially after seeing the *mujahidin* last night. As she went into the kitchen to reheat the *reshta* from yesterday's dinner, she found Ahmed making tea. She kissed him and announced, "I'd love to go out for a cup of coffee!"

"What did you say?"

"I wish we could go out for coffee, just the two of us."

"This is not America, my little one–we can't do that."

"There are bazaars, restaurants here; they serve coffee, don't they?"

"Andrea, we are not tourists nor villagers; just now we can't be seen on the streets around here. Later we'll be able to move about more freely, not now. Come here, my sweet, let me hold you. I can see you're upset." She came closer to Ahmed and he playfully grabbed her, locking her in his arms.

"Please let me go, Ahmed."

She was serious–what was it? "Look at me, Andrea–tell me why you're angry."

"I dreamed of the wonderful smell of coffee brewing; I'd die for a good strong cup of coffee right now. I'm tired of Afghan tea, Afghan music, Afghan whatever, and I'm tired of being cooped up in this house! I want to ride Buttercup, I want to run, I need to see people, talk to them. And…I need music." She almost cried.

Ahmed was stunned, but not surprised. His wild bird needed to fly. He held her face in his hands, looked into her green eyes, and kissed her.

"My sweet American, you are the beating of my heart. No Afghan culture, no language lessons for the rest of the time I'm here. Today, something different." He was relieved to see two reluctant tears fall from her eyes.

"Thank God. I'm so damned tired of the lessons." They ate their breakfast together while Abdullah was busy in the stable with the horses. "Abdullah takes good care of Buttercup, I must admit."

"Yes, he knows horses; do you know the story of the Arabian?"

"No, I only know they are beautiful creatures."

"I will get Abdullah to tell you about your Buttercup." Brushing the hair away, he kissed the back of her neck. "You have a long scar here; what happened?"

"Wild horses."

"So, you tame horses, do you?"

"Yes, you can see I've got the scars to prove it, sweetie!"

"You're in the right place for wild horses," he laughed, "one day I'll take you to where they are wilder than any you've seen!"

"I'll talk to them first!"

"No, not these. Come with me, Andrea, we've got work to do." She felt better, a little guilty about her outburst, but glad Ahmed understood.

It occurred to Andrea it must not be easy for him to live with the infidel she appeared to be; she hadn't given it a thought until Abdullah offered to teach her about Islam. She politely refused the offer. They assumed she was Christian; in fact she was not. Her only belief was that God is God, however he is worshiped. As a result of her life with Wenonah and Patrick, Andrea did not believe in icons, heroes, role models. If there were such beings, they were ordinary people who simply persisted and survived with a certain amount of honor, grace, and humor intact. She respected the shamanism of her

Indian culture as much as anything. Yet she did ask Ahmed on occasion about the prayers. He recognized the questions as Andrea's polite interest in his faith. So the subject was put aside for another time, one Andrea hoped would be in the distant future.

Ahmed went to the stable and brought out two shovels, rakes, and hoes, and put them in front of Andrea. "We'll start here in front of the door, and make a track about three feet wide."

"A track to where?"

"All around the buildings, on this side of the wall–inside."

"What's the track for?"

"For you, wild child. For my restless one's exercise."

"Oh, Ahmed, sweetie, what a great idea! And–could I have music to exercise with? A Walkman with tapes, so no one else could hear."

"We'll find something for you. Now start scraping and digging."

Together they worked most of the morning clearing rock and stones, smoothing the path. Abdullah watched from the house where he made himself busy, watched and wondered what was going to come of all this; he was deeply conflicted about Andrea and her influence on Ahmed. She was only nineteen; Ahmed was ten years older. She was American; he could not imagine her becoming a Muslim. He felt she would always be American, that she would never embrace Afghan ways. Perhaps…if she loved Ahmed enough and remained loyal. She didn't yet know of Ahmed's significance, his importance to this country–and what about her parents? So many questions, so many problems. Abdullah again caught sight of them working, laughing at how dirty they were getting. He saw Andrea run up to Ahmed and throw her arms around him, giving him an enthusiastic kiss. They looked carefree, unabashed at their happiness, like children at play. Maybe…Abdullah's thoughts were going in too many different directions–it was too soon to decide anything about this relationship. He stopped himself from more thinking. But he did know she was going to cause trouble somehow, intentional or not.

For all their play, Andrea and Ahmed worked hard on the track and finished just before it was time for prayer. She and Ahmed washed off the dirt from their project, and while Ahmed and Abdullah prayed, Andrea walked around the track meditating, trying to decide when she would confront her father; she thought of Laura and John and their unborn child. *I hope they're in a good place, angels together. Angels? I don't believe in angels.* She had believed in Laura. What irony–Laura had been spared the horror of the World Trade Center attack only to be killed in Afghanistan. Involuntarily, she said the Lord's Prayer as she walked and looked out on the Islamic nation she was beginning to think of as home.

It had been a good day. As she came to the front of the house, she saw Abdullah preparing their evening meal over the fire. "Umm, something smells so good. What are you cooking, Abdullah?"

"We will have kebabs–this one is *kofta*–and some fresh fruit."

*Meat–I hope I can eat it.*

"The meat is fresh, Andrea."

Andrea smiled, "I'm sure it is." This was a sensitive problem–she ate the fruit, the vegetables, the curds, but meat and water were questionable. The meat needed to be fresh from the butcher and the water boiled for at least twenty minutes, unless one used the water purification tablets which were not always practical. Andrea had a dread of getting sick from food. She had been in too many countries where foreigners contracted any number of disabling diseases, but she put her trust in Abdullah's assurance of "fresh meat" and the three of them ate generous portions of the *kofta*. She and Ahmed complimented Abdullah on his cooking. He in turn presented Andrea with a small package.

"I found this in a village shop; the owner had hidden it away from the Taliban, along with other forbidden items. I hope it is what you wanted." Andrea was stunned that Abdullah had thought to bring her a gift.

"Open it, Andrea," said Ahmed.

She tore off the wrapping–a Walkman with music tapes! She stood on tiptoe and gave him a kiss, showering him with a string of profuse thank-yous.

"Think of it as a graduation present, Andrea."

Ahmed, Andrea, and Abdullah all had a similar thought at that moment: *There's more learning to come.*

After evening prayers, they strolled around Andrea's track. The exhilarating freedom of work and play led them to reveal another layer of their personalities, leaving their deeper beliefs and potential problems for another time. For this moment, they simply reveled in the newness of love and physical attraction.

Awaking from a pleasant dream she wasn't willing to let go of just yet, Andrea luxuriated in a mellow serenity, let out a relaxing yawn, and stretched her arms and legs. Opening her eyes, she looked at Ahmed beside her still asleep, stroked his beard, brushed the hair away from his eyes, and kissed his lips. Suddenly, she was trapped by his arms tight around her. "Oh!" she cried, startled, "I didn't know you were awake; you scared me!"

"Good!" He laughed as she struggled to get free.

The wrestling match ended in a win for Ahmed.

"Not fair," Andrea protested, laughing with him.

"I don't play fair," he replied.

The last day of Ahmed's stay was spent in serious talks with Abdullah and difficult answers to Andrea. She insisted, demanded, finally begged Ahmed to take her with him, but he was adamant and harsh on the subject. "We have no women fighters. Women are expected to work in the home–wash, clean, cook, sew, and keep their men happy!" He almost said "husbands," but caught himself in time. His lecture met with a reaction not unexpected.

"Damn it, Ahmed, I'm not one of your Afghan slave women!"

He met her outburst with a cold, hard look; no woman could be allowed to dictate to him. She turned away from him, but he spun her around to face him and said, "I heard some words from one of the CIA men to a soldier, 'I may not always be right, but I'm never wrong.' You'd do well to remember that."

"Oh, hell, Ahmed, that's a silly old saying, one of those things they print on coffee cups!"

"That may be, but it's true. And stop your cursing."

The idea of Ahmed quoting a saying she had seen on one of her father's coffee mugs struck Andrea as hilarious, and she couldn't help laughing; once started, she couldn't stop, and finally buried her head in Ahmed's chest. She hugged him, then looked into his eyes, said, "I'll stay here this time, but please, Ahmed, think about it. I can help you; I'm a good fighter. I was trained to…"

"Trained–how–by whom?"

"Never mind, it doesn't matter now."

Ahmed said nothing more, knowing he would soon find out about this "training."

Later, Andrea told him Abdullah said he could accompany her to the village if she wanted to go; would it be all right? Ahmed gave his reluctant permission, went to a closet, and pulled out a *burqa*. He put it over her head, telling her this was what she must wear anywhere outside the compound. It was the first time Andrea had the garment on and it was smothering, insulting to her, but she would tolerate it if it meant even a modicum of freedom. She couldn't resist leaving Ahmed with a final thought about a "woman's place" in Afghanistan. "You know, sweetie, women will be doing a lot of things besides keeping house after the Taliban are finished. Teachers, doctors, reporters–they can help make wonderful changes here!"

Ahmed smiled at her naïve talk of change for women. He was well aware change was inevitable; he would, in fact, have the responsibility for implementing some of those changes. But there were too many battles to be fought before he would discuss it with Andrea. Andrea's mind was already on her visit to the village.

"Ahmed, what about Abdullah being seen by the Taliban?"

"They don't know Abdullah's connection with me; he'll just be your wise old uncle. Only one man knows Abdullah, and he's not here. But be careful, my love; let Abdullah do the talking. Your bit of American accent could give you away."

Ahmed left the next day after morning prayers. Andrea watched them pray, envying the certainty of their faith. She tried to suppress a *frisson* of anxiety and apprehension as she said goodbye to Ahmed; he saw it in her eyes and held her in a long embrace. "Everything will be fine. Give me a long American kiss!" As always, he made her laugh.

"As opposed to a short Afghan kiss?"

"Exactly." Then he was gone. She went into the bedroom and looked at her Kalashnikov–soon, Ahmed, she thought. Trying to erase her worrisome thoughts, she went out to Buttercup's stall; as she curried, combed and fed him, she talked softly to him. "Buttercup, sweetie, I want to get in the saddle and ride and ride. Down in the valley, we could really let loose, even go to the front. But I'm not allowed –hmm, that never stopped us before when we wanted to do something, did it?"

She felt a presence in the stable, turned and saw Abdullah. Had he heard her? He looked his usual stern self, such a killjoy sometimes; "Andrea, you must not take Zabuli out. I know he needs to be ridden– I will exercise him for you."

Andrea was incredulous, forgetting the lessons, his present, his kindnesses. *Does he hear everything? He's a goddamned spy! Zabuli, hah!* Apparently he could also read her mind.

"We will go to the bazaar tomorrow."

# IV. A Dangerous Place

The next day, Andrea dressed in nondescript gray pants and tunic, then the *burqa*. It was a voluminous blue thing–a great disguise, thought Andrea. It seemed to reek of generations of women whose main purpose in life was to obey; she felt anonymous and claustrophobic. How could women stand this for any length of time? Abdullah looked her over to be sure nothing said "foreigner" and they set off for the village in the donkey cart. Andrea was as excited about going to a village market in Afghanistan as she would have been about going to Saville Row or Rodeo Drive. This was to be her first taste of everyday life in Afghanistan. The main street was full of people, almost all of whom were men; the few women there walked in groups. Andrea was dismayed at the poor condition of all the buildings. Their compound was luxurious in comparison to these structures, damaged first by Russian bombs, then sacked and burned by the Taliban. Nevertheless, on this sunny, mild day, the marketplace was busy with the babble of the bargaining sellers and buyers, colorful with cartloads of *naan*, a variety of vegetables, fruits, and other foods unidentifiable to Andrea.

It was a social affair, this Afghan supermarket, and the sellers and buyers were having a good time, considering the calamities taking place daily in their lives. So many men; few women. Abdullah had come upon a group of men he apparently knew well. So there are people who know him, not just one man, thought Andrea; strange. Leaving her alone in the cart, he and the others greeted one another with effusive hugs and kisses and cries of *salaam aleichum* (peace be with you). They gathered in a little circle to exchange the latest news, jokes, and probably gossip–just like the ladies, thought Andrea. Yes, they reminded her of an Apache gathering of men on the reservation, or men sitting around the old stove in the general store swapping tall tales. Circles, the same all over. Finally, the group broke apart, thank God. She was feeling uneasy in her role of Afghan woman. Abdullah stowed his purchases in baskets on the cart and indicated to Andrea it was time to leave. Near the end of the street, she saw what looked to be a small shop, and signaled Abdullah to stop, asking him to see if they had any American music tapes.

"Andrea, the Taliban do not allow music to be sold."

"Isn't this where you found the Walkman?"

"Yes, but he only had Afghan music."

"Maybe if he looked…"

He hesitated, then agreed after strict warnings not to speak to anyone, and went into the shop.

Andrea waited in the cart, feeling alone and strange in the *burqa*. In the distance, she noticed an old pickup truck filled with men coming down the road. She felt a shiver of warning and the truck came to where she was waiting. Oh shit, Taliban! The soldiers jumped out, running into the crowd, singling out and seizing a woman who was walking alone. One of the men looked up at Andrea; she knew she had to respond. With her hand on the trigger of her revolver, she said in Dari "husband" and indicated the shop; just then Abdullah came out. The soldier shrugged–thank God, thought Andrea.

The Taliban started in the direction of the bazaar; suddenly gunshots erupted. Another woman who had been seized and was resisting the soldiers' beating fell to the ground; someone in the crowd decided he would challenge the beating of the woman and started shooting. The soldiers, in turn, sprayed the crowd with bullets from their Kalashnikovs. Andrea, infuriated at what she was seeing, lifted her gun and shot through the *burqa*, hitting two of the soldiers in the back. In the shouting and confusion, no one saw a woman wearing a *burqa* and shooting.

Andrea motioned to Abdullah to start back to the compound. They left without being stopped. Andrea looked back once, and saw the Taliban soldiers carrying their wounded into the truck after leaving the beaten women and the bodies of two men they had killed in the dirt. Andrea and Abdullah were silent as they arrived at the compound; they had not spoken since leaving the village. Abdullah brought in the provisions he had purchased, looked at Andrea removing the hated *burqa*, and said, "Our meal will be ready soon."

"Abdullah, I want you to know…"

"I need no explanation. Oh, here is the package from the shop."

Andrea opened it to find two tapes: an old Billy Joel tape, and one of classical music. She smiled at Abdullah, said "Thank you," and a little later ,they ate their evening meal.

Abdullah said nothing throughout the meal; the calm indifference was too much for Andrea. "Well, what do you think about—" she started.

He stopped her. "You have much to tell Ahmed."

"So that's it–no opinion of your own? Well, I have opinions, and I have questions!" Abdullah had no wish to deal with her anger–another Westerner who did not understand or appreciate Islam. But she persisted. "Why are women being so abused; what's their status here, or don't they have any? Why should they be kept hidden under *burqas* or behind walls?"

"Actually, women are revered."

"Revered?" It seems to me they're more reviled than revered!"

"No, women must be protected, kept separate from men other than family. It is called *purdah*. They are the childbearers, but they are also a temptation to other men, a temptation that is looked upon as a weakness in a man's character, unacceptable in a country of strong men."

Andrea interrupted, speaking in the sweetest tone she could manage, "Obviously, that's not a problem for Ahmed; he's very strong." Abdullah, outraged by such disrespect, went on, his words now more a lecture than an explanation. "Women should not dress or act in such a way as to entice men. They should not go about alone. Perhaps you should read the Qu'ran."

"No thanks, not now."

"East and West," he said, "it is a big problem."

Amused at his impassioned pronouncement, Andrea couldn't help laughing, adding her bit of humor. "You got that right; is a puzzlement."

"Puzzlement?"

"Anna and the King of Siam. Whenever the King couldn't understand something, he would throw up his hands and say, 'Is a puzzlement!'"

"Hah," he grumbled. "An appropriate conclusion to this discussion." Ahmed needs to know more about her, he thought.

All was quiet when Ahmed entered the compound; as he neared the door, he heard faint notes of Andrea's beloved music, this time a soaring wave of rich melody sung by her favorite tenor. He remembered her words during her first days here; when she told them she "needed" music, she meant it. The door opened and Ahmed was swept up in the glorious wave of sound as Andrea, joyful at his homecoming, greeted him with an excited kiss.

"Your Italian tenor?"

"Yes," she admitted with a laugh. "I think you're jealous of him," she teased.

"And I think you love him as much as you love me!"

"Almost!" she answered. Her smile faded when she saw the fatigue in his eyes. "Come sit down, sweetie. I'll bring you tea; you need to rest."

"I'm all right. What I need most is you." His tired eyes devoured her; Andrea felt a delicious tingling racing through her body.

"Oh, Ahmed, I love you so."

He took her hand, leading her into their bedroom. She had unrolled the bedding earlier; now she removed each piece of his clothing lovingly, like a bride unwrapping a precious gift. Her heart ached for him; the weight of his responsibilities was obvious–his devil-may-care decisiveness did not fool her. She poured a little of the herb oil in her hand and massaged his body until their passion led them into a different world.

The routine of their days together resumed. Implicit in Ahmed's news about the front was the knowledge he would soon be going back. The next time, thought Andrea, I'm going with him. Ahmed and Abdullah worked on the old generator, made sure the compound looked worn and damaged, and checked to make sure the tunnels behind the house were open. The first morning of Ahmed's return was spent in long talks with Abdullah. Andrea was not included in these discussions; she wondered if Abdullah would tell Ahmed about the incident at the bazaar; probably not. That would be her responsibility, and she wasn't looking forward to it. She had no inclination to answer to anyone for her actions.

After the evening meal, Andrea and Ahmed went to the stable to check on Buttercup. "Isn't he a love, Ahmed? He's been so good, letting Abdullah ride him–he's my baby." And she gave her horse a kiss.

Ahmed took a dim view of all this affection being lavished on a horse. He had a love and respect for horses; he knew how valuable they were, especially the remarkable animals he rode when playing *buzkashi*. But he also had a fighter's detachment from the horse he rode.

"Enough about Buttercup, who, by the way, has another name befitting an Afghan horse. Abdullah calls him Zabuli."

"Yes I know; well, he's still Buttercup to me."

She had put off as long as she could her news about the bazaar, so she started by saying, "Abdullah was kind enough to take me to the bazaar. I wore that *burqa*, a horrible piece of sh...uh, clothing. And Abdullah bought two music tapes for me. So ..."

Ahmed stopped her. "What happened, Andrea?" He knew there was something she was trying to tell him. A flurry of quick words came out.

"Taliban soldiers came, they beat some women, someone in the crowd started shooting, and the Taliban shot at the crowd; they hit a couple of the men. I shot two of the Taliban. They didn't know it was me; nobody saw me. Then we left." Andrea waited. Ahmed had a serious expression on his face, not speaking for long minutes. She couldn't stand the silence any longer and said, "Ahmed, I had to do it! They might have killed more people!"

"Do you know how close you came to being killed yourself? Look into my eyes, Andrea, you must understand it is my duty to protect you; you're making it very difficult."

*Tell him, tell him!* "Ahmed, listen to me. I need to get out of this house, do what I was trained to do, I want to join your *mujahidin*." She hesitated, uncertain how much to tell him. "In that marketplace, people were having a good time, laughing, even when they knew they could be killed that very day. They accept all of it with such"–she searched for the right word–"grace."

Ahmed smiled. "It's our faith; Allah will lead us on the right path."

Andrea felt diminished in the face of such strong belief, yet doubtful about divine intervention.

"I hope so," she said.

Ahmed changed the subject; he wanted his questions about her answered. "Where did you get training for battle–a nineteen-year-old, a girl? Who taught you?"

She answered, "My father, Patrick McAlister. The training started long before I was nineteen."

"Your father? I thought he was a physician in Pakistan."

"He is for now, and I hope to God for the rest of his life. I don't want to talk about him. Oh sweetie, I need to go with you, to fight beside you. That's where I belong!" Ahmed gave her a long, thoughtful look, put his arm around her, and led her back to the house.

"Ahmed, women in this..."

"Andrea, changing the Afghan culture and attitude about women will take more years than we both have; customs in many areas may never change."

"Women could contribute so much more, Ahmed!" she exclaimed. "We need to try!"

"We?"

"Well, no, me. It'll be my gift to Afghan women!"

"A gift Afghan men will not appreciate!" Though he laughed as he said it, he knew the reality of American life was not the reality of Afghanistan, and his anticipation for their life together was mixed with an equal amount of apprehension. When they went to bed that night, Abdullah guessed Andrea had told Ahmed about the bazaar; he doubted that was the end of her misadventures. Andrea fell asleep quickly, relieved she had told Ahmed something about her father. Ahmed was glad she was safe; he was awed by her composure under fire, her accuracy with a gun, her determination to right what she saw as wrongs. What he first saw as a spoiled, reckless American girl to fulfill his sexual need was turning into something more ominous: a crusader, not a welcome thing in Afghanistan. What kind of man would have no qualms about teaching his only child, a girl, to shoot with deadly accuracy, and willingly place her in danger? *A fighter–she's too young–what if she's injured or Allah forbid, killed?* He could no longer imagine life without her. She still had a certain reticence; was it a fear of complete surrender? Her father–the key to the mystery?

He fell asleep, weary of battle, verbal or physical. They slept soundly, Ahmed with his arm around Andrea. He felt her turn away;

a little later, he was awakened by the sound of her crying, calling out, "No! No!," then gasping for breath. *Wake her.* He stroked her softly, whispering, "Shhhh, it's all right, my love, I'm here. Everything is all right. You're safe." She sat up abruptly, and he held her fast. "Did you have a bad dream?"

"A nightmare that comes to me sometimes."

"It's over, Andrea. Don't think about it; just think about us." Then he whispered endearments to her in all the languages he knew.

"Oh, Ahmed, so many languages!" The corners of her mouth turned up in an uncertain smile; then she solemnly declared, "You're a very smart man, Ahmed…but you know that, don't you? Can you love me in Russian?"

Ahmed laughed at her. "We can love in any language you like; I'll teach you some Russian if you want me to." Then he spoke in Persian, saying, "This is a little story my mother told me in Dari, but I'll tell it to you in English." And he recited such a wonderfully silly fairy tale that Andrea couldn't keep from laughing. "So," he ended, "they lived happily ever after and the prince told his bride, 'You're my sun, moon, and stars.'"

"That's what you must tell me!" said Andrea.

"And I will, at least once a week, because you are," he replied.

# *V. Devils and Angels*

Abdullah knew Ahmed was different from the time the little boy was eight, as he tried to explain to him why his parents were dead, killed by assassins from Kandahar. Ahmed's older brother, Rashid, twelve, accepted the news stoically, sure his parents were with Allah in Paradise; he was proud of them, proclaiming he would be a fighter and avenge their deaths–he would be honored to die for Allah if necessary.

Neither this statement nor Abdullah's explanations satisfied Ahmed; he had to know exactly why his mother and father were killed, what made the Pashtuns want to kill them. It was hard for him to understand why the killers wanted the Tajiks' territory and control of Afghanistan. His eight-year-old mind did not yet grasp the concept of war. But Ahmed was always an intensely curious and restless child; he asked questions about everything and had a deep desire to learn. Abdullah had made the most of his own education in France and was well respected as a professor at Kabul University, but he wanted a change, and the position as tutor and guardian of the Sharif children intrigued him. It worked out well; he found he loved the Panjshir Valley and the children he was teaching. Ahmed, he knew, was the one who would excel; at a very young age, Ahmed's intuition told him that knowledge meant power, even though at six, power simply meant outsmarting his brother or Abdullah. By the time he was fourteen, he knew what power really meant. As Ahmed grew into a strong young soldier, he developed the political art of persuasion and conciliation. He was easy to talk to, with an air of innocence and a ready smile. Ahmed learned how to get information; secrets that began as casual conversation were often shared unintentionally with this handsome, empathetic young man. Only Abdullah knew the iron determination beneath the guileless exterior; Ahmed's skills served him well until the battle at Mazer-I-Sharif.

The killing field of Mazer-I-Sharif was quiet. All that remained was the collection and disposition of bodies and body parts to families or unmarked graves. Ahmed stood outside the prison, directing his soldiers to round up RPGs, Kalashnikovs, artillery, and whatever else of value to them. The uprising had finally been quelled–at a terrible price. The Northern Alliance prevailed after a hard-fought battle; Taliban had surrendered and been taken prisoners, Ahmed was ordering his men to seize weapons. Suddenly, Sayed Rasoul, the Uzbek warlord, appeared accompanied by a contingent of guards and press people.

"Let them go," he ordered, "they will go home to their families." Ahmed, furious at this announcement, faced Rasoul and shouted, "Do you know what you're doing? We can't trust this group of Taliban! I'm telling my men to take arms and prisoners!"

Rasoul shrugged his shoulders, posed for the press, and was driven away by his officers. Ahmed stationed his men to guard the prisoners. With five hundred Taliban and one hundred Northern Alliance soldiers, the Taliban refused to surrender, one blowing himself up, and the revolt started. Rasoul's men had left the area. The Americans who were there called for reinforcements; the planes came and dropped their bombs on the wrong targets, killing some Northern Alliance fighters. British forces and American Special Forces moved in; more bombs came down, blowing up an ammunition dump and killing Taliban soldiers. Combat between the Northern Alliance and the Taliban inside the fortress became a deadly hail of bullets sprayed in every direction. Ahmed's men fought desperately, winning a costly victory. Many were lost during the three days of fighting, all due to a foolish mistake.

When he returned the day after the battle, Rasoul made a theatrical show of anger at the debacle, seemingly incredulous that the Taliban did not honor their surrender. No words were exchanged between Ahmed and Rasoul, but Ahmed would neither forget nor forgive this disaster.

How had the Taliban gotten access to the armory after their regular weapons had been confiscated? Something was very wrong–a betrayal-his men-Rasoul's? Ahmed stood alone on the field with its litter of corpses and body parts and watched his men. Even the most ribald of his soldiers were quiet after the bloody victory. Then he saw the five men huddled together under some trees, seemingly euphoric-hashish? No, cocaine! Ahmed approached them, and in a voice both commanding and menacing, demanded, "Where did you get the drugs? Who gave them to you, what did you give in return?"

They would not answer. Ahmed had his suspicions, but could not be sure. But he was sure of the disposition of the five traitors. There was only one conclusion for them. As he prepared to leave, Jeff, the CIA man he had been introduced to, walked up to him. "This was a damned messy operation, but I think your guys are gonna roll right over the Taliban from here on in. We'll be into Jalalabad and Kabul before you know it."

"The sooner the better-winter's coming on," replied Ahmed.

"Uh, I have a little piece of information you'll want to take care of; got this from a good source." Ahmed already knew what it was. "It will be handled," he said curtly.

Jeff shrugged his shoulders. "Okay, Ahmed-hope to see you in Jalalabad. Keep your eye on Rasoul."

Ahmed didn't answer. He kept his distance from men he didn't know, especially foreigners.

That evening, Ahmed gave instructions to his deputy, made sure his five prisoners were shackled, then headed south to the foothills of the Hindu Kush. They trotted at a moderate pace, appearing from a distance to be a group of soldiers with no heavy arms, on their way home. They came at last to an area about an acre in size, almost a circle, secluded by shrubs and some trees. Abdullah had called this place Golgolha (sound of the dying) and told Ahmed of its use in the past as a place for prisoners who committed serious crimes.

On one side of the land was a crumbling structure that may have been a jail of sorts; on the side was a deep trench. Ahmed led the men along a narrow path into a walled courtyard. His prisoners had no saddles, no personal belongings, no arms, nothing but the clothes on their backs. Ahmed dismounted and pulled each man off his horse. The five men guessed their fate, resigned themselves to it; all prayed they would be with Allah that day. Ahmed's voice was low and without emotion as he said, "You think Allah will receive you into

Paradise? I wonder if he welcomes turncoats, traitors, scum that you are."

His own men had betrayed him, he had no mercy on them. The man behind the betrayal he would punish in good time. It was an unpardonable offense, and there was only one punishment for these five men. They flinched and prayed softly as Ahmed, gun drawn, stood directly in front of each one and fired straight into the heart. As he prepared to shoot the fifth one, the man threw a knife. It landed in Ahmed's shoulder, throwing him off balance. He fired, dropping the gun–the bullet went into the man's leg. A bad outcome, and Ahmed knew it; the injured turncoat lay on the ground bleeding, writhing in pain. Ahmed felt the cold metal of the knife tearing his flesh, forcing his blood out in small spurts. He struggled to his feet, tried to mount his horse, but he had no strength–he would have to walk. First, he wanted to finish the man off, but where was his gun? He cursed himself for missing the knife concealed on his prisoner, for not having killed the man, then losing his gun and not having strength enough to mount his horse.

Andrea had been waiting for three days. This time, she knew where Ahmed was; knew, in fact, about the uprising at Mazar-I-Sharif, and she was worried. Ahmed and Abdullah were unaware that she was listening to their discussion. They saw her going to Buttercup's stall, not knowing she climbed back through a small window and hid near them. For once, she overheard information she needed.

Abdullah wanted to go with Ahmed, but Ahmed's instructions were terse. "Stay with Andrea. Protect her with your life, if need be."

And Abdullah growled, "That girl to be the death of me? What a sorry end for an Afghan! She has put a spell on you."

"I'll put a spell on you if you don't stop complaining–do as I say." Then Ahmed smiled; he couldn't be angry with Abdullah for long. "She's put a spell on both of us–I know you're fond of her."

Abdullah couldn't deny it. "Possibly, but be careful of her; she's dangerous."

Then their voices lowered, but Andrea had heard enough. Adding to her torment, the nightmare was visiting her again, a vague omen of evil. None of it was clear, but all of it was bad.

On the third day, she decided she could wait no longer; wrapping herself in her cape and scarf, she looked into the parlor where she saw Abdullah guarding the door, absorbed in the Afghan music on the radio. Hoisting herself up into the window opening, she slipped to the ground. It was almost dark. She freed Buttercup's reins, mounted him, and rode off, following the rough road that Ahmed had mentioned.

She had ridden for almost an hour when she heard a clanking sound like metal–what was that? Following the sound, she rode Buttercup on a path leading into a walled compound. Andrea turned on her small flashlight and took out her gun. She was totally unprepared for what was in front of her. She came upon the scene of an execution: five men shackled to one another, four looked to be dead, shot in the chest, and a fifth, with a gunshot wound in his left leg, was moaning in pain. He looked at her in shock. Was this someone to help him, this girl dressed in black? She got down from her horse, came close to him, green eyes surveying him sadly.

"Help me, I've been shot by a madman–see, he assassinated my companions, that devil…black eyes, black heart. I got him with my knife, though. He can't get far with all that bleeding."

"What is his name?" She didn't need to ask–she knew.

"It was Ahmed Sharif, Ahmed, Ahmed the murderer!" he shouted. Yes, he had killed them–why? They were his prisoners–Taliban, or did his own men deceive him? She felt something hard under her boot, reached down, and picked up Ahmed's gun. Andrea knew what she had to do. She said, "Go with God," aimed the gun and fired. The fifth man died.

Where was Ahmed? She mounted Buttercup, rode back on the path, crossed the road, and carefully picked her way through the brush. He had to be somewhere on this path, she thought. At last she heard the sound of labored breathing; cursing and then flashing her light, she saw Ahmed struggling to walk, leading his horse. At the same time, she heard Abdullah's voice in the darkness, "Andrea, help me get Ahmed on his horse."

After Abdullah applied a tourniquet to Ahmed's arm, they got him in the saddle and slowly made their way back to the compound. They carried Ahmed into the house and placed him on the bed. Until that time, Andrea hadn't allowed herself to feel panic, fright, or worry. It was clear Ahmed had lost a lot of blood.

Abdullah quickly produced medical supplies and applied compresses to stop the blood flow, cleaned the wound, and made a poultice, which he placed over the wound, finally bandaging the area. As Abdullah was caring for him, Andrea sat by Ahmed's side putting wet cloths on his forehead. The night's events finally penetrated her consciousness. Ahmed was weak from the loss of blood, in pain, but he knew he would be all right with Abdullah and Andrea caring for him. Still, he had unfinished business to take care of. He saw Andrea trying to control her crying. He wanted to comfort her; she had found him, how far had she gone to...? But she came from the wrong direction, from Golgolha! What did she know?

"Andrea, Andrea," he whispered before exhaustion and sleep took over. Andrea's tears spilled out even as she knew Ahmed would live. They were not just for Ahmed; they were bitter, angry tears for man's passion for war. She mourned the wounds laid bare in Afghanistan; men had made this country a playground for terrorists. Good old Dad would say, "Well, it's the way things are, love." Her mother would say, "Cry, Andrea, that's what women do." Tonight she killed a man with ease and deliberation; it seemed familiar, a cloudy image from childhood.

Patrick McAlister was one who was never caught, the clever one, a man in the shadows. But Andrea knew things she was not supposed to know, secrets she couldn't share. On her fifteenth birthday Andrea was introduced to terrorism. She met "Uncle Tim" that day.

Her father bellowed, "Come meet your Uncle Tim, he's a distant relative, very distant, all the way from Ireland." Patrick laughed. Uncle Tim reached out to shake her hand, and Andrea instinctively recoiled at his touch. He was a dark-complexioned, muscular man, six-feet-four, quiet, with a menacing air about him. She disliked him immediately; he had the cold eyes of a snake, she thought. He shouldn't be here on her birthday. Why did her dad invite him?

Her father and the unwelcome uncle went out of the house to the barn. "I'll just show Tim what we've got here," boasted Patrick. They didn't notice her as she followed them, running around to the far door and hiding in one of the stalls. They were deep in conversation as they entered–her father was angry.

"Damn it, Tim, I told you to leave McShane alone. He needed no punishing; he was a good lad, just a little impetuous."

"You're too patient with these young bastards for your own good, Patrick. It had to be done, McShane was doing a lot of talking to the wrong person. I took care of him; we'll have no more trouble there, but I'm watching Shanahan. We must act fast to stop these leaks."

Her father's tone changed upon hearing this news. The two men looked around, lowering their voices. Andrea couldn't hear all the words, but the few she did hear were chilling. "...make it quiet...river...McShane...no loose ends...end it."

Then they walked back to the house from their "tour" of the ranch. The "uncle" left soon after. When he said goodbye to Andrea, she knew she was looking at a killer, and when her father gave her a birthday kiss, she looked in his eyes and saw a terrorist.

The shock of her new knowledge about Patrick left Andrea feeling bewildered. Her father, after all, was the one who had taught her to ride, to shoot, to ignore the kids who teased her; he was painstaking in cultivating the fearlessness and toughness she displayed as a very young child. She knew she was the son he wanted. But Patrick was a paradox; he was tender with her, talked of his pride in becoming a doctor, told her tales of ancient Ireland. Her mother looked forward to a career for Andrea in the world of music; Patrick had other plans. About a year after that, her father took her to Ireland where he bought horses, two Connemaras and two Arabians. This was the stated purpose of the trip; Andrea didn't question the reason. It was the first time she saw the place where her father was born, Northern Ireland.

The small cottage in the Sperrin Mountains was nestled in a beautiful valley. It was an enchanting land, green and lush, unlike Arizona–a bucolic, peaceful scene with no hint of the "troubles" that took place in Belfast. They had lunch in Omagh, the county town;

Patrick pointed out on their way the places he had known as a young boy before the family moved to Belfast. He was strangely subdued; most of her questions went unanswered. He had never talked much about his parents; Andrea's impression was that her grandmother had had a hard life before she died at the age of forty-five, and her grandfather had not been a nice man. "Oh, he'd take the stick to me now and again, and to Ma when she got uppity." Andrea felt no ties to either one of them.

On their last night in Belfast, Patrick took her to a small pub where he was greeted like a long-lost relative, with laughter, handshakes, slaps on the back, and pints of ale. Patrick introduced his daughter in his usual boisterous manner. Here he was in his element.

Andrea was given a pint; "Just one, my girl, thank God your mum's not here." Young Sean O'Malley started playing his accordion.

"Ah, a good Irish tune; sing along for me, there's a good lass."

Andrea felt herself being drawn into the camaraderie of the evening, sipping some of the strongest drink she had ever had. They were all in high spirits; it's time to go, thought Andrea. The fun gradually slid into an almost whispered level of jokes and curses, then into ominous, quiet conversation. Andrea glanced across the room and saw someone she had hoped never to set eyes on again. It was "Uncle Tim." He was in deep discussion with Sean O'Malley. A voice inside her said "go, go."

"Dad, I want to leave. We have to be up early tomorrow to catch our flight." Andrea made a quick exit without being seen by Tim; Patrick spoke to him on the way out.

"Andrea was here somewhere–I guess she left ahead of me." He caught up with Andrea outside. "Andrea, why didn't you say hello to your Uncle Tim?"

"I didn't want to; I don't like him."

Nothing more was said, but Andrea remembered that night for years, and by the time she met Laura at nineteen, she had had enough of the Irish conundrum. My father calls those men patriots, freedom fighters. I know better, she thought. They're conspirators, assassins. The hell with the lot of them. I wouldn't trust any one of them.

Ahmed awoke the next morning from his drug-induced sleep feeling hazy and unrested. He remembered that Abdullah had given him medications, antibiotics and a sleeping pill. He felt his forehead–the fever had subsided. *I have to get up–where is Andrea?* He remembered her crying last night; she had looked like a frightened little girl. Ahmed tried to raise himself from the bed; a sharp pain took away his breath and his strength, and he lay back down. As he made a second attempt to rise, Andrea came in.

"Ahmed sweetie, no, you can't get up yet–oh, Ahmed." She kissed him and felt his head. "The fever's gone down, but you're not ready to do anything but rest."

"Andrea, I need to get up–right now the only thing I want to do is get to the bathroom."

"Just a minute." She left, returning with Abdullah. The two of them supported Ahmed as they helped him to the bathroom, Abdullah staying with Ahmed.

When they came out, Ahmed said, "I'll be all right," and waved them away. He made his way to the parlor and sat on one of the cushions. "Don't worry about me," he said as he saw the look on their faces. "Andrea, come here. I need to talk to you."

Abdullah left them alone. She sat by his side, reluctant to face him.

"Andrea, tell me about last night–you found the prison, didn't you–"

Andrea interrupted him. "Ahmed, you don't need to go back there. The fifth man is dead." She spoke in a confessional whisper. "I shot him; I had to, of course. I don't need to know about any of it, I just knew he couldn't be left alive. Abdullah took care of the horses. Oh, Ahmed, seeing you wounded with all that blood was…very hard."

"Did you think I was going to die?"

"I wasn't thinking, I was just scared to see you bleeding and helpless–thank God for Abdullah."

"Yes, I do thank God for Abdullah. But if he hadn't come, you would have gotten me home. I thank God for you, my love. I'm sorry you had to kill a man for me. It was a stupid mistake on my part–but then, the whole affair at Mazar was wrong," and he told her about all of it, ending with his suspicion of one who engineered the betrayal.

When he finished, he was quiet, keeping to himself the names of two men who would pay for their deception. Andrea was ready to help him as he got up and started walking. "Not back to the bedroom, my love. We're going outside; just put your arm under mine, I'll be fine."

They walked out into the brisk morning air, pungent with the faint fragrance of artillery rounds and mortar fire, and stood looking out over the mountains. Ahmed seemed distant, his expression the reflection of Afghanistan's countless conquerors and warlords-grimly calculating, assessing time and distance, planning the next maneuver. He was quiet, studying the beautiful deception of mountains with their promise of death. Ahmed turned to Andrea. In a tone of resignation, he spoke in a low, meditative voice, "Sometimes we forget we must understand our enemy, though once you know him, he may no longer be your enemy. It is easy to lose one's identity. I must be more careful of friends as well as enemies." A long pause. "Trust is a tricky thing in Afghanistan."

"Yes," said Andrea. "It's tricky everywhere–it doesn't pay."

"Andrea, tell me about your father, your childhood."

She had never told anyone the secrets she held inside about her father; if ever there was a time, this was it. *How can I do this–how can I put into words…I'm not sure what my feelings are.* Ahmed was waiting for her to speak. *You don't know how hard it is, Ahmed. The words are there inside of me; how can I say them? Oh God, what would Ahmed do–avenge me, somehow? No, his temper is measured–he's much more deliberate than me. Still, he would not forget it.*

"Andrea?"

She spoke, hesitant at first. "My father…my father, is part, a big part, of the IRA." She paused, her voice low, as she struggled to speak. He taught me about guerrilla warfare, survival techniques, how to shoot like a sniper, how to make bombs, how and where to acquire weapons–oh, Pakistan's a terrific source, by the way! How to be a soldier. Soldier, shit! I was supposed to become his number two terrorist! I thought he was wonderful when I was very young. He loved me, he read poetry to me, encouraged my dancing, let me roughhouse with the cowboys. I got to travel with him to other countries." Silence again. "I guess I was a good cover. I didn't know about the IRA until I was fifteen. Lucky for me, I was old enough to know that wasn't what I wanted to do with my life, so I tried to change it."

"Change it?"

Andrea sat with her legs crossed, eyes cast down, hands clasped tightly. "After my fifteenth birthday, I decided… decided not to go with him anymore, to concentrate on my dancing; I told him I wanted to finish high school in Arizona and spend some time with Mom, but everything was coming apart–he was very angry. I went with him when he got the teaching job in Pakistan, then came home. That summer, my mother and I went to New York and I met Laura. She changed my life." She looked directly at him for the first time. "After you told me Laura and John died, I had a strange feeling…"

"These nightmares you have, are they about your father?"

"I don't know. So, now you know about my childhood and my father who's still with the IRA. Funny, you might like him if you ever meet him–he's a big, blustery, good-looking Irishman full of stories and fun, an evil man."

She helped him out of his chair, putting her arms around him. He looked at the girl he had first thought of as a diversion to give him comfort and relief from war; now he saw the damage carelessly inflicted on her by a father who had no conscience. His instinct told him there was something else, but it lay hidden in the nightmares.

Ahmed awoke to see Andrea's curls on his chest and hear her soft breath sounds: relaxed, contented–no bad dreams last night. Weeks had passed since she reluctantly told him of the recurring nightmare. He ran his hand through the curls; at times he felt as much like a father to her as he did a lover. Disturbing thoughts flooded his mind and his face took on a grave expression, a mirror image of his father. It would not be easy, this choice he had made. But it wasn't a choice, it was a stroke of fate, like lightning, a destiny inescapable. Thinking of the troubles it would bring upon him, he absently stroked the curls of his sleeping beauty and smiled. She will be the mother of my children, my sons. Her blood will strengthen our people for generations. If only they could understand, but tribal loyalties run strong and deep.

It was almost time for prayers. He gently moved her aside, looked down and whispered, "I love you–it is time for prayers."

She opened her eyes. "Oh–say just one for me."

"Yes," he answered, as he prepared to place his problems in the hands of Allah.

# VI. Road to Hell

*Take my hand, you must lead,*
*soothe my soul when it's bleeding*
*teach me how to understand*
*so much death in this strange land.*

Patrick McAlister embraced the terror he had been born into. He was a tall, strong boy with fiery red curly hair and a temper to match, softened somewhat by his jokes, stories, and loud laughter. For all his vulgarity, he was a clever lad who knew how to keep his mouth shut when it counted. A collector of information and a firebrand, he joined his gang in the streets of Belfast to harass the British, but soon realized there was no percentage in unimportant battles. As he grew older, he developed his skills at using information to organize, blackmail, to put the right person in the right job; he knew how to instill fear in friends and enemies. Patrick became an elusive operative; to the unpracticed eye, he was just a bellicose, loudmouthed Irishman. Few knew him for the menace he was.

At some point in his life, Patrick knew he would not die an old man. After the wild joy of his youth was spent, after he ceased to believe he was immortal, reality took hold hard the night he barely escaped from an English bullet. A bad night, a bad decision, doing the job himself; he had given in to temptation after one too many pints. "Not like yourself, Paddy, my boy; time for a change; time to leave."

With money, and papers that looked real enough, he left for America. In his overwhelming egotism, he decided he would become a doctor, directing his considerable intellect to the pursuit of an education. Eight years later, with an M.D. after his name, he moved to Arizona. Patrick always had a foreigner's curiosity about America's Wild West, so he bought a ranch near Tucson and set himself up in practice. It seemed Belfast was far behind him; he was now a respectable physician with a charming Irish accent and smile. He loved Arizona: its climate, the desert, the openness of it, the bizarre rock formations, and the lingering aura of its ancient peoples.

Escape from Ireland was easy; escape from his past was not, and one day he found the past at his door in the form of an old friend, Sean Murphy. At Patrick's look of surprise, Sean smiled. "You know the IRA, Paddy, we have our ways. 'Tis quite a place you have here; by the look of things, you're doing quite well."

"Aye, I've done all right for myself." Patrick couldn't resist a little bragging.

"And you a doctor now, I'd not have thought it! You must have the ladies wrapped around your little finger," laughed Sean. "It's in high society you must be now, my boy."

Patrick returned the laughter. "No, Sean, I'm not quite civilized and refined enough for what passes for aristocracy in the good old USA. But they pay well; that's what counts."

"Ah, yes, so you're quite content, Paddy?" Sean looked at Patrick in some amusement, guessing he was far from content.

"Well, I should be, shouldn't I? Sure, and I miss the old life a bit. Mind you, I have no intention of going back. Is that why you're here, Sean?"

"No, my boy, we know you can't return to Ireland just yet."

"Oh, is it money you're after, then?"

"That would be very helpful, Paddy. And a little of your expert knowledge would be even better."

That was the beginning of Patrick's re-emergence as a master of covert operations. He welcomed the intrigue, the secrecy, the plotting, and the danger. His medical practice was lucrative, but it was becoming stultifying–he needed more–even with the work on the ranch, he'd manage it all. So it started again. A slight complication arose when he met Wenonah, a striking Apache Indian. He decided he would court and marry her–he was drawn to her exotic beauty, her background and heritage. Wenonah fell in love with him easily. She knew life with Patrick might be more complicated than life on an Apache reservation, but she had her art, her pottery, and basket weaving to sustain her. It worked out well; they were both happy when Wenonah was pregnant, Patrick hoping for a boy. His disappointment at the birth of a girl was never obvious; he had to admit she was a beautiful baby, with green Irish eyes and curly red-blond hair.

Wenonah's life revolved around Andrea until the little girl was six years old. But somewhere in the halcyon days of her daughter's childhood, she had to face the reality that Patrick controlled the little girl. Andrea's life became filled with guns, military tactics, hard labor on the ranch, as much as it was with the music she loved. He took her with him to Ireland, to Indonesia, to countries that did not welcome Americans.

As time passed, Wenonah became aware Patrick lived a secret life; he was not an unfaithful husband but something far more disturbing–a manipulator of men; she knew it had to do with the IRA, but exactly what he did she never knew and never questioned, accepting and loving Patrick as he was. To almost everyone, he appeared to be a respected physician and a hard-working rancher. When Wenonah visited her father on the reservation, he would take her to the shaman, Satanta, who prayed with her to the Great Spirit and gave her special symbols of her ancestor, Cochise. Wenonah was keenly aware she was one of a very few of his descendants, and she felt a duty to keep as many of the old ways as possible. She never forgot the words of Red Cloud: "They made us many promises, more than I can remember, but they never kept but one; they promised to take our land, and they took it." She in some way connected the rape of the Indian lands to Patrick's cause; it calmed her when, deep in her heart, she suspected him of vile deeds.

Though looked down upon by a certain segment of Tucson society as "that boorish Irishman who married an Apache," it was a triviality that meant nothing to Patrick and Wenonah. It suited Patrick's activities. Never did it occur to him his daughter would pay a high price for such a father. Wenonah was a loving mother who took refuge in her art. For her, the paintings, pottery and baskets were the life of her people; she was grateful she had the skill to preserve her culture, for her mission in life was to keep her heritage alive.

Wenonah was disappointed Andrea didn't pursue her education to the highest level, but not surprised. None of the succession of schools she attended suited her. Because she threw away the notes that were sent home with her, teachers and principals called the parents–earnest discussions usually concluded with the cliché, "she doesn't get along well with others." Of course not, thought Wenonah; she's an adventurer. The "others" she did get along with were cowboys, strange old characters who lived in ramshackle housing near the ranch, and her grandfather, Jack Redbird, who lived on the reservation.

Patrick had done his work well. Andrea wanted nothing to do with formal education after she finished high school at sixteen. Early in her school life, she had been dubbed a near genius; when Wenonah mentioned her daughter, she referred to her as "our wayward prodigy." She's going to live a dangerous life, thought Wenonah, I just hope she finds happiness and love somewhere along the way. There were days when the sight of Andrea's baby pictures on the dresser would tear at her heart, so deeply did she want her own little girl back. Some day, she thought. Then she walked out to her garden to say hello to the creatures who lived there and knew her–ah, the freedom of her garden! Her comfort lay in the ephemerals of life and her strong Indian connection to nature. On warm, sunlit mornings, she could feel sunshine rushing through her in giddy abandon. In the big living room, at a certain time of day, she would look up and see the water in the birdbath outside reflected on the ceiling. It would quiver and dance, be still, then dance furiously again, shooting its rays over her ceiling. She laughed at the dancing water caught by the sun, and a new design evolved in her mind for the next pot.

Ahmed's wound was healing well; he was ready to go back to the front, and Andrea knew it was time to assert herself. She made her declaration of independence one morning a few days before Ahmed was to leave. "This time I'm going with you–from now on, consider me a Northern Alliance soldier. I'll be worth any inconvenience I may cause."

This was met with little protest from Ahmed. He had discussed the subject with Abdullah; he knew, after the debacle of Mazar-I-Sharif, that Andrea could not be contained as a virtual prisoner in the house, and Abdullah agreed. "You can't keep her here, Ahmed; she needs to be free to do as she feels best, otherwise you will have real trouble on your hands. Take her with you; you'll have better control of her. She'll be a good fighter."

"Yes, her father would approve," Ahmed said with some sarcasm, to which Abdullah retorted, "I doubt if he'd approve of her living with you, and neither would your father. It is wrong; you are flouting our religion, our culture. You know your father had planned for you to be married to your cousin Saira; she knows how to keep a home and serve her husband!" Abdullah's usual calm demeanor had changed to a low-voiced, agitated storm of rebuke. "I am concerned for you, Ahmed. You have responsibilities to your country. "You may be chosen for a high office in the new government. But with Andrea-imagine the problems!"

Ahmed had indeed imagined the problems, but he also imagined the joy; his path was different from the one others had envisioned for him. "Please say no more about the matter, Abdullah. We will overcome whatever problems there may be."

Abdullah sighed. He prayed he could smooth the rocky road laid before these two who would not listen.

Jalalabad–War is hell, but it's a little bit of Paradise if you have your woman right there beside you! Bombs rained down like manna from heaven, crushing everything in their path. The mighty American firepower produced results as advertised, and the Alliance welcomed this turn in their fortunes even as they viewed it with a jaundiced eye; one never knew, in Afghanistan, how long victory would last. Ahmed took her into battle with him, treating her as a soldier, giving up the Afghan principle of *purdah*, and protected against danger or temptation–at least until the time was right to resume control.

Andrea watched the exploding American bombs with satisfaction-smart bombs, they'd minimize casualties. To reach their *marcaz* (military base), Ahmed's *mujahidin* traveled the narrow passes of ragged mountains, up and down switchbacks, crossing streams and fording rivers. They passed villages decimated once by Russians, once more by Taliban artillery. A soft shroud of snow descended, sent perhaps by some sad angel telling them they must stop and rest. Weary and hungry, they came to a village *chaikhana* (tea house) and were welcomed by an old white-bearded wraith of a man. His weak voice was laced with bitterness as he declared, "Taliban devils destroyed my family. If I see them again, I kill them!"and he brandished his old carbine rifle. "Taliban not far away!"

Then Anwar's shout came, *"Awan ast, awan ast!"* (Incoming mortar)

They dived into the snow as a deafening blast exploded over top of them. Andrea's sorrow for the old man turned into terror. She crouched on the ground, shaking with fear. But she was alive–Ahmed? He was standing, binoculars in hand, searching out the enemy position. The *chaikhana*, where? Leveled, and in the ruins, the old man lay dead, still clutching his gun. War had become real; death, a wily miscreant, waiting in the wings.

They were snow-covered, the Afghan mountains, but far removed from the summits of the Alps, the Rockies, or any of the slopes of pleasure-seekers. Forbidding inclines made desolate by wars, they were peppered with land mines, filled with the ghosts of hope, defiled by cruel intentions. Abandoned bits of life told their tale: tattered school books, a headless doll, scraps of bright fabric, pieces of homes whose hand-hewn log supports lay haphazardly about.

Andrea found it hard to shake off a sense of doom, yet the men joked and laughed as usual. These were hard men and Ahmed was one of them. Their pursuit of the Taliban was relentless; they wanted their country back. As they crossed the Konar River, she felt they were crossing the river Styx, dead souls along with them. How holy could this struggle be?

They plodded on, stopping only for prayers. Reaching the *marcaz*, the *muj* rested, cleaned their weapons, replenished supplies from the arms cache stored there, and waited. Waiting's the worst, thought Andrea. The Taliban had been located not far away, to the north of the

Alliance. Soon the enemy would be in their gun sights. The men were quiet.

Andrea shut it all out; to slow her racing pulse, she thought of Arizona–warm, sunny, safe. *God, I wish I were there now.* As she pictured herself riding Satanta, hat off, wind blowing through her hair, she heard a shout, "Fire!" A tumult of sound assaulted them; bullets whizzing by, machine guns hammering, RPG trails hissing. The cacophony of battle wrapped her in its fury as she discharged her rifle at random. Then a calm determination took over; she found her targets and shot with an accuracy born of desperation and training. Though she showed no sign of weakness, her heart beat with an alarming fluttering.

Hassan, a seasoned twenty-three-year-old, told her, "*Natars*, it gets easy; everything be all right, all crazy in Afghanistan. Trust in Allah. You good soldier!"

Ahmed took advantage of a lull in the fighting to check on her. "Are you all right?"

"It's harder than I thought... I didn't expect so much..." She gestured toward the dead fighters. "I'll be all right... just so much death." He had tried to prepare her, to make her understand about the horrors she would face, things her father could not teach her. She must get used to it, and quick. He had no more time to comfort or protect her now.

"You're a brave soldier," he said, and left to resume his position.

Another volley of artillery shells and RPGs. At last Andrea breathed a sigh of relief at having dodged the second wild burst of gunfire, but she stood up too soon.

"Stay down!"

At the same time she heard Abdul's shout, she felt a pressure on the right side of her head so intense it knocked her down. She lay stunned, in pain, as Abdul knelt beside her; there was just time to see his anguished eyes and wonder if she was dying before she lost consciousness.

Andrea awoke to see a very anxious Abdul by her side. "Oooh, Abdul, my head–what happened? I've got a terrible headache."

"Thank God you're awake. I've got to tell Ahmed. Don't get up!"

Andrea felt for blood; there was a bandage around her head. *Grazed by a bullet because I stood up too soon! Now Ahmed will have an argument to use against my fighting with him. Damn!* She forced herself to stand, holding her hand over the bandage. Abdul and Ahmed walked into the cave, Abdul babbling something about guarding her.

"I'm fine," she announced. Abdul looked at her in disbelief, and Ahmed put his arms around her. Before he could deliver a lecture, she said, "Don't fuss over me; it was just one of those things that happen."

Abdul made a hasty retreat as Ahmed scrutinized her. "You're lucky-next time pay better attention."

"I will; do you have any aspirin?" she asked, determined to say nothing about the throbbing pain in her head.

He gave her two tablets. "I know damn well how much it hurts."

So she became a seasoned Alliance soldier, fighting alongside Ahmed, impatient to rid this quixotic country of its ancient tyranny. But, after that, what? Freedom has its price, and like the Hindu Kush, the problems that loomed ahead seemed insurmountable. Ahmed, the orphaned little boy who wanted only to be a soldier, knew Afghanistan needed a miracle. He was painfully aware of his country's needs, and his prayers to Allah were urgent. Andrea, succumbing to her perverse nature after exhausting days of grime, dust and gunfire, asked Ahmed if they were on the Road to Paradise-a bad metaphor that amused her-an Emerald City in Afghanistan? Ahmed knew her so thoroughly that he ignored her barbed remarks, merely commenting, "What an American thing to say!"

In a cold sweat, Andrea struggled to sit up. She felt imprisoned by the dream, and it took what seemed too long a time to fight her way out of it. Finally, she crossed over from dream to reality. This was a new nightmare-she saw pieces of men falling into a black chasm, saw herself shooting until the pieces disappeared into a bottomless void; then more pieces fell... She looked at her hands-empty, no gun-heard the men snoring, heard the sentries laughing softly as they compared Indian movie stars, heard distant gunfire, then a gentle question from the darkness.

"Andrea all right?"

Startled, she recognized Anwar's voice.

"Yes-you'd better go back with the men."

Then he was gone-speaking to the commander's woman in the dark of night was risky. Andrea looked for Ahmed among the men; he was asleep, thank God. She wouldn't tell him about the dream even if it came again; it would only reinforce his opinion about her presence among the *mujahidin*. The dream visited her a few more times, then faded away along with her qualms about killing men whose wives and children were waiting for them to come home. She was accepting the cost of war, immeasurable in every way.

Tough as his Alliance was, Ahmed's men were physically and mentally tired; admired as Andrea was, she belonged to Ahmed, not to his soldiers–they wanted to go home to their own women. There was a certain night when Andrea acknowledged to herself this was not an adventure. That night, her monthly period had finished; what a damned nuisance to cope with, she thought. She was unusually tired. Ahmed came into the room of the bombed-out structure and lay beside her, covering them with their now dirty *patous* (blankets). It was very cold; the two of them huddled together under the blanket. They were not the only ones in the room. At least twenty-five of the men were nearby, sleeping under their thin coverings. Andrea felt Ahmed unbuttoning her shirt, her pants, cupping her breasts, kissing her, tongue reaching deep into her mouth.

"Andrea, I'm so hungry for you–I can't wait."

And he was on top of her, penetrating her with an intense, furious passion, quick, animal-like. After he finished, he lay beside her, wrapping them tightly in the blanket.

"I'm sorry, my sweet, I didn't mean to be so rough. Forgive me."

In other circumstances, Andrea might have considered the apology an advantage, a tiny edge in the ancient game of sex–that momentary rush of power over man. But that was play; she had no interest in such games anymore. Andrea looked over at him to tell him "it's all right," but he was asleep.

The building was dirty, the floor hard, they themselves were unwashed, and then there were the men near them, all of whom seemed to be asleep–at least she hoped so; it would be embarrassing to know they witnessed such an intimate moment. Afghans never allowed outsiders to see their women, much less be witness to such private acts.

She looked around. Close to them was Rashid, the old soldier, seventy, whose wife and two sons had been killed and thrown in the road by the Taliban, and Amin, twenty, trying to make money to feed his parents and sisters. Farther away were the three brothers who

hated the Taliban for their savage interpretation of Islam–
Mohammed, Abdul, and Abdur, who jokingly declared that "too
much Taliban interferes with our lifestyle." They wanted music and
movies, Eastern or Western, showing erotic scenes of dancing
women. Andrea knew all the men and felt comfortable among them.
She was treated with respect and a certain deference, partly because
she was a foreigner outside the Islamic culture, and partly because of
Ahmed's status beyond that of a commander. After more weeks of
fighting, there was nothing that embarrassed her. She had to laugh
when she thought of Patrick's training–little did he know he was
training her for fighting with the savages in Afghanistan! If he could
see her now! Her poor mother would be horrified–or would she?

Ahmed's army was fighting its way to Kabul and Kandahar.
"Army" was a fluid term, as it applied to Afghanistan. Men left the
*marcaz*, returning as needed. They had little use for military
ceremony. But Ahmed was their commander, and, except for the five
men who met their fate at Golgolha, their loyalty was unquestioned.
He knew this rag-tag band of soldiers, without proper uniforms,
without decent shoes, without water for long periods of time, was
determined to rout the Taliban; now that the Americans were
bombing, his Alliance had the opportunity to finish an enemy that
had robbed Afghans of the smallest joys in their hard lives. With old,
poorly working equipment, they were dependent on the help of the
Americans, but they had their Kalashnikovs and their rocket
propelled grenade launchers, weapons they valued above all else.
There was a variety of weaponry that might need to be surrendered
some day, but it would take a very long time, if ever, before they
would give up their guns. Victory…peace…those were commodities
too fragile to be counted on in Afghanistan.

Ahmed had no illusions about the Alliance. They could be every
bit as cruel and capricious as the Taliban; they considered tribal
conflicts ordinary, warlords and banditry an unchanging fact of life.
But they were fighting for their unique brand of culture, their own
interpretation of Islam, not something imposed on them by
foreigners. And now, brought into sharp focus by Andrea, was the
status of women. She was free-spirited, strong, independent, while
his country's women were seemingly punished for such qualities.
Worse, he thought, they are being abused and raped at will, even by

this Alliance. Ahmed felt ashamed of them, ashamed of himself for accepting such abuses as part of the privilege of being a man. He would never be at peace with this situation, and he knew Andrea would not ignore it. Another goal, another fight. Acutely aware of the deficiencies of his country, he knew it was the height of naiveté to envision a rosy picture in Afghanistan's near future. Yet he also knew that things must change; he believed it was possible–this was a moment to be seized. Whatever he did would be done in honor of his mother and father. Theirs was a lonely vision of a new Afghanistan and they lost their lives because of it.

To Andrea, life with the *mujahidin* was a blend of desperation, devastation, and broad humor punctuated by the warning to "trust only in God." All of it got to be a wild mix of tears and laughter, which of course was the way of war and life itself–but the Afghans had a special gift for the ludicrous, the wild, the cruel, the comic, the improbable, and in the end, the giving.

With the Hindu Kush winds roaring down upon them, they rode in the old Russian truck over the spine-jarring road. Too late, Andrea covered her face to avoid the choking dust assaulting her eyes, nose, and mouth. The howling wind swept up everything in its fury. Breathing became difficult.

"Cover up your face–cough it up, spit it out, spit it out!" shouted Ahmed.

When they finally settled into a bomb-damaged *chaikhana* for the night, Andrea in a space by herself , and Ahmed with the men, he came over to her. "Now you know what turbans and scarves are for!"

I don't need his shit, she thought, and started to snap back at him when he put his arms around her, holding her close to his chest. "Are you...?"

"I'm all right." She feigned a casualness she did not feel, "just careless."

"Afghan wind across your face will always be with you."

He held her for a moment longer, then went back to his men. Reconnaissance had shown the group of Taliban numbered about one hundred, clustered together, no reports of any more nearby. They scrambled down out of the truck, unloading the machine guns, RPGs, tins of ammunition, mortars, and mortar shells, and hauled them up the steep slope to a ridge. Pulling scarves over their faces to fend off the wind and dust, they prepared to meet the enemy. As the guns were placed on their mounts, mortar fire started raining down upon them. Ahmed checked the positions; no one had been hit, but Taliban held the high ground. Andrea had settled in place with her Kalashnikov when she heard an American voice. Surprised, she turned to see what she guessed was a CIA operative. Their eyes met, his openly curious. He said, "Good luck," in a slightly mocking tone. Andrea didn't answer–who the hell was he; he looked more like a reject than an active agent. Then she noticed nineteen-year-old Anwar standing on the ridge-line, looking down the mountain.

"What is it, Anwar; what do you see?"

Flashing a happy smile at her, he said in his shy manner, "A vision; better country, no Taliban–maybe peace long enough to stay home. I think we will win–hope we behave better than Taliban!"

He knows, Andrea thought; he sees the promise as well as the danger in victory.

The two sides exchanged fire for about an hour with a couple of minor injuries to three men; they were not making much progress in their attempt to move up the mountain. Darkness was starting to fall; gunfire stopped for prayer, ablutions having to be made with handfuls of dust for lack of water. After rice, cucumbers, *naan*, and dried fruit were shared, Ahmed ordered them to advance to a higher position, spreading out so they might avoid the direct line of fire, and took a quick moment to make sure Andrea was all right.

She was climbing along with the men, carrying her gun and ammunition when Ahmed came behind her and said, "Careful–these rocks and peaks are very sharp."

"I'm okay, sweetie; you stay safe." She was already bleeding from small cuts, her hands and legs testament to the piercing mountain ridges.

Jeff Scott took long drags from his cigarette–damned stupid habit, he thought, but the smoke dulled the confusion pounding away in his head. All of Afghanistan seemed to be descending upon him; he saw a collage of scenes running together like Easter egg dyes mixing into an ugly muddy gray. *Nothing's clear in this country; no black and white here, just this shitty in-between crap. Friends, enemies–they're all alike. I'm tired of it, I don't belong here anymore. Mazar-I-Sharif was it for me. We're almost to Kabul, thank Christ.*

He thought of Ahmed Sharif; at least he tried to give Ahmed a warning, but Ahmed must have found out in some way about the five men. Jeff figured they were probably dead by now. Good. He wouldn't need to worry about that anymore. Oh sure, pat yourself on the back for that one; what about Ali and that slimy piece of shit, Sultan; can't depend on them, he thought. Taliban! They'll turn on you at the slightest provocation; why the hell had he worked out the deal with them and Rasoul? They had almost gotten what they paid him for at Mazar.

Well, so what if it hadn't quite worked out? He did what he promised. All this trouble with drugs and guns so Rasoul could look good. *Jesus, I'll be glad to get out of here, won't be long now. Lay low, Scottie.* The cigarettes lulled him into a fantasy of sex. He saw an Afghan girl, a cousin of Ahmed, a while back when he went to the family compound with his boss. She was really something; even with her face partially veiled, he recognized a beautiful woman. He gave her a long look, custom be damned. She met his eyes for an instant, then looked away. *Hmm, I wonder; better not.*

Jeff woke up suddenly to the sound of gunfire close to his head, jumped up, grabbed his gun, and checked the range of the Taliban. Close. He walked over to the Northern Alliance soldiers, greeting them in Dari. "How you boys doing–any good information for me?"

Smiling, they said, "Good morning, Mr. CIA. No information today."

It was then he saw the woman in black with a Kalashnikov slung over her shoulder, taking her place on the front line. *My God, he really does have her here with him.* He had heard that Ahmed was living with an American woman, an almost unheard-of relationship for an Afghan, but he had never seen her. Okay, Ahmed was not the average Afghan, some sort of aristocracy here. But he might be screwing things up for himself with that girl.

At the thought of Ahmed's possible downfall, Jeff felt a surge of satisfaction. Ahmed was too sure of himself, too aloof for his taste–and quick to take revenge. He thought of the five men; he was taking his chances going along with Ahmed's *mujahids* to Kabul. He'd have to be more careful from now on if he expected to reap any benefit from the CIA status. When Jeff first met him, he thought Ahmed, a Westernized Tajik, would be receptive to his offers of information, open to deals, but this Afghan reminded him more of the Afridis. He was a dangerous man. And Ahmed did not welcome foreign interference, only foreign bombs.

Jeff was right. Ahmed was not impressed with foreign diplomacy or foreign aid. Even as he welcomed the bombs and humanitarian aid, he took a dim view of all of it, knowing it would not last–tribalism had always prevailed in Afghanistan. He wanted nothing to do with Jeff Scott and his machinations. Jeff couldn't contain his curiosity about Ahmed's woman; he made his way to the firing line ostensibly to speak to a deputy. When the woman heard his American accent, she turned briefly and looked at him. He met her eyes, saying, "Good luck."

She said nothing, resuming her position. But Jeff had seen a striking young woman, very young, well able to handle the AK 47. Forget Ahmed, thought Jeff, he's almost incorruptible, except with women, apparently. What's he doing with a young American girl–how did that come about?

"Nadar!" he called to the sixteen-year-old fighter near him. "Who's the woman here?

"She's with Ahmed–her name is Andrea."

"I see she's American. Interesting to see an American woman at the front. Tell me about her."

Nadar smiled. *The CIA man thinks he's clever.* "Nothing to tell; know nothing about her. Ask Ahmed," he said, knowing that would be the end of it.

"Okay, just thought I'd ask."

*Leave it for later, don't push your luck.* He'd had a close enough call at Mazar.

They made their way up the steep slope to a relatively level ridge where they settled into what they hoped were advantageous positions. With sentries posted, the men and Andrea settled down for the night under a sky showing off its new moon with stars sparkling in all directions. *Reminds me of all the guns firing over Afghanistan,* mused Andrea. *But stars are peaceful, stars are beautiful...*Her fanciful comparison was at last replaced by much needed sleep.

She awoke about five in the morning to the sound of gunfire and jumped up, Kalashnikov ready. Bullets whizzed by her. *Damn, where are the RPGs?* As she reached for a grenade launcher, she saw Rahim, at fifteen, the youngest of the *mujahidin*, firing his RPG in the direction of the gunfire. There was a small explosion as the grenade seemed to find its mark. They heard loud curses coming from the Taliban position; Ahmed had all the men on their feet. *Closer than we thought; can't tell anything in this darkness.* The gunfire from above stopped. Dawn would be breaking soon, along with the day's fighting. All was quiet; they waited, said prayers, had their rice and tea, and admired the kaleidoscopic dawn as it smiled down on them.

"Wait," commanded Ahmed. He heard a faint stir from above, spotted some activity in his lens, and gave a signal to advance in silence. To the background thunder of bombs in the distance, with no talk and as little noise as possible, they scrambled up the slope, coming closer to the Taliban than expected. It was an abrupt confrontation. The Alliance fighters found themselves face to face with their enemy and opened fire–machine guns, Kalashnikovs, RPGs. The surprised Taliban, unprepared, sprayed their gunfire aimlessly. Ahmed's soldiers discharged their weapons with deliberation and accuracy, decimating the Taliban, until most were killed. About twenty terrified men held up their hands in surrender. Three of Ahmed's men had died in the fighting, four were wounded.

One of the dead was Anwar–the happy young warrior. Andrea looked at his body waiting to be taken away for burial and felt a fierce anger raging through her, anger she could not suppress. She found Ahmed and looked at his resolute face revealing no emotion. He stood alone, withdrawn, an observer. He must feel something, she thought, he must, and she gave voice to the anger. Her loud, emphatic, bitterly edged words cut through Ahmed like a sword.

"God, Ahmed, sometimes I want to pound and pound and pound on heaven's door and say hear me! Hear me! Help us! Give us at least a little of your Paradise here on earth, now! Not later–now!....now."

The last word was quiet. The brief outburst exhausted her. He stood unresponsive, watching the valley below. Taking her hand in his, he said, "Yes. I know."

She turned away from Ahmed and started down the slope.

They were getting closer to Kabul. Leaving their wounded to be treated in a village clinic, the *mujahidin* deposited the captives in a prison compound on the way to Kabul. They traveled several miles before descending another rock strewn, snow-covered slope. Andrea was grateful for her Indian buckskin boots; going up is easier than coming down, she thought. As she made her way down, she heard a shout–"*Allahu Akbar!*"

Almost on top of her, she saw the Azeem brothers lined up with Mohammed above the other two as he shouted a triumphant "God is great!" and laughed. They seemed to be playing some idiotic game; Mohammed gave Abdur a push, Abdur tumbled into Abdul and all three came rolling down like circus acrobats, barely missing Andrea. She stared at them, open mouthed, curses forming on her lips, as the three lay in the snow. *Oh, my God, are they alive?* As she broke into a run they stood up, shaking with laughter at their antics. Andrea's anger and concern dissolved into laughter. War in Afghanistan: tears and laughter, grief and comedy.

A grim sadness settled on Ahmed's face as they passed through devastated villages where women and children gathered around them, pleading for transport to safety. Ahmed met Andrea's look with a cold detachment. "We cannot take them with us."

Close to Kabul, they came to a bomb-shattered, abandoned village and took shelter in the mud brick houses, paused for prayers, and ate the last of their rice.

"My God, it's cold. I wish I had a cup of hot coffee."

Coffee again! "You can't seem to get used to the cold. Too much Arizona, perhaps?"

"I've been in mountains before," protested Andrea, "the cold here is different."

"Cold is cold," was Ahmed's comment.

"Whatever…I just know I'm freezing. And I'm sore," she added. "I feel like I've broken ten f…bucking horses!"

"Count yourself lucky, my little American, you have warm boots."

"Yes sir!" She gave him a mock salute. "I'm sorry, I have no business complaining, it's just…"

Ahmed walked away. He knew Andrea was tough; she had proven herself time and again, climbing mountains in the thin air with the rest of them, going without water, but she wasn't hardened over long years of deprivation; how could she be? Let her complain, thought Ahmed; he knew she would complain only to him, never to his men. Andrea had grown to love those men; they were like the boys at Paloma–tough, irreverent, smart, with an innocence and a wild sense of humor. She saw the *mujs* and her cowboys as a brotherhood. They had the same sustaining faith in Allah and God, and they treated her as one of them. The Afghans laughed at her jokes and stories of Arizona, telling her she was a good soldier, "better than the TV men. Afghanistan is only for the tough, the faithful or the crazy, mostly crazy!"

But she decided to keep some distance between herself and the men; she was tired of the pain of caring. The grief for Anwar, for the man who one moment she was joking with and the next viewing as a corpse, was too much. The *mujihidin* grieved; they raged and cried and called on Allah for help; that was their way. But Andrea had stubbornly maintained her composure; from childhood, displays of emotion were discouraged. Until now. If Ahmed needed her, she needed him even more, and before he could say another word, the pent-up grief came pouring out. She couldn't look at him, ashamed of her weakness, and buried her head in his chest, sobbing uncontrollably, holding on to him as she drowned in a sea of sorrow. Andrea couldn't hear his words, could only feel his arms around her, his hand stroking her head, his lips kissing her hair. Finally, she heard the comforting sounds a father would make to soothe his hurt child.

"Andrea, we have this place to ourselves for the night. I'll keep you warm." Ahmed kissed her and started unbuttoning her shirt.

"Oh God, Ahmed, I wanted to heat some water for washing. I still feel dirty."

Ahmed shook his head. "It doesn't matter."

With that, he kissed her lips, her throat, continuing to ravish her, from her mouth, to her breasts, on down her body to her clitoris. Whatever inhibitions Andrea had left were obliterated by his lips and tongue insistently arousing her to a frenetic climax. "Oh my God," she moaned. Every inch of her body seemed to be pulsating. Ahmed's lovemaking before had been conventional, satisfying her romantic idea of sex. But now, he gave himself to her with a passion that demanded the same abandonment from her. A revelation, it set her free to give back, no holds barred. She had been reluctant when he started, but the ecstasy he gave her was so great, she felt only wild desire to give him the same joy. She kissed him until she lay between his legs, placed his hard penis between her breasts, stroking and kissing it until he said, "stop," rolled her over and thrust his penis into her with a quickening rhythm, kissing her lips as he reached a climax. Again she felt the thrill of the climax shooting through her. Now she was warm.

She looked directly into his eyes for the first time. It was Alexander who gazed at his Roxane, victorious, triumphant, and humbled.

# VII. Strange Players

Ahmed's *mujahidin*, settled into their position about twenty-five miles west of Kabul, were poised to take the city. They were attracting the attention of TV crews who were playing their show-and-tell game in Afghanistan for as long as the war was exciting enough to bring in good ratings.

Lauren Bannister studied the *mujahid* commander, wondering if he was important. Why hadn't she heard of him before now–she had sources, well-paid informers, staffers who were supposed to do the investigative work and present her with stats, background stuff. But none of them seemed to know much about this guy. It was by accident she came across two *mujahids* discussing him. Thank God she knew some Dari. Ahmed Sharif. Her interest was aroused as she saw him standing on the hilltop–tall, handsome, erect, giving orders to his lieutenants. His dress was the usual *shalwar kameez*; instead of the *pakol* he wore a bandana tied around his head.

She asked for an interview; it was agreed upon under the condition it be short with no video. She was looking forward to meeting this mystery man. He at last walked toward her; finally, she thought, and prepared to write.

"Miss Bannister, I am Ahmed Sharif. You have questions for me?"

Lauren's professionalism was shaken somewhat by Sharif's imperialistic manner, his good English, his good looks–chiseled features, brown skin and dark eyes with an Asian cast. These Afghans have gorgeous eyes, thought Lauren; he could be a film star. After an awkward silence on her part, Lauren started the interview. Her questions were pointed and specific; his answers were polite, general, and just informative enough to be of interest without revealing anything significant. She felt she was dealing with a highly skilled diplomat, sure as hell not the usual savage warlord.

"Perhaps I could have another interview when you reach Kabul?" No harm in asking.

"Perhaps," was the succinct reply.

"I wanted to give our audience a sense of what life is like personally for an Afghan commander. For instance, do you have a wife and children?"

"No," he said.

"Well, perhaps we can get together on a personal basis."

Ahmed held the laughter that started to surface. This woman was idiotic. But he answered her with a cold courtesy, "No, Miss Bannister, that is out of the question."

"Ah....well, thanks for your time," she said, but Ahmed had already walked off to another area.

He was watching Jeff Scott, who had rejoined them after Jalalabad. The man did not look well; he seemed distracted, smoked incessantly. Ahmed saw the American's gaze fixed on Andrea–simple curiosity, or something more, lust? Well, Scott wouldn't be in Afghanistan much longer.

Andrea had been watching the reporter with some curiosity–an American, interesting; she thought about talking with her, but decided it wasn't a good idea. The woman had not noticed her at all– she was too busy looking at Ahmed. She was flirting with him! It had never occurred to Andrea to be jealous of other women wanting Ahmed; suddenly she felt embarrassed, insecure and very young. Lauren was attractive, poised, and sophisticated in her designed-for-Afghanistan outfit, and...hell, predatory, while she was in her usual pants, boots and head-scarf; she needed washing.

"Oh, damn," she muttered to herself, "I don't look like a woman anymore. I can't even shave my legs." She wondered if Ahmed was tempted by Lauren Bannister; then the scene of their lovemaking in the bombed-out house flashed before her, its honesty, intensity, and sweetness wiping out any doubts about Ahmed's commitment. The media people, meanwhile, took off for positions away from the line of fire.

"Andrea!" Andrea was startled out of her moment of uncertainty by Ahmed's shout. "We're moving up–here, take these RPGs." They scrambled over the stony ground, wind flogging their faces with stinging sand, and climbed into the truck. The *mujahidin* moved forward, carrying gun mounts, RPGs, artillery, the old Russian machine guns, and ammo cases. The Americans had bombed Taliban positions into a wretched semblance of an army and the Alliance took full advantage of the American fire power. This was the time, the moment they fought so hard to reach, the capture of Kabul. As they advanced toward Kabul, Taliban retreated.

"We will not move into Kabul as an army just yet," Ahmed announced. "The situation would be too chaotic; I'll send in a contingent to keep order."

"How long can you keep the men here?" asked Andrea.

"I don't know; we'll see, but I won't be ordered about by Americans for long."

"Did she get her story?" Andrea couldn't help herself–she had to ask.

Ahmed smiled slyly at her. "Don't worry, that woman could never compare to you!" Again, she felt embarrassed–Ahmed saw right through her. Oh, well, so I'm transparent, so what. She looked forward to entering Kabul.

When they finally went into Kabul, Andrea felt no triumph. The capital of Afghanistan was the saddest place she had ever seen. All she could compare it to was the World Trade Center–its devastation seemed complete. If the gods of war were determined to bomb Afghanistan back to ancient times, they must be pleased with their work in Kabul.

The once-beautiful city lay crushed almost beyond recognition; it was a shock for Andrea to see the place where Laura and John, from the purest of motives, came to help Afghanistan. She briefly wondered where, in this destruction, they had died, but put it out of her mind–would they be happy for her–glad to know Afghanistan was now her home? She turned to look at Ahmed's reaction to the wild victory, and saw a different look in his eyes, a look she guessed came from childhood memories. He saw in his mind a scene in a park–they walked beneath trees green and lush with mulberries and apricots. He saw himself at twelve, with Rashid, Soraya, and cousins Saira and Assif, eating ice cream, laughing at the boy who looked like a monkey.

"Half human, half monkey! Come in, watch him do tricks! Learn your fate from Aiza, who knows all!" The monkey boy, prodded by his master, teased the audience with one of his tricks, then disappeared behind a curtain.

"Can we go in, Abdullah?" begged Rashid.

"No, you may not. I don't approve of such things; you shouldn't laugh at that child's misfortune."

Disappointed, they soon forgot the monkey boy and bought a *tulchan*–a cake of dried mulberries and walnuts. Soon they would be flying their new kites, and ...the vision was suddenly erased from his mind by gunfire. The park with its beautiful trees was now just a dusty mix of dry grass and rubble. One tree struggled to live, a sad remnant of a different age.

The streets of Kabul were a cauldron of joyful bedlam; the dregs of Taliban perversion were snatched off shop windows and pulled from street posts. Some beards were shaved off, windows displayed CDs, videos, books–a myriad of once-banned items. Most of the celebrants were men. Andrea saw a few women; most would not want to be caught in the middle of all this. Would there be women later, without the *burqas*? Probably not. Paradise is in ruins, thought Andrea, then caught sight of the public transport of Afghanistan. She laughed, in a rare joyous moment, at an object straight out of a fairy tale. The old Russian bus was a fantasy of color in this land of Oz. It dazzled the eye with bright colors, scenes of Afghanistan and Mecca, Arabic inscriptions, red tassels, jingling bells and bright plastic flowers springing from every opening. Written in large Arabic script on the sides were the words TRUST IN GOD, advice which Andrea would thereafter complete mentally as NOT IN YOUR DRIVER.

Ahmed was not the only commander with *mujahidin* entering Kabul. The Uzbek warlord, Sayed Rasoul, led a small army into Kabul from the north, and the meeting between the two factions was strained, to say the least, after the battle of Mazar-I-Sharif. Press corps, TV correspondents, cameras were all there in force to record the meeting between the two leaders; Kabul was a confusing mix of soldiers, press, jubilant Kabulis, and a small number of ineffective policemen.

It was a bizarre scene, one that Ahmed did not want Andrea to be part of; he noticed Lauren Bannister among the press people–a presumptuous woman, thought Ahmed. He was worried about Andrea. He wanted her protected; she must go back to the safe house with Abdullah. In the meantime he had no choice but to publicly meet with Rasoul in front of the TV cameras; the bad blood between the two would have to be suppressed for now. They were supposedly fighting on the same side. But neither trusted the other. Rasoul's allegiance wavered between the Northern Alliance and the Taliban; his loyalty had always been for sale. Rasoul thought Ahmed Sharif too Western, too impractical, too secretive. He himself reveled in the TV coverage, but he would have to watch out for Ahmed. Andrea, in the meantime, was getting impatient with the intractability of Afghanistan's numerous tribes and their resistance to compromise. Men! The women could do a better job of it. Thank goodness Abdullah was traveling with them now; he provided a bit of sanity in the craziness as he attempted to give her some understanding of the complexities of the divisions in Afghanistan.

"Oh, Ahmed, don't leave me; take me with you to Kandahar."

"I'll come back to you."

"But you can't guarantee that, can you?"

"Of course not–I can only promise I will always be with you."

But she didn't want to hear his lofty reassurance and couldn't disguise the angry desperation in her voice. "Oh, sure, I know what that means. Damn it, Ahmed, it's your body I want next to mine, you in the flesh!"

"My darling, my darling," he said over and over as he tried to comfort her.

Islamabad–It fell into his lap. Wrestling with a plan to foil this outrageous living arrangement of Andrea's, Patrick was suddenly presented with the chance to bring down the arrogant Ahmed Khan

Sharif. When opportunity knocked on the door, Patrick was always first to seize it, and it came in the form of Rahim Gul, the twenty-three-year-old son of Mohammed Gul, a highly placed official in the Pakistan Foreign Office. Rahim happened to be in the path of an out-of-control car bomb. The Arab driver had bailed out, leaving the car and its bomb to speed aimlessly into a group of young Pakistanis at a coffee shop. Rahim arrived at the hospital bleeding, in shock, close to death. Patrick immediately took charge of the extensive surgery required after Rahim was sufficiently stabilized, the most complicated operation he had ever performed. After six hours, the procedure was pronounced a tentative success. Patrick cautioned Mohammed not to celebrate just yet. "It will take at least a few days to know whether he will have a full recovery."

But Mohammed believed Allah would complete Rahim's healing; his gratitude was overwhelming and could not have come at a better time. "I am in your debt, Dr. Patrick, anything you want..."

"Get me into Afghanistan, to Kabul."

"It is a very dangerous place, doctor; I would rather give you money."

"I'll accept that when I come back."

"Why must you go to...."

Patrick interrupted, "There's no need for you to know—I can only say I have a friend who is waiting for me."

Patrick had been shocked at the letter from Ahmed Sharif—how could Andrea have fallen into his hands? Kidnaped by a Tajik soldier! When he got to the part about their living together—"Andrea is living with me by her own choice; I very much love and respect her and will keep her safe"—it couldn't be! Well, it was, but not for long. He would cut short his daughter's unfortunate venture into exotic romance. Didn't she know how dangerous this man was? Had he trained her to love danger so well she would run recklessly toward it?

He was alone in this effort to rescue Andrea; there must be no one else who could tell his daughter about the assassination of her lover. When Patrick finally saw Ahmed Sharif standing atop a tank amidst a rabble of Afghans, he understood what had drawn his rebellious daughter to Sharif. The *mujahidin* was a commanding presence, tall, good looking, with mesmerizing eyes. There he was, the savage, standing like a conquering hero, giving orders to his men as they occupied Kabul. It was an unsettling reminder of himself in the old days when he savored a successful bombing or assassination. Even at a distance, Patrick saw the fury in the black eyes. The Taliban prisoners, at least the foreign ones, would soon feel the exquisite pain of Afghan revenge–death–but first, torture.

Patrick's hand on the trigger of his revolver was sure and steady. He cautiously withdrew the gun from the baggy Afghan trousers, aimed, and shot. The rabble of Afghans scattered, *mujahidin* charged into the crowd. Patrick let the gun fall to the ground, easing his way through the still bearded, clamoring mob of confused Kabulis.

He looked back and saw Sharif still standing on the tank, Kalashnikov in hand–and smiling? What kind of devil was this? A sudden thrill of accomplishment surged through him. He had not succeeded in killing Ahmed Sharif. Yet, he laughed; I'm still a soldier, aye, I can still do it, by God. Then he felt *mujahidin* eyes watching him, waiting for a threat, a mistake, a sudden move. He slipped away, melting into the mob of Afghans. Bide your time, my boy, he told himself–wait and see. In the end, his windfall from Mohammed came in handy. He sent the money to Sean Murphy in Ireland.

Ahmed put down the Kalashnikov and smiled–there was no need to kill Patrick McAlister. Patrick had lost his daughter some time ago; just when, Ahmed didn't know, but lost her he had. Patrick's terrorist skills were no longer sharp enough and his judgment was clouded by jealousy. Let Andrea put the final nail in the coffin–sooner or later he knew she would do it. Ahmed almost felt sorry for the man trapped in the cross-hairs of his gun.

# VIII. Politics

Andrea inhaled the clean, crisp German air; it was a perfumed mix of newly mown grass, late blooming roses, soft gray stems of lavender and the raspberry smells of butterfly bush and phlox. Germany was a startling contrast to Afghanistan. What an orderly, neat, predictable world, thought Andrea, and they have plumbing here!

As their car rounded a curve lined with linden trees, the small hotel came into view. Andrea gave a gasp of delight. The half-timbered structure with its ornamentation took her back to a fantasia of childhood fairy tales. "It's right out of Hanzel and Gretel! she exclaimed.

"Hanzel and Gretel?"

"Oh," she finally answered, "They lived in a cottage like this, only smaller, and…"

Ahmed laughed. "You're a real storyteller, my Andrea."

"It must be the Afghan in me!"

"Well, enjoy it all while you can, but don't get used to it."

"If there is dancing, could we dance together in public; would it be permissible?"

"The fact that we are living together outside of marriage is what is not permissible."

"Oh," she replied, subdued by the feeling she had been reprimanded.

Ahmed smiled and rumpled her hair. "We'll correct that situation, my darling." She turned away so he wouldn't see the doubt in her eyes. They entered the rococo-style lobby and were shown to their room–no gingerbread there. They shared a look of wonder, then laughed.

"Now I know we're not in Afghanistan anymore!" joked Andrea.

"What room are your parents in, Andrea?"

"Uh, I think it's room 227. Oh God, I haven't seen them together in over a year or more; I'm starting to feel guilty about inflicting them on you when you have this conference."

"Don't worry about that. If they're here, I'd like to meet them right away."

"Oh sh.... oh all right, I'll find out if they've arrived yet."

So he would soon meet formally the man who had tried to kill him. Patrick McAlister would learn the depth of Sharif's love for Andrea and the lengths to which he would go to protect her. This meeting would serve as an agreement not to be broken.

"Oh, Ahmed, come look, we have a shower–and hot water. Yippee!" She ran over to him, giving him an enthusiastic hug.

"All this is going to spoil you; you won't want to go back to Afghanistan," teased Ahmed, enjoying Andrea's happiness.

"We'll have a shower, with hot and cold running water, in Afghanistan some day," pronounced Andrea. She turned on the radio and danced around the room to the music. Ahmed, sitting at a table, chin resting in the hand of his propped up elbow, smiled. The sight of her filled him with a pleasure that reminded him of the affection between his parents so long ago.

Sometimes Ahmed forgot that Andrea was only nineteen; she was so matter-of-fact, quick, and tough in battle. But here, she was a sprite again, his "wild child." At her age, Afghan women had been married for three or four years and might have several children. And old before their time, he thought. If Andrea was atypical, so was Ahmed, still unmarried at twenty-nine. His mother had instilled in him a deep respect for women, not by words, but by her loving nature and relationship with his father.

Romance was not an important part of Afghan life; women were generally viewed as embarrassing necessities, hidden away, protected from other men. Even the end of Taliban rule would not necessarily change that, at least in rural areas, for the villages of Afghanistan were still rooted in ancient times. The fact was repugnant to Andrea, even as she grew to understand it. Ah, but Ahmed, she thought, Ahmed is a gem amid the rubble. And me, what am I? Hmm...a thorn in the side of Islam; what can we do? Well. There is only one way, and I don't want to think about it now.

She unpacked their few belongings, inspecting the silvery blue dress she would wear that night and a suit to wear at the conference—and shoes, real shoes, not boots, shoes with heels! *I hope I don't trip; Ahmed chose these things—he wants me to look good, to show me off. Can't do that in Afghanistan, but in Germany… And Ahmed will dress in Western clothing; it's going to be interesting.*

She was beginning to get butterflies in her stomach. Andrea rang Room 227; her parents were there.

"Well, sweetie, I guess we may as well go into the lions' den."

"Andrea, it will be all right. Calm down, love."

Easy for you to say, she thought. As they entered the room Andrea saw her father with his "you can't get the best of me" look on his face, while her mother looked happy to see her. The introductions were awkward for Andrea, but Ahmed was polite, diplomatic, friendly. He got a good look at Andrea's father for the first time—curly red hair, blue eyes, ruddy complexion. A pugnacious, "I dare you" face, ready for a fight, then, an impish smile just like Andrea's, luminous and magnetic. But Ahmed wasn't drawn into the Irish charm. Already they knew one another in the most grotesque way. From the day in Kabul when Patrick attempted to assassinate him, the day he could easily have killed Andrea's father, Ahmed knew their tenuous relationship would continue; the time for killing had passed. His love and concern for Andrea outweighed any murderous thoughts about her father. *It must be erased, that day in Kabul, as though it never existed.* Ahmed's instinct told him he would always be friends with Wenonah; she reminded him of his mother.

The meeting went well enough—just a few thoughtless comments and jokes from Patrick. Then Wenonah announced she had brought a video of 9/11 and thought they should watch it.

No longer in her carefree mood, Andrea started to protest, but Ahmed said, "I would like to see it, Wenonah; I've never seen the entire thing."

The four of them sat watching the graphic video. They were silent; even her father didn't speak. Thank goodness her mother had gone back to Arizona before 9/11. The attack on the towers was seared into Andrea's soul; the horror, the indignity, and the insult of it was something she had buried too deeply to speak of to anyone. The tape ended.

Patrick's only comment was, "Damned CIA dropped the ball; all the information was out there and they couldn't connect it– incompetents. Sure must have been hell to pay for the drones; what a mess."

Wenonah looked sadly at Patrick. "I don't think that's fair, Patrick. I'm sure it was a complicated situation, not as simple as a small operation in Ireland, for instance."

Patrick was taken aback. Wenonah had never defied him openly, never had talked about Ireland. He started to say something, then held his tongue. Wenonah saw that Andrea was very quiet. Ahmed said, "Wenonah, were you there in New York when this happened?"

"No, I had gone back home, but Andrea was there–she and her friend saw it happen; two of their friends were lost there."

Still Andrea said nothing, just stared at the blank screen. Ahmed went to her, saying, "We're going out for a while. Thank you for the video, Wenonah."

As they left, Ahmed heard Patrick remonstrating his wife. "Wen, you shouldn't have brought that damned thing."

Keeping a tight hold on her, Ahmed led Andrea out into the quiet courtyard; they sat on a bench surrounded by asters still blooming under the late autumn sun. "Andrea, please talk to me. Why didn't you tell me–I think I understand, but you should talk about it. I can't make it go away, but I can help if you let me, love."

She forced herself to speak, to relive the hideous scene. "My friends...firefighters...policemen. So many people. Videos can't make it real, Ahmed, you had to be there; the smell, the dust, the ash, people jumping to their deaths...it was like being in hell..."

They sat without speaking for a long time. The Americans had come to root out an unspeakable evil in his country; he understood, but he wished they didn't have to be there.

"I'm sorry, sweetheart, so sorry." He held her; in a little while, she lifted her head from his chest, smiled, and kissed him.

"Thank you...It's a relief to say the words and to have you understand."

"Andrea, you don't need to thank me."

"Well, I think I do; I love you so." They sat in the sun, safe and content.

Ahmed broke their meditation. "This is a good time to give you my gift. Andrea, I want you to marry me. Please accept this, my love." And he took out of his pocket a small velvet pouch, opened it, and pulled out a ring.

Andrea was speechless. She wasn't sure how their living arrangement would be resolved–she knew it was unacceptable to Ahmed and to his religion. The ring would change that. It was a brilliant emerald surrounded by small diamonds.

"When I saw this, I knew it was for you; it matches your eyes." He put it on her finger. "Will you marry me?"

"Yes," she said without hesitation. His expression was one of surprise. "Did you doubt that I would say yes?"

"I wasn't expecting an answer right away, but I had no doubts."

Laughing, Andrea said, "Well! You're very sure of yourself, Afghan."

"I'm sure of you. Now, we must go tell your parents."

"I'm surprised you didn't ask my father's permission first."

"I thought it best not to, but if you like, you can take the ring off and I will ask him."

"No, no, I'm kidding, no sweetie, I'm not taking this ring off! I love it, I love you and I'm so happy I could…."

"Dance? We'll do that tonight. This will be a Western engagement party–we'll have an Afghan wedding when we go back home."

Home. Afghanistan. An uncertain life–the only certainty was their love. Andrea thought, I'm sure as hell that will be tested.

Back in their room, she heard splashing water as Ahmed turned on the shower; oh, how wonderfully decadent, such a different world. She undressed, went into the bathroom, and squeezed into the small shower stall with Ahmed. Andrea wasn't sure whether the look he gave her was disapproval or desire, but he stared as though seeing her for the first time. She returned his gaze, her eyes roaming over his body. He opened his mouth to speak; Andrea put her fingers to his lips and smiled. "Shhh," she whispered. Ahmed poured shampoo into Andrea's hair, sculpting it into stiff, fantastic designs.

"Am I not a good artist?" he asked.

"Stop it, Ahmed, stop! It's getting in my eyes–you crazy Afghan…ooooh," she yelled as he rinsed her hair and gave her a soapy kiss, laughing all the while. "I'll get you, just wait!" But she surrendered to his playfulness; he was not often this carefree. They made love in the cramped space, luxuriating in the water splashing over them, then wrapped one another in towels, refreshed and relaxed.

Ahmed dried her hair; "I love your hair."

"So I've noticed; I think I'll cut it short."

"No, no Andrea, you may not cut it, no."

"So you can torture me again in the shower?"she teased. "I absolutely hate my hair–oh well, for you, my sweet savage, I'll do anything," and she reached up and ran her fingers over his rough beard.

He smiled. "That's a dangerous thing to say, my love."

Ahmed lay on the bed watching Andrea dress. "What were you like as a child, Andrea?"

"What a question. I was a holy horror!"

"I don't believe you."

"Well, you should ask my mother. Ahmed, you haven't said much about my mother and father–what do you think? The truth, now."
"I like your mother very much; your father is, I think, a difficult man to understand, considering what you've told me about him. And…perhaps we have too much in common. I think he's trying to hold on to his little girl, even when he knows he can't."

"Oh it's always about control!" exclaimed Andrea. "He created me like a designer creates a costume; well, no more. Let's not talk about him now. I wish your mother and father could have been here with us. Do you have a picture of them?"

"Yes, wait," and he produced a photograph. There were his parents sitting on a wall in a garden, smiling. His mother was beautiful, with black hair and dark eyes, dark skin. His father looked light complexioned with dark curly hair and the dark Afghan eyes, a handsome man just like Ahmed.
"I can picture you as an adorable little boy."

"A stubborn, curious little boy who drove them all crazy."

"Including Abdullah, I bet."

"True. That's enough of old times. Whatever we were as children, now we need to make things happen. Come, put your dress on."

Andrea slipped the dress over her head, put on her high heels and stood before Ahmed. The long-sleeved dress covered her body completely; the mores of Islam were beginning to sink in.

"Am I all right? I feel strange in a dress and these shoes. Heavens, I had to get a bra, slip, panty hose. Too much." Ahmed took a moment to admire her; he had never seen her in any clothing except shirts, pants and scarf.

"Andrea, you're beautiful–you look like a princess."

"Like Princess Soraya of the sun, moon and stars?"

"Any princess."

"Do you know who I really am? I'm Cinderella! and if you don't bring me home by midnight I'll turn into...God knows what." Then she looked at Ahmed in his suit, tall and handsome. He would pull at any woman's heartstrings.

"You look so distinguished I can't stand it. Umm, you look good enough to eat."

"Come on, Cinderella, we're going to celebrate."

That day in Kabul had already revealed what Patrick needed most to know about Ahmed Sharif–he was a man who tolerated no interference from anyone. They met Patrick and Wenonah in the lobby.

"Well! I must say, Andrea, you look a proper young lady," pronounced Patrick.

Her mother said, "Andrea, you are beautiful."

"Thank you. Shall we go in the dining room?"

"Not yet, Andrea; Dr. and Mrs. McAlister, please have a seat," said Ahmed, and he led them to a sofa in a corner of the lobby.

What's going on, thought Andrea. She felt confused and nervous; she wasn't used to this extremely polite Ahmed in his Western dress. Oh, the ring, she thought, but... When they were all seated, Ahmed spoke, "I'm happy to tell you that Andrea and I are engaged to be married–I hope both of you approve."

And he took Andrea's hand to show them her ring. His English was correct, a little stilted, formal. Andrea felt herself on the verge of hysterical laughter, but just smiled instead. She didn't know that Wenonah and Patrick had been notified of the plans by Abdullah; or that Ahmed had written a long letter of explanation about Andrea and himself. Since Andrea had not contacted her father or mother after her first message about Laura and John, Ahmed had taken matters into his own hands. The McAlisters were grateful to know that Andrea was safe, stunned to hear about her living with Ahmed

Sharif.

"An Afghan! And she's living with him!" Patrick had blustered.

"And fighting; Patrick, this was your doing!"

"Hell, Wenonah, do you think I want her in that dung heap of a country!" In the end, Patrick and Wenonah had resigned themselves to the situation–Wenonah hoped she was happy, Patrick raged, yet admitted to himself, "Well, she's my daughter, all right. An Afghan!" They had graciously accepted Ahmed's invitation.

Wenonah admired the ring and gave Andrea a hug, saying, "Be happy, my dear. I think Ahmed is a good man; he seems very wise. And he's sweet."

"Yes, he is, Mom; don't worry about me."

Patrick examined the ring, hugged Andrea, and whispered, "You're in a real adventure now, lass. Be careful."

Wenonah embraced Ahmed affectionately–Patrick shook his hand, no Afghan embraces for him. A nice ring, looks pretty damned expensive, thought Patrick. At least this Afghan seemed civilized; he had manners, and probably money; he was not a mere savage. Patrick recognized a soldier when he saw one. The eyes gave it away. He almost felt a kinship with him–never!–but there were no more thoughts of assassination.

Then, he saw what had to be the rest of the party: a man in his thirties who looked like Ahmed, an attractive woman of about twenty-five, an important looking older man and a middle-aged woman. The men had beards, the two women wore head-scarves, but all were dressed basically in Western style. Ahmed got up to greet them and made introductions: his brother Rashid, his sister Soraya, Mohammed Khalis, the interim Afghan ambassador, and Halima Gul, one of two women delegates to the meeting.

Ahmed introduced Andrea last. "This is Andrea; we are engaged to be married." My baptism under fire, she thought. I hope I don't blow it; oh well, what the hell. So she stood and smiled, saying, "Hello, it's wonderful to meet you" to Ahmed's brother and sister and "How nice to meet you" to the delegate and the ambassador. Andrea spoke to the Afghan dignitaries in Dari, the language she had been using since meeting Ahmed. When English did wend its way into her new language, it was a different English. Gone was the faddish teenspeak; in its place was a more adult speech pattern, on occasion slightly formal. The profanity, not as frequent, remained. "There are no other words that will do!" she would tell Ahmed when she saw his disapproving look.

They all went in to dinner, where Patrick was the only one to order beer–hell, it was Germany; the others had mineral water. Andrea was seated between Ahmed's brother and sister. Soraya was fascinated by the ring. "Oh, it matches your green eyes. Ahmed told us about you; I understand you are with him fighting?"

"Yes, I know it's not....I know I'm not traditional for Afghanistan; I hope both of you will understand."

Rashid spoke, "We're not surprised that Ahmed chose an American. He has Western ideas and the soul of a poet. I'm afraid that Ahmed is ...well, a romantic," he said, as though to apologize for a failing. "Of course, he is an excellent commander; his men like him. We respect you as Ahmed's future wife; you'll be treated in the same way any foreign woman would be, uh, that is," he paused as if forgetting part of a rehearsed speech, then smiled, "Afghanistan will not expect you to put on a *burqa* and behave as an Afghan woman."

Soraya attempted to make things clear. "Rashid's right. You will have more freedom, even though you'll be married to an Afghan. I think it will be good for Afghanistan; you know, Ahmed is expected to hold an office in our new government. It's all very exciting; this is good for Ahmed–he needs a wife. People will like you, and Andrea, I like you, we'll be sisters!"

Even as the idea of belonging to this family excited her, it also scared her. Will I fit in–I can't be Afghan–will they accept me? Is Rashid afraid I'll corrupt their Muslim values?

As though he knew her thoughts, the dialogue went on with Rashid observing, "Ah, Soraya, some things may be changing for women in Afghanistan, but not everything, the changes will be slower than you want." He gave Andrea a rather stern look. "Tonight is not an example of what Afghanistan will be like anytime soon."

No kidding, she thought, but sooner than you might want, future brother-in-law.

After the bombardment of helpful hints, Andrea managed to say, "I understand, but I'm glad we're here enjoying this evening." *God, let me come up for air.*

As the dinner went on, she began to feel more comfortable with

Rashid and Soraya and more at ease with Mohammed and Halima. You'll be living among Afghans, she told herself, get used to them.

As soon as she heard music, Andrea started to relax and enjoy the evening. The German band was playing one of her favorite pieces–did Ahmed arrange that too? She saw him stand; he was going to dance a waltz with her in public. She hardly heard him asking her to dance, bemused by this celebration he had planned some time ago. He took her in his arms and led her to the dance floor. Ahmed had a sure feel for the rhythm of music, and they danced together with a natural flowing grace.

He looked at her gravely, then smiled. "Are you angry?"

"Yes, I don't know, no. How can I be mad when we're dancing together to this beautiful music and you look so handsome? You're amazing."

"Stop talking, everything is going well, just stay close to me." He kissed her as they were dancing and said, "How is my Cinderella?"

Andrea laughed, replying, "I'm beginning to think I'm Alice in Wonderland!"

"Another fairy tale?"

"Sort of."

Soraya watched her brother as he whispered in Andrea's ear, then rose from his seat to lead her onto the dance floor, taking her in his arms with a delicacy she hadn't seen since they were children. Ahmed absolutely adores her, she thought, and unexpected tears filled her eyes. I wish Abdul was here dancing with me. But such a thing was unimaginable; he would never allow it. It was enough that Ahmed had insisted she come, assuring Abdul it was proper and appropriate. Abdul had no choice but to agree.

Andrea saw that there was a steady flow of conversation around the table. Her father seemed to be behaving, keeping all amused with his stories and his accentuated-for-the-occasion Irish brogue. As the dance ended, she kissed Ahmed and said, " I love you."

At the table, Ahmed's brother whispered to him, "Ahmed, you really love this girl, don't you?" "Yes."

The group toasted Andrea and Ahmed with an Afghan wish for happiness, ending in *Allahu Akbar*–God is Great.

The conversation around the table grew animated, some of it in Dari, some in English. There was a rather heated debate between

Halima and Rashid, something about a girl's school in Herat, laughter from Ahmed and Soraya over childhood misdeeds; Patrick and Wenonah seemed to be having a serious discussion. The ambassador asked her if it was true that she was half American Indian, how interesting. Andrea answered yes and went on to explain her mother's people were part of the Chiricahua Apache tribe; the ambassador seemed very pleased–what does that have to do with anything? thought Andrea. Oh right, it's the Mad Hatter's tea party.

Just then Ahmed whispered they would dance a last dance and leave. Andrea gratefully stood and melted into his arms. Patrick watched with envy and a hint of regret. He had never seen Andrea so radiant, so happy, so sure. Hah! trouble was, she hadn't chosen an American or an Irishman, but a goddamned Tajik, fighting for that pile of rubble that was Afghanistan. Andrea could feel all eyes upon them–the whole table was watching them. Ahmed was showing off, daring anyone to object, in effect saying he would not be intimidated by custom. But she was wrong–to all the watchers except Patrick, the dance, the music, was simply balm to their bruised spirits, a rare moment of beauty. Nervous, Andrea said, "Oh Ahmed, I think we've all fallen down the rabbit hole."

"What?"

Andrea laughed, looked into his dark eyes and said, "Never mind, sweetie, it's just a silly part of the fairy tale."

"I see."

"Here we are, Cinderella, or Alice, whoever you may be, home by midnight."

"Thank goodness."

"Well, what do you think?"

"I think I can't trust you, you with your surprises, I think your sister is sweet, your brother not convinced I should be your wife, my father respects you, my mother is crazy about you, and the ambassador and the delegate seem to be favorably impressed and somewhat accepting. So there. Ahmed, I've never been more tired in my life. Politics is exhausting."

"Politics?"

"Well, that's what it was, wasn't it? I know you did it for me and I love you for it. Now I'm going to sleep."

With that, she undressed and got into bed, soon falling asleep;

Ahmed picked up his Qur'an, looking for some divine guidance. Too tired to concentrate, he put the book aside and got into bed beside Andrea, who seemed completely content as she murmured his name.

Andrea awoke, hardly believing the happiness bubbling inside her. *I'm engaged, I'm going to be married. Laura, Ahmed gave me a beautiful ring, it's incredible! Where is Ahmed? He's been quite the diplomat since we got here.*

Just as she turned on the radio, he walked in carrying a tray with a breakfast of scrambled eggs and apple strudel.

"Good morning, are you Andrea this morning?"

"Yes," she giggled, "that food looks delicious."

"Take note—I'm serving you breakfast in bed with coffee and you don't have to go to any parties; just enjoy the day," he said with a kiss.

"How did you get to be such a romantic Afghan?"

"Paris."

"Plans, Ahmed, plans—tell me our plans." He didn't miss the sly dig.

"Well, our wedding will be in the Afghan custom, more or less. My parents were married in the old tradition; it took days for all the ceremonies to take place, but our wedding will take just one day. Weddings are not as elaborate as they used to be."

Andrea hardly heard Ahmed's explanation; she didn't care whether or not she had a big part in the planning. All she wanted was to be Ahmed's wife. Wife! It was a word that applied to others, not to her. Never had she thought about being a wife. She didn't even like the word. Yet she was anticipating her marriage, a contract making her a wife.

"Andrea, Andrea, where were you—not in a fairy tale again!"

"No, sweetie, I was just thinking about being your wife." She laughed. "Love is so strange—I can't believe how it changes one's life."

He reached over and ran his hand through her curls, smiling. "It certainly changed mine the night you almost killed me!"

"We won't talk about that," she chided. "About the wedding plans—whatever you decide is fine with me, except..."

"Tell me, Andrea, I want to include whatever you would like—you can choose at least one piece of music, and you must decide what to wear, of course."

"And can we dance together to my one piece of music? I know, I know, men and women dance separately, but ..."

"Yes, my love, we'll dance together to your music." Ahmed was silent, considering if this was the right time to tell her the rest of the plans. Yes, better all at once. "Andrea, after the wedding."

"A honeymoon?–I don't think Afghanistan is exactly..."

"Andrea, be quiet and listen to me. We're going to Ireland with your mother and father, then America, and last stop, Paris, by ourselves."

"Good heavens, Ahmed! How are you going to manage all that– what about money, what about coming back to Afghanistan, how long is all this going to take?" Most troublesome in the plans was the thought of going to Ireland again. "Why Ireland?" she asked.

"I've never been there, I'm interested to see where your father came from. And there is no problem about the money. We won't be staying away for very long, probably about three weeks or so. I think Afghanistan can get along without me for that long," he said. And Ireland? He had his own reasons for that. He needed to find out more about Patrick and his hold over Andrea–it was not the firm grip he had on her when they first met, but there was something evil still lurking beneath the bellicose good cheer. Patrick's assassination attempt was a mere glimpse into a portrait of darkness.

"Part of the trip will be business. I need to go to Washington on a small political mission. Then we'll go to Arizona," continued Ahmed.

Andrea didn't know what to say. She was stunned by Ahmed the eloquent politician, with his VIP persona. It wasn't easy to grasp these new components of his life, but she accepted them as she accepted everything about Ahmed, feeling a little like Alice again, just along for the ride. Where was the wild, savage Ahmed she had met on the Khyber? So he has lots of plans. *Well, I'll do my own thing in Afghanistan after we're married.* She too had plans.

She was a glowing presence, the girl who sat alone on the white leather sofa, eyes downcast, hoping to appear inconspicuous. Dressed in a soft green business suit, her form and face were entirely feminine, and if the silk scarf over her head was removed, a stranger would be struck by the red-gold ringlets drawn up in a hastily arranged bun. Andrea McAlister was waiting to find out how her life would be changed again, a life she never dreamed of in any of her considerable flights of fancy. Ahmed had finally satisfied her curiosity about his Afghan heritage and status. His family was related to an obscure Tajik, Bacha-I-Saqao, who ruled as Habibullah Ghazi II for about nine months, then met the not uncommon fate in Afghanistan of execution in 1929.

"My grandfather likes to think of him as royalty, but he was just an ordinary Tajik, probably a bandit or warlord. Apparently, that old Tajik gave the Sharifs a higher status in Afghanistan, I don't know how. You ought to know by now we're all crazy!"

Andrea joked, "Would you like to be king of Afghanistan?"

"Absolutely not!" Ahmed said in a more serious vein, "I do want to be part of the new government; it would be an honor to my parents. One other thing, Andrea. Don't be upset if my grandfather disapproves of you. It'll have nothing to do with you personally, it's just politics. They'll all love you in time."

"That doesn't upset me; I care nothing about what people think of me."

Ahmed knew that wasn't quite true, and he was determined to protect Andrea from any more hurt in her life.

The last Bonn meeting had ended in surprising general agreement between the various factions of the delegation. The interim leader they chose was worldly, cultured, diplomatic and patient, a resolute man who wanted Afghanistan to be a viable, cohesive country, even as he knew it was a close to impossible goal to achieve. As they stopped for tea, Ahmed brought Andrea in and introduced her to everyone. The Afghans met face to face the woman they had only heard about. She was beautiful, respectful, even spoke Dari. Halima and Mohammed spoke to her as an old friend, Mohammed putting aside Afghan custom in this exceptional circumstance. Andrea's new clothes gave her a confidence she hadn't felt before last night; the evening had been a success in spite of her fairy tales. She knew she looked good; Ahmed had chosen the right clothes for the occasion. It did make a difference. She felt comfortable as she talked to the delegates, finding herself more than a match for them–many looked rather fierce, uneasy without a Kalashnikov in their hands. Ahmed studied Andrea as they were packing for their return to Afghanistan. "What did you think of the delegates?"

"Oh, they seem to be intelligent, powerful people."

"Andrea, the men you just met are some of the most dangerous in the world."

"I've met men like that before."

"And they may think you, my love, are a dangerous woman!"

She laughed. "No, I'm just engaged to one of the dangerous men."

❈❈❈

Under an icy blue December sky, Ahmed led his men into Tora Bora, knowing it was a futile mission. He had made his decision after Kandahar; Tora Bora would be his last battle, his last effort to cooperate with the American forces. He had had enough. From now on, his war would be waged in the political arena. Ahmed Sharif had been fighting since he was fourteen–Russians, rival Afghan tribes, Taliban and their Arab cohorts. At twenty-nine he was a hardened, often brutal, soldier of God. For all those years, he believed his cause was holy and just, and he still believed it; as a faithful Muslim, he loved his enigmatic country. A commander who earned his rank over those long years, he would not be told how to fight by Americans. No, there were better ways to heal Afghanistan's long agony. When he told Andrea about his plans, she gave him an understanding look and said, "I'm glad."

He would not permit her to do any more fighting–"stay with Abdullah and wait for me." So he left her, in spite of her protests. His assurance that he would always be with her was small comfort. Though Ahmed missed Andrea, he thanked God she hadn't been caught up in the maelstrom of Kandahar and here now in this Tora Bora business.

This is so damned useless, thought Ahmed, this searching cave after cave for one who has escaped. All the Afghans he talked to told him the same thing–the man had passed through Tora Bora and was now into Pakistan. They saw him. Well, maybe they had and maybe they hadn't, but it didn't matter. He wasn't here in Tora Bora. The thunder of the bombs became irritating background noise to him. In spite of the Americans' highly successful campaign, all the bombs in the world would never completely penetrate so many caves, and bombs could not tell you the names of those who were in the caves. *They should have let us do the searching before they started bombing; we could have found him, now it's too late.* Ahmed's men were cold, hungry, and running out of motivation for this operation. The bombs were coming in closer; Ahmed hoped they had been targeted correctly.

Abdullah saw that Andrea was restless, worried about Ahmed. He tried to interest her in a new game he had purchased at the bazaar, even asked her to explain American music to him, but she was preoccupied with concern for Ahmed.

"He should be coming soon," she said.

"These things cannot be timed, you know that; he's not on a schedule, Andrea."

"But they're bombing the hell out of Tora Bora, he can't stay there long."

"Ahmed knows what he's doing, Andrea, stop pacing."

"I can't stay here another minute. I'm going out; I'll ride Buttercup."

"Andrea–you're taking the Kalashnikov?"

"Yes, and my handgun."

"What about the *burqa*?"

"No, I'm not wearing that."

"But–"

"No buts about it–nobody's going to bother me," she said firmly. She walked outside.

"*Allahu Akbar*," called Abdullah.

"*Allahu Akbar*," responded Andrea.

Mounting Buttercup, she started in the direction of Tora Bora. As she rode, truckloads of *mujahidin* came toward her. She didn't recognize any of them; they were not Ahmed's men. They looked at her with some curiosity but didn't stop. "Ahmed Sharif?" she called out. They shook their heads–haven't seen him, he might be back there somewhere. A little further along, she met another group of *mujs* on their way home; this time she recognized their commander, Mahmood Qadir, a big burly bear of a man with a huge moustache and black rapacious eyes. He was riding a donkey–poor donkey, thought Andrea. When he saw her, he got off the donkey and walked up to her. Andrea dismounted and greeted him, "*Salaam.*"

"Ah, Andrea, I haven't had the pleasure of seeing you since Bonn. Why are you riding this road by yourself?" He had a faintly suggestive look in his black eyes. Andrea felt a little uneasy, but made a show of handling the Kalashnikov.

"Well-armed, I see."

"Yes, I'm looking for Ahmed."

"Well, you'll see him soon. He is behind us, not very far."

*Thank God.* "Thank you, Mahmood. *Allahu Akbar.*" She had heard some wild stories about Mahmood, and he sure looked the part; you can never tell about these crazy Afghans–their half true stories grow to mythical proportions.

Where was Ahmed? She was getting anxious, the cold was penetrating. Oh, there he was, climbing out of a truck, coming to her! She spurred Buttercup on a little farther, dismounted and ran to Ahmed.

"Andrea, slow down." Tired as he was, Ahmed had to laugh at Andrea's exuberant welcome; she was like a puppy greeting his master with endless kisses.

Finally, she realized that Ahmed was tired and limping a little. "Oh, I'm sorry, sweetie."

"You almost knocked me over, cowgirl."

"Cowgirl! Are you learning American?"

"One of the men picked it up from a–what do you call it–a Western. Isn't that what you were?"

"Cowgirl, ranch hand, whatever. Ahmed, don't start calling me a cowgirl!" But it pleased Ahmed to tease her, and he would use the word on what he decided were appropriate occasions.

He stood behind Andrea, arms wrapped around her as they waved to the men going home. Ahmed had no reservations about showing his feeling for Andrea in public; the battlefield was a world apart from the decorum of village life. His men knew Andrea almost as well as he did; she looked perfectly appropriate in the arms of her lover as they called *Allahu Akbar!* to the tired soldiers.

# IX. East is East

When Ahmed told Abdullah he intended to marry Andrea, he was met with a long silence, pregnant with disapproval. As loving and progressive as Ahmed's parents were, Abdullah felt they could not have imagined any of their children marrying a Western nonbeliever, willful, outspoken and disobedient, albeit intelligent and, unfortunately, very much in love. The catalog of imperfections and problems raced through Abdullah's head. It was clear Ahmed would never fit into a mold. From childhood, he had questioned and evaluated answers given by others, in the end depending on his own analysis.

At last, Abdullah spoke. "I fear for your soul, if you do this, and worse, I fear for your vision, your ambitions for Afghanistan. Please consider the implications of marriage to an American."

Now here they were, engaged, Andrea waiting for their wedding day. Ahmed had not planned to ask Andrea to become Muslim, though the problem of religion was in his thoughts since the moment he knew he loved her and wanted no one else. There was no requirement he marry within his faith, but Abdullah was right. His wife should be Muslim. But Andrea a Muslim–how incongruous, his independent Andrea. Obedient? She would never willingly be subservient to anyone. After much prayer and thought, Ahmed concluded she could be a beautiful example of his faith. Muslim women were not necessarily meek, *burqa*-clad phantoms. He liked strong, fun loving, smart, affectionate women. Ahmed quite naturally considered himself superior to women; it was, after all, as Allah intended. Yet he went his own way in a country of invisible, servile women, encouraging their education and participation in the wider fabric of life.

When Andrea came into his life, he discarded the Afghan tradition of separate sleeping quarters–he wanted her in his bed every night, and he knew she would accept nothing less. Islam didn't demand that women be slaves; on the contrary, they were meant to be treasured partners of their husbands. A growing number of Afghan men, mostly in the cities, believed women should have rights equal to a man's, that they need not wear the *hijab*, and they respected the desire of women to be educated participants in government. All these thoughts seemed to him to make a perfect case for convincing Andrea to become Muslim. And it was interesting that Andrea had always shown deference to him. Patrick's control, Apache philosophy, the difference in his and Andrea's ages? He didn't know, but Andrea looked to him for guidance. He told himself she was already Muslim, all she had to do was make it official.

Convinced he could persuade her to Islamism, he took her aside in the courtyard; under a moon that made the night almost day, he assured a worried Andrea his limp was the result of a bad bruise from a misfired RPG, and taking a deep breath, he started, "Andrea, about our wedding. I want us to be married very soon, but there is one thing…" How can I tell her, he thought, asking, "Do you love me?"

"Ahmed, you know I do. This one thing…it must be a problem, a big problem, it just might be a huge problem; I knew it was there somewhere, waiting for me."

Islam. She could not dismiss it. It was a wall she could not knock down, a challenge she could not conquer. Andrea's Indian forbears were not Christian, their religion was related to the elements of the earth and the mysticism of the shaman. But Islam? That was another story. She would be expected to obey a man, have limits on her freedom; all the lofty idealism of the Qur'an would not change that. And she was modest only in the way she dressed. She looked men straight in the eye, she questioned anything or anyone she didn't trust. Her intellect had a sharp edge and her spirit revealed an infectious joy of life. How could she subjugate herself to the requirements of Islamic faith yet retain her innate sense of self?

As she expressed these thoughts to Ahmed, he assumed a tone of confidence he did not feel.

"We can work it out together."

"Don't patronize me, Ahmed. How can I…" Her sentence trailed off, but she already knew the answer; she must be the one to submit. Surrender. The word was anathema to her. It struck him then how hard, how painful this might be for her.

Taking her hands in his, he said, "I love you so much–I know this is very hard, but it would not be so different from what it is now, and there will be times away from Afghanistan; we'll visit your parents in Arizona, we can go to Paris."

She shook her head and scolded, "You make it sound so casual. I may not have the freedom I have now–worship Allah–obey Islamic law? Oh Ahmed, how can you ask me to do this?" she ended in an anguished cry.

"Hadn't you thought about this before?"

"No–I guess I was too naïve to care about religion...I just thought...hoped, I guess...everything would stay the way it was!" She ran a hand through her hair in frustration.

"I can't tell you what to do. Possibly we could stay as we are," he said without conviction.

"No, Ahmed, I no longer believe that." There was a long pause. Then, a whisper, "I have no choice."

"Andrea, do you love me?" he asked for the second time.

"Yes! Yes! Yes! You know...I don't have a choice." She shrugged her shoulders and threw her hands up in frustration to Allah, to God, to the Great Spirit. It was an awkward, uncertain moment for them. Then Ahmed stepped closer and took her in his arms.

"My darling, Islam is a beautiful faith. I'll see that you have all the freedom you need. We will be free to love one another in whatever way we wish, and free to say whatever we wish. I don't expect you to change; just be my Andrea." She took a deep breath, and wondered if she could do it.

"After all, you're my sun, moon, and stars–I'll keep you safe from any danger, even Islam."

She finally got tired of fighting with her conscience and just followed her heart, telling Abdullah she was ready to learn about Islam. He put booklets in front of her, then held up a copy of the Qur'an. "This is the word of Allah, or God. It is both simple and complicated, and requires more time than you can spare to study and understand it. I have studied for years."

Andrea smiled, "School time again, isn't it? Is that copy in English–

I can't read Arabic."

"Yes, and Andrea, I would like to believe you are doing this because you sincerely wish to embrace Islam."

She let out a loud sigh of frustration, "Oh, Abdullah, you know better. I'm doing this for Ahmed–I'll study, but make no mistake, I do it for Ahmed. So let's get started."

Andrea was nothing if not honest. In spite of his misgivings, Abdullah agreed to be her teacher once again, deciding she must learn to read and write in Arabic. She found the words of the Qur'an beautiful, inspirational, surprisingly practical. The grace of Muslim prayer pleased her–the ablutions, the surrender to Allah in each prayerful movement, the prostration before him. She wondered if prayer five times a day helped keep one's worst impulses in check, or at least caused one to think before acting. The problem she struggled with was that Islam seemed to require complete, unquestioning, even rapturous faith, and obedience to its laws; there was no separation of church and state. Her deep need to be Ahmed's wife pushed her to keep studying, though it tried her patience. Then she came to the fifth pillar of Islam, the Hajj, a pilgrimage to Mecca. After Abdullah's tale of his journey there, she concluded it was a torturous, cleansing pilgrimage that ended in ecstatic submission to God and rebirth of the soul.

"Ahmed performed the Hajj when he was eighteen." Andrea made no comment, thinking, all religions have their tests, even Apaches. She doubted if she would ever be ready for that journey.
She was eager to learn Arabic, but a sense of guilt plagued her, as well as a feeling she was denigrating every Afghan's religion in order to be married. These tormenting questions she kept to herself, wavering between studying with renewed energy and giving up, deciding she was a hypocrite. Abdullah, though pleased with her willingness to learn, was troubled by hints of conflict within her. Her eyes held a trace of sadness and distance; she didn't eat well, looked thinner–most pronounced was her serious demeanor. In the past, he would have welcomed it, but now found he missed her teasing, her challenges to him, her sly impudence followed by mock apologies.

Abdullah took over the meal preparation to give Andrea a rest from the household duties she carried out as though possessed by demons. He decided this would not do–she needed Ahmed, who was in the middle of the political confusion at Kandahar. No matter. Let others deal with the Taliban supporters. Ahmed was needed here; he sent a message for Ahmed to come home.

Andrea was sound asleep after a day filled with study, housework, and exercise. The exercise helped ease her mental stress and made her too tired to stay awake at night. She was dreaming that Ahmed was brushing her hair back and kissing her. Then his voice–a whisper, "Andrea, my love, I'm here with you." It wasn't a dream–she opened her eyes, he was really there.

"Ahmed, Ahmed...." He was smiling at her, his eyes full of concern for her. "Why are you here–what happened–is something wrong?"

"No, everything is all right. I need to be with you; I think it's time for us to be married."

Now fully awake, Andrea said, "How did you know I....did Abdullah call you?"

"Yes, love, and it's a good thing he did."

"That old Afghan–he should mind his own business!"

Ahmed laughed. "You are his business; so am I, for that matter. Don't you know that?"

Yes, of course, Abdullah the angel, always hovering over them! "Yes," she answered quietly.

"You look pale, Andrea, you've lost some weight, but no more. Study is over. And–if you want to change your mind about becoming Muslim, I understand. I can't have you made sick over this–we'll be married no matter what you decide."

"Ahmed, I've been trying; oh sweetie, I love you so and...I want you to be proud of me."

He looked at her in surprise. "Andrea, I've always been proud of you. I'll be proud of you whether you're Muslim or...whatever you choose to be." Ahmed didn't know that Andrea would want to be anything at all; he realized he would accept any decision she made–he would never give her up. He told her, "Think about what I've told you. I'll accept whatever you decide."

Andrea awoke early the next morning knowing her decision; she would tell Ahmed that evening. Sleepy eyed, she lay beside him, happy and secure in the warmth of his body against hers, reluctant to rise.

"Good morning, cowgirl, are you ready for a day of excitement?"

She broke into a smile, wan and unenthusiastic, but a smile nevertheless. "I'm ready for something different."

"This is a sport you've never seen before, an Afghan version of any of the most exciting games of the West."

"Are horses part of it?"

"Ah, you know what I'm talking about."

He picked her up, stood her before him, and looked at her as Abdullah would just before a lecture. "Dress warm. It's very cold and not an easy ride–be sure to carry the Kalashnikov. I don't expect any trouble, but you never know."

Andrea thought, even when you think you know, you don't; there's no easy ride in Afghanistan. But none of that worried her; she felt she was being released from prison. The journey to Charikar was uneventful. They passed American soldiers on patrol and Ahmed stopped briefly to talk to their commander. Andrea pulled her scarf over her face–no use causing comment. For the moment, she was at peace with the world and with herself; the freedom of a day without duties was intoxicating. Riding Buttercup, she breathed in the intense cold, dismissed Afghanistan's ever-present dangers of the road, pondered the regurgitating remnants of exploding bombs over the mountains, and looked forward to the game.

*Buzkashi!* The word itself sounded violent and harsh. Ahmed was greeted with a "*Salaam Aleichum*" by the local warlord, Abdullah Khalev, who knew Ahmed's prowess at their national game; Andrea was introduced as an American come to see this Afghan sport. Khalev was impressed by Andrea's Arabian and her presence on the horse, seeing she was expert at handling the animal. He knew she was engaged to be married to Ahmed, a somewhat sticky situation, but he was not concerned enough to make anything of it, being a devout Muslim when it suited him. Khalev warned her to stay well back from the loosely defined field of play.

"More than one spectator has been trampled when he got in the way!" A trace of uneasiness rippled through Andrea at the sight of the wild-looking men on their horses. She positioned herself among the other onlookers on a slope slightly above the horsemen and hoped that Ahmed would not be injured. No football, no soccer ball–a headless goat carcass was used to score a goal, and soon after play had gotten underway, Andrea realized these were the best horsemen she had ever seen–the game was ferocious, the players swooping down to snatch the carcass for their team, the horses making dizzying twists and turns, almost careening into one another, the players shouting loud directions and curses to their teammates. And she saw Ahmed in a very different role, that of a member of a primitive tribe, uncivilized, un-Westernized. My God, he looks like an Apache on the warpath! But pumped with excitement, she loudly cheered him on, so in the spirit of the game she was tempted to shoot her gun into the air, catching herself just in time. She understood Khalev's warning–there was no real "field" in this game, no boundaries, few rules except to get the carcass into the opponent's territory and score a goal. Typical, she thought–symbolic of Afghanistan. Ahmed was right. She would not talk to *Buzkashi* horses.

Ahmed was triumphant after his team's hard won victory against Abdul Rahman's team. This was a man's event; Ahmed was in the middle of a rough, laughing, welcoming group of men, giving one another enthusiastic Afghan hugs. Andrea had no part in this celebration, so she made her way over to the courtyard of Abdullah Khalev's house and was welcomed by his wife, daughter-in-law, and two sisters. They greeted her as though they were old friends, offering tea and a special fruit-filled *naan*.

It was the first time Andrea had been in any family social gathering in Afghanistan. Everything before had been lessons with Abdullah, staying in a safe house, or fighting. Except for the engagement party at Bonn, her involvement in everyday Afghan life was nil. Andrea suddenly realized how much she missed normal social interaction with other women, and she thought of Laura. What good times they had had in New York! This was a world away, yet it was the same. All the women were full of questions about American women, about their home life–"do women really go out alone–no *hijab*–they have jobs–they earn money?" and on and on. They were incredulous that women had such freedom, and expressed their reservations about such a decadent life.

"Of course, they are not Muslims, so one cannot expect them to honor Allah or their husbands," commented Sarina, Abdullah's wife. Andrea tried to explain the women of America. It was not a matter of religion, or superiority or inferiority–it was just different. They talked about men; Andrea was amused by their candid, gossipy comments about men, their faults, their virtues, their sexual exploits. Zohra, sixteen, asked Andrea about Ahmed. That opened the door to a laughing explosion of opinions–"He is rich and so handsome. What is he like in bed? You are very lucky. Isn't he different from American men? Will you obey him? He doesn't beat you, does he? No, he's an aristocrat!"

Then Sarina said in a low voice, "You should be careful, Andrea, he can be a very dangerous man."

Andrea smiled, her green eyes veiled, "Don't worry, I can match Ahmed in all kinds of ways; you're looking at the daughter of a terrorist."

She regretted the words as soon as they were out of her mouth, but at least these women knew who they were dealing with. I'm not going to be that poor American girl, victim of Ahmed Sharif. Shades of Patrick McAlister! Keep your mouth shut–too late now. The catharsis of talking with women again had freed her thoughts and, unfortunately, her tongue. Oh well, she thought, what the hell. I can't pretend to be something I'm not. But the women didn't seem to think less of her for the statement.

Abdullah's wife had a feeling Andrea was a power to be reckoned with, and liked her more for it–it's about time, she thought.

They spent the night with Abdullah's family but, as guests, did not sleep together. Andrea had a moment with a jubilant Ahmed:"Congratulations, sweetie, you'd make a good cowboy; you'll show those old boys a thing or two about horses!"

Ahmed, still full of the excitement of *buzkashi*, grinned. "Did you like the game? It's been so long since I've played, I'd forgotten how it feels to win."

Andrea laughed. "You're really high, Ahmed. I love seeing you so happy; I was a little nervous at first but once the game started I loved it. I felt like yelling "ride 'em cowboy!"

They hugged each other, caught up in the joyful freedom of the day. After a moment, Andrea remembered what she needed to tell him.

"Ahmed, I've decided to become a Muslim; no more study, I'll learn as I go."

"Are you sure? I want a happy bride on our wedding day."

"Yes–sleep well, my victorious savage!"

Ahmed was glad to see Andrea happy and content; again he was grateful for Abdullah's wisdom. Intoxicated with the excitement of the game, Andrea's decision to become Muslim, and thoughts of his marriage, he slept the sleep of the happy warrior.

# X. Visions That Dance

"Afghan wedding"–not exactly. Two days before the wedding, Andrea made the required, brief declaration of faith, the *shahada*: I bear witness that there is no deity worthy to be worshiped but Allah, and I bear witness that Mohammed is His servant and messenger. What was in her heart as she said the words that made her a Muslim only she knew, but the declaration brought her to a place of acceptance, and she was able to look forward to her marriage with a clearer conscience.

Ahmed made arrangements for the ceremony to take place in his uncle Abdul's spacious, still intact home in Kabul. There, the *mullah* from the family's native Panjshir Valley performed the Muslim rite (*nikah*) and Andrea and Ahmed exchanged vows of their own after signing the Islamic marriage contract. A simple statement was made, each saying to the other, "I promise to love and honor you, Andrea (or Ahmed), before all others, all the days of my life, into Paradise." There were some puzzled looks, some disapproving expressions, but the Eastern and Western guests accepted their union. There was an audible murmur of approval from Ahmed's *mujahidin* lieutenants. At the end of the vows, Andrea added softly, "I'll love you forever, my beautiful Afghan."

"Beautiful! Andrea, you're impossible," whispered Ahmed, then spoke so he could be heard, "And I'll love you forever, my beautiful wild child," an exchange that seemed to amuse everyone. The party began with the Afghan national dance, the *attani mili*, danced by the men, slowly at first, building to a frenzied climax to the tumultuous music of the small band. Following custom, the men danced separately from the women, Andrea in the group of women, and

Ahmed with the men. The erotic Eastern music was hypnotic. It rushed through the women with an electricity that transformed these hidden beings from phantoms to real women who possessed a mysterious authority men could never achieve. A simple expression of joy, the dance contained a message for Andrea–there must be many independent-minded women in Afghanistan preparing to change their destiny, their country.

The music stopped, and food and drink were placed on a long table– it was a feast of meat and vegetable dishes, kebabs, salads, *qabuli*, pastas, fresh fruit and various sweets, a rare feast. Uncle Abdul was giving them a party in grand style.

Ahmed retrieved Andrea from the admiring, inquisitive ladies, some unveiled for the day. "Come, Andrea, we'll eat with your parents and Abdullah."

"Oh, Ahmed, I'm so delirious with it all, I don't think I can eat anything. What a beautiful day you and your uncle have given us."

"You deserve it, my love. I insist you eat something, perhaps a salad, at least. I want you to have enough energy to dance with me."

She laughed and said, "Oh, in that case, I'll manage a little salad." The banquet table was beautiful–exquisite china and silverware. What a party; Afghans know how to have a good time, thought Andrea, then spied the rather dour countenance of her *father–lighten up, Patrick; bye-bye IRA, won't go there anymore, thank you.*

Ahmed was amused to see Andrea's father in a friendly discussion with some of his *mujahidin*–terrorist tactics? He didn't care. He had no illusions about Patrick's opinion of Afghans. But this was not the day to think about Patrick; this was his wedding day. Andrea is mine, this girl who fought on the front beside me, who killed for me, who torments me, enchants me, who loves me without question. I love her, Mother and Father, and you would too. His reverie was ended by Andrea's voice. "Ahmed, do you think I should tie down my father– he's starting to tell his stories."

"Andrea, he's behaving very well–they like him."

She put her arms around him. "Thank you, sweetie, thank you for this day, for the feast, for putting up with my father…"

"Whoa, Andrea, enough of the thank yous. Listen, do you hear music?"

"Oh, Ahmed!"

"Yes, your Italian tenor. It's time for us to dance together." She looked like an Afghan princess in the green silk dress that matched her eyes. Soraya had helped her pin back the unruly curls with beautiful gold barrettes studded with tiny emeralds, and had given her a matching head-scarf for the ceremony. They waltzed to the soaring melody of the warm, sensual voice; all the ugliness of war vanished under the spell of the music.

As Ahmed brushed an escaping curl from her eyes, he said, "I love you; are you happy?"

"I never dreamed I could be this happy."

The two looked at one another almost shyly, hardly believing they were now husband and wife.

Wenonah watched her daughter dance with Ahmed; she seemed a vision from ancient Persia in the silky green dress, skirt swirling around her ankles. Ahmed took Andrea's hand to spin her around in a slow, undulating movement, then reached down to tuck an errant curl back, a gesture that Wenonah remembered from somewhere in time. How sad, she thought, it's been so long. They are so much alike, but Ahmed is the stronger, more stable of the two. The dance over, the pair came to the table. Andrea looked at her mother in surprise.

"Mom, you're crying–I've never seen you cry!"

"Oh a bit, after all it is a wedding, and I do find tears come more easily now." No one else noticed, the men being involved in lively conversation; Ahmed had gone to find his sister.

"Is anything wrong?" Andrea asked her mother.

"No, I've just been thinking how difficult this might be for you. Do you know what you're getting into, Andrea?"

"Not entirely, but I have a pretty good idea."

"It's hard to know when you're so much in love." Andrea saw an unfamiliar look on her mother's face. Which of them was she talking about–mother or daughter?

"Ahmed is a sweet man, Andrea, but it's hard to think ahead, and..."

"Sweet? You've said that before about him; not many would describe him that way."

"He's also a very strong man..."

"I would have to have a strong man, wouldn't I, everything considered."

"Yes," said Wenonah.

"Don't worry, Mom, I'll be all right," she said, and gave her mother a hug. Andrea, unlike her mother, knew exactly what and who her husband was. She accepted his Eastern character, knowing Western standards would never apply to him.

Jeff Scott smoked his cigarettes one after the other, looking around the room, trying to blend into the crowd. Some of the guests wore Western dress, some were in their best Afghan dress. Ahmed was dressed in an obviously custom fitted *shalwar kameez*, looking the part of a prince. This was one invitation Jeff wanted to refuse; he couldn't, it was extended to him by Ahmed's older brother Rashid, who knew him from the days before the Taliban. Their exchange of information for arms had been good for both Jeff and the Alliance; Rashid had more respect for Jeff than any other agent–he was as tough as any *muj*. Jeff liked Rashid, but things were getting too complicated with his brother; it was a miracle the two brothers hadn't made contact before now, thank Christ they operated in widely separate parts of Afghanistan. But it was only a matter of time, a short time, he thought. *Quite a party, what's to celebrate? an American girl marrying an Afghan; that might go over big with some idealists I know, but not with me.*

Jeff sat in a far corner of the room watching as the Afghan music picked up its frenzied pace and the dancers, all men, whirled in a crescendo of sound to end the dance. *Reminds me of home–some comparison!* He saw himself dancing with Carrie at the American Legion–rock, some slow stuff, that old Willie Nelson number, Crazy–they both loved that song. They'd dance close together, not just swaying in place the way they do it now, but doing the steps right, and sexy. They had a comfortable routine after they got home, not quite sleepy enough to go to bed. Carrie would make cocoa and they'd sit in the bedroom by the fireplace drinking it, reviewing the evening–the latest gossip, who had made a fool of himself–"Jesus, he must have had five pitchers of beer!" how good or bad the band was, their friends' latest escapades. The assessment of the night usually ended with "It was a good time." Hmm, a good time–seemed like just yesterday, yet very long ago. Jeff wondered what his two young sons were doing right now. Well. When he got home he'd take them to a ball game, they loved baseball. Suddenly he felt tears on his cheeks, sat bolt upright and wiped them away. How had he gotten so far from home?

The music had stopped–standing not far from him was Ahmed's cousin. She recognized him with a look of curiosity mixed with fear. Carrie had looked at him in love and contentment. Why would this Afghan woman fear him–he was American, here to help her country. Damn this country! Then he heard Western music, some romantic Italian song, and saw Ahmed and Andrea dancing together. She wore a long green Afghan dress, no scarf, and looked up at Ahmed with an intimate smile. They were alone on the floor and alone in their own world. Jeff's body was suffused with envy, longing, loneliness and desire. He got to his feet. With a practiced stealth, he followed Saira to a small room where he saw her looking in a mirror, rearranging her head-scarf. Soft melody drifted into the room and he visualized Carrie and himself dancing. He came up behind her.

"You're very beautiful–are you enjoying the Western music?"

She turned in surprise to see a man in this room–the American CIA agent, the one who had seen her before! Saira said, "Please leave, you should not be here."

But Scott came closer. "Dance with me, just one dance."

"No–leave me alone."

Scott stood in front of her, looked in her frightened eyes, saw Carrie, and kissed Saira. His rough, homesick hunger forced her mouth open; he reached for her breasts, tearing at her clothing. Saira fought him, but he was too strong. In desperation she lifted her leg and jabbed her knee hard in his groin. Jeff let go of her so suddenly she almost fell. Groaning in pain, his glazed eyes finally focused, and he looked at Saira in shock. This wasn't *Carrie–oh my God, he thought, what the hell have I done?*

Saira looked at him in disgust–her cousin's CIA friend. She stood frozen, aware he was dangerous. And pitiful, looking like a man come to the end of his rope. She forced her feet to move and ran out of the room, deciding she would not tell her cousins exactly how close she had come to being raped; she would warn Ahmed and Rashid about Jeff Scott's disloyalty and potential betrayal in some way. He was not to be trusted.

Jeff Scott had not expected to be in Afghanistan for so long. He was one of the CIA's best; he knew the country intimately, not just present-day Afghanistan, but the ancient land that it was. Many changes since the days of Alexander and Roxane, yet much the same. He always liked studying the ancient history of countries; he found Afghanistan's history especially fascinating because so much of the country remained in the middle ages. If you were in a village in the mountain stronghold of the Afridi's, you were living in ancient times–there, time literally stood still.

When he first came to Afghanistan, the place had enchanted him–mountains, sky, ether air, the simplicity and friendly hospitality of people who lived their religion every day. Their most valued possessions were their families and their guns. There had been no time of peace in recent history; war was all most of them had ever known. After the Russians left, the country plunged into its tribal warfare mode. Change in Afghanistan could be dizzying; after supporting the Taliban and Bin Laden, America found the Northern Alliance a little more palatable, so Bin Laden and the Taliban were now the villains of the piece. *And here I am, CIA, come to rescue Afghanistan from itself and the Taliban. Now the bombs are falling–what's a little more destruction in a country with mud brick structures. I bring order along with chaos–I am the harbinger of death and devastation, but I'm here to do good things for your country. In the end you will thank me.*

He had been home with Carrie and his sons for only a month when he got orders to leave for Afghanistan.

"Oh, Jeff, why so soon? Can't you turn this assignment down? We've had so little time. Daniel and Adam need you here. I need you." She was on the verge of tears.

"Carrie, I can't refuse this–it's high level. It won't be for long, just a few months." Carrie had looked at her handsome husband and wondered, will we ever live a normal life? Then she had remembered his occupation was one of his attractions when they met. Now she was growing to hate it, and she knew it showed. No longer was she the strong, supportive wife of their early years. Keep it together, Carrie, she had told herself.

"I love you, Jeff. I worried about you when you were in Europe, but Afghanistan–I don't like it. That's a whole different ball game. From the little I've seen on TV, it's a wild place with a bunch of guerillas fighting the Russians. Oh Jeff…"

He had interrupted her, "Carrie, sweetheart, I can't tell you anything about all this except that I've studied the history of the place, the geography, you know, the usual things, but that's all. Don't worry. I know where not to go and what not to do; I've got good contacts and good security, so I'll be fine. Carrie, I love you, you know that, and soon I'll be out of the CIA and home with you. Then you'll have a boring husband; hell, you won't know what to do with me!"

"Oh, yes, I will, I'll know exactly what to do with you," and her smile had beckoned him as they went to bed and made love. Carrie had stayed awake for a long while, already feeling lonely and sad. *Please, God, let Jeff be safe.*

Jeff Scott was weaving through the crowd trying to make a hasty retreat when he brushed by Andrea; she was speaking to Mohammed Khalis, "Yes, Afghanistan is my country now, my home."

"But you are still American?"

"Of course. I…"

Scott interrupted, "Afghanistan is your home–that's obscene! I remind you, Andrea, you are a citizen of the United States."

Andrea faced him alone; Mohammed had walked away. She remembered the look he had given her when he had seen her on the front lines near Kabul, the mocking tone he had used when he spoke to her. She knew he was supposed to be a friend of Rashid, but there was something wrong with this man; she knew Ahmed didn't like or trust him. She had also heard he was being investigated by CIA officials.

Angry at his insulting tone and words, Andrea answered him, "I hardly think you are the one to be reminding me of anything, much less my citizenship status. As a matter of fact, isn't that shoe on the other foot now?"

Scott blanched, then recovered; affecting an unconvincing

indignation, he replied, "I work for the American government, remember. Why would you want to spend your life in this miserable country?" Andrea's sardonic laugh told him she suspected, or worse, knew too much.

"I'll spend my life wherever Ahmed is and wherever I please. My life is none of your business, whereas what you do might turn out to be my business."

"What do you mean?" he asked in a sinister tone.

"Oh, it's just a feeling; I don't trust you. Remember, Ahmed is not someone you'd want for an enemy."

Scott saw Ahmed coming towards them and left the house. Better have a talk with Ahmed, try to diffuse this situation. He hoped he could rationalize his small defection in some way. He didn't like this growing feeling that his fate was sealed. Ahmed appeared, putting his arm around Andrea as Jeff Scott retreated.

"Jeff Scott left in a hurry. Was he bothering you, Andrea? We're watching him. I don't want my wife to have any unpleasantness on her wedding day; what did he say to you?"

"Oh, nothing much. I noticed him earlier charming the ladies, but not me; there's something wrong about that man. But he's not worth talking about on our wedding day; I'm too happy to care about him."

"Exactly–I want you to think only about happy things today. He won't be talking to you anymore."

"Oh he's not important. But I think he's been in Afghanistan too long."

The band started to play again; the music had a haunting melody that sounded to Andrea like a *chaconne*, a graceful, slow Spanish movement. Ahmed led her onto the dance floor; he wanted her to forget everything unpleasant. He had worked to make their wedding day perfect–it was his composition, an "esthetically unified arrangement of parts," an example of his talent for diplomacy. The delicate dance of East and West was always on the verge of disaster, but today it was a joyful step to the edge.

"I don't know how you did it all, but you're amazing. I think I've married a master strategist." Realizing that term also referred to her father, she exclaimed, "But....oh, I didn't mean...Ahmed..."

Ahmed laughed at her. "I know what you meant. Time to go, my darling, let's say our good byes."

As they prepared to leave, Abdullah took Andrea aside. He gave her a polite embrace, kissing her on both cheeks. With a slight smile that accented his solemn eyes, he said, "I know how much this day means to you." He glanced over at Ahmed, standing a little distance away. "Ahmed is happier than I have ever seen him. I pray that your marriage will bring blessings to both of you and to Afghanistan."

Their wedding day was an amalgam of Afghan grace and eccentricity; the genuine pleasure at their union was a promise of what their country could some day achieve, but the decision of the disparate groups to forego their differences was the truest gift of all.

Northern Ireland–County Antrim. The four who arrived at Belfast Airport from Afghanistan were not tourists, though the one Afghan among them had never seen Ireland. They had no plans to tour Belfast; their destination was the Sperrin Mountains in County Tyrone. As soon as she stepped from the plane into Ireland, every antenna in Andrea's body was quivering with anxiety. It was not a beautiful Irish spring day, this Saturday in January. The mild Irish winter kept the land green, but the cold, unfriendly dampness intensified Andrea's foreboding. Wenonah was biding her time, wanting to get home to Arizona. Patrick and Ahmed were here each on his own mission. They piled into the rented Land Rover, Andrea at the wheel under protest.

"Dad, you know the road better. You should drive."

"Andrea, lass, do your old dad a favor and drive. I'll navigate."

At Patrick's direction, she drove over the winding road to Plumbridge village, between the Sperrin and Munterlony Mountains, then on to Sperrin village.

"We'll go to the Sperrin Heritage Centre; you might find it

interesting, Ahmed."

Ahmed didn't answer–he was speechless at the sight of the lush green landscape. The mountain roads of the Sperrins were civilized and tourist-friendly, unlike the pitted, suicidal roads of Afghanistan that were bordered by land mines. Easier driving, thought Andrea, but I'd rather be back in Afghanistan. She pulled off the road near a cottage advertising crafts, food, and traditional Irish music. Wenonah decided to go into the cottage, where she was captivated by the Irish rendition of pottery design. Andrea followed Ahmed and Patrick up the slope, keeping well behind them, to the top.

She heard Patrick's loud voice talking about his childhood in these mountains, "Ah, yes, before Belfast." He left Ahmed to follow a different path. Andrea watched Ahmed, who had been very quiet on the entire journey, climb another grassy slope to discover what had always fascinated her, relics of the ancient people who had been here– stones, grave slabs, a few crosses.

As Ahmed looked across the wooded glen to the mountains in the distance, he felt the pull of long-ago peoples who lived, struggled, fought in this wild land. Every stone, every cross, every piece of the earth sang its somber song to him. Ghosts are here; they were warriors, fierce and determined to preserve their land, their ways, their freedom. With a wild fury, they fought to the bitter end for survival. I can feel them in my bones, I can hear their music, their laughter when they rested, see them as they danced, loved, and thought long thoughts. I know them well. They are my people, whether Norman, Celt, Afghan or Indian. He knew it would be the same in the Indian lands Andrea knew as a child. A deep heartache gripped him as he heard the mournful sound of Irish song. *It's eternal, this terrible struggle to win at all costs. What religion of man could possibly be greater than this earth? I wonder if God weeps for us; I'm afraid there is much for me to question. I'm afraid I'll find no answers.* And as he stood beside the ancient graves in Ireland, he saw himself standing among the fresh ones in Afghanistan. His heart wept, as only a soldier's can, for the folly of men going to war.

Patrick McAlister stood on the hilltop staring at an ancient stone. From the cottage came the Irish music he had long ago dismissed. He saw his son-in-law looking at a grave slab, deep in thought; under the spell of the Sperrins, perhaps? Well, he should be, thought Patrick;

this is his kind of country, these mountains, the misty vales–ah, but no dusty desert, thank God. It was good to be in the green wet lushness of Ireland. Yet the serene setting was *deceiving–quiet it is for now, but go up the road a bit, have a look at Belfast, there you'll see a wee bit of Afghanistan. Ah yes, Ireland is well rid of me; I won't be coming back again after this trip.* Wenonah wanted to leave Northern Ireland, but it was Andrea who felt its threat more strongly than any of them. She had resisted coming to this place; it held dark memories for her, yet she sensed Ahmed had a strong need to be here. Patrick felt both nostalgia and finality for a life he no longer really wanted; he looked at his son-in-law, trying to guess his thoughts.

Ahmed sat on the stone bench thinking of what he needed to do when Andrea came over and sat down beside him. He took her hand in his and smiled at her, hoping her mood would change. "This is a beautiful land, Ireland, these mountains here are quiet and peaceful. Andrea, how many times did your father bring you to Ireland?"

"Only once–remember, I told you about coming to buy the horses, when I saw that man Tim. Why do you ask?"

"You seem to know this area so well."

"Good memory, I guess. I'd just as soon forget it, Ahmed." He put his arm around her and felt her shivering in the warming sun.

"Andrea, are you all right?"

"I'm cold, that's all."

"Well, we are in a graveyard of sorts, aren't we?"

"It is a graveyard," she said in a voice filled with despair.

"But my darling Andrea, these are ancient graves."

She corrected him, "They aren't all ancient."

"What do you mean?"

"I'm not sure, Ahmed. Look at those girls down there. They're about my age; they're having fun, they don't seem to have a care in the world."

"My sweet, do you have so many cares?" It was unusual for her to fall into such a sad, solemn mood.

"Cares? Only when I'm in this place. It occurs to me I've seen death too often for being twenty years old, but maybe those girls have seen it too and they need to pretend. This place is evil, Ahmed, and it's not finished, it's not finished!" she cried out.

Ahmed held her. "Shhh, we'll leave now, Andrea. You'll soon be in Arizona; think of all the things you'll have to show me."

He knew she was deeply disturbed; something here haunted her. He cursed her father for the kind of life he had bestowed upon his daughter, for whatever he had done to rob her of her childhood. There was a reason for her nightmares, and it had nothing to do with Afghanistan.

Patrick was ready to leave the Sperrins; time to go to Arizona, but...he had a sudden, sharp twinge of nostalgia–Belfast, why not? The others could stay here, he'd go alone. Take a day and look up some old mates, if they were still around. Wait a minute, why not take Ahmed? That might be interesting. What would he think of Belfast? His old haunt seemed more inviting every minute. He caught up with the others and took Ahmed aside.

"Ahmed, I've decided to take a little trip to Belfast; want to come along?"

Feigning some reluctance, Ahmed asked, "Are you sure you want an Afghan with you, among all those Irishmen?"

"Sure, I'm thinking you'd be a good conversation piece–no offense."

Amused at Patrick's casual insult, Ahmed agreed to go. It was the opportunity he had been looking for.

When he had asked Wenonah about Andrea's trips to Ireland, she had said in some surprise, "Oh, Andrea went only once with Patrick, when he bought the Connemaras. Other times he went by himself. I used to go with him before Andrea was born, but I preferred to stay at home after that."

She was not a good liar; what were they hiding?

Andrea protested at first when he told her he was going to Belfast with Patrick, then decided it might help Ahmed get some questions in his mind settled. After she and Ahmed left the graves on the hilltop, she knew he had decided to find answers to questions she couldn't answer. Her happiness and safety were always more important to him than anything else; it was one of his most endearing traits. So Andrea and Wenonah checked in at MacDonnell's guesthouse with its comfortable, understated Irish décor. Mother and daughter found themselves looking forward to this little bit of time together.

"Mom, let's go to lunch at the Mouse Hole; we'll have some wine and get a little high!"

"Andrea!"

Andrea laughed, "Well, this is my chance. When Ahmed gets back, I'm sure I'll never have another drink again!"

"Do you really like drinking?"

"I don't care about it one way or the other. I just thought we might as well make it a fun time for the two of us."

Wenonah smiled, "That sounds nice." Mother and daughter. Their thoughts, specific to each, meshed into the same command–break out of the mold, use all those hidden desires and drives. Dance, use every joy, every tragic moment, every lovely imagining, music, art, use it all, show it to the world. Ah the power of liberation, helped by a little wine and good humor!

The pub that evening was just as Patrick remembered, but there was no riotous welcome this time. Old Hugh O'Connor was no longer tending bar, the crowd seemed either too young or too old to be planning anything too strenuous. But there were Brian McGee and Daniel MacCarthy, shocked to see Patrick.

"It's a ghost I'm seein'–my God, Patrick McAlister!"

Patrick burst out in laughter. "It's me in the flesh, no ghost yet. Boys, meet my new son-in-law, Ahmed Sharif."

"Well, pleased to meet you," was the acknowledgment of their second shock.

Patrick was quick to explain Ahmed. "Now you've got to know Ahmed is not Arab, he's Afghan, a commander in their war there."

"And how is your lovely daughter? 'Tis hard to believe she's old enough to be married."

"Well, she thought so; the lass has a mind of her own, you know." Patrick felt like he was back where he belonged–a warm feeling, but it couldn't last. There had been too many changes, can't go home again. He stood for pints all around; Ahmed, of course, would have to drink imitation ale–ah well, at least he was being congenial, making himself one of them. Brian and Daniel were curious about the fighting in Afghanistan, and Ahmed was quite willing to talk about it, giving as many bloody details as they wanted.

He waited until Patrick left the table to comment, "Andrea knows Northern Ireland well, doesn't she, even though she's been here only once."

Brian answered, "Aye, she does but you've got it wrong, Ahmed.

Her dad brought her here when she was a wee lass only ten years old."

"And remember the time she came with Patrick when he bought those Connemaras. Ah, those were beautiful horses."

He knew all along Patrick and Wenonah were not telling him the truth, but why not? He knew now he needed to follow this to the end. The next morning they returned to Plumbridge, Patrick having decided after their somewhat rollicking evening that Ahmed was not too bad after all; he admitted to himself he had shown off his Afghan son-in-law.

His friends were impressed–"he's a tough young fighter, that Ahmed. He'd do well with us, if he knew something about covert operations!"

Andrea's lively description of the mother/daughter day together pleased Ahmed; their relationship was closer than it had been for years. Good, thought Ahmed. They left Ireland under a sunny January sky; from the plane they looked down at the magical green isle of mysteries and friendly people, bitter struggles and ancient stones. The last time.

America–the country of Andrea's birth. Though Abdullah had provided Ahmed with a working knowledge of the USA, as Andrea said, "you have to be there." And he was glad to be here, glad Ireland was behind them–too many ghosts, too many demons to catch up with. It should be better for Andrea here. He loved her so deeply, it broke his heart to hear her cry out in her sleep over something so terrible she had no conscious memory of it.

Ahmed had planned this trip as a gift to Andrea; it turned into a quest for the truth. Patrick and Wenonah had no interest in Washington; they went on to Arizona, Patrick deciding he needed to be sure the ranch was in tip-top shape to be shown to Ahmed. He had depended on Billy, his foreman, to keep things up to snuff; he'd show Ahmed what a first class operation he had. He wondered if Ahmed would be successful in Washington. *He's got gumption, I'll say that for him, meeting with that son of a bitch, that so-called senator, Everly. Trying to get the goods on me, is he. Well, the honorable senator will not have any success with his little project–I've taken care of that; they'll never find McCarthy.*

The limousine driver who picked up Andrea and Ahmed from

Dulles gave them a short tour of Washington through a sight-seer's eyes, and Ahmed saw for the first time the seat of power in the country whose bombs helped destroy his enemies, and in so doing, killed innocent Afghans.

Ahmed had come to terms with the American military presence in Afghanistan; he understood the price of conducting war. At some point, he knew the U.S. would leave; Afghanistan would raise itself from the ashes as it did so often. But Afghans needed help now, and he, who resisted all foreign influence, was chosen to ask for that help. The irony of it did not escape him; he would do it as a duty to his country–and there were others in his government who were asking. As they drove through the capital, Ahmed was struck by the variety and splendor of its monuments, the quiet majesty of the Mall, and finally, the Capitol building itself.

"This is where..."

Ahmed broke in, "Yes, Andrea I know all about Congress."

"Oh that's right–of course. Sort of a Loya Jirga."

"I doubt that. Everything looks so clean and white–and big," commented Ahmed. "I'm surprised it's so cold here."

"It's not usually this cold; twenty-five degrees is freezing, all right. Well, what do you think, sweetie?" She waited several minutes for him to answer. Ahmed's eyes were looking far away, as though seeing a vision. How could one not envy this extraordinary country. "This really is a new world, isn't it? Still fresh, clean, proud–and powerful."

Andrea saw in his eyes and felt in her heart his anguish, his longing for even a tiny corner of a new world. She looked into her husband's eyes. "We'll start making our world new, too, something to be proud of–I'll help you." There was no more time for sentimental exchanges.

Andrea did not accompany him into the senator's office; instead an assistant showed her around the complex and requested that she stand beside Ahmed and the senator when the public relations photos were shot. A reluctant Ahmed and Andrea posed with Senator Everly after the meeting. There had been many promises made for Afghanistan–assistance in revitalizing the mines, promoting the exportation of wheat, fruit, nuts, carpets, sheepskins, all of which might give incentive to the people plying the opium trade to turn to other sources of income. Promises–he could only hope some of them might be kept. America, as it revealed itself to Ahmed throughout the journey, was an amazing melange of landscapes and people. It was an unexpected breath of air–not the alluring, siren scent of Paris he remembered, but the aromatic, astringent smell of the *santolina* in Andrea's herb garden. Its scent was in the air throughout his journey in America; this was the fragrance of freedom, strong and indomitable.

Ahmed was still troubled by Ireland. Had he helped Andrea by going there? He had gotten information but no real answers. On their arrival in Tucson, Ahmed was struck by the contrast between the east and the west of America. The phrase "e pluribus unum" was an apt description of the USA, thought Ahmed–out of many, one. Yes, many people, many states, all with their own identities, somehow united, however loosely, and all with that same acerbic air.

Ahmed pondered this phenomenal country as it related to Afghanistan–would that his country could become united. Arizona was familiar; the desert, the mountains reminded him of home, and Paloma, with its horses and hard working ranch hands, suited him. He was impressed with the cattle, sleek, well-fed, and the proficiency of the men who wrangled them. He found another parallel–the game of *buzkashi*, skillful men who played on wild, wonderful horses. The house was not what he expected–certainly not an American mansion; it was not luxurious, but the main room was very large, a multi-purpose room. An eating area held a long table where the cowboys usually ate, and in a smaller room off the kitchen was a table for four to six people; it was a rambling old place, a true ranch house of the old West.

When the cowboys saw Andrea, they broke into smiles and loud shouts of, "Yea, Andrea, welcome home!" Andrea laughed; Ahmed was glad she was in a place where she was loved, protected, and free of troubles. She quickly ran to them, pulling Ahmed along.

"Come on, Ahmed, when you get to know them, you'll feel like you're at home in Afghanistan, except for the language; they sure don't speak Dari. Billy, my God, what's with the long hair? Jack, I see you're still here!" The laconic Jack continually threatened to quit. "Ed, are you taking care of my Danny? Danny, I hope you're behaving yourself for a change–I expect not. Oh well…"

She went on teasing, praising, flirting with them all. Billy, the foreman, had indeed let his hair grow to shoulder length in the hope of attracting a young girl he had his eye on; Ed, a muscular 5'9," claimed he had to guard Danny, 6'4," so he wouldn't make someone named Vera his fourth wife. They all had a story and Andrea knew all their stories. Ahmed stood back a little, enjoying this wild reunion. He could understand how Andrea so seamlessly blended with his *mujahidin*. She was in her element, loving all of them. Finally she took Ahmed's hand and introduced him.

"Boys, please welcome my husband, Ahmed Sharif." They welcomed him with slaps on the back, handshakes and friendly greetings, "if Andrea thought so much of you to get married to you, you're okay in my book!" Ahmed, not yet used to American idiom, wasn't sure how this was meant, but it was said with much laughter and back slapping.

Andrea knew Patrick would have to throw a party for them. To be fair, thought Andrea, it would celebrate his homecoming as well as their marriage. Dad showing off for Ahmed; perhaps this was his farewell gift to her. She wouldn't protest it, Ahmed could handle it as he did everything, with enthusiasm and grace. The surprise was her mother's participation. Their relationship had reached a new level of warmth and understanding, and it felt good: the one happy thing that came out of Ireland.

A delicious lunch and good wine had put them in a mellow mood, making their afternoon at the Mouse Hole relaxed and free–no Patrick or Ahmed. As Andrea had said, "We don't need to behave!"
She asked her mother if she needed any help; Wenonah said, "No dear, not really–your father e-mailed Maria to make all the preparations; food will be catered, band hired. And Maria's going to do her special *gorditas* and *churros*; oh, Miguel in Tucson will do flower arrangements."

"My God, he's going all out, doing the whole bit."

"Let him have his party, Andrea; you may look back on it some day as a good memory. One other thing–your grandfather will be here, along with Uncle Joseph and Uncle Naiche, and the cousins with the children."

Andrea stared at her mother in amazement. "Well, well, Mom, you must have twisted his arm a couple of times, or did you get him when he was feeling romantic in bed?"

"Andrea, really! Sometimes you can be so, so..."

"Vulgar? Honest?"

"Aren't you pleased they are coming?"

"Yes, I'm just in shock." Wenonah ignored this.

"I thought Ahmed might like to see a real Apache ceremonial dance, or at least a mini-version of it, and I want you to dance too. We'll make tomorrow a happy day for all of us–now go make sure Ahmed is comfortable."

"Yes ma'am!" Andrea went to look for Maria, who was in the garden cutting cilantro.

"Maria, what can I do to help for tomorrow?" Maria looked up at her, the weathered, still pretty face happy to have Andrea home; she couldn't believe their wild, rebellious teenager was a married woman–and her husband, *que hombre!*

She scolded happily, "Don do nothing. But go talk to Jack–tell that devil to tie up that bad horse of his. He stepped in my flowers again. I'm gone to smack him one of these days."

"The horse or Jack?"

"Both."

Andrea laughed. The running battle between Maria and the boys had been going on ever since she came to work for her father ten years ago. This party was going to be a big deal; how to dress, fancy Western with her best boots? She would have to wear her Apache dress for the dance; wait 'til Ahmed saw her in those outfits! Her mother needn't have worried about Ahmed. He was at the corral explaining, with extravagant gestures, the game of *buzkashi* and admiring the horses; Billy was demonstrating his skill with the lasso. Andrea watched him, smiling; she was still surprised a man could fill her heart with such joy.

He felt a gentle breeze rustling over him; pleasurable sounds and fragrances crept into his naked body–it was almost a dream–bird song, squirrels' chatter, a horse's whinny, soft morning music, smells of freshly baked bread, pungent spices. He felt like staying in bed for the day, but it was time for morning prayers. Later he would need to get ready for the party; the early morning sweetness would soon fade. Ahmed turned, eyes half open, reaching for Andrea to pull her into his reverie, but she wasn't in bed. As he got up, she walked in, flushed, exultant from riding, and ran over to him, putting her arms around him, kissing him.

"Oh my, you'd better put some clothes on before some crazy female makes improper advances."

He laughed. "Yes, that could be very embarrassing." She smelled of fresh air and lavender, along with a touch of horse or dog. "You've been doing something that's made you very happy–tell me."

"Umm, been riding Lightning–he's big and fast, different from Buttercup."

"Be careful, Andrea, no broken bones, please."

Andrea pulled away from him. "I'll be careful, sweetie. I've got to go help Maria with some stuff–I'll see you a little later." Then she turned around to kiss him once more. "Love you."

Ahmed dressed, said prayers, and went down to the kitchen. Maria greeted him with an ingratiating, *"Buenos dias, senor."*

"Good morning," responded Ahmed.

"I fix you eggs," said Maria, and at his doubtful look she explained, "I don give you no meat, just eggs and my fresh bread; made tea for you too."

Ahmed smiled at her. "Thank you, *gracias*. I thought Andrea was helping you."

*"Si,* she is in the garden, working." He decided not to interrupt Maria's schedule, and went to the corral, where Billy and Jack were examining one of the quarter horses.

"Put him in the stall. Dr. Joe will have to check him–don't like the look of that leg," said Billy. "Mornin'," they acknowledged his presence; Ahmed knew they were too busy to talk, and he leaned on the rail, looking at the Arizona grasslands, its mountains and desert in the distance. He thought about his wife; after he saw Paloma and met the ranch hands he could easily envision Andrea growing up here, strong and determined, under the watchful eye of her father. Yes, he could see her through the eyes of her "boys," a tough little tomboy of a girl who felt a sense of belonging only when she was among the ranch hands. What she really loved, she told him, was breaking horses, and she was good at it, having a special knack for communicating with them.

"And she sure loved music, why, that little gal could sing and dance like an angel."

"Yeah, and cuss like a sailor," laughed Jack.

"Well, she spent too much time around you, you no good cowboy! Yep, she's a prize, our Andrea. You seen her ride, Ahmed? She rides like the wind."

"Yes, I know."

"Now, you take good care of her, Ahmed, cause I know your country's a hell of a dangerous place," pronounced Jack.

"Well that's what he's doin', ain't it?"

Billy didn't have a high opinion of Jack's intelligence or his diplomacy. However, Ahmed assured both he would always take good care of Andrea.

When they finished showering and were dressed for the party, Andrea pulled Ahmed over to the full length mirror and exclaimed, "Now isn't that a good looking couple–I think they're in love!"

"I can't imagine how an Afghan came to be in love with a cowgirl from Arizona–strange."

She gave him a playful punch. "Let's go, Afghan, it's party time!"

Where did all these people come from? Andrea couldn't remember when they ever had so many party guests. An unpleasant thought occurred to her and she looked carefully at the partygoers, but couldn't spot any who looked like IRA–better not be, she thought. The house and courtyard were filled with the music of the *mariachi* band, Mexican food was piled on platters, and Miguel's flowers were everywhere.

Patrick greeted them, "Andrea, you look like my daughter again, a proper cowgirl. Now be sure to save me a dance, lass. Ahmed, enjoy yourself–plenty of food here, not all of it's Mexican. Just ask if you need something special–'tis a happy occasion; nothing like a grand party for an Irishman!"

The lilting Irish accent was triumphant. Andrea had to laugh–she knew all her father's moods, and this one was over the top. I know all his blarney too, she thought; he's happy–back in his own little kingdom. Whatever, as long as he's nice to Ahmed. Ahmed was not surprised at Patrick's overblown hospitality–he has a lot of weapons in his arsenal, thought Ahmed, but none of them will bring Andrea back to him; let him have his day.

"Oh sweetie, come meet my Apache relatives."

Ahmed was introduced to Jack Redbird, Andrea's grandfather,

her Uncle John and Uncle Naiche, four cousins and their children, ages two to eight. He could see their relationship to Wenonah, but little of it to Andrea, except for the skin color and cheekbones. They greeted him with hugs, expressing their wishes for Andrea's and his happiness; her grandfather's kind eyes looked at Ahmed for long minutes. Jack Redbird, smiling all the while, took a stern measure of the man who married his wild granddaughter–she who most needed love. It was one of the few times in his life Ahmed felt ill at ease upon meeting someone, yet he liked this Indian immediately. Andrea and three of the cousins, all female, were chattering away, catching up on one another's lives, and, Ahmed noted, expressing dismay that Andrea was really going to make her home in Afghanistan.

"You know, we hardly ever saw each other when I lived here," said Andrea. "I'll be back now and then."

Her cousin Juanita eyed her shrewdly, "It sounds like you're going to be a pioneer, and in a dangerous place. You ought to know that doesn't work well."

Cousin Rosita retorted, "Don't pay attention to her. You'll have a good time trying, with your handsome husband!"

Laughing, Andrea told them, "Enough, enough, tell me what's going on; where are your moms?"

"Oh, they said to tell you they're sorry they can't be here; they're in Alaska, something about a casino up there, we don't know anything about it–they're always involved in politics."

The conversation ended when Robert Armiger, a state senator and close friend of Patrick's, called for a toast first to Patrick, then to Andrea and Ahmed. The guests toasted Patrick with an affection that surprised Ahmed; the toast to Andrea and Ahmed was proposed by Patrick, who took the opportunity to bestow on them a classic Irish blessing: " May the road rise up to meet you, may the wind be always at your back, may the sun shine warm upon your face, and the rains fall soft upon your fields, and until we meet again, may God hold you in the palm of his hand," which they acknowledged with a nod and smile.

"The lord of the manor, has condescended to bless us! What bull!"

"Andrea, don't let him upset you. Come dance with me, be happy." She let go of her anger–after all, the verse was beautiful, one of her favorites; as they danced she forgot everyone but Ahmed.

.They moved in time to flamenco rhythm, slowly, then faster, with an exuberance and joy that evoked the same passion and wild urgency of the dance of Afghanistan. Andrea and Ahmed sat down, filled with a pleasurable triumph at having danced so well together. The *mariachi* band, delighted with the enthusiastic response to their performance so far, started playing an old Mexican folk dance, a *jaranas*, and Juan Garcia, one of the cowboys, got up to dance. More dancers joined him and became a circle. Caught up in the joy of the music, Ahmed was drawn into the circle between Andrea and Rosita, following the steps of the others. This was new to him, this dance with both men and women, but the circle of dancers was as old as time. As the *mariachi* band took a break, a D.J. switched gears and played rock and country, music Ahmed neither liked nor understood. But he wasn't surprised to see Andrea's cousins get up to dance–this was the music they liked. For them, the Apache dances and rituals were not relevant to modern American life, even when they understood the value of preserving them.

Andrea turned to Ahmed to speak; he stopped her by saying, "Go ahead, wild child, dance with them!"

"Come with me."

"It looks foolish."

"Oh, come on, let me corrupt you with just one American number, it's one of my favorites."

"Everything is your favorite! But I'll be American when I'm here with you, may Allah forgive me!" He got up with Andrea and let her dance as she wanted, while he simply kept time with the beat of music he would never appreciate. The party spilled out into the courtyard; the children's games ended in the late afternoon under a surreal orange Arizona sky.

As Patrick watched, euphoric with the success of his party, a hypnotic drumbeat sounded to start an Apache tribal dance. Oh Jesus, he thought, not that damned Indian dance, and he saw Wenonah and Andrea, in Indian dress, in the circle of Apache dancers. As he watched the tribal ritual, his heart sank; in the midst of this celebration of home and family, there was an odd void. Loss. His training, his ambitions for her–all gone in a marriage to an Afghan. It seemed an abrupt, almost casual, dismissal.

Ahmed was intrigued by the ceremonial dance. "It's the dance of the Ganhs, mountain spirits sent by the Great Spirit, who tells us how to live a good life. We dance to summon the mountain spirits to help us live well," Andrea explained.

"So many beliefs in America."

"It's a big country, sweetie."

The celebration had woven itself into a tapestry of the American Southwest–*mariachi* music, Mexican food, Spanish dance, Apache ceremony. Ahmed thought of the conversation he had earlier with Andrea's uncle, Naiche.

Naiche asked, "What do you think of Andrea's father?"

Ahmed replied, "He's not an easy man."

"Irish–he took Andrea away from our people, but what a joke on him! Now she'll be an Afghan; he'll never get her to Ireland again; she won't follow in his footsteps now."

"Andrea will always be American, too."

"Yes, I hope so. Just watch out for Patrick; he has blood on his hands. But then, you're a soldier, you know all these things. What do you think of America?"

Ahmed picked his words carefully, "You have so much...yet..."

"Yes," Naiche agreed. "Some have much, too much, others have little, but no one starves in America as they do in Afghanistan. We're rich compared to everyone else, but I think...I think there's a hunger in our souls."

"A hunger, for...?"

"Oh, I don't exactly know; I'm not a philosopher, or a psychiatrist, it's just something one feels...a true purpose, a true course, some kind of nobility...who knows? I wish you well, you and Andrea, in Afghanistan."

Ahmed awoke early; he looked at Andrea sleeping, and decided not to wake her. Let her sleep–he kissed her lightly, not wanting to disturb her, and proceeded to pray. When he went downstairs, he found Wenonah and Maria already at work cleaning up the remnants of the party. Waving away Maria's offer of breakfast, Ahmed helped himself to cereal and fruit, deciding on coffee for a change. Outside, he admired the crystal clear blue sky that whitewashed Paloma in a brief burst of purity. It was an exciting subject for the artistry of a landscape painter or Wenonah the potter. Afghans wove carpets and cloth of beautiful colors and patterns; they could learn other crafts, some day there might be a cultural exchange of arts and crafts; no doubt Andrea had already thought of it. He went to the stable where Patrick and Ed were discussing a horse sale in Tucson.

"Well, good morning, Ahmed, what did you think of our little party yesterday?"

"Andrea and I both enjoyed it; I was happy to meet Wenonah's relatives."

"Aye, the Apaches; they went on the warpath for you," Patrick joked.

"Andrea explained that the dance was something like a prayer to their Great Spirit."

"Oh, to be sure–now, would you be wanting a good horse to take out? I've got just the one–now, this is one of our splendid Arabians and I've got to admit that is one good thing that comes from your part of the world. Here you go," and he led Ahmed to a beautiful chestnut Arabian named Satanta.

"He is a fine horse," said Ahmed, ignoring Patrick's commentary on Indians and Afghanistan. "An interesting name, Satanta."

"Well, it's an Indian name–Andrea had her way with that. Ed can saddle him for you."

"Thank you, but I can do that myself."

"Enjoy your ride."

Ahmed saddled the chestnut stallion and set out to explore some of the vast acreage owned by Andrea's father. He looked in envy at the cattle, well fed by the grasses of Paloma, being herded into another section by Billy and Jack, and almost felt like one of the cowboys. Laughing to himself at the thought, he loped over to the two ranch hands.

"Where's your hat?" they asked. "You need a ten-gallon hat to be a real cowboy!"

Ahmed laughed. "I don't have one; my bandana will do; I'm not going much farther. This is a big ranch, those are good looking cows."

"Yep, this spread ain't so big compared to other ranches, 'specially the ones in Texas, but it's a pretty good size."

Billy commented, "I see you got Satanta. Patrick likes his Arabians; they're beauties for sure–don't work like quarter horses, though. Andrea's got one, ain't she, over in Afghanistan?"

"Yes, she named him Buttercup, and Abdullah and I gave him an

Afghan name, Zabuli. Arabians are known as drinkers of the wind."

"Yeah, they got a lot of wind to drink in your part of the world, goin' without water for a long time –and the way their head is carried, they're made for the wind; sure are different. Buttercup! Well, that sounds like Andrea."

Jack called, "I expect she's got plans for you today, gonna do some sightseein' up to the Canyon, I bet."

Ahmed realized he had been out longer than he intended, said goodbye and started back.

When he returned, Ahmed didn't see Andrea anywhere outside; he entered a quiet, put-in-order house, and went up to their bedroom, where he heard Andrea in the shower, singing. He stood still, smiling and listening to her song–though he teased her about it, he loved hearing her sing.

Opening the bathroom door, he called, "Andrea!"

"Come on in, sweetie, the water's fine!"

"Not with my clothes on, wild child."

"Take them off, silly!" Her invitation was too tempting to resist. She had resumed her song, "anything you want, you got it…" Ahmed stepped in the shower and kissed her, pressing his body against hers.

"Where did you go, sweetie?"

"Riding on an Arabian stallion, Satanta."

"Ah, he's a beauty. I was so sleepy I just stayed in bed thinking about you, feeling very lazy today."

"You smell so good," he said. "You taste good, too. Sing that song for me again."

Andrea laughed. "You are one sexy Afghan, Ahmed Sharif!"

"If I am, you are to blame. You're a temptress; I can't resist you!"

Laughing, Andrea said, "Then don't."

As they were dressing, Ahmed, in a thoughtless moment, said, "I couldn't blame you if you wanted to stay here. You must feel like you're home."

Andrea looked at him after a long pause. "But I'm not home. This was my home, I lived here once, I love the ranch and the boys, but there's a lot I hated when I was here. My home is wherever you are." Her voice grew quieter as she went on. "You're my heart and home, husband. This is fun, our honeymoon, and it's like…like a little package of happiness. No, Ahmed, my home is with you."

"Forgive me; it was just seeing you happy and relaxed … Afghanistan is not where most people would choose to live."

"It's our home, Ahmed, and we'll be happy there, whatever craziness is going on."

"Yes, as long as you trust me."

He knew she couldn't understand his words; she frowned, a quizzical look in her eyes as she said, "Always."

Jack was wrong. Andrea had no plans to show Ahmed Arizona's wonders that day; they spent the day quietly, Ahmed learning about the day-to-day operation of ranching in the American Southwest, Andrea critiquing Wenonah's latest designs and suggesting subjects for paintings. Andrea promised Ahmed, "Tomorrow I'll show you an Arizona that's almost as old as Afghanistan–we'll see some amazing cliff dwellings."

They ate lunch together, Maria sitting with them telling stories of her family in Mexico, her twelve year old nephew's aspirations to become a matador, "now that would be *un milagro!*" As she was speaking, she abandoned English for a rapid Spanish which, except for Patrick, who understood only a little, they followed.

"Speak English, Maria, this is the USA!"

"Oh, *si, senor,*" she replied, said nothing more, and rose to clear the table.

Bullfighting interested Ahmed. He had seen a *corrida* in France and was impressed with its beauty, formality and discipline; though he would like to attend another one, he deferred to Andrea and her plans for tomorrow.

Patrick looked at Wenonah; what was she so excited about?

His usually calm wife was laughing at some comment from Maria, then said to Andrea, "Oh, I think that would be fun, Andrea. Ahmed, we'd like to take you to the Casa Capricho; it's a little club near Nogales, just over the border." He had not seen her so animated since…he didn't know when.

"Please, Dad, you've got to come; it'll be a pleasant evening for the four of us."

As Maria came by the table, they heard her muttering, "Little club, hah! It's just a saloon, with *muchos vagabundo.*"

"What's that you're grumbling about?" asked Patrick in a loud voice. The new intimacy between his wife and daughter felt like a plot in which he was the victim. This rediscovered relationship made him uneasy. Maria merely shrugged her shoulders and smiled. And Ahmed knew that Andrea and Wenonah were in control of the situation and enjoying it. Whatever this place was where they wanted to take him was sure to be interesting.

Casa Capricho was not an upscale nightclub, nor was it a saloon full of bums, as Maria had described it; they entered a Mexican *cantina* where talk revolved around one sport: the *corrida*. Heated discussions could be overheard about the quality of the bulls; now and then came a boast from someone who had been invited to the *tentadero de eralas*, testing of the heifers; debates raged regarding which matadors would become the heroes of the coming season. A few curious looks were directed at Ahmed and Andrea. The Casa held an eclectic crowd–office workers, gypsies, city sophisticates, laborers, there to hear the music of renowned flamenco guitarist, Jose Ballardo, who was playing a slow, melancholy Spanish melody. Ballardo was watching Andrea intently; could this be the girl of fourteen who had danced so gracefully to his music some years ago? He was almost certain it was she–who could forget that glorious hair? All grown up–*es una belleza!*

Andrea exclaimed to her mother, "He's still playing here!"

"Oh, he comes and goes–Europe, South America, many places, but Andrea, he wasn't so old. Did you think he had died?"

"I probably did," she said, laughing, "when I was fourteen, a lot of people seemed old!"

Patrick had ordered *sangria* and fruit drinks for Andrea and Ahmed, and was making an effort to ingratiate himself with a wealthy tourist from Alabama; there was always a good deal to be made.

"So you know him, lass? Go speak to him, ask him to play an Irish tune," he joked.

Andrea ignored her father. "Ahmed, come with me."

Ahmed smiled; "I like this place; it has a certain flavor: Spanish, Indian, Moorish perhaps."

They had no sooner reached Ballardo's table when he cried out, "*Si*, I remember my young dancer; you are Andrea, the girl with the beautiful hair." Laughing, he kissed her on both cheeks. "Have you come to dance for me again?"

"I'd love to, if my husband agrees," and she introduced Ahmed to

Ballardo, who studied him with an uncertain look. Husband! Well, she was too beautiful to be single for long.

"But you are not American–you come from the East, is that not so?"

"Yes, Afghanistan."

"Aha! I traveled to India and Iran to learn the music, now they know a little flamenco from this old gypsy! Will you two be going back to Afghanistan?" At the question, Ahmed put his arm around Andrea, evoking a poignant memory for Ballardo of the tenderness he had always shown his wife. They told him yes, they would return to Afghanistan.

"That is our home."

"Well, *vaya con dios*, my children, *vaya con dios*."

"Thank you," said Ahmed.

Ballardo handed Andrea a pair of castanets. "This piece is going to be northern Spain's traditional fandango; do you remember the steps?" and he placed his hand on her arm. "Even if you have forgotten them, I'm sure you will dance like an angel, or in this case, like a devil!"

He needn't have been concerned; Andrea that afternoon had found time by herself to try on the dress she had left behind at Paloma. After much searching, she found the shoes she needed; putting in a flamenco guitar tape, she started dancing–the music guided her; she felt sure of the steps.        Ballardo spoke quickly before starting, "Enjoy, Andrea, enjoy the dance!"

Ahmed sat with Wenonah and Patrick to watch Andrea. "It will be a professional performance. All those dance lessons, all part of her education," explained Patrick.

No, thought Ahmed, this was Wenonah's training, not Patrick's. To Ahmed's surprise, a young man in dance costume appeared opposite Andrea. Ballardo started with a slow, tender rhythm; with castanets clicking and feet stamping the dancers picked up speed as the music became faster. Then came the breathless, sudden pause as both music and dancers were completely still for a moment before once again, in turn, resuming their teasing and pursuit of one another. They moved voluptuously to the cadence of the music, ending in a whirl of ecstasy. Ahmed was enthralled by the fandango, only wishing he could be her partner.

Across the table, Wenonah gave him a knowing look and said quietly, "Yes, she's my daughter too," and there was a small, triumphant smile on her usually expressionless face. At that moment, Ahmed knew Andrea belonged in Afghanistan; the dance seemed to erase any of his doubts.

"My God, I'm sinfully happy," said a breathless Andrea as she sat down.

"It was a beautiful dance; I'm surprised you're not on Broadway," said Ahmed with a touch of sarcasm.

"Oh Ahmed, you're pouting." She placed her fingers on his lips turning them up into a smile. "I didn't know I was going to have a partner, that was a surprise; turns out it was a good thing for Ballardo. That was his son, and he's trying out for a Broadway musical. Please don't be mad, sweetie."

As the guitarist started playing again, Andrea whispered to Ahmed, "Dance this with me."

It was a slow, seductive *bolero* with an insistent, throbbing beat–Ahmed could not refuse. He took Andrea's hands, pinning her arms to her side with his; Wenonah watched, admiring their passion. The music lulled her into a vision of her people and tribes everywhere, dancing sacred rituals on desert floors hundreds of years ago. The ancients respected nature's force and recognized a supernatural will; at least some vestige of the old ceremonies lingered in today's dance. As Andrea sat down, Ahmed stood behind her, his hands lifting the shower of curls, stroking her neck. Wenonah was amused at the loving gesture; Patrick's attention was diverted from horse trading by the sight of it. *Fondling my daughter in front of me, is he, claiming ownership of my daughter–I'll show him!* But he knew he couldn't. Instead, Ahmed's overt sexual caress aroused his desire. He looked at Wenonah, laughing at some remark from Andrea; by God, she was radiant tonight–I need to make love to her.

"Let's dance, Wen," he ordered. She surrendered to his arms with her usual grace, and they danced briefly; it was not his kind of music. He smiled at her in anticipation of a sensual night of lovemaking, and Wenonah returned his smile with a playful gleam in her eye. The discussion with the wealthy tourist from Alabama was soon abandoned for something far more promising. It was time to go home.

After they made love that night, Andrea abruptly turned away from him, but he turned her to face him, and saw that her eyes were closed.

"Asleep already?"

"No."

"Look at me."

He saw tears in her half-open eyes. "Crying, my love, what's wrong? I haven't beaten you lately!" She did not answer. "Andrea, look at me!"

She opened her eyes. "I love you," she cried.

"I know that. What's making you so sad?"

"I'm afraid…"

"Afraid? There is nothing …"

Panic in her voice, she interrupted, "I don't know if I can be the wife you need, and there's something else, but I…I don't know what it is…something…flashing…"

Ahmed held Andrea in a tight embrace, whispering reassurances to her until she was calm. The sadness he felt for her since Ireland had eased somewhat; she seemed happy here at Paloma. Yet he felt there was an evil shadow following her. *I think there's a lost child inside my beautiful wife–lost since her father took her to Ireland years ago. What happened in Ireland? No matter how I try, I can't get hold of that damned shadow, but…*A sudden realization struck him–Andrea's beloved Paloma was a poisonous place. Desperate as he was to find an answer before they left Arizona, he knew he had to take her away from here. Thank God they would soon leave.

They lay together, breathing in the cool air, listening to the night sounds. The answer he had been searching for would come soon.

There was something foreboding in the purple Arizona sky that enclosed them. Since she was very little, Andrea heard faint notes of Indian flutes rising from the canyons, floating on the slightest current of air. He looked into her half closed eyes, ready to vanquish any enemy for her.

Curious at her half-trance, he asked, "What do you see; what do you hear?"

"Ghosts," she answered, and blinked to clear her eyes. "You'll hear them, you'll see them for yourself soon."

"Are you sure you want to go?"

"Very sure," she answered, and they climbed into the Land Rover.

Andrea and Ahmed had allowed themselves five days to see the historic sites she wanted to show him. He was aware of her hesitation in sharing with him the forces that had shaped her life, but he knew she needed him to see and feel all the bits and pieces, good or bad, that made her what she was. Their first destination was Fort Apache Indian Reservation. As they traveled, the purple sky turned to a bright blue interspersed by wispy white clouds; Andrea pointed out the bizarre, tall saguaro cactus here and there and named a few of the rather gaunt, colorful desert plants. They crossed the Gila River, going into the Superstition Mountains and the Apache Trail.

"This was an Apache warpath; now it's just scenery." Ahmed made no comment, imagining savage Apache warriors on their horses plunging headlong into battles they would never truly win. Soon they were on the reservation.

"This is what the Apaches ended up with, a small piece of the lands they once called their own."

There was a harshness in her words.

Ahmed was puzzled. "Why are you angry, my love?"

"Angry—what do you mean, sweetie? Oh, the Indian thing. It's not so much anger, more of a sadness. Apaches were a very proud people, and intelligent, with a culture as legitimate as any other tribe. But they weren't as easily tamed as the others and...they did have some cruel customs."

"Scalping?"

"Yes, but other tribes practiced that too. Scalping is an ancient thing; it goes back further in time than the American Indians. Anyway, I think my mother was always made to feel inferior, not quite as good as the whites. So I feel a little defensive about the Apaches. At least my father didn't care about her race or background, though he puts Indians down—but then, he puts everybody down who's not Irish; he's sort of an equal-opportunity racist."

"Andrea, who are these ghosts you see?"

"When we go to a place called Cochise Stronghold, you'll know."

As they drove, Ahmed could see a wide variety of housing, nothing approaching the level of housing in Tucson. These were modest homes, as though the owner had resigned himself to build a basic shelter out of sheer necessity. And Jack Redbird's house was one of these. As they approached, Andrea and Ahmed saw her grandfather digging, pulling up carrots, harvesting squash. He smiled broadly as he saw them, giving both a hug, his long graying hair escaping from its knotted band.

"Welcome, Andrea; welcome, Ahmed. Come in, we'll have sandwiches and tea and talk." As they entered, Ahmed could not contain his surprise.

"This is beautiful–your coverings and the carpets!" He examined them in detail.

Jack explained with pride, "They are the usual Apache designs. The Navajos are really the better weavers."

In the large kitchen, Ahmed stared in admiration at Wenonah's pots and paintings surrounding them. As they ate sandwiches and Jack's spicy squash casserole, Ahmed commented, "Much I've seen here in Arizona reminds me of Afghanistan."

Jack Redbird pondered this, then asked, "Does Andrea remind you of Afghanistan?"

Ahmed smiled, remembering her fandango dancing last night, and replied, "She is very much like Afghanistan–beautiful, wild, stubborn, and a little dangerous."

Jack laughed, "Ah, granddaughter, I see this man knows your soul."

"Hmph–the only part of that description I like is the first word!" Andrea cleared the table and washed dishes as Ahmed inspected the weavings more closely. "Grandfather, that was a good lunch; Ahmed loved your squash casserole. I should try it when we get back home; will you give me the recipe?"

"Of course; I'm surprised to hear that you cook."

"Well, I'm sort of learning."

Good, he thought; she could use some domesticating. "I'm glad to hear it. Now we'll go on a little tour of the reservation."

Except for the subtle beauty of the desert plants and the striking sunlit red of mountains and rock formations in the distance, the reservation could have been called desolate, with its ramshackle houses and slightly unkempt appearance. Jack took them past the school and two churches, and a small museum where Ahmed noticed a braid of hair adorned with various beads and feathers. Jack confirmed Ahmed's suspicion. "It's a scalp; was used in the victory dance." Ahmed was fascinated by the Apache ceremonial trappings, especially the pipes and flutes.

"We have a pretty good medical clinic, and there, see, a police station. Never needed those in the old days. Not many Chiricahuas on this reservation; most live in New Mexico or Oklahoma. We do all right, the timber operation makes money. Now, at San Carlos, they've got a cattle operation, some mining, good hunting and fishing, even got one of those casinos, but I like it here. Quiet–doesn't always pay to get rich, too complicated."

Andrea laughed. "My grandfather's a wise man!"

Ahmed agreed.

In the bracing dry air and bright sun, they said goodbye to Jack Redbird. He called out a warning to Ahmed as Andrea started the car. "She drives too fast; better keep a tight rein on her." He wondered about his granddaughter; she dances to her own beat–may the Great Spirit protect her. He was sorry to see them go, for he had many stories to tell them, more stories than he had days, he thought, but that is the way of old men–his stories would find their way to their hearts, would live with them for a while and become part of their children's heritage. Andrea wondered if this would be her last visit to her grandfather.

"Our next stop will be the Grand Canyon; it'll be dark by the time we get there, so we'll stay at a hotel and you can see it in the early morning in all its glory, from the south rim."

The long drive to the canyon was tiresome; Andrea let Ahmed convince her to give him the wheel for a while, and he took over. Jack had warned Ahmed about Andrea's driving; had he known about Ahmed's, he would have beseeched the Great Spirit to protect Ahmed as well. A typical Afghan driver, Ahmed drove as fast as he did around Kabul, where there was no such thing as an enforceable speed limit.

Andrea cautioned, "Ahmed, slow down! We may end up in jail at this rate!" The open road, smooth and almost traffic-free, was intoxicating; he couldn't resist it. But Andrea was right–he didn't want to be arrested in America with the way things were right now; he reluctantly turned the wheel over to her, kissing her and laughing. "Drive on, my cautious one."

As the sky became darker, Andrea pulled into the parking lot of the rustic old hotel at Grand Canyon Village. She had been there once with her parents and loved the aura of the place and its unpretentious comfort, the smell of it, and the feeling it had grown out of the rock of the Canyon. How appropriate that Hopi Indians had helped build this place.

They slept well that night, tired from the boring inactivity of riding so long in a car; when he awoke, Ahmed reached for Andrea, then saw her, praying, facing Mecca. He was surprised she had decided to honor a vow he knew she took only for him. She had ignored Islam since their wedding–what inspired her this morning? Whatever it was, Ahmed had no intention of making anything of it; he felt patience was the best policy. As he rose to join her, the sight from their window was unbelievable, even to one accustomed to spectacular mountain vistas. He saw a small portion of an enormous geologic spectacle–an overwhelming, surreal proof of nature's power.

Andrea waited until he had finished his prayers to speak, then asked him, "Is this sight worth the drive?" She didn't need to ask; the wonder in his eyes answered her.

"I'd like to see it all."

"Let's eat breakfast first, then we'll explore a little. We'll go to Desert View and you'll see the Colorado River."

By the time they went out, Ahmed had read how this huge gorge was formed over time, how rain and the Colorado River had cut through and eroded the plateau, leaving a continuous castle-like fantasy of cliffs, valleys, and peaks. Always there was the deep russet red of Arizona dominating the palette of sunset colors. Andrea and Ahmed exchanged no words–they simply breathed deeply of the majesty before them.

Their journey into the world of the Indian took them to the Navajo reservation and into the Navajo National Monument, home of the Kayenta Anasazi, prehistoric people who lived there until 1300. There they saw Keet Seel, a cliff dwelling once occupied by the Anasazi, who farmed the valley below. Andrea's first visit with Wenonah and Patrick was a guided tour by permit only, so she applied for the permit in advance; led by a park ranger, they rode on horseback to the ancient dwellings. The primitive cliff houses were amazingly well preserved, considering the village was first occupied around A.D. 950. It was with a sense of gratitude that Ahmed, an Afghan, inspected those ancient dwellings. His country's ancient structures and artifacts had been largely destroyed–one or two Buddhas were left intact. In the end, it mattered not to him where the traces of history had been preserved, only that there were still human beings in the world who knew and appreciated their value. Afghan or not, one could not help but feel the connection with these people; he understood Andrea's feeling for the graves of Ireland and the abandoned cliff dwellings. They were her people, reaching out for her from the mists of time, playing their music for her, as did the tribes of Afghanistan, who whispered warnings to Ahmed–be careful, change is coming, caution...!

They had one more stop before returning to Paloma–Andrea wanted him to see Cochise's Stronghold–there were many more footprints of almost obliterated places and people, but time was running out; they had to make the long trip back to Paloma.

Ahmed and Andrea drove past Willcox and the sign that pointed tourists to the Cochise Information Center and Museum; Andrea was not interested in museums. A magnetic force had always drawn her to the canyon where Cochise took shelter and hid, with his warriors, from his pursuers.

"Is this the place where you hear the flutes?" asked Ahmed.

"Yes, all around here."

"Do you hear them now?"

"No," smiled Andrea. "But we must be quiet; my ghosts are here–they may not show themselves to you."

Ahmed was silent, not sure if he believed her. As they stood in the shadows of the canyon, a light wind whistled past them; Ahmed felt a heaviness in the air, and a familiar longing rushing through his body. He saw no ghosts–he felt them in his bones, as he had in Ireland. Andrea was still, her eyes reflecting a kinship and a knowledge of her ancestors' acceptance of defeat. She needed no monuments, no tombstones, for they were here in the earth, everywhere.

Paloma–Ahmed was glad to be back and looking forward to leaving; Paris lay ahead–Andrea needed Paris, he thought. He watched her as she dressed, pulling jeans up over long, shapely legs; she grabbed a white shirt off the hanger, starting to put it on.

"Andrea, your bra."

"Oh Ahmed..."

"No." Giving him a look of exasperation and frustration, she put the bra on, then the shirt.

"There–does this suit your sense of propriety?" And, pirouetting before him, she leaned over to kiss him.

"Yes, wild child, you know…"

"Yes, I know–you're such a, a, oh, whatever, but I love you anyway. Now may I go ride Satanta–it's a beautiful morning; said my prayers and I'll eat breakfast when I get back."

"Yes," he answered. "Andrea, don't get too caught up in these…these ghosts, please. I like seeing you happy." For one moment, Andrea felt fear, then cast her eyes down to avoid his gaze.

"Tomorrow we'll be on our way to Paris–that will be our real honeymoon, just the two of us."

Ahmed hoped there would be no one else with them; ghosts, begone! He sat thinking about the Indians, about Andrea–how dark and tanned she was, like an Indian or an Afghan, but the hair–that was Patrick's. He loved to watch her getting dressed; the elegant curved body, feminine, strong, moved with a dancer's grace. Ahmed was worried about her–the nightmare had not been coming as often, but he knew it wasn't over, and he hadn't solved it for her.

Even after questioning a reluctant Wenonah, the only information he got was a nervous statement. "Oh, yes, perhaps Andrea went with Patrick to Ireland more than once…it's been so long…I've forgotten…"

Ahmed dressed, ate Maria's pancakes accompanied by her comments about sausages. "Would you not like just one? They're *delicioso*, Senor Ahmed," then, muttering to herself, "I no understand *el problema*."

Patrick appeared as Ahmed started to leave and told Maria, "Stop your complaining; you can fix pancakes and eggs AND sausage for me. I'm hungry. Well, Ahmed, how did you like the Indian tour?"

Not waiting for a reply, he went on, "Those old Apache chiefs were tough fighters–they knew a thing or two about the fine art of torture; learned that from the Spanish, you know. Well," he said expansively, "Afghans too, maybe Irish know how to get the message across, eh?"

Ahmed stared at him, his eyes hard and cold. Patrick frowned, his mouth turning up in a small, superior smile. "You don't like the comparison? I think Andrea would like it–she has a bit of knowledge about such things."

A furious Ahmed strode over to face him; if Patrick felt threatened by Ahmed, he didn't show it.

He placed his hand on Ahmed's shoulder, "Just a little joke between warriors, my boy, 'tis nothing to be concerned about. What concerns me is Andrea's safety in Afghanistan. Take good care of my lass."

The condescending son of a bitch, thought Ahmed. Resisting a strong impulse to strike him, Ahmed realized this was not the time for confrontation–he had no ammunition yet.

In a voice that matched the coldness of his eyes, Ahmed said, "You need not concern yourself with Andrea. She is my wife; she'll always be safe with me," and he walked away from Patrick.

Andrea packed a lunch and the two of them spent the day exploring the country around Paloma, relaxing and enjoying the sunny crispness of their last full day in Arizona. Ahmed made love to her that night in an unusually tender fashion. Afterwards, Andrea lifted her head from his chest and stroked his face, smiling. "When are you going to grow your beard again?"

"I may not–don't you like it shaved?"

"Either way is fine with me, handsome," she said.

He whispered to her in Dari, "Go to sleep, my Indian princess."

Ahmed woke abruptly to the sound of sobs from Andrea. That damned nightmare–he held her tight, but she couldn't stop crying; at one point a small scream came from her lips, and Ahmed put his hand over her mouth to muffle another scream–he didn't want anyone coming in to check on them.

"Andrea, my darling, I've got you, you're all right. Shhh, darling."

She uttered a stream of words, almost unintelligible.

"What? Slowly, Andrea, tell me slowly."

"Ahmed, he made me do it, he made me, I didn't want to, he said I had to do it!" After ten years, she was reliving the nightmare, putting its evil into words for the first time.

"Who made you?"

"He did–Patrick–my father!"

"What did he make you do?"

"He told me to do it," she said between sobs. "I shot him, killed him–there was blood, a lot of blood!"

Ahmed kept hold of her, calming her as best he could, but he knew she needed to rid herself of the dream's haunting misery. "Andrea, please, my darling, try to tell me what happened."

"It was in Ireland, a place in Belfast; I was ten years old. I remember being in a house, in a room with two men and my father. They were arguing–ooh–my father was bleeding, his hand. Another man was standing in front of him, he was bleeding, too. I don't know, they must have shot each other. I picked up my father's gun, the man who was with my father ran away–then I had to shoot the man who was bleeding…he fell down…my father went to him…stood over him…he said…'you killed him.' He said it over and over–'you killed him, you killed him.' I don't remember after that."

She spoke the words in staccato-like syllables, in a voice unlike her own. The sporadic pauses and sudden stops were clear evidence of a child's efforts to wipe out part of her life.

Ahmed wiped her tear-stained cheeks–he was not shocked at her dramatic revelation, but his fury and hatred were overwhelming; if Patrick had been standing there, Ahmed would have killed him on the spot. But Patrick was in his own bedroom with Wenonah, and Andrea needed his strength, not more bloodshed. How could a father do such a thing to his only child, a daughter he professed to love–and telling him to take good care of his "lass," that he was concerned for her safety! Apparently he had no concern for her feelings, her emotions, her heart.

Ahmed said in a low voice, "He is a monster."

At this, Andrea exclaimed, "Oh, Ahmed, please don't say anything to him or my mother–it won't do any good now–promise, please. I feel a little better. Oh, my God, Ahmed, I finally know…I can't believe…"

"Andrea, do you realize what he did to you?"

"Yes."

No. She didn't. Patrick's deed had taken away much of her childhood.

"Yes, I do, but he can't control my life any longer; he has no more power. I almost pity him; he's so contemptible, but I won't go back to the past. Some day I'll go to Ireland and settle what happened that night, but it can wait. Ahmed," here she paused, looking at him in wide-eyed wonder, "I'm free!"

Ahmed tried to suppress his seething anger, realizing this was the time for support, not lectures.

Holding her face in his hands he told her, "I don't think you will ever have that nightmare again, my darling. But your father…"

She interrupted him–Patrick–that was her job. "I'm going to talk to him before we leave and I'll do it by myself. He's going to know that he's not important to me anymore. Don't worry, it's going to be all right."

She placed her hand on his face in a gesture of reassurance. "One thing–I will not involve my mother; she fell under the spell of a charming Irishman when they met, and I'm sure she knows what he is now, but…she still loves him." She sighed. Yes, he thought, confrontation with Patrick must be left to her.

The next morning, Ahmed found Wenonah sitting by the window in the big room downstairs, deep in thought. As he came closer, she stood up and kissed him, Afghan style, on both cheeks.

"You're a dear man Ahmed; I couldn't have asked for a better husband for Andrea. Take care of her–she'll need you now more than ever."

She certainly will after last night, he thought. "Thank you, Wenonah; I'll keep her safe. You…you must come to see us."

"Yes–*Vaya con Dios*."

What he wanted to say was left unspoken. He went out on the porch, set their bags down, and waited for Andrea. She walked out, saw the boys waiting to say goodbye, and gave each one a hug; Ahmed shook their hands.

Andrea announced, "If any of you boys ever happen to be in Afghanistan, look us up!"

They roared with laughter, Billy saying, in a perfect imitation of John Wayne, "That'll be the day!"

More laughter, and a final goodbye. Wenonah stood watching the farewells, then sat again by the window. As Andrea entered, her mother was looking at the squirrels in her garden devouring birdseed. "Gluttonous little devils–there's nothing that stops them–I've tried everything!"

"Mom, I don't think you want to talk about squirrels."

"No. I wanted to say goodbye to you alone. Andrea, do you know how glad I am that you're married to Ahmed and you're going to live in Afghanistan? I want you to be happy; don't let anything or anyone come between the two of you. Just stay close to Ahmed always. Now go say goodbye to your father–he's in the stable."

Giving her mother a final hug, Andrea turned to leave. "I'll write to you. Love you, Mom, and thanks."

Wenonah went out to the garden and put more birdseed in the feeders. An idle thought came to her–I'd love to be able to drive anywhere I want in my next life, like Andrea. She's not afraid of anything. I'll drive everywhere–and won't need any gas! Drive? Maybe I'll just fly like Peter Pan! And she laughed and laughed at the lengths to which her ridiculous visions took her and settled into the private, secret world where no one could touch her, especially Patrick. Lost in the splendor of earth and sky, Wenonah smiled at her garden, thinking of bluebonnets and sunflowers.

Andrea went to Satanta's stall, offering him an apple and giving him a kiss. She felt a presence–Patrick–and turned to face him.

"Well, lass," he said, "sorry to see you go–be careful in that crazy country. I told Ahmed he'd better take good care of you. You know, I wish it could be you and me going off for adventure again. Well…if you need me, just…"

Andrea steadied her voice as she answered him. "No, I won't need you, ever again."

He flinched just a bit. "Listen, my girl,"

"I'm not your girl, I no longer belong to you, and what's better, I don't think I'll have any more nightmares about you! Maybe it will be your nightmare now!"

Patrick bristled, not believing her words, that she would actually talk to him this way. "Oh, nightmares, is it–about what?" He felt an almost forgotten dread of discovery in the pit of his stomach. "That was an accident, that night, not your fault, though if you think you're just an innocent little lass...."

"I was, until you took that away from me!"

"'Tis your own father you blame for it all–why, you learned valuable lessons from me!"

"Oh that I did," she responded, in a bitter mocking of his Irish accent that had become more pronounced as his anger grew. "Yes, I learned how to become superior to other people, how to deceive them, how to get what I wanted for myself, how not to care about anyone else," and in a low voice she said, "and how to kill and justify it."

"Ah, lass, you did it for the cause, for freedom."

"No, I was never interested in the cause, as you put it. I did it because I was your little puppet!"

"What about Afghanistan? I didn't make you kill there; that was your own doing!"

"Yes, for Afghanistan's survival; it was a war, I was a soldier."

"Precious little difference, girl!"

"It was completely different–just as I'm completely different from you; I am not you, I will never be you. I'm not an assassin! My nightmare was always of you; now it's over, I know what you did; you have no power over me anymore, thank God."

"Well, Andy, I wish you luck," and he let out a sardonic laugh, "the luck of the Irish. May it always be with you." God, that name he tried to pin on me because I should have been a son!

She yelled, "Don't call me that! And I don't need your Irish luck!"

"Ah, perhaps I should have said the love of the Irish? God knows your mother hasn't much to give you."

"What a hateful thing to say!"

"Ah, well, I was hoping the Irish in you would take over, but I guess you're just a half-breed at heart, one of Cochise's progeny. Go off to Afghanistan–you belong in that mad mistake of a country!"

He stormed out, nearly tearing off the door of the stable. She felt strangely calm and rested; she knew she might never see her father again. Andrea walked out to meet Ahmed, waiting for her in the Land Rover. Jack was at the wheel, ready to take them to the airport.

As she got in, Ahmed kissed her and asked, "Are you all right?"

"Yes," she answered, "it's over."

# XI. Black Taffeta

Not long after boarding the plane, the calm self-control she achieved upon leaving Paloma deserted her. A sense of doom stealing into her heart muffled the sounds of in-flight routine and muted Ahmed's voice; she had to ask him to repeat a question or comment–even then she didn't respond. After three or four requests, Ahmed refrained from talking, realizing she was experiencing more emotional stress than either of them expected. He asked the flight attendant for sherry–she needed more than tea or coffee.

Ahmed held the cup and ordered her to take sips; she finished the drink, saying, "I'm sorry, I don't know what's wrong with me–I'm so sleepy."

"Rest, my love," said Ahmed; she leaned back, resting her head on the pillow, and fell asleep. The older woman across the aisle watched them with a remembering smile and a touch of longing. Her eyes met Ahmed's; it was as though he was seeing a fond, approving look on his mother's face. As soon as they landed at Orly, Ahmed took charge. This was their most private time, their own bit of happiness–he wouldn't let anything spoil it for Andrea; she had been through enough, and more hardship and danger lay ahead. He couldn't prevent it all, but he would make Paris her sweetest memory. Sleep and sherry seemed to have worked a miracle. And, thought Ahmed, the very nice American lady who watched us. As they filed out of the plane, she touched Ahmed's shoulder and said, "Godspeed and good luck to you both–I'll be thinking of you."

Ahmed watched over Andrea with some anxiety on their first day as they walked the avenues and boulevards of Paris, from the Arc de Triomphe down the Champs-Elysees to the Place de la Concorde, then strolled through the streets of the left bank to the Eiffel Tower.

The somber mood became lighter, and her excitement and enthusiasm greater. By the time they got back to their hotel, she couldn't stop talking about everything she had seen. Ahmed smiled– she was genuinely happy. Happy but tired; he had supper sent up to their room, along with a bottle of expensive champagne.

"But Ahmed, you can't–and I shouldn't."

"Never mind–we are Parisians now."

He laughed at her disbelief as he poured the sparkling liquid into their glasses. Ahmed's carefree manner and the champagne released tension and inhibitions as she sang, told him lewd cowboy jokes, then seduced him with love and laughter. Ahmed let her make love as she wished, seeing a wanton side of her that both worried and pleased him. They lounged on the sofa, her head on his lap; she was falling asleep. He gathered her in his arms and put her to bed, as she whispered, "No more champagne."

"No, go to sleep."

She awoke the next morning with a headache; Ahmed was still sleeping. As she leaned over to kiss him, pain shot through her head.

"Ouch!" she exclaimed. "Oh I didn't mean to wake you, sweetie."

"Do you need aspirin?"

"Yes–Ahmed, I don't remember…"

He brought her two tablets and water. "Well, you were having a good time, singing…"

"Did we…?"

"We made love, yes. You know a lot of very, very dirty jokes!"

"Oh no! I didn't really tell you…?"

"Yes, you did; then I put you to bed."

"I feel like…like…"

"A naughty child?"

"Worse." But Ahmed smiled, enjoying her embarrassment, pleased he had discovered another facet of his ever-evolving treasure. Andrea was captivated by the City of Light and all its wonders. They spent hours at the Louvre, explored Montparnasse and Montmartre, ate lunch at a bistro Ahmed remembered in the Pere Lachaise neighborhood. Eating became an adventure and a challenge; the restaurants were very expensive. Andrea said no to most of them–the prices were shocking, but in the course of their walks through the city, they found many small bistros and cafes that were good, with reasonably priced menus.

Andrea, finally feeling free and in love with Paris and Ahmed, followed his lead even as she tried to rein in his spending–he had been transformed into a Parisian, giving her a tour of some of the less celebrated and more interesting *arrondissements*. In the chill of the Paris evening, they strolled the bridges of the Seine, stopping at a bistro for coffee and a croissant, sometimes catching a drift of music coming from one of the clubs. Entranced with one another in this most romantic of cities, they became equally enchanted with the people of Paris, who gave the city its sophisticated, insouciant air.

Andrea observed the women in some awe; they were elegant, rather aloof, always chic–from rich to poor, Parisiennes had style.

"Oh Ahmed, I love Paris, let's not ever leave."

"All right, my darling, we'll stay forever."

And Paris seemed to embrace the two of them; they were careful to respect French custom, spoke French, and carried no cameras. Memories would be their photographs. While Andrea wore her jeans and T-shirts, she also wore a vintage Dior jacket bought by her mother in Tucson.

"Andrea, you can't go to Paris looking like a ranch hand!" Well gee, thanks, Mom, but the jacket and scarves from her mother did lend a kind of thrift shop chic. When Ahmed took her to a boutique on the Rue St. Honore, she protested, "This isn't my kind of place, Ahmed, I don't belong here; anyway, it's much too expensive."

"Andrea, no arguments; come," he commanded, and propelled her into the shop.

She felt totally out of place, but the attendants seemed eager to serve them. He was handsome, looked rich, and she was lovely; it made all the difference. This project of Ahmed's was obviously giving him great pleasure. Andrea's excitement grew as the haute couture gowns were shown.

"Your wife would be lovely in any of these, monsieur, green is a wonderful complement to her hair and complexion, though it must be a certain green, deep, emerald, or something very light; she can wear almost any style."

Ahmed agreed, but decided, "Black, something modest."

The dress shown next was breathtaking; Andrea loved it immediately, and Ahmed said, "That's the one."

A bewitching confection of black silk and taffeta, it had a high-necked bodice, a suggestion of cap sleeves; the waist was encircled by a slim silver belt and the long skirt of black taffeta ruffles was dotted with tiny, shimmering silver beads. "Oooh, Ahmed," she whispered, "it must cost a fortune."

"Probably," he laughed, ignoring her concern over the cost, and in the end, adding an evening purse, sandals, and a black silk cape to complete the look.

When Andrea tried on the dress, the attendant asked her, "What do you think, Madame?" Andrea hardly knew how to respond; she was stunned by her appearance–even her wedding dress, beautiful as it was, had not had such an impact. She truly felt like Cinderella, in black.

"Don't you like it?" asked the woman.

"I don't know what to say–it's stunning, I can't believe it!"

"Madame, you make the dress stunning–your husband is very discerning, he knows what suits you."

"Yes," smiled Andrea, "he certainly does."

So this is what Laura used to talk about when she told Andrea she just had to go shopping–"I need a lift, and it gives me a high, better than alcohol." *That's how I feel–high–like I've just had champagne, but what an obscene thing to do when Afghans are without jobs, food...*

Ahmed interrupted her thoughts. "This is a special occasion; tomorrow, my darling, is our last day here, we'll have it always."

Evening in Paris–magic! A wand full of its fairy dust bestowed upon Andrea a sexual, worldly sophistication, for at least this night. In the dress Ahmed had chosen for her, she felt exquisitely feminine. All was a dream she had never dreamed, a story no one had ever written for her, a scene no one had ever planned or directed; this was Paradise. And Ahmed–oh God, she thought, he looks so handsome. She had erased Ireland and Patrick from her mind, erased Afghanistan, for that matter; tonight there was just this moment.

Ahmed couldn't take his eyes off her–his wild child was a lovely, sophisticated Parisienne. Even on their wedding day, she was not so tempting, so markedly a woman. He wished he could make it last forever for her. Tomorrow they would leave for Afghanistan.

She was almost ready when suddenly she threw up her hands and exclaimed, "This hair has got to go–I can't stand it–oh damn!" and reached for her scissors.

Ahmed took them away from her, saying, "No, Andrea." He gathered her hair up, twisted it into a bun and put in a barrette and some silver clips.

"There–isn't that better?" She looked in the mirror.

"*Merci, monsieur, vous etes une artiste!*"

"Any style you wish, *ma petite*." They made a game of it, laughing. Then Ahmed said, "We'd better go to the theater now, unless you want to be ravaged by your hairdresser."

"*Mon Dieu, non, non!*"

As they sat in the lavish splendor of the Opera Garnier, the music of Mozart seduced them; Ahmed saw tears falling on Andrea's cheeks. He offered her his handkerchief; with an apologetic smile, she squeezed his hand, grateful for his understanding. Hearing this music from the past turned Ahmed's thoughts to Afghanistan's agony, piercing his contentment with a sorrow he soon suppressed. The final curtain call over, the crowd descended the grand staircase, Andrea still under the spell of the music and the grandeur of the old theater. As Ahmed observed the throng of glamorous Parisians, he noticed Andrea was the object of some admiring glances, whispers of "who is she?," and a few envious looks, which she wasn't aware of or simply ignored.

"Andrea, do you know you are being watched like a celebrity? I expect someone to ask you for your autograph soon," he said in amusement.

"That's ridiculous," she answered. "I would hate to be a celebrity– what a nuisance! Let's get out of here–I need some fresh air."

Once out of the theater, Ahmed decided they should go to a club for coffee and sandwiches. "And dancing," added Andrea.

The club in Montmartre was a mix of the fashionable and the funky, lots of beautiful people, all with the Parisian savoir-faire. The dress was worth every *sou*, thought Ahmed. I'm a lucky man to have this beautiful girl on my arm–men look at her in admiration, perhaps they even desire her; my wife–I can't allow this in Afghanistan. And Andrea–she is blind to her beauty, her effect on men; so young and innocent in certain ways yet so determined and headstrong. How can I protect her without controlling her.

Suddenly he heard Andrea's voice–"you look like you're thinking long thoughts, Afghan, and this is not the time. Come on, they're playing our song."

"Our song?"

"Oh," she laughed, "any song is our song. Let's dance."

"*Oui, mon chere.*" On the dance floor, Ahmed pinned her arms to his side as he had when they danced to the flamenco guitar.

Andrea smiled up at him, "When are you going to let go of me?"

"Never," he replied. Andrea looked into her husband's enigmatic, commanding eyes; Afghan eyes, she thought, analyzing, planning, and she smiled–I'm pretty good at that too–life will be interesting. The fun-loving crowd was lively, oozing Parisian charm and wit, sharing casual tidbits of conversation with Andrea and Ahmed as they danced to a wild variety of music.

Finally, Ahmed told her it was time to leave; "Andrea, I can't make love to you here, and you're becoming irresistible."

"So are you," she said "Let's go, Ahmed."

Andrea looked into his eyes as Ahmed slowly unfastened her necklace, the barrettes in her hair, and the zipper of her dress, letting the black taffeta drop into a pool around her feet. She stepped out of the rustle of black and unbuttoned his shirt. Ahmed picked her up, carrying her over to the bed where they slowly finished undressing one another. The electricity of the foreplay excited and exhilarated them; often it made intercourse intense to the point of desperation; tonight was one of those times. An element of sadness crept into the sexual moment. Andrea saw tears in Ahmed's eyes; she kissed them and murmured, "oh, my sweet savage, I love you so."

They lay together, silent, each with different thoughts–Ahmed anticipating the war's end and its complications, Andrea with a question lurking in the back of her mind like a mischievous leprechaun.

"Ahmed, I'm…curious about something–I'd like to know…maybe I shouldn't, but I will anyway…"

"Well, go ahead and ask."

"Am I…I mean, did you ever…am I the first…," she stumbled over the words, embarrassed.

"The first what?" he said, a knowing glint in his eye.

"Oh you know what I mean. You're so…skillful, so sophisticated….so good. You must have had girlfriends."

"Girlfriends! In Afghanistan! There are very few, if any, relationships like that there. I've never had a girlfriend."

"But you must have had sex before, didn't you?"

"Now why do you need or want to know that?"

"Oh, I just want to know everything about you; it makes me feel part of you, part of your whole family, closer somehow, and..."

"And having sex with another woman before you would make you feel good? That's not a question to ask a man. No, I think your motive has more to do with your insatiable curiosity."

"Like the elephant?"

"Well, you know what happened to him!"

She laughed. "Okay, to be honest, the other reason is, well, it sort of turns me on."

"Oh, you find it an attraction?"

"Ahmed, stop tormenting me! Oh, forget I asked. I should have known better."

"Well, curious one, I'll tell you. Yes, I had sex before you, but not in Afghanistan. Abdullah arranged for me to come here to Paris to finish my education and get my degree. I was fighting with the *mujahidin*, but I wasn't an officer yet, I was only eighteen, so I came to Paris. Abdullah gave me his lecture about foreigners, religion and so forth, but he told me if I wanted to become intimate with a woman, he would tell me what place I should go to so it would be safe–a special place."

"Abdullah directed you to a brothel? I can't believe it!"

"He didn't call it that–it was a special place he had recommended to Afghans before."

Andrea started to laugh. "Oh, a special Afghan/Muslim brothel, an exclusive brothel for Afghans–it's too much. Did he get a percentage for his referrals? Oh, I love it!"

Ahmed didn't know whether to be angry or laugh with her; his story did sound ridiculous. "Well, my passionate Afghan, did you go?"

"Yes."

"So...so, how was it?"

"Well, it solved my problem. But you want to know the rest, I can see. I went back to the war and that was the end of any love life until you."

"You're kidding! You went that long without sex?"

"I had no time for anything but fighting. I could have married my cousin Saira, but I didn't love her in that way. I don't think marriage between cousins is good, so I satisfied myself in other ways."

"That's an incredible story. I bet that Frenchwoman was one hell of a teacher!"

"Andrea! Stop cursing."

"Sorry." And she started laughing again. Gone was the sophisticated Andrea of the opera and nightclub. Ahmed joined in the laughter, and they finally went to sleep. What Ahmed didn't tell her, and what she suspected, was that there were at least a few other sexual encounters in his life. To Ahmed, they were a lifetime ago–Andrea was the only one that mattered.

The following day Andrea and Ahmed were back in Kabul. Abdullah was there to meet them as they got off the plane. Ah, he thought, they have the glow of newlyweds. Andrea was more radiant than usual, and quieter. Where was the wild child? *She'll be back soon enough.* He smiled at the thought–Andrea smiled back at him–a truce, an understanding–an acceptance? He had to admit it was a good feeling.

The two were glad to be back on Afghanistan's dusty soil, anxious to help a country whose hopes had been crushed so many times. That evening, as they watched the sunset after prayers, Ahmed talked of his brief time as a child, his mother's hopes that he wouldn't have to be a fighter, his terror the first time he saw a friend blown apart by a land mine, his grief at seeing children orphaned and crying for their mothers, teenage *mujahidin* fighters struck down, innocent villagers suffering from diseases most of the civilized world had long since eliminated. Andrea listened without comment, her heart aching for him. Ahmed put his arm around his wife, admiring her profile and hair that matched the setting sun. He loved every inch of his harsh, impossibly landscaped country, a land replete with history, full of strange, exotic stories and people. And Wenonah had passed on to her daughter an abundance of Indian history; between them were many tall tales and history lessons waiting to be told to children that, already, he was eagerly anticipating.

Ahmed smiled as he thought of Paris, remembering their talk about Abdullah's solution to his problem about sex and Andrea's amusement. He thought of women he had been intimate with over the years; it was an education he found valuable, learning that caution and safety served him better than his wilder impulses–unbridled ecstasy had too high a price. Of the women he had sex with, none had been as challenging as Andrea; none had inspired his love. In his mind, she was his first and only love. He hoped Paris had eased the pain of her final separation from Patrick. As the sun set, Andrea felt the warmth of Ahmed's embrace and the strength of their commitment to each other and to Afghanistan.

Though Patrick was no longer haunting her dreams, pieces of his observations wandered into her mind now and then, no longer traumatic, just leftover crumbs of moldy bread. "Men are natural born killers, Andrea," he had once pronounced, and she had answered, "but they are not all assassins."

"Quite right," he had replied, unconcerned.

# XII. Challenges

With Ahmed's new position came a modest house in Kabul, and wonder of wonders, it had plumbing–running water, a bathroom with shower, a kitchen with a stove, plus a large living room and two small bedrooms. The walled compound contained enclosures for goats or chickens and a few stalls for donkeys and horses. Andrea was dazzled by such unexpected luxury. "Ahmed, I didn't think there was anything like this left standing in Kabul!"

"You saw only the devastation; true, there's not much left of Kabul, but now and then, by some blessing of Allah, the Russians and the Taliban missed something."

"But can we afford it?"

"Yes," said Ahmed.

Abdullah closed the book he was reading about tribes–tribes everywhere in the world. His eyes were tired, and he was tired of the battles between the tribes in his country. Now it's the bombs of the Americans, he thought, where could one turn for relief from this madness?

The screaming jets above demanded his attention–on their way to another target, somewhere near Kandahar, he guessed. He pictured the young American boys at the controls and even younger Afghan boys firing their guns at the Taliban. All so young, ready for battle, thinking they would settle things. Ah, old warriors know better; such sadness, such waste. But none of it was up to him anymore; he had other things to do–get the house in order–how long would they stay in this one. He couldn't erase the picture of the bombs' destruction; well at least it was generally aimed at the Taliban and most of the bombs hit their targets.

Andrea helped Abdullah clean the house; part of the back wall had been damaged by mortar fire, but that was minor–a hole here and there didn't matter. A garden did matter to Andrea, and she was determined to have one. Ahmed and Abdullah shook their heads–a garden in this barren, stony dust! But she had decided; making a plan, Andrea eventually put it all together–she scrounged small plants from other homes they visited, even the old king's residence, rescued a sapling of a tree she was totally unfamiliar with from a pile of rubble, collected the animals' manure, letting it age, and found some old rotting wood for her fence. Her forays into various parts of Kabul had unexpected consequences. When Ahmed found out she had taken the Jeep and gone by herself to an area known for its lawlessness and banditry, he was furious. "How could you do such a thing? You could have been killed–don't ever do that again, Andrea!"

His words did not have the effect he intended. "I'm not a prisoner. I can go where I like," she protested, then softened in the face of Ahmed's obvious concern for her. "I won't go there anymore, but..."

He interrupted her, "This is something I cannot let you do by yourself. Andrea, you don't understand. If you were not yet known here in Kabul, you are by now. I'm a government official, not a safe position to be in, and my wife must have protection. You may go about Kabul, but not without guards. And," here he paused, "you should wear a *burqa*, or at the very least, the *chaadar*."

She said curtly, "I choose the veil." Andrea wasn't surprised to hear his cold reply, "Be sure you cover your head and face completely, especially your hair."

Escaping to what would be her garden, she made vicious stabs in the soil with her trowel, thinking unkind thoughts about Ahmed. She knew Afghanistan was going to be a huge challenge for her, but gave specific problems and obstacles very little thought. That day, Andrea began to understand that Islam would dictate much of her life. Discouraged, she sat on the old chair, thinking about what to do, when she felt his hands caressing the nape of her neck, fondling the tangled curls.

As she tilted her head back, he leaned over and kissed her mouth. "I brought you some petunias for your garden; we'll plant them together."

Andrea easily adapted to the female version of the *shalwar kameez*.

It was not all that different from her usual dress, and more comfortable. Since fashion meant little to her as a teenager, she was never caught up in the Western penchant for showing off her body. Dressed as an Afghan woman, she found the *chaadar* useful; though the *burqa* was a choice for many women, she hated its obsequiousness, preferring to take her chances with the veil.

Andrea thought of her wedding day often; its absurd contradictions made her smile. The tug of war between East and West had given that day an almost dark excitement, especially now, when she remembered Mahmood's grim, well-meaning predictions, "You'll live in a house with no running water, no washer and dryer, nothing Western; you must be a true Afghan wife who will be obedient, hard working, neither seen nor heard unless your husband permits it!" And a few of Ahmed's lieutenants had nodded solemnly.

But the three brothers, the video enthusiasts, had said, "Don't pay any attention to those old goats. They just want to scare you to make themselves important. Ahmed will be a good husband; he is very lenient about women. But it is good to obey him; he is wise–and powerful," they added.

Andrea's smothered laughter bubbled to the surface as she said, "Thank you for the advice; I'll remember it." As comic-opera as it seemed, she knew she was no longer the free and easy Western girlfriend of Ahmed Sharif. Now she was his Afghan wife.

At first, Andrea found life in Kabul confusing. Ahmed was chosen for a position in the new government by the "powerful men" she met in Germany; suddenly he was one of them, and Andrea, always suspicious of men in high office who possessed immense power to persuade others, was seized by a vague, inexplicable fear for her husband. Germany…Bonn. She remembered the meeting between her father and Ahmed there, the thread of recognition between them– acknowledgment of some sort? She knew, if it hadn't been for his love for her, Ahmed would have killed Patrick, and Patrick let Ahmed live because he no longer had the skill to assassinate without detection and reprisal.

*Oh, hell, I'm sick of obsessing about all this crap*; donning the *chaadar* and slinging the Kalashnikov over her shoulder, she saddled Buttercup and started down the dirt road at a leisurely pace. Coming to a once-prosperous neighborhood occupied by wealthy merchants, she looked curiously at the little she could see of a home set upon a hill, surrounded by a wall enclosing a lush garden bordered by poplar trees. Most of the merchants had fled Afghanistan for sanctuary in Pakistan, but there were signs of return. Well-dressed children played here and there; kites were flying. A wonderful sense of normalcy took hold of her; wispy clouds, warming sun, and the distant purple of mountains carried her back briefly to Arizona. She felt utterly at peace, at home.

The orderly neighborhood disappeared; intoxicated by the open road, she yelled, "Let's go, sweetie pie!" and spurred Buttercup to a gallop, flying down the road until her pent up energy was spent. The road became rougher–they slowed down, Andrea leading the horse carefully around deep potholes. Noting brightly colored disks alongside the road, she looked at one, half tempted to pick it up.

"Don't touch it–get away!"

Startled, Andrea looked up and saw an American soldier shouting at her; more soldiers appeared, all motioning her back to the middle of the road. The first soldier came closer and said, "Don't you know what those are?" Andrea, immersed as she was in the magic of the day, suddenly realized in horror what she was seeing. Mines! on both sides of the road–butterfly mines, not toys. "Yes, I see," she answered in English. "I won't pick them up."

"You'd best turn back, Ma'am," the young GI said.

Andrea held back laughter as she replied, "Yes, I will."

Ma'am! He was probably older than her; he mistook her for an Afghan woman. He stared at her rifle, keeping his weapon trained on her. Good for you, soldier, she thought, and started back home.

She had never mastered Afghan cooking; her efforts were half-hearted at best, but now her flourishing herb garden inspired her. She decided to fix lamb *lawand*, cooked with tomatoes, mushrooms and herbs, topped with yogurt and sour cream. As she brought it to the table, she thought, let it be good. Andrea watched Ahmed, drinking in his flowing gestures, his deft hands choosing rice and vegetables. Impatient, she picked up a piece of lamb and plopped it into his open mouth. His frown of annoyance became a surprised look of pleasure. "It's delicious," he pronounced.

Andrea, exultant, exclaimed, "It's about time!"

That evening, Andrea asked Ahmed, a touch of sarcasm in her

voice, "What's your title, Minister of Public Relations?"

He was evasive about his job, not wanting her to know how much was involved or how many dangers he faced. Andrea didn't mention her ride on Buttercup. It had been a beautiful day–she no longer cared about the mysteries of men.

Ahmed was tired, she could see it in his eyes; his smile held little of the excitement of their days in Paris and his face looked drawn. When she teased him, he didn't respond with his usual indulgent "such a wild child!" She had promised not to question him about his "public relations" duties–whatever they were, they took him away at intervals for five or six days. When she struggled with her garden, she daydreamed of Ahmed, picturing his strong hands, stronger even than her father's, taking apart steel and metal, forcing the old weapons to work, saw his long fingers reach for her curls with delicate grace to brush them away from her eyes; she went to sleep imagining he was there beside her and she fingered the black hairs of his chest, tracing the bones that had sustained the blows and bruises of battle. When he returned, sometimes elated, other times discouraged, she kissed him with a thankful, tender passion, knowing he was, at all times, in danger. *And here I am, nothing but a housewife–this will never do!* This place of proud, passionate people, whose first allegiance was to Allah and family, was now her home, and she needed to help in some way, to be useful.

Soraya came to see her after a visit to the clinic. Newly pregnant, she was worried about Andrea, and hoped to ease her anxiety about Ahmed.

"He's very smart, Andrea. Ahmed has always come out ahead of everyone; now that he has his beautiful wife to come home to, he will be more careful about taking risks."

"What risks? What is he doing, Soraya? Where does he go?"

"I don't know, only that he has always had to do that; he was always a…a, what is the word…a negotiator. Oh, that Ahmed! He could talk anyone into anything, even as a little boy."

Andrea was not impressed by this resume of her husband's abilities.

Soraya suddenly realized she was making things worse; fumbling in her mind for a more cheerful topic, she asked, "Andrea, have you been to the school or the clinic here–I think we'll be sending our little one there," and she patted her slightly protruding belly. "You know, Andrea, I didn't see much of my brothers when I was growing up–they were with the *mujahidin,* my grandfather was always away on business, and Abdullah–Abdullah stayed with Ahmed as a sort of advisor after he turned eighteen. I lived with my cousin Saira's family and then I was married to Mohammed at seventeen."

"An arranged marriage?"

"Oh yes, of course–arranged by my grandfather. Dr. Ducasse at the clinic is very nice; of course I'll give birth at home, but he is monitoring my pregnancy. Whatever happens, I won't go to the maternity hospital–it's disgraceful the way women are treated there. Barbaric! But Kabul is becoming almost civilized again. Why don't you visit the school, if Ahmed thinks it is all right?"

If Ahmed thinks it is all right–what if he doesn't, how about that? thought Andrea. The thought of talking to a teacher, seeing Afghan education in action–well, who knows where it could lead; suddenly ideas were leaping around her brain like electric conductors. Hmm, I wonder if any of the kids are as miserable as I was in school.

Another night without Ahmed. One day, Abdullah came upon her in the parlor, sobbing softly, hands clasped tight behind her neck, arms pressed against her ears to shut out devilish voices running rampant in her mind. Abdullah watched her surrender to the pathos of the music. He wanted to tell her, "music is not always good–it's only making you sad!," but he didn't have the heart.

The next morning she called in her "guards," the video boys, told Abdullah where she was going, adjusted the veil, and took off in the old Jeep, promising Abdullah to bring back fruits and vegetables. The school was not very far away from their house. The brothers Azeem, with their Kalashnikovs, were ready to escort her into the damaged concrete structure, but she waved them away. "You'll only scare the kids!"

She tried to hide her nervous anticipation as she entered the school, scoffing at herself for the bit of leftover dread from her childhood. The school was bereft of books, desks, posters, paintings, everything that gave it the unique feeling and smell of a place of learning. But there were no miserable children. All were girls, paying rapt attention to a teacher so engrossed in her pupils she didn't see the American girl standing at the back of the room in her Afghan garb and veil. And Andrea stood still, fascinated by these children who were as hungry for knowledge as they were for food. She had been looking for her place in Kabul, and now she found it. This damaged, desolate place was school as it should be.

Triumphant, knowing this was right for her, she drove through the streets of Kabul happier than she had been since Ahmed's job had become a mission, diplomatic or otherwise. Her offer of help with supplies and teaching assistance had been gratefully accepted; she couldn't wait to get started. The streets were a busy, noisy hodgepodge of Afghans plying their trades–carpet sellers, dressmakers, bookstores, office workers. She knew of certain neighborhoods where phantom-like cocaine peddlers beckoned, mingling with small arms dealers and prostitutes; these areas she avoided. Most of the Kabulis were men; women, still in their *burqas*, patronized the beauty salons and clothing stores. Some in Western dress, still veiled, worked in business offices.

Andrea stopped at the bazaar for the vegetables and fruits she had promised Abdullah. She was hungry, and the aromas were tempting; the brothers got something for themselves and, against their advice and her own judgment, she bought a spicy, luscious-looking kebab, eating it on the spot. Laughter and noisy debates were punctuated by extravagant gestures, but a *chaikhana* here and there provided quiet reflection with a relaxing glass of green tea and music. Andrea loved it–Main Street in Afghanistan, where any day could be your last, depending on who was bent on revenge that day.

Arriving home that afternoon, she couldn't contain her excitement about the school–she had to share her news; if anyone could understand her enthusiasm, it would be Abdullah, the teacher.

"Abdullah, Abdullah," she called.

He came in from the unfinished garden, wondering what she had done now. "What is it, Andrea?"

"I'm going to help teach at the school–I'm actually going to be back in a school and this time, it's going to be fun!"

"Sit down and explain, I don't understand."

"Let's go in the garden."

Her face was flushed with what he thought was excitement. As she explained the eager acceptance of help and donations, and described the students' obvious joy in being in school, Abdullah nodded approvingly. She would make a good teacher, though just an assistant; she needed a certificate, he could help with that. Would Ahmed agree to her new venture?

"I'm pleased you've discovered something useful and important; it will be...." He stopped in mid sentence. Andrea had doubled over in pain, clutching her stomach, her flushed face a picture of distress.

"Oh my God, ooh....I've got to throw up."

Abdullah was so surprised he couldn't move for a moment. Andrea was never sick, always so careful about diseases and organisms that plagued Afghans, so strict about boiling water, making sure meat was fresh, well cooked.

"Oh, Abdullah, my stomach is killing me."

"You must lie down; come, I'll help you to bed."

"What's wrong with me-oh my God, the kebab."

"You ate a kebab at the bazaar?"

"Yes, I was so hungry. Oh," and she disappeared into the bathroom. Abdullah anxiously waited-finally she came out, looking weak, pale, and drained from vomiting.

"No more bazaar food for me! Do you think I've got some fatal disease?"

Abdullah smiled. "No, you probably got a bad piece of goat meat, not fresh enough. You'll be all right-don't worry."

Stars in the thin mountain air bejeweled the Afghan night. So many constellations-they reminded Andrea of the poem she loved as a child, Wynken, Blynken, and Nod. Her father used to read it to her when she was very young.

Ahmed's voice cut through the memory, "Are you all right, my love-do you feel any better?"

"I'll live, but believe me, I've learned my lesson. No more *kebabs* for me, unless Abdullah or I myself make them."

"Are you sure you're all right? My sweet, lonely wife, I hate being away from you, and look what happens, you get sick." He held her in his arms in the cold night and led her inside. "It's too cold outside for you, come get into bed–I'll make you comfortable."

Tell him, thought Andrea. Without any preliminaries or requests for approval, she said, "Ahmed, I'm going to help at the school."

"Hmm, how will you help?" As vaguely as possible, she answered in generalities, though she had some very specific plans. But Ahmed didn't need to know all that.

A nervous but enthusiastic Andrea was about to start "teaching" the children for whom she felt such empathy; she knew it might not be easy. And she wasn't an accredited teacher, to her an insignificant drawback. All she wanted to do was help in some way, so she brought with her some of the things she had mentioned to Nuria Agha, the teacher. Pencils, pens, note books, crayons, paints and brushes, poster board paper for their paintings, and a gift she had not mentioned–a small atlas for each child. Andrea had not been able to find any in Arabic, but perhaps translating from English to Arabic could be part of their lessons. She had thought ahead to what the girls and the boys, too, would like; for now this was enough–she didn't want to overwhelm them the first day, and Nuria might resent such American overkill. But Nuria was pleased to get these basic tools; she liked this effervescent American girl who spoke good Dari and took her status as Ahmed Sharif's wife seriously. Some of the girls were shy, some very talkative, very curious about America; all were eager to learn. None possessed an atlas, and Andrea explained how they could use it, how they could find all the countries in the world.

"Are they all Muslim countries?" asked one of the girls.

"No," said Andrea. "But that's what makes the world interesting."

She hoped Nuria would teach them the things they needed to know about the world, not just Afghanistan. Nuria wondered if she had opened a Pandora's box–would Andrea try to turn them against their Islamic faith? She thought it best to confront Andrea with boundaries beyond which she should not go.

"Nuria, I have no intention to try converting the students to another religion. Why, I am Muslim; Ahmed would never approve of my doing such a thing!"

Nuria knew Andrea was sincere; she wondered how faithful a Muslim she really was.

Andrea managed to get through the days without Ahmed–school kept her busy–but night without him became a cold abyss that brought forth visions of Ahmed injured or dying at the hand of a ruthless warlord or an old enemy. Often, the relative peace of Kabul was shattered by an errant American bomb or old Russian ones being detonated. Though she had fought on the front, the nights without Ahmed mocked her supposed fearlessness. Trying to sleep without the warmth of his body made her feel naked, exposed to dangers she had all but forgotten. Gathering up clothing to wash, she found a shirt of Ahmed's that brought tears to her eyes as she picked it up. She held it for a long time, pressing it against her face, breathing in his scent, reluctant to let it go. I won't wash it, she thought; oh that's foolish, and she plunged all the clothing into the washtub. She wondered if Ahmed had a similar reaction when he looked at the lock of hair she gave him before he left.

Thank God for school. Each day she looked forward to discovering the personalities inside the increasingly self-confident girls. Some were still shy, but she knew she would win them over. The boys, who came in the afternoon, were a different story. They were more serious, intense, anxious to learn as soon as possible so they could get jobs. Their first duty was to feed their families. Some had higher goals–engineers, doctors, computer experts, not impossible objectives, if they could continue an education uninterrupted by the necessity of providing food for their relatives. The boys loved the atlases and Andrea, inspired by their enthusiasm and hard work, decided to ask Nuria if she could bring some fun things. "Fun!" exclaimed Nuria. "They need to learn, that's what they're here for, Andrea."

"Yes, and they are learning, they're all so quick, and smart, but what would be so bad about having a little joy in their lives while they're learning?"

"And this little joy would be…?"

"Kites–beautiful kites–I know they make their own, but these would be special, and music–flutes, a CD player, music of countries around the world. Music is very inspirational."

"It depends on what you're inspiring them to do. We certainly can't have wild rock music, or martial music; I have to be careful about these children, Andrea."

"I know; Nuria, don't you think they need to learn about the whole world, not just Afghanistan?"

"Yes, but I don't know if we can work all these extra things into their schedule. You know, I lived in Connecticut while I got my degree, and life there was good. I have nothing against America; I just want my country to be a good place to live in again. You've worked hard with the children, you've been a real asset and help to me."

Smiling, Andrea asked her, "Is that a yes?"

"For now–we'll see if it works."

She brought in flutes, the CD player, and music she hoped was appropriate, and for a brief half hour, turned the schoolroom into a theater featuring music of other countries. Some of the children knew how to play the flutes, and most of them wanted to dance; Andrea was so pleased to see them dancing that she danced along with them, until she realized they had stopped and were watching her. Nuria was watching too, a calculating expression on her face. Andrea stopped; I hope I haven't screwed up, she thought.

"Andrea, where did you learn to dance?"

"Oh, I had some training back home; I wanted a career in music, but…well, things happened and it didn't work out. These kids are natural dancers; they love music."

"Of course; they're Afghans, just like you and me!" Nuria and Andrea both laughed; change was coming to Kabul. Women might not be visible, but their presence and power, invisible and subtle, would move the stubborn mountains of Afghanistan.

Andrea was saying the required five daily prayers on a regular basis. Ever since their return from Paris, she seemed somewhat subdued; Abdullah was surprised, expecting little evidence of a practicing Muslim. *She's learning; I hope she appreciates the wisdom of Islam and prays sincerely.* While she followed the Muslim ritual, Andrea added instructions rather than pleas in the name of Allah. She prayed for Ahmed's safety, then prayed for all the things that were needed at school. Coincidentally, she received a shipment of long-ago ordered shoes, a large, elaborately detailed globe, material for new kites, and head-scarves for the girls. Nuria was shocked to see all these new, and expensive, gifts.

"Andrea, does Ahmed know what you are doing–he has money, I know, but all this is…well…"

"Oh no, Nuria, Ahmed isn't paying for it; I am, and please don't ask me anymore about it. I assure you, it's all paid for. Do you like the materials for the scarves and kites? I wanted to have the shoes sooner for the really cold weather, but I think the children will be pleased. It's like Christmas!"

"Christmas? We don't have Christmas!"

"Well, you know what I mean." Andrea caught a word of Nuria's muttering under her breath–"impossible," but she didn't care.

There was an excited reaction to the globe. As they turned it and explored the world, she heard expressions of wonder mixed with doubt.

"But Afghanistan is so small compared to America,"

"Look at Russia, it's bigger than America!"

"Is Canada part of your America?" and it went on.

These children would start to understand, for all its vastness, how finite the world was. Their curiosity about America was boundless–they wanted to know about the Wild West, the cowboys and Indians, and could hardly believe Andrea when she told them that she was half Indian, so she gave them a brief lesson about present-day Indians. Was America a bad country, where were the bad countries, show us the Islamic countries. Knowledge seemed to unlock all their latent abilities; though they were eager to see the rest of the gifts, the shoes, scarves and kites could wait until tomorrow. They're smart, thought Andrea, they really want to learn.

That evening, her prayers to Allah were first for Ahmed, then for the children who were discovering the world. "Please let them grow up using their knowledge well. Peace, bring us peace. And oh, God, please let Laura know I'm trying to do something for children. She'd be happy. John, too." She sighed, content, though it was not a Muslim prayer. Ahmed would be home tomorrow.

"Andrea, what is this?" Ahmed's stern voice had an edge to it as he held out in front of her what looked like a letter, written in Arabic.

"I don't know; I haven't read it yet." Andrea had a feeling she had been caught in the act–*what did I do now?*

"I'll read it for you." And he read a letter of thanks to himself and Andrea for the wonderful gifts the children at Kabul School had received from them; how happy the children were to have these special things–shoes, boots, books, kites, paints, and flutes. Oh no, thought Andrea.

"Oh, Ahmed, I did mean to tell you, but you've been away and ..." Her voice trailed off into silence. She looked at him in front of her, his eyes black with anger.

"Andrea, how could you do this without asking me, without my permission? I need to know about things like this–you had no right!"

Permission! No right! This was too much–she erupted in a fury of words. "I did this on my own; why should I need permission, I can do things by myself–you know I've been helping at the school; did you think I was going there just to pass the time? I've told you I want to be useful. Those kids need so much, they've been so damaged by stupid wars and stupid men who only understand power. Sometimes I hate men!"

"Do you hate me?" Her anger was spent but she had uttered hurtful words.

"Oh, no, Ahmed, I'm sorry. I love you. Men like my father, men in general, I don't know. Men can be very frustrating. And the thing is...I owe something to Laura and John, they came here to help children; I think that's what I should do–continue what they started. John would love to see how happy those kids were today."

"And who is paying for all these things?"

"That's the good part." She flashed a wicked smile. "My father is paying–I have his credit card. He gave it to me when I first came to Pakistan and told me to charge anything I needed. I never used it until now; just think, it's helping Afghan children. It's an absolutely perfect joke on him."

Ahmed stared at her, then said, "I need to see Abdullah."

Ahmed couldn't contain his indignation; he needed to express it to someone, not Andrea–how difficult she could be, not asking him first, not telling him! As he told the story, Ahmed saw that Abdullah was smiling, on the verge of laughter. Ahmed finished, frowning at Abdullah.

"Why are you laughing, you think this is funny?"

"It is a wonderful joke on her father–she's doing good deeds, the children are happy, she's making a hero of you; why are you so angry, because she didn't ask you first? Ahmed, Ahmed, Andrea is simply being Andrea. It is not a serious thing. You must let her use her judgment and go her own way from time to time. You know she'll never be Afghan. But she has a kind heart. It is a good trick she's played on her father," laughed Abdullah.

An astounded Ahmed said, "You've certainly changed your opinion of her. As I recall, you rolled your eyes more than once because you thought she was impossible."

"Ah, yes, I still do, but I understand her and I admire her. She's your match, all right–the two of you are a strong pair. Now go speak sensibly to her. She loves you very much, Ahmed."

By this time, Ahmed's initial outrage had dissipated. He's right, of course, thought Ahmed. He sat for a few minutes thinking of Andrea's strong will and his own sense of superiority over women, realizing he would not really want a woman who would obey him without question. The tug and pull between the two of them, East and West, was part of the magnetism that brought them together. Back in the parlor, he sat down, putting his arm around her.

"Andrea, I don't want you to be angry. I understand what you are doing for the school. I'm sure your friends would be happy to know about it, but I need you to tell me about these things before you do them. And by the way, love, I can pay for things you want." Andrea didn't reply. "Andrea, look at me, look into my eyes, tell me you understand." She looked into his eyes, a hint of rebellion on her face, then smiled, acknowledging his authority.

"I'm sorry I didn't tell you first, I suppose I wasn't sure you would agree and I had made up my mind, I was determined…"

"Miss Determination, yes, I know you well!"

"I'll tell you if anything comes up again, I'll talk to you first…now what do you think about the things for the kids?"

Ahmed, his anger gone in the face of her apparent submission, smiled, "It is time we helped them, and if I know you, you'll have them singing and dancing. And Andrea, you may not realize it, but women can be extremely frustrating!"

Abdullah looked in on them, relieved that the issue seemed to be resolved. She could be annoyingly American, but Abdullah watched her as he would a difficult daughter; she had charmed her way into his heart, and there she would stay.

In the contentment of sleep just before dawn, Andrea felt Ahmed, nestled snugly behind her, move to the rhythm of desire. He whispered her name again and again. She stirred, unwilling to wake up just yet, as he murmured, "My darling, you're too tempting."

"I'm too sleepy," she mumbled.

Ignoring her protests, he kissed her, entering with a gentle movement that soon aroused her. Half scolding, she murmured, "Not even dawn. Oh well–fill me with your love, my poetic Afghan!" Finished, their sleepy reverie lasted until the *azan* broke the spell with its ancient summons.

"I feel so good, nice and warm; let's stay in bed," said Andrea.

"Allah calls us, both of us, my reluctant follower. Time to rise."

Ahmed watched her with undisguised pride as she danced to a bit of Tschaikovsky's Swan Lake. He had never seen her dance professionally with plies, pirouettes and spins, blissful amidst shattered buildings, rubble, and unpredictable dangers. Andrea's heart beat with joy at the passion that moved the instruments and filled a broken world with such beauty. At the end of the performance, the children clapped and called out to her in excitement at the music and dance they had not known before.

Andrea bowed in acknowledgment of their praise; flushed with the satisfaction of sharing her passion, she told them, "You see, music makes you happy, in here," and she put her hand on her heart, "it can be Afghan music, American music, any music you like; you must always have something to make you happy, even when terrible things happen, even if it's just for a little while; always put music in your heart."

Twelve-year-old Meena said, "But when you go to Paradise, you'll always be happy."

"I don't know…"

"But aren't you Muslim?"

"Well, I am, but I'm not a full-fledged Muslim; I have a lot of studying to do."

Then she noticed Ahmed, standing in the back, watching her, shaking his head, hands raised, laughing silently. She joined him, felt a momentary rush of guilt, then laughed with him.

"Would you like me to present you with a Muslim diploma when you are full fledged? When are you going to graduate?"

"Only Allah knows."

"Andrea, wear the black taffeta." Was this embassy reception that important?

"Do you really think I should?"

"Yes, why wouldn't you want to?"

"It's so special to me…."

"It's special to me, also," he said, "please wear it."

She put it on, deciding to pack it away after tonight. The reception at the American Embassy was an occasion–Andrea wished there were as many solutions as there were occasions. It was a silly idea, her not wanting to wear this dress again, but it represented the magic of Paris, the most exquisite night of her life. In the end, she was glad she'd worn it. As they went through the receiving line, she noticed on the far side of the room a woman she had seen twice before. Lauren Bannister. The two had never been formally introduced; they moved in different circles. Andrea had no interest in the political or social life of Kabul; she worked at the school, kept house, and was now staying close to Soraya, soon to give birth to her second child. It's about time we met, thought Andrea.

"Introduce me to that TV reporter, Ahmed–I'm surprised she's still here in Kabul. I thought she'd have been long gone by now."

Ahmed felt strangely uncomfortable with this request. "She's not important," he said.

"Since when do I care who's important? I've never met a celebrity; I'm just curious."

Lauren knew Andrea was Ahmed's wife, but she wasn't prepared for the beautiful girl in her black designer gown, no veil concealing the glorious hair this time; the green eyes, polite and cold, met hers. Andrea felt a moment of triumph as she saw the impact of her presence on Lauren Bannister.

The introduction confirmed Andrea's first impression of the woman–sophisticated, smooth, ambitious, predatory. She knew Ahmed had some contact with her in his effort to enlist American government help in the clearing of land mines. Not too much contact, thought Andrea. The introduction over, Ahmed led Andrea to the dance floor. She knew Ahmed loved to show her off when they were among Westerners; he kept her by his side until he was summoned by the Afghan ambassador for a brief meeting. Andrea scanned the room for Lauren Bannister, but did not see her. Hmm, just when I wanted to talk to her–I feel absolutely wicked right now; maybe it's just as well.

A high pitched voice behind her said, "Oh my dear, what a lovely gown," and she turned to see a very tall American woman in a colorful Afghan or Indian dress holding a drink in her hand.

"Thank you," said Andrea. She vaguely remembered having met her in Germany at the conference.

"So you're still with your Afghan, dear?"

"Yes, the Afghan and I are still together–we're married!" Oh boy, thought Andrea, she's had one too many; the woman was having trouble keeping her balance.

"Ah, of course...one of those Arab names, uh..."

"Ahmed Sharif, and I am Andrea Sharif."

"Yes, well, my Edward and I have been married twenty years now–it can get a little boring–he's British, you know."

"Oh, I'm sorry."

"Your Ahmed, he has such an exotic look, interesting."

"Yes, he's exotic and endlessly fascinating."

"Tell me, my dear, Afghans...does he, well, you know...is he..."

"Oh yes, he does and he is–anywhere, any time; as I said, endlessly."

"Oh, oh my, I do think I need a little air–excuse me."

Ahmed came up behind Andrea. "Perhaps I should go fan the lady; Andrea, you are very bad."

She couldn't stop laughing. "She might be society, but she's an insulting old bi..." Ahmed interrupted her before she got the word out and gave her a look.

"Well, she is. I like to stick it to people like that. But she's so dumb she probably didn't even get it." Ahmed gave her a quick kiss just as the lady in question came teetering by, looking at Ahmed with wide eyes.

Andrea smiled. "That'll give her something to dream about, poor thing."

"Andrea, you're evil," he said, " but I love you! Come, you must meet a few friends of Abdullah–they are scholars, deep thinkers like Abdullah; unfortunately, wisdom alone cannot turn Afghanistan around. *Mujihidin* are the other side of the equation–together we will prevail, if..."

"If all of you stop fighting among yourselves!"

"Ah, well."

"I don't see that CIA guy, Jeff Scott." Now, why should I think about him, thought Andrea. As far as she was concerned, Jeff Scott was a loser. She knew he had been involved with the debacle of Mazar-I-Sharif and the five traitors; Ahmed never said his name again after Scott left their wedding reception. She had seen Rashid and Ahmed watching Jeff Scott on the day they left for Ireland and noticed Scott standing some distance away, surrounded by some of Rashid's *mujahidin*. But that day her thoughts were only on their journey to Ireland. Andrea's habit of observing her surroundings opened a previously dismissed picture in her mind of Ahmed and Rashid hugging one another and exchanging documents of some sort. Something was significant; she had seen nothing of Jeff Scott since that day. For him not to be at the reception was unusual. Would Ahmed tell her what happened?

"Ahmed, do you know where he is?"

"No, I don't, Andrea, but I don't think we'll be seeing him again."

She said, without emotion, "Is he dead, did Rashid have him killed, or...was it the two of you who ordered it?"

Ahmed looked amused and replied, "Of course not. We let him go–he may be on his way home." This sounded sinister, and final.

"He was the traitor behind the Mazar-I-Sharif business, wasn't he?"

"A traitor, and a would-be rapist, a bad combination. There is just one more."

Andrea looked into his eyes, understanding this was Afghan justice and she had nothing to say about it; she knew the results of betrayal and the consequences. There was only one who was not yet erased from existence, but Ahmed was patient, he could wait. Jeff Scott had protested at first, and in the end, pleaded.

"Oh shit, it's a convoluted world, Ahmed. Sometimes you don't know which end is up, who's your friend, who's your enemy."

"And which are you, friend or foe?"

"I'm somewhere in no man's land–ready to get out of this damned business." He let out a bitter laugh, "I'm ready for expert commentating on TV!"

Ahmed's eyes were cold as he said, "I'm sure you'd be good at it, but you may not get the chance."

"Oh, come on, Ahmed. I'm an American, first and foremost–my country would hunt you down if anything happened to me. You'd have hell to pay."

"I have no intention of doing anything to you, Scott. We're going to let you go."

Scott felt a faint chill at the back of his neck. He knew this handsome Afghan was a fair man who tolerated foreigners; after all, he had just married the American girl he had been sleeping with.

"Hell, Ahmed, loyalties here in Afghanistan change like the weather, for God's sake, get real."

"My loyalty does not change–yours is available for a price. That isn't the worst of it. In Afghanistan, the crime of attempted rape brings a death sentence. As for being American, that doesn't matter to me. You not only betrayed me, you betrayed your own country. You're a traitor, any way you look at it. We deal with traitors in many ways. If you were Afghan, I would simply kill you. You want leniency because you're American. I won't harm you. But you must leave Afghanistan now."

Scott felt some resurgence of his confidence and daring. "Damn right–I'll be glad to get out of here."

"You will be taken to the northeast, to the Wakhan, from there you'll go the rest of the way alone."

"Wakhan, the Nowshak–you can't be serious! No, no, just give me a horse or mule, I'll go over the Khyber to Peshawar and be out of your way!"

Ahmed ignored this protest and continued, "There's a way to northern Pakistan from there, the Baroghil Pass. You will be given food and water. Don't try to turn back; you'll be monitored."

"Ahmed, wait–listen to me. We can make a good deal..."

Ahmed cut him off. "I'm finished with you. May Allah have mercy on you."

Jeff Scott knew that Allah might have mercy on him; Ahmed would not.

# XIII. Patriarch

Mohammed Shah was a shrewd Tajik business man who could never understand his son Haroun's passion for politics. Unwelcome thoughts of Haroun stole into his orderly mind–how he had not truly appreciated his son's Afghan love of poetry and music or his determination to change the political face of Afghanistan, and he shook his head in sad resignation at the memory of his only child. Just a faint vision remained of his wife; no longer did he try to remember the day she died giving birth to Haroun. But his grandsons, now there was a wild pair! Suppressing his misgivings about them, he prayed they would not be assassinated. Abdullah had, after all, done his best for Haroun's children. Rashid and Ahmed were well-educated and Soraya was a good wife; Mohammed congratulated himself on arranging a fine husband for his lovely granddaughter.

Tall, still erect at eighty, clean-shaven, he had Ahmed's arresting eyes, but there was a circumspect look about him, correct, precise, and Western. "Emeralds, lapis lazuli, carpets–they are the wealth of Afghanistan and most important, the wealth of our family." Mohammed made sure that that wealth was kept in the family; his two grandsons, who took their dead father's struggles from the conference table to the battlefield, would need it. His family must never go hungry. After Haroun's death, he was more determined than ever to increase his wealth, and when he found Abdullah, he was relieved to be able to turn over his son's family to Abdullah's excellent care; he could devote his time to business and the travel it demanded.

Upon his return from Iran, Mohammed found that Ahmed, shrewd as himself in business, was becoming a politician–a grandson he could have been proud of had it not been for two troublesome problems. In his suite at the presidential palace, he stood facing Ahmed, livid with anger.

"I always told you the wealth of Afghanistan lay in its jewels and carpets. Now–hah! our country's wealth lies in its poppy fields, in the hands of the Taliban and local warlords! And you, my grandson, have reaped profits from its evil, stinking crop!"

The words burned themselves into Ahmed's brain; they were bitter, sarcastic words he had never before heard from the mouth of his benevolent grandfather.

"This is how you help your people?"

Ahmed could not deny the charge; a sullen resentment rose up in him as he shouted at his grandfather. "It was for my men–for equipment and weapons! The money was used only for these things, not for personal gain! We needed modern weapons. Enfield rifles are no good against RPGs–it was for my men–I could not stand to see them cut down in battle by machine guns, while we stood there like chickens waiting to be plucked, with nothing but Enfields and old broken-down Russian equipment!"

After a moment of silence, Mohammed spoke. "A case of means justifying the ends, eh?"

"No, I knew it was wrong. I'm not trying to justify it! I'm no longer involved in it, and in fact, I'll be working to eliminate the poppy fields."

"I see, and do you think the Alliance is going to stop using drug money because you have developed a conscience?"

"It's not something I'm proud of."

"Perhaps not, but you won your battles–and Rashid–what about..."

"I cannot tell Rashid what to do, I have no knowledge of his arrangements."

"Now, about your American woman..."

Ahmed's voice was cold as he interrupted. "She is my wife, her name is Andrea, and she has nothing to do with any of this."

"She doesn't know, does she?"

"No."

"I understand she is beautiful, has strong opinions, fought on the front with you, helps at the school–trying to remake Afghanistan in America's image?"

"She's not involved in politics."

"Ahmed, Ahmed, why couldn't you have taken an Afghan wife?"

"When you meet her, you will understand."

"May Allah understand. I heard your introduction to her was a violent one!"

Ahmed was silent, seething with the knowledge Abdullah's first duty was to Mohammed, reporting not only business matters, but even revealing personal details of his life with Andrea.

"Aha! I detect some surprise. Abdullah, by the way, talked of your wife with much affection." He let out a sardonic laugh. "So the worlds collided that night, did they?" Ahmed decided there was no use responding to Mohammed's comments. His grandfather's sudden interest in his life could not make up for all the years of seeming disinterest and lack of personal involvement.

"I must be serious, Ahmed. I am disappointed in you. It will be hard for you to overcome the evil of those poppy fields, now that they are providing a good living for the naïve innocents who grow the pretty flowers, and an even better existence for our enemies who control the provinces there."

Two days later, Andrea was introduced to Ahmed's grandfather. After speaking with her for an hour or so, without mentioning the poppy fields, Mohammed fell in love with his new granddaughter, especially pleased she had become Muslim. Probably did that for Ahmed, he thought, but it was a good thing no matter the motive. Yes, an asset for Ahmed, a bit young and wild, but one must accept change. My days are almost over; this is the time for the young ones, even a young American. And Ahmed must somehow make peace with himself about the damned poppy fields.

Before he left for Iraq on business, he advised his grandson, "Whatever you do, trust utterly in God."

When Ahmed asked Andrea for her opinion of his grandfather, she smiled. "What do you think I thought of him?"

"Oh, I guess I know, since you were on your best behavior, flattering him, charming him–you made him do the same. If he were younger, he'd probably try to steal you away from me!"

She laughed. "Shame on you, Ahmed–but I bet he's popular with the international set, Muslim or not. You're right, he's a charmer. And you know I do have a thing for grandfathers!"

# XIV. Endless Round

Andrea read a line of her story to Abdullah.

"As Afghanistan played its infinite canon of tribalism..."

"What is infinite canon?" asked Abdullah.

"Well," answered Andrea, "It's a round of music. The end of the song leads to the beginning,
so that the song goes 'round and round' and may be repeated endlessly –an infinite canon, an endless round."

"Appropriate," muttered Abdullah.

As Andrea went about Kabul, she came to know the neighborhoods, some so devastated they looked uninhabitable, houses cut in half by mortar fire or smashed into rubble by bombs, destruction meted out to the city impartially by Russian, Taliban, American, and Northern Alliance forces. But people lived there, behind the walls, somehow eking out a living, slowly rebuilding the houses, if not the lives, they once had. Children played, but most worked in the streets of Kabul; many spent their days weaving carpets to help their families buy food. *If only I could scoop them all up and take them to school*–well, some day they would all come. There were small moments when she almost imagined she was in America, in the bustle of people shopping, doing errands, going to work. But her American illusion was regularly pierced by the guttural, sonorous tone of the *azan* echoing loudly throughout the city, commanding the faithful to pray, or sharp metallic drumbeats accenting Eastern music. It was a land like no other; though it bore a resemblance to its neighbors, Afghanistan was unique, an Islamic nation that worshiped Allah in its own pragmatic fashion. There was little gentleness here–most of it lay behind walls and doors, hidden away in the domain of women or sitting pitiably on the street, hand protruding from the *burqa*, begging for food to sustain a fragile life.

While the bazaars could not compare to the glamorous shopping malls of the West, they were immensely more fascinating. Andrea loved Chicken Street, with its shops of genuine and fake antiquities, sensuous, lovely fabric, and wonderful carpets. The carpets, thought Andrea, are the real jewels of Afghanistan. She knew nothing about them; they all looked beautiful to her. But Ahmed told her not to buy any without having Abdullah or himself examine them first.

"You must know their true worth before you choose one, otherwise you will be cheated." So Andrea blended into the daily life of Kabul, the Azeem brothers trailing after her. They sometimes became distracted, letting her get ahead; she carried a gun and she could shoot straight, they reasoned. Still not satisfied with her limited supply of CDs, she left school one day on a search for more music. The sounds of Kabul in mid-day were always raucous, but a woman's terrified screams attracted her attention. Placing her hand on the trigger of her gun, she hurried to see what was going on and came upon an ugly sight–a man yelled curses at a woman as he dealt blow after blow to her body with the butt of his Kalashnikov. The woman had fallen to the ground, curling up in a fetal position and sobbing. The evils of Eastern culture were captured in the brutal scene. Andrea, gun drawn, was ready to shoot when the video boys surrounded her.

"No, no, no, Andrea!" They snatched the revolver from her hand.

Andrea shouted at them, "Stop him, you cowards, stop him, damn it!" Unveiled, she glared at the man, hissing, "Evil, evil, evil, you will be punished by Allah!" then helped the woman up, telling her she could take her to the hospital.

The *burqa*-clad woman protested, "No, please leave us alone."

"But..."

"No! You cause more trouble. Go away!" Infuriated by all this interference with the discipline of his wife, the man abruptly took aim at Andrea and her guards; a bullet caught Abdul in the leg before Mohammed and Abdur subdued him. Andrea left the woman to her fate, and looked in alarm at Abdul, blood streaming from his leg. "We're going to the hospital."

Andrea always avoided the hospital–she had no desire to see any more of war's sad consequences, but Abdul needed a doctor. It was what Andrea expected and didn't want to see–boys, men, children

190

and a few women missing limbs sat in wheelchairs, resigned to the wait for prosthetic arms and legs. As they helped Abdul into a treatment area, a woman doctor came in. A brusque German woman who cleaned and bandaged the wound, she gave Abdul some antibiotics and dismissed him. Andrea thanked her, and the doctor turned to her and asked, "Who are you? Not Afghan."

"No, American. I'm Andrea Sharif."

"Ah, I know the name. Are you here to help? We need aides. You help at the school; that's fine, but you could be more helpful here. Do you have any experience? Well, no matter, really; you can learn."

Andrea thought, lady, you presume too much, but it was obvious there was a shortage of everything here. She answered, "Doctor...?"

The woman broke in, "Sorry, my name is Emma Schilling."

"I'm not a nurse," said Andrea, "I have some limited knowledge; my father is a doctor and I used to help out at his office sometimes."

"Good enough. Come tomorrow, we'll put you to work–don't worry about school. I'll speak to Nuria about it. Now I need to get back to my patients."

That quickly, Andrea became a hospital worker. Dr. Schilling had left no room for hesitation or debate–she needed Andrea at the hospital, and that was that. Andrea had not met any woman as decisive as the weary, too-busy doctor; she called Nuria to tell her what had happened. Feeling uncertain about the hospital, she was hoping Nuria would persuade her to stay with the school, but Nuria knew Dr. Schilling.

"Oh, she's a drill sergeant, but it's true they are very short-handed there; it's certainly a more critical situation."

"I suppose, but I love the kids, I'll miss them; I had more things planned for them."

"Come one or two days, divide your time–you just need to tell the good doctor in no uncertain terms how important the school is to you."

"Don't worry, I will–thanks, Nuria."

Divide her time? Ahmed should be home soon, the house needed cleaning. The hospital's needs, however, were more compelling than anything else. After five days of training, she gave injections, drew blood, bandaged minor wounds, cleaned up the messiness of injury, death, or sickness, and harangued aid agencies for more supplies. Her hardest duty was reading stories to young children, letters to young fighters, and comforting those near death. Their pride dulled by pain, they looked at her with sad, unquestioning, yet puzzled eyes that made her want to turn away; she couldn't, so she faced them honestly, with understanding. How could Emma Schilling deal with this for any length of time? There were only two other doctors in attendance–it seemed impossible to give everyone the care needed. And it was. They finally got word another "staff" was coming to relieve the three doctors.

When Dr. Schilling left, she said to Andrea, "I'll be back; you've done a wonderful job–you should study; become an M.D."

Andrea replied, "Never."

She was done with the hospital duties, but her immersion in the aftermath of war's effect on the people of Afghanistan had yielded a strange benefit. Every day, as she came and went, she passed by an Uzbek fighter, a fierce-looking man who could have been twenty-five or fifty-five; who knew? He had lost both legs at Mazar-I-Sharif and sat sullenly waiting for artificial limbs. Passing the row of intensely red roses leading to the entrance, Andrea greeted him daily with a smile and a *Salaam aleichum*; he never returned her smile or greeting, just glared at her.

She finally decided to return his black look one day instead of smiling–he suddenly barked at her in English, "You Miss America, you smile!" then burst out in a fit of laughter. "Legs come today; I go."

"But you can't go just yet, you'll…"

"No! I go, soon be fighting again."

"Who will you be fighting?"

He gave her an evil smile. "I fight Tajiks, maybe Americans who bomb my family–maybe they leave Afghanistan. You American, you stay, make music, carry a gun. Good."

A few days later, she saw him walking awkwardly on his new legs, carrying his Kalashnikov, triumphant, ready for battle; his tribe needed him. Andrea smiled in acknowledgment and a sudden surge of joy rippled through her body. "Make music," he had said. Yes, yes. Music, dance that spoke of Afghanistan's spirit. The joy produced a composition in her mind, complete in every detail. I'll have to ask Ahmed, she thought.

It felt good to be spending most of her time now with the children.

Their thirst for learning keen as ever, they were sometimes absent due to some unfortunate circumstance at home, but Nuria understood the problems of families struggling with hunger and the loss of their breadwinners. Andrea's geography lessons and musical periods were the dessert after the main course; now, Nuria had fewer qualms about the music since it included many countries and languages, painting a mosaic of the world. Andrea led the children in dances, went kite-flying with them, marveled at their vividly colored art works. She became a bit of a legend in Kabul; she wore the *chadoor*, but much to the consternation of the video boys, she was promptly recognized, veil or no veil. They were dedicated to protecting her, and knew how Ahmed would deal with them should anything happen to her–why couldn't she wear a *burqa*? that would be much easier. No, she always answered. The boys gloomily told themselves it was only a matter of time.

"I will not allow you to leave yourself open to danger–school is one thing, the hospital quite another! Wear the *burqa*!"

It was not a request. Ahmed came home to find the Azeem brothers in a mild state of rebellion. With much gesturing, and all talking at once, they complained about Andrea's refusal to wear a *burqa*.

"We cannot be responsible–she takes too many chances, talks to Taliban prisoners and Uzbeks at the hospital, everyone knows her, she faces men in the street and scolds them about their wives! It is too much; we must be relieved of this duty."

"She works at the hospital?"

"Yes," answered Abdul.

"No, not now," corrected Abdur.

He protested his brothers' criticism of her; she was high-spirited and difficult, but always ready to help others–"she works very hard at the school; the children love her," he said as he glared at his brothers.

But Ahmed decided this must be the end of Andrea's freedom from the *burqa*; when he issued his command to her, she said nothing at first, stung by Ahmed's angry order. She knew his first responsibility was to protect her. He couldn't be by her side all the time; that was why he hired the video boys, and still she rebelled. Why couldn't she understand? He could no longer contain his anger.

"Why do you disobey me–you must obey, obey!"

"Obey? Shit! We're not on the battlefield, I don't obey just because you say so..."

"It is for your safety!"

"For your pride!"

He looked at her in disbelief, forced himself to speak quietly, and said, "For my peace of mind."

Though Andrea listened to the voices inside her, she didn't always like what they told her. I don't want to hear it, she thought, trying to ignore the message throbbing in her brain, but she couldn't. This was the man who loved her, the commander who carried the dead home to their families, who made painful decisions for his soldiers, who had to accept the foreigners he didn't want in his country, a man who was always in harm's way for his cause. My commander, one way or another; I love him. "For my peace of mind." Of course. *Surely you can grant him that much.* Ashamed of her childish behavior, she crossed the space between them and embraced him.

"You're right, Ahmed." His eyes softened as he kissed her.

"I don't want to shout at you."

"I know. Ahmed?"

"Yes?"

"You know you're my hero, don't you?"

He laughed. "For how long?"

"Forever. I never wanted to work at the hospital in the first place; I only wanted to help at school, but once I went, and saw the..."

"What did you see that you hadn't seen on the battlefield?"

"It was different, closer. It wasn't just the injuries–it was their eyes...beautiful Afghan eyes, your eyes." She laughed. "Sometimes I'd sing to them–it made them smile, even laugh. Maybe they were making fun of me; well, that was good. I wanted to be busy so I wouldn't have much time to think about...I did stop working at the hospital, and I've been checking on Soraya. I'm going to help when the baby comes." She stopped for a moment. "I never used to worry, but..."

She frowned, scolding herself for such a failing, then admitted, "It was so hard not knowing where you were...whether you were dead or alive... the nights were...I can't sleep well, Ahmed, without you to keep me warm. It was easier on the front!" she cried out. He smiled, holding her face in his hands.

"I understand it is hard for you; you've never been good at waiting. Andrea, listen to me. I cannot tell you what I do or how long I'll be gone. I do what I must." He walked across the room and gazed at his parents' picture on the wall. It was the photograph he had shown Andrea in Bonn; she had presented it to him just before his thirty-first birthday, enlarged and framed. For a moment, he was lost in thought, then turned to her and sighed. "The desire to fight is stronger than the will to make peace. His voice was almost a whisper– he was far away, contemplating some sadness; coming back to the present, he asked, "Do you really worry so much?"

"No, not so much," she lied.

"Look at me; tell the truth!"

"Oh for God's sake, Ahmed, what do you want from me?"

"Everything."

And I've given it to you, she thought, my body, my soul, every last bit of me.

"Andrea, do you know what I see when I look into your eyes? I see the wife I love and the mother of the children we will have. You must wear the *burqa*." He held her and said, "Stay with me, Andrea, stay with me."

She groaned silently. Oh no, she thought, I'm not ready. Yet she knew his decision was final.

Andrea put the *burqa* over her head, told Abdullah where she was going, and went out to start the motorbike. She was anonymous now, no Jeep, no video boys, just one muj who followed at a discreet distance. The voluminous garment billowed around her feet; she secured the hem to keep it up and away from the wheels of her bike. My fashion statement–one of these days, I'll burn this God-awful outfit. She had to hurry. Soraya had started in labor and needed her; the midwife would be there for the delivery, but Andrea wanted to be with her sister-in-law from beginning to end. Of course, Soraya's husband, Mohammed, would stay well out of the way, following the custom of Afghan husbands, who thought it shameful to see a woman's vaginal area during delivery. They sure as hell don't mind seeing it when they want sex, thought Andrea.

Andrea found Soraya pacing up and down the bedroom, clutching her belly. "Oh Andrea, I'm so glad you're here. I hope Fahima comes soon–I think this birth might be much quicker than Ahmad's."

"Fine, but I hope she gets here soon. Can I get you a glass of tea? And I should put some water on to boil. Have you got clean cloths?"

"Over there on the table–tea would be good. Don't worry, Andrea. If the baby comes quickly, I'm sure you can handle it."

Andrea had never been so unsure of anything in her life, but she tried to appear calm. *Poor Soraya, if I have to deliver this baby.* Soraya's pains became more frequent, more intense. Andrea placed a large piece of plastic on the mattress and clean cloths on top of it, and helped Soraya to the mattress, propping her up on the cushions.

"Don't push too hard yet, remember to relax and breathe between pushing."

As Soraya struggled to follow directions, Fahima came; thank God, thought Andrea, then wondered if she could have managed the delivery by herself. But Fahima was experienced–she monitored Soraya's labor, telling her when to push, when to breathe and relax. Andrea comforted and encouraged, gently wiping Soraya's sweating face, rubbing her forehead.

"You're doing well, Soraya."

"I'll help you when it's your turn," said Soraya.

Her labor lasted just under three hours. She gave a final, hard push, and delivered a boy; Fahima suctioned the baby's airways, cut the cord, and handed the little one to his mother. Finally, an anxious Mohammed was welcomed into the presence of three women who were supposed to stay hidden away and provide their husbands with sons. Soraya was happy–she knew her place; Andrea and Fahima were not so compliant.

Zibak, Afghanistan: Under the pastel paint colors of the sunrise, he walked down the stony road, a lonely man, carrying his carton of bottled water. Jeff Scott looked over at the mountains, marveling at the sight of the bombs leaving their proud trails of black mixed with the soft pinks and blues of early morning. Just another day in Afghanistan. He knew he was being watched, but he didn't care, finding himself in a philosophical, Zen-like frame of mind. His body moved with a calm, sad purpose. Free of obligation to anyone but himself, he allowed his mind to wander into a delusion of expectation–there was Carrie waiting for him, reaching out to him; this time, he'd stay home…he was so tired…But he suddenly felt light as air, at one with the elements, then came a rush of enlightenment–he knew all, and the knowledge gave him a special vision. He saw them–Darius, Alexander, the Hephalites, Genghis Khan, Tamerlane, Babur, all the ghosts of Afghanistan come to life, determined to win their battles. He heard their siren songs in the relentless winds of the Hindu Kush, in the far reaches of the Safed Koh, and in the furious swirling dust of the desert. He plodded on toward Nowshak, almost triumphant.

Wardak Province–Ahmed faced Halim, Kalashnikov slung over his shoulder. He felt no need to use it yet. Halim, tall, white haired and bearded, had piercing blue eyes, an emaciated frame that looked as though it might collapse in on itself any moment, and an eerie elegance. Russians, Taliban, Afghans–it mattered little to him what or who his enemies were, though he hated the godless Russians most; his mission was to keep his power, his faith, and his fiefdom alive. He occasionally made a truce with a fellow warlord, though it didn't last long–as soon as any triviality occurred (a woman's name being spoken or a favorite horse stolen) the deal was off and the battle was on. He spoke some English, French, and Russian and loved using the foreign phrases to impress his sophistication upon friends and enemies. Ahmed didn't expect any concessions from Halim; he was there on a "good will" visit. Halim had known Ahmed as a young boy, clever, trustworthy up to a point, and here he was, a grown man with an American wife.

"Ahmed, *salaam, salaam aleichum.* Come, have tea and food–we will talk. When did I last see you–*mon Dieu*–a long time ago, before you were a commander, when we were fighting the Shurovee."

"We met briefly about two years ago."

"Ah," sighed Halim heavily, "I am getting old and forgetful. Now, why have you come–to take away my humble position? What would my people do without me? They honor me, depend upon me. You come from Kabul, an evil place of many conspirators; I am disappointed that you chose to be their messenger."

Ahmed ignored the exaggerations, shaking his head. "I come in peace, Halim, to ask that you not molest the people of Kowt-e Ashrow."

"By God, Ahmed, those thieves cross my boundaries, steal my horses and women; I kill them in the name of Allah and *nang*!"

"That I understand, and that problem can be quickly solved; after all, we are all Afghans."

As he spoke, one of Halim's men, testing this Tajik who seemed to think he was another Massoud, reached for Ahmed's rifle; Ahmed spun around, striking the man on the head with the butt of the Kalashnikov. Halim watched the scene, commenting, "I see you're still a *mujahid*." Ahmed shouldered the Kalashnikov and faced Halim.

He stared at the elegant warlord a minute before speaking. "This is not a good thing to do. Don't antagonize those you cannot conquer."

Halim laughed, slapping Ahmed on the back. "Just a little joke. Why do you stay in Kabul?"

"I won't be there forever; then you'll have no friend in Kabul, only unfriendly *mujs* and possibly American bombs to deal with. You will be much better off when you help us. We'll meet again to talk about it. Thank you for your hospitality," he ended with a wry smile.

Halim watched him, signaling his man to take his finger off the trigger. He knew Ahmed had his guards ready, their sights trained on him, and he didn't want to die today.

This old man still has fire in him, thought Ahmed.

The guards were well-armed, expert marksmen, but when they climbed the Safed Koh range of the Hindu Kush they had no expectation of easy negotiations–they were going into the mouth of the dragon. Pashtun territory–numerous ethnic groups, tribes, bandits. Ahmed was doubtful much could be accomplished here; certainly no lasting agreement, a contradiction in terms, he thought, in Afghanistan. Villagers here were suspicious, even as they gave freely of traditional Afghan hospitality. They were in the cross-hairs of American firepower, houses destroyed, innocents killed and injured, teams of American soldiers searching their villages. Living in their midst was the cause of much of the trouble–Taliban–and the Afghans' support of those fundamentalists exacted a price.

Ahmed understood the desire of Afghans to retain a traditional, fundamental Islamic culture; he himself was struggling with his conflicting views of Islam. More often than not, he found it complicated having one foot in the East and one in the West. He was troubled by criticism of his marriage, on one hand resenting it, on the other unable to deny his concessions to Western culture.

As they wound around the bleak, rocky slopes of the Safed Koh, Ahmed thought of Andrea; he was glad he insisted she wear the *burqa*–she would at least appear to be Afghan. Two things in his life he was certain of: his faith, and his love for Andrea. When they stopped for prayers, Ahmed prayed for guidance.

The small force approached Zawra, a small village jammed into the mountainside, one house almost on top of the other. Ahmed stopped the small caravan–no eager children, no curious teenage *mujihids*, no one came to greet them. Something was wrong.

"Mahmud, find the *mullah*–no, wait!"

From the peak above them, he saw Taliban, at least fifteen, pointing their Kalashnikovs at his men, then heard the scream of a jet engine. He yelled to his men to get down under the shelf of the ledge, then ran to Mahmud, falling on top of him. He felt a searing pain in his side; all was darkness after that.

Her herb garden needed attention; Andrea apologized to her plants for her neglect and hummed as she cut oregano and thyme for the mid-day meal of *aushak*, and lavender for her hair rinse. Thoughts of Ahmed made her glance at the mountains with their snow-covered tops glistening in the sun. She was captured by a moment of reflection, content among her plantings; taking her gaze off the mountains, she shook off a chill that ran through her. As she gathered up the herbs and started toward the house, Abdullah appeared; Andrea knew immediately something was wrong. She dropped the clippings, a terrible anxiety overwhelming her. "Oh no, oh no–Abdullah–is he…" She didn't dare finish the question.

"He is alive, Andrea."

He put his arm around her shoulders and led her to the Jeep. "Wear your head-scarf."

As Abdullah drove through the streets of Kabul, Andrea sat silent, wrapping her arms close to her body, rigid with fear. They passed Kabul Hospital.

"Where are you going?"

"Ahmed is in the clinic at Bagram." The American airbase–that must mean…

"They took him there, there were no appropriate beds at Kabul. Andrea, remember, Ahmed is very strong; he'll be all right." But Andrea's mind leapt to the worst conclusions–missing limbs, paralysis, death. Oh God, she prayed, please help him, please.

They had no difficulty getting into tightly secured Bagram; the military there had gotten word of their coming; a soldier guided them to the medical unit. Dr. Fitzsimmons met them in the clean, well equipped infirmary. Calm, kind, and matter of fact, he explained that Ahmed had been brought in early this morning.

"This happened two days ago, but it took time to bring him down from the mountain, an unfortunate situation, as he lost a lot of blood. By the way, the bombing was intended for the Taliban; our people didn't know of your husband's presence at Zawra. We've done what we can, performed immediate surgery to remove shrapnel and clean the area. There was minor damage to the liver and other organs, some of which we repaired–most will heal on their own."

Andrea received this information in a mild state of shock, unable to absorb all the details.

Abdullah nodded solemnly as the doctor spoke and asked, "What is his condition now?"

"Well, he's still unconscious, and may be for some time, but on the whole I'd say he's a pretty lucky fellow. We'll watch him carefully, and I'll check on him again soon. Ah, Mrs. Shar–"

"Oh," she said, "Just call me Andrea."

"Fine–don't be alarmed, Andrea, when you see your husband. He has a couple of tubes in him, antibiotics, glucose, and a catheter. I'd say his chances are good."

"Please take us to him now," said Andrea. "I want to stay with him; is there a cot I can use?"

Surprised, the doctor answered, "Stay–over night? I'm not sure. This is a military installation; I'll need to speak to the commanding officer."

Andrea had already made up her mind.

They were led to a cubicle where the sight of Ahmed dealt a physical blow to her heart. For one horrific moment, Andrea stood paralyzed, unable to breathe. She knew he was not indestructible, though she had almost convinced herself he was. Pale and weak, he lay helpless, his fate in the hands of doctors and scalpels and tubes– and Allah. Andrea bit her lip to keep from crying. Abdullah prayed.

"I want to take care of him," she announced. "Please arrange for a cot and a pitcher of ice water and cloths, and anything else you need me to do."

Dr. Fitzsimmons saw her distress and her determination; it would be helpful to have her with him. "You will be a good nurse."

Andrea prayed as she moistened Ahmed's lips. She uttered so many supplications, made so many deals with Allah, so many promises to God, she was aware nothing she said made any sense, yet she couldn't stop herself. She kept talking to Ahmed, hoping he heard her.

The third day at Bagram–he should be awake by now, thought Andrea. That evening after prayers, she gently washed his face–*oh, Ahmed, open those beautiful eyes*. The infirmary was quiet, there were a few men being treated for minor injuries they had sustained during a Taliban attack near Bagram; soft music came from someone's CD player. The nurse came by to check the IVs; impressed by Andrea's care of her husband, she took a few minutes to reassure her that Ahmed was doing well. "Don't worry, he'll be waking up soon." She wondered what it was like for an American girl to be married to an Afghan *mujahidin*–a fate worse than death? Hardly–she seems to be very much in love with him.

Dr. Fitzsimmons had come several times to examine him, urging her to be patient. "Heart sounds are good, blood pressure a little low, temp normal–it's a waiting game; I know it's hard." A sudden burst of activity caught their attention; the doctor took one look at his pager and excused himself. "We have new casualties coming in–I'll see you before Ahmed's released."

"American soldiers?"

"Yes–bad." Andrea felt her heart pounding with the knowledge she had to face fellow Americans injured in this alien land she had chosen. She had to see them. As she approached the ER, dread settled itself in her stomach; trapped by fear, she could hardly move. Then the scene, like a movie, unfolded before her. The worst cases were being prepared to be taken to Germany for extensive surgery. Some men were still conscious, faces blank, a few still unaware or forgetting their arms or legs were gone. Then there were the young, once-handsome boys whose damaged faces resembled grotesque Halloween masks. Andrea's eyes met those of a nurse whose blue eyes were vacant with exhaustion.

"Can I help?" asked Andrea.

"No," she said. "Go back to your Afghan husband. He's lucky."

Andrea's green eyes glared at her with intense anger; ignoring her, the nurse turned away to continue her duties. Andrea had been chastised and dismissed. She wanted to yell, "what the hell do you know about it?" She had come face to face with prejudice and disapproval, and it hurt.

The commanding officer came in one day asking about Ahmed, but he was mainly concerned with Andrea. Trying to cheer her up, he told her he was from Arizona, and the two of them shared stories and memories of their native state. Then he became serious; "You know what happened at Zawra was a mistake."

"Yes, Dr. Fitzsimmons told me."

"Perhaps he didn't mention it, but it was a mistake on the Afghans' part. Someone failed to communicate to the pilot that Alliance soldiers were near that village. So often, these failures to communicate are blamed on us–and we do make mistakes, but not this time. Of course, all that is beside the point now. Did you know your husband saved the life of one of his men? Mahmud, I believe."

"What about the rest?"

"They suffered some injuries, but all of them will be all right. Some

Taliban were killed, a few brought to Kabul Hospital as prisoners."

He left after Andrea thanked him, saying, "Everyone here has been so kind; we won't forget that, believe me."

"I only hope all of this works out well," and he gestured to show he meant all of Afghanistan.

Andrea leaned close to Ahmed's face-"Ahmed, you're a hero, you know that? You saved Mahmud and probably all your men. They're all okay. Come on, sweetie, it's time to wake up-I need you, please wake up; I love you." Then she kissed him and said, "We need to go home." Holding his hand, she began singing an old song from childhood. As she sang, there was an answering pressure on her hand. She looked at Abdullah, eyes shining; he returned her look with a nod and a wide smile.

"Ahmed, oh Ahmed!" His hand clasped hers, strong and sure; his eyelids fluttered uncertainly.

"Andrea."

Thank God he was awake. She called to let Dr. Fitzsimmons know, then turned to Ahmed.

He spoke hoarsely, "Andrea...I want...to sit up." She protested, then helped him into a reclining position, a movement that took all his strength.

"I'm so happy to see you open your eyes."

He saw the infirmary with its up-to-date equipment and asked, "Where...what is this place? Tell me... what happened." She told him about all, except the part about the mistake being Afghan. Ahmed guessed from her tone what had gone wrong. So Mahmud was all right, along with the rest of his men-good.

He felt a terrible thirst. "I need water."

She gave him sips of water, not sure how much he should be taking. His speech was still slow, hesitant, but his eyes had lost none of their sparkle. Noticing the cot next to his bed, he said, "You've been here the whole time? Sleeping here?"

Her relief at seeing Ahmed awake and alert dissipated the dark thoughts and worries-she kissed him and laughed. "Of course-and don't scold me; I've been very proper. Now I'm so happy I could dance an Irish jig."

Ahmed managed a smile. "I heard your song... about sunshine...." he broke off as Dr. Fitzsimmons appeared.

"Well, Ahmed–I'm Dr. Fitzsimmons; looks like you'll be leaving us soon."

"I want to go now, doctor."

Andrea mouthed the words no, no, at Dr. Fitzsimmons and rolled her eyes. Abdullah shook his head.

"We'll release you as soon as possible; tomorrow, perhaps. I want to be sure you're all right."

"I'm fine now," insisted Ahmed.

"Tomorrow, I promise," said the doctor on his way out.

"Andrea, I am all right."

"I know, sweetie, but they have to check everything out first. Please, Ahmed. We'll be home tomorrow."

Ahmed thought, why do they want to keep me here, I can…the rest of the thought escaped him as he fell asleep.

Andrea smiled at her stubborn husband; *you're not quite as strong as you think, my sweet Afghan.*

They came home the next day. No more tubes, no catheter. Ahmed admitted to himself he needed the extra day, and thanked Dr. Fitzsimmons for his care, saying, "If I can be of help to you in any way, you've only to ask."

"I appreciate that, and I'll remember–one never knows here."

He knew this Afghan meant what he said. It was just another wound in Ahmed's years of fighting, but this time there was Andrea; Ahmed knew her care would be dutiful and loving, probably excessive.

Andrea was so ecstatic to have him home with her for an extended period of time, she sang all the verses of all the silly childhood songs she could remember, until Ahmed said, "Enough, enough–go tend to your garden!" *Andrea, Andrea, let me be!*

Four weeks of rest and light activity helped restore Ahmed's strength; after that he was called on to resume the fruitless campaign of conciliation and acceptance of the Kabul government. Traveling with the same men in whatever mode of transportation the mountains would allow–Jeep, horseback, or climbing on foot the unforgiving peaks of the Hindu Kush–Ahmed persisted in his efforts to unite, in some measure, his countrymen. But he couldn't work miracles. After any small success, failures followed. He came back to Kabul physically and emotionally tired, disturbed that Afghans were unable or refused to understand the importance of a central government. Often he thought of united America, a dream that was fading. And there were ominous developments in the wild, lawless border lands–a regrouping of Taliban and Al Qaeda camps. American bombs had been silent for months; where were they now?

Home at last, tired and discouraged, he responded to Andrea's hugs with a kiss and few words; it was easy to see how he was feeling about this latest mission. Andrea couldn't bear his sadness; as they ate their afternoon meal, she told him, "One of the girls asked me today if you were a prince."

Ahmed gave a small laugh. "And what did you tell her?"

"I said that you are my prince."

"Ah, that was the right answer."

Andrea saw a hint of desire in his eyes. As they prepared for bed that evening, he watched her as she removed her clothing.

"Am I tempting my prince?"

"Yes."

His expression became dark, almost hostile; he pulled her roughly to him, pressing against her, "I'm weak with desire, under the spell of my princess," and he guided her hands down his body.

"So, you think I am stronger?"

"I'm unable to resist your temptations."

"But you are always in a position to decide my fate."

"Andrea, closer, closer."

"If I'm really stronger, perhaps I'll refuse," she teased.

"Andrea."

As he started to kiss her, she backed away. "What happens if I refuse?" she asked, without any laughter this time.

"You can't," and he grabbed at her, but she slipped out of his grasp. Enough of these games.

"Andrea, come here when I speak to you–why are you doing this!"

"You're a man, stronger than me, make me."

What had gotten into her?

"Men do what they want with women in this country and they get away with it–beat their wives, rape women, even the Qu'ran says it's okay!" Ahmed realized her tirade had nothing to do with him, she was reacting to something else.

"What happened?"

"Nothing remarkable for Afghanistan, just seeing one more man abusing his wife on the street and I stand there, not able to do anything about it. I came close to shooting the son of a bitch, but that's no good, I'd only have caused more trouble."

He was quiet for a moment, studying her. "Sometimes you're too quick to use that gun, cowgirl."

"That's not funny, Ahmed."

"I didn't mean it to be, I'm serious. American men don't abuse women?"

"Yes," she admitted, "they do. It's against the law in America; but yes, they do. It's always the power; men need the power." He saw the torment in her eyes, and she saw Ahmed's understanding.

"I will not force myself on you, my love."

"Oh, I'm sorry, sweetie..." She sighed, "I almost wish I were a man."

Ahmed smiled, "Well, thank God you're not. Come to bed with me."

"Make love to me, Ahmed."

"Yes."

After making some difficult recommendations in a conference with government officials, Ahmed offered to resign; refusal of his resignation was both frustrating and flattering. He would stay on, he told them, if he could work on the problem of clearing land mines-thousands of them lay in wait for their victims. Perhaps he could accomplish something real; he knew he could not turn Andrea's dreams into reality. After she expressed her anger at the abusive treatment of women, Ahmed thought about it and repeated what he had told her before. "It will take time for change, it may never come. You know Afghan history; I don't feel hopeful about a central government right now."

"I just wish they would all get on the same page!"

"Same page? Ethnic groups, tribes within the groups-same page-it would be an accomplishment to get them in the same book! Ah, Andrea, you're thinking like an American-logic, efficiency, immediacy. Wishful thinking. I do what I must, I try. We will both do what we can. But please, Andrea," he said with a smile, "you cannot shoot people."

As she watched her husband in his troubled, fitful sleep, she prayed, asking for his safety from the warlords that threatened his life. The call to prayer had started beckoning throughout the city; Ahmed awoke and obeyed its summons, as did Andrea. She prayed again for Ahmed's safety, and saw a vision of gardens, fountains, museums, forests, green, mine-free fields, plentiful harvests, carefree children, tourists coming to see the ancient artifacts, to hear the poets' eloquent recitations of Islam's history and beauty.

"Andrea, are you going to school today?"

She was abruptly snatched back to reality.

# XV. Afghan Eyes

*Afghan eyes, warm and wild,*
*So commanding, so beguiling…*

She had not heard from her father since leaving Arizona. It was a relief, yet–a story with no conclusion. His silence left a somewhat guilty uncertainty in her heart.

"This is my dad; he's DOCTOR McAlister!" the eight-year-old Andrea would proclaim defiantly when introducing him to her teachers or schoolmates. A spasmodic, chilly pain passed through her body. She could only wonder…

The letter from Wenonah lay unopened in her closet; Andrea didn't want to read it. "Andrea, open it, you can't ignore a letter from your mother." I wish I could, she thought, but of course Ahmed was right. Pulling the envelope from her jewelry box, she sat in front of Ahmed and opened it, reading aloud to him.

The first few paragraphs were chatty bits of news about the ranch, the family, the boys–"it's a nice letter," said Andrea, relieved.

But in the end, it was disturbing–Andrea's voice faltered a little as she read the last paragraph. "I have bad news to tell you about your father–he has prostate cancer, diagnosed late, and hasn't responded to chemo or radiation. He's very ill. I feel sorry to tell you this, Andrea, but I must. He has only a few months left." Here Andrea stopped, dropping the piece of paper; Ahmed picked it up and finished reading it aloud. "Please know that I am all right. Your grandfather, Naiche, John, and your aunts are helping me with everything, and the boys are handling the ranch work as usual. Don't worry about me;

you don't need to come here. Your father said it's not necessary, and said to tell you he loves you and wishes you and Ahmed well. I know this news might be hard for you in many ways; I'm so glad you have Ahmed. His love will help you through anything. Tell him I love him. Love, Mom."

Andrea couldn't speak at first; she looked at Ahmed, shaking her head. "I wouldn't go to see him anyway. Poor Mom, but she'll be okay. She thinks of you as a son, Ahmed. Oh God, for him to say he loves me–wishes us well–in control to the end."

"Are you all right, love?" He was touched by Wenonah's feeling for him.

"Yes," answered Andrea, "but it's not over yet. What will he do for the finale?"

"Shhh, Andrea."

A year of living in Kabul brought Ahmed and Andrea to an unexpected crossroad. Since the day they entered the city as victors over the Taliban, Kabul had become more orderly, happier than the hysteria they experienced just after the defeat of the enemy. But the political power play that emerged, and the rivalry among the tribes, did not go away just because the world was impatient for a new Afghanistan to rise from the ashes. Too much had gone before; a modern, productive, educated Afghanistan would be only a dream for years. Yet Ahmed, his dreams more realistic than Andrea's, worked for it, making deals with more than one devil who had the potential for plunging his country back into war or moving it forward. He played his role of the handsome, educated soldier/diplomat well, charming foreigners into believing their money would be well-spent.

Andrea wanted no part of the political party circuit, although she appeared like an elusive star with Ahmed when it was necessary. She was a low-profile American phenomenon in Afghanistan.

Eager to take her place was Lauren Bannister, the darling of cable news. She came and went in Kabul, issuing lengthy "special reports," a little fluff and a little substance thrown together to entertain viewers with short attention spans. Her contacts with Ahmed increased; he found her less and less objectionable, easy to talk to, and pleasant to have tea or a chat with at a social occasion. Most important, she had many good contacts that might be useful.

Ahmed knew she was after more than interviews and stories. During one of their meetings at a high level conference, she spoke about the countless number of mines, especially the ones that maimed so many children who, because they resembled toys, innocently picked them up–butterfly mines, a perpetual evil.

"Ahmed, I think I have a source of a great deal of money for your mine clearing operation. I need to see one of those mine fields and the people that have been injured by them. What do you use, how do you go about clearing a minefield?"

"We use primacord."

"What's that?"

"It's a rocket-fired cable; it explodes about two feet above the ground and clears a path through the minefield."

"How interesting. Take me with you when you go out to inspect the work; then I can document the operation and convince my source of your needs."

"I don't know, Lauren–it is very dangerous, not a place for a woman." Lauren felt a warmth rushing through her–he was concerned for her safety, he cared about her! "You do want the money, don't you; I can be very useful in many ways." She appeared cool and confident, knowing her blue eyes, blond hair and long shapely limbs proclaimed her American and desirable. Ahmed suddenly became aware of the strong aura of sexual invitation. She placed her hand on his arm; "Ahmed, Ahmed, we can work well together–it will be so good." As she lifted her lips to his, he pushed her so hard she almost fell from her chair.

"What do you think you are doing!" he exclaimed in a low, angry tone.

"Why, darling, nothing that you haven't thought about; I know desire when I see it, and I saw it the first time we met near Kabul–how can you deny it?"

"You're mistaken, I have no desire for you! Any desire you think you see is for my wife! You have misjudged me, Miss Bannister, and unfortunately, I've misjudged you! Please don't bother your source about money for clearing land mines or anything else. We will manage without your help. It is best that we have no more interviews or discussions of any kind. If you remain in Kabul, you will need to contact someone else." And he walked away.

She couldn't believe it–he had rejected her, but she took it in stride. One couldn't always have what one wanted; still, she held a feeling of triumph inside her. She was sure he had been tempted. And Ahmed knew at that moment what he dreaded and disdained in others who wielded power was also a demon in him; he was no better than them. This day would mark the end of his duties in Kabul.

Ahmed stepped into the shower with Andrea–she was not pleased to have him there with her; she needed to be alone to think about what was happening with Lauren Bannister. Laughing, Ahmed said, "Andrea, you look too serious, put a smile on your face for me."

"I don't feel like smiling."

Ahmed guessed what was bothering her. "You know that Lauren Bannister doesn't..."

"What–doesn't compare with me, doesn't mean anything; I don't want to hear it. She's very sophisticated, that's something I'll never be–you love to hear all that crap from her oh-so-carefully painted mouth. She tells you what you want to hear and you're flattered by it, you believe it. If she had her way, she'd have you in bed by now! But I don't think you've let yourself go that far yet. And let me tell you, my worldly Afghan, you've become as sophisticated as she is, and that's not a compliment. You're telling people what they want to hear, making deals with people you would have gotten rid of before– you've become a politician, sophisticated like the smooth-as-silk Miss Bannister!"

Ahmed could not believe what he was hearing.

"You must have been quite honored by all her special attention to you and only you!" Her words dripped with sarcasm.

He waited a few minutes before answering. "Flattered, perhaps, but never tempted."

"Well, that's cutting it close, Ahmed."

"Andrea, Andrea, my little one."

"I'm not little, and I'm not your play toy or your possession! I will never again be owned by anyone! My father did that for years, and I was too young to stop him. No longer–and you will not own me, either. I'm telling you, Ahmed, you've changed. I don't even think it has that much to do with Lauren Bannister. She's nothing to me, I could cut her down in a New York minute!"

"Andrea!"

"Don't look so surprised. I call it as I see it, I won't pretend anymore–I won't charm people I don't like or trust."

"What about Mahmood?"

"He's a savage, but an honest one; I like him, he knows the score. He'd never try anything with me." She had come to the end of her diatribe, exhausted. Her voice was cold as she said, "This is not a good time to be in the shower with me." No sooner had Ahmed left her in the shower, Andrea burst into tears.

"Oh my God, what have I done, what have I done."

Abdullah caught sight of Ahmed storming out of the house in a black rage. What had happened? He knew Andrea was not happy about Ahmed's new lifestyle, especially as it concerned Lauren Bannister. This cannot continue, thought Abdullah, and he went to look for Andrea. She was in the stable with Buttercup, crying. He had seen her upset before, but never like this. She tried in vain to hold back the tears when she saw him.

"Do you want something, Abdullah?"

"Just to see that you are all right." He knelt next to her and put his arm around her, comforting her.

"Everything will be all right, Andrea."

"You know what happened?"

"No, but I can guess."

"I've tried to behave as an Afghan wife; I've tried, but I can't. It's not just Lauren Bannister; it's the whole thing–this political crap. I know he's proud, I know I've hurt him; oh, I never wanted to act like this, it's just...what will he do? He'll hate me for this. Oh, God, I want my old Ahmed back. What shall I do?"

"Be patient with Ahmed. He has to find himself again; he has lost his way a little. When he was a boy, he always seemed to be in trouble, so restless, doing dangerous stunts, so curious–how and why this, why that, oh, he was a rascal."

Abdullah's eyes held a touch of nostalgia as he spoke of old times, then he remembered the subject at hand. "He is at heart a loving, kind man, a man his parents would be proud of, and he loves you. He'll do what is right for both of you." Abdullah paused, then said rather shyly, "I think of you as a daughter."

Andrea smiled through her tears, "You make a wonderful father."

Ahmed was furious; he did not trust himself to respond to

Andrea's angry outburst. He dressed and saddled his horse, spurring him at a fast clip down the rough trail outside their compound. How dare she talk to him that way. Yes, she had a temper, a fierce independence, and a will of her own, but their love had seemed to lighten her spirit and the effects of her unfortunate relationship with her father. Andrea was his gift, he was her protector; he loved her with a wild passion. Afghan women did not defy their men, they obeyed. But Andrea was not Afghan. For all his understanding and acceptance of her as an American, he was not prepared for a scathing lecture from a woman, any woman.

As he brought his horse down to a slower pace, he thought of her words. Lauren Bannister–yes, he was flattered by her praise, how she deferred to his judgment–that was the way it should be–but he had no intention of becoming intimate with her, though he knew she could be his for the taking. He could never imagine himself with anyone but Andrea. Had he changed so much, lost his direction, his honesty? Andrea called him sophisticated, as though it was a bad word. He had always been sophisticated; she knew that. Was she resentful because she didn't have the sophistication of a Lauren Bannister? But she never wanted it. Ahmed's head was pounding from his attempt to sort it all out. He turned back, went into the house to find Abdullah, who was waiting for him.

After hearing Ahmed's tale of Andrea's temper tantrum, Abdullah asked quietly, "Do you think Lauren Bannister was the cause of her anger?"

"Partly, but it seemed more about my position in government–she's not used to seeing me in that role. I don't know, I would think she'd be glad I'm not at the front anymore or going into Waziri territory."

"Do you think Andrea is jealous of Miss Bannister taking the time that used to be hers? Perhaps Andrea feels insecure about her place in your life right now."

"But she is very busy herself with the school. The children love her; she's become very important to them. I don't understand, but she cannot be allowed to talk to me the way she did, Abdullah."

"That may be, Ahmed, but she has some genuine concerns for you. She sees you becoming a political figure who must compromise. In her eyes, that means consorting with the enemy, giving up your principles, in effect, becoming a different person from the man she fell in love with, while she's still the same."

"Yes, she is," muttered Ahmed grudgingly, smiling slightly at the picture in his mind of the wild, determined girl he had met on the Khyber Pass. "What shall I do?"

"Do you love her?"

"Of course."

"You must decide this for yourself. Remember when you were a boy and you did something bad–your mother would tell you to pray and read more passages from the Qu'ran?"

"Yes, do you really think I'll find my answer there?"

"Perhaps. Your mother also said you must not merely say the words; you must think about why you're praying and what the words are telling you. The answer will come."

"Thank you, Abdullah; you've always been my best teacher."

Abdullah shook his head in mild despair–he had come from Andrea's side to counsel Ahmed. Such unhappiness! But he had no doubt they would find their way together.

After talking to Abdullah, Andrea busied herself making bread and preparing their meal. Ahmed had come back and gone directly into Abdullah's room. Finally, he came into the kitchen where Andrea was baking, flour on her hands and arms. He kissed her and said, "I have some reading to do, I may be studying well into the night–please get provisions together for a journey tomorrow. We'll be leaving at dawn."

Oh, God, she thought, what does that mean? *At least he kissed me.* Still she was nervous–he had shown nothing of what he was feeling. *Should I apologize? No.* Sometime in the night, she was aware she was crying in her sleep, and felt Ahmed turn to her to hold her in his arms.

"I love you," she whispered.

"You know I love you," he said softly.

The next morning dawned to the noisy cackle of blackbirds and chirping sparrows. Andrea awoke feeling contemplative and drained from yesterday's drama. In the kitchen, Ahmed and Abdullah were eating, having said morning prayers. Andrea had not meant to sleep this late; she started to serve the men their tea, but Abdullah stopped her.

"Sit down, Andrea." Ahmed spoke in a serious tone, "We're going to the Panjshir Valley."

Panjshir–Ahmed's boyhood home, home of the Tajiks. She had heard wild tales about the Valley of the Five Lions, stronghold of the Northern Alliance, almost impenetrable. Andrea asked herself what was Ahmed's plan; surely he wouldn't leave her there with Abdullah. She felt uncomfortable, uncertain of his mood, even after last night's tender kiss, and it showed on her face.

Abdullah left the table to stow their things on the packhorses.

Ahmed saw Andrea's uncertainty and reached over to take her hand in his, saying, "It's all right, Andrea. You'll see; this is something I've thought and prayed about very carefully. It will be a surprise for you."

A surprise? *Is he going to drop me off in the Panjshir? Oh stop, that's ridiculous.*

Ahmed answered her thoughts. "Andrea, I love you, I'll never leave you. We will be together in the Panjshir."

"Why are we going there..."

"No more questions; you'll see." He kissed her, saying, "We must get started. Come, sleepy one, let's go."

They mounted their horses, two packhorses bringing up the rear. Andrea sent a note to school that covered her absence for several days; she wasn't sure how long they would be away, since Ahmed wouldn't be specific about his plans. The Panjshir Valley lay between the foothills of the Hindu Kush, buttressed by steep, craggy, almost inaccessible slopes. This was Massoud's land; his aura permeated the region with a mystical invincibility. The Panjshir mourned him, its sadness palpable. They stopped for the night on a small stony plateau. Andrea was grateful for the rest; the air here was pure, thin ether, harder to breathe than the air in Kabul. After eating a light meal, Abdullah and Ahmed said prayers; Andrea prayed, speaking to whomever there was to hear her. *Please let whatever it is we are doing here be a good thing.*

A swath of ruffled clouds scudded across the late evening sky, bathing everything in a bright pink; the moment of splendor was soon extinguished as the sun gave way to the mystery of night. Andrea wrapped herself in her blanket and settled into the sleeping bag; Ahmed crept in beside her. "Good night, my love," he said. They were both tired and fell asleep. Sometime in the cold night Andrea awoke, feeling, as she had the night before, wet tears on her cheeks and Ahmed's arms around her.

"Andrea my love, I'm here; please, you don't need to worry."

"I'm sorry, Ahmed, I didn't know…I didn't know I was crying."

"This time, my love, I know it was because of me, not your father."

"All of this is confusing for me."

"I wanted to surprise you; a good surprise!" he exclaimed when he saw the look on her face, "but I need to know something. The other night when I left you in the shower, what did you think?"

Now that's unfair, thought Andrea. "My first thought was, my God, what have I done."

"And what did you decide you had done?"

Andrea hesitated, took a deep breath and sighed. "I knew I said awful, mean things to you–I knew I hurt you, and I know Lauren Bannister isn't really important to you. I do feel you've become different–maybe a little too smooth, too important, too pleased to have such power, and I can't deal with it. I just wanted my soldier back." She looked into his eyes imploring him to understand. "I'm truly sorry to have hurt you."

"Yes, your words hurt, hurt my pride."

His half-smile told her he wasn't angry, he understood, but she needed to express her misery, and in a low voice, told him, "I promised myself I would never hurt your pride and I did, that I would be understanding and I wasn't. I think I broke a lot of promises." The last word ended in a whisper.

"Andrea, you were right about Kabul. None of it is as important to me as you. I thought I could accomplish something, but Pashtuns rule. I need to be back in the Panjshir. No more tears; we are finished with Kabul. Now go to sleep–we'll soon be home, my love."

Physically and mentally tired, they slept, problems settled for now.

Ahmed was full of enthusiastic excitement about the return to his birthplace, and Andrea was glad to leave Kabul behind. Her only regret was having to leave the schoolchildren she loved.

Their travel to the Panjshir took them over rough trails and steep rocky slopes where they were forced to make their way on foot, carefully leading the horses. On the side of a high, vertical gorge, Andrea looked at the swirling river at least fifty feet below, unconsciously holding her horse's reins tighter. Ahmed knew his decision to come back to his home had been made on a strong, sudden impulse, but it was the right moment. Now was the time. It would be slow going by horse and on foot–unfortunately there was no choice; the old Jeep had finally given up. They would manage, and Andrea would have a very good idea of the difficulties, the beauty, and the remoteness of this piece of Afghanistan.

Russia's helicopter gun ships and bombers had been relentless–they had delivered death on schedule, and thousands of people fled the carnage to become refugees. Those who stayed took shelter in caves during the day, emerging at night to plow fields and plant, in the hope their crops would endure.

What did endure were the Russian remnants of war. The uses to which Afghans put the rusting hulks of tanks, bombs, and trucks amazed and amused. They were the masters of recycling. Now the rusted trucks helped support the wooden bridges over the river, old wheels of tanks blended into the stone walls separating the crops, other relics were used for rooftops. It was heartbreaking, disappointing, strangely inspiring. "All the king's horses and all the king's men...." Yet this place had a lilting beauty, a buoyancy, a fierce and wonderful spirit, a true path. It was home.

Ahmed watched Andrea carefully, hoping she would not be too discouraged by the sad fruits of war. She became silent, introspective. He guessed the destruction she was witnessing was affecting her as it had many who came to see and write about Afghanistan; they were never able to erase it from their hearts and minds.

But she turned to look at him in wonder, saying, "It's beautiful, Ahmed." Gradually, the slope leveled off into a wide valley of one village after another, ensconced in the high rock above them; farmers plowed their fields, unveiled women turned away, and children flying kites waved to them. They left the villages behind and followed the rising trail as the valley became narrower. The day was growing shorter, and the temperature plummeted; a bruising wind assaulted them, causing them to wrap their scarves over their faces and forge ahead in silence. Arriving at a *chaikhana* very near Kafjan, they were met by Haroun, an old friend of Abdullah. "Come, we will have tea and something to eat."

He saw Andrea; taking Abdullah aside, he said, "We must make other arrangements because of the woman; she cannot stay here. There are only men here, there is no place here for a woman."

Abdullah thought of all the places in which Andrea had stayed with numbers of *mujihidin*. "Then we will make our own arrangements."

"No, no, you are my guests. You will come to my house. It is not far; I would be honored to have all of you for the night. I have heard of Ahmed's wife; we know all about these things. I didn't expect her to be along."

Abdullah wasn't sure what he meant by "all these things," possibly the lewd modernity of goings-on in Kabul; he knew Haroun was not being disrespectful, simply honest. So he told Ahmed of the slight change in plans and suggested he formally introduce Andrea to Haroun. Andrea kept her veil on during the dignified introduction, sensing her presence might not be accepted.

After a meal of *quabuli*, tea and fruit–Andrea eating with the women of Haroun's household–they slept well, Andrea with the women. Travel the next day was difficult over the mountain passes, but the sun was shining, the narrow valley had once more become a broad swath of lush green beside the Qonduz River, and all seemed right with the world. Andrea saw Ahmed's growing excitement, rode up beside him, and asked, "Are we there yet?"

He smiled at her joking, saying, "We'll be there by nightfall, love," and leaned out of the saddle to give her a kiss.

Rounding a curve on the sinuous path, they were confronted by a group of *mujahidin*; as soon as they saw Ahmed, they called out greetings–"*Salaam aleichum, Allahu akbar!*" All dismounted, embracing one another, and Andrea recognized most of them; they were Mahmood's men.

"Andrea, *salaam aleichum*," and she responded in kind, asking them how they were.

"We are going home–Sadar's house needs repair."

"What happened?"

"Hit by a bomb. Hamid's wife bore a son, praise be to Allah, but she is not well."

"Where is Mahmood?"

"He's coming; he's been negotiating with that old bandit, Ali Khan."

"Negotiating–Mahmood?"

"He wants Ali Khan's house, but he'll have to pay a good price to that thief."

Bits and pieces of news were related to her with a flourish of arms and hands picturing all the lurid details. Ahmed was glad to see them, glad to see Andrea talking and laughing as they regaled her with their fantastic stories, and Andrea felt good to be one of them again. She looked up to see the imposing form of Mahmood in front of her, a mischievous smile on his face. The smile disappeared as he greeted Ahmed, but Ahmed had seen it, deciding he would not kill Mahmood that day. As they shared their afternoon meal of grilled meat, *naan*, and tea, Ahmed kept his eyes on Mahmood, who had not yet spoken to Andrea. Andrea tried to hide her discomfort with the licentious commander as he approached her; she knew Ahmed was watching.

He greeted her politely, then whispered, "You are looking quite fetching today. Ahmed must be treating you well."

Andrea, startled, prayed Ahmed had not heard his words.

She lamely replied, "I am well, thank you," then excused herself and walked over to Ahmed.

"Ahmed, it's getting late, are we going to go on?"

"Yes, Andrea, stay with me."

Finally, with much confusion and a seeming lack of any plan, Mahmood and his men went on their way after extensive farewells; Andrea, who hated long good byes, was no longer feeling hospitable.

"Did Mahmood offend you in any way?" asked Ahmed.

"No, but I hope he gets to see his wife soon."

"Which one? he's got two!"

"The youngest one, if she's the strongest!"

Twilight became a night lit by a glowing moon whose beams created eerie designs of light and shadow. No bombs, no mortar fire punctured the silence; all they heard was a *muezzin's* call to prayer and the faint howling of wolves in the distance. Andrea rode beside Ahmed; in a low voice, he said, "This is where I come from, this valley." She saw the old wildness in his black eyes and felt his happiness; it was perfect for him, the moonlit night, the peace–it's his citadel, thought Andrea. Kabul could never be home to him.

"We will stop here for prayers."

They passed a small village and a few miles further on came to a walled compound fitting snugly into the hillside. Ahmed stopped, Abdullah at his side.

"This is my home, our home," he proclaimed. It was a solemn statement; he couldn't have been more proud had it been a declaration about a king's palace.

"Do you like my valley?" he asked Andrea.

"Oh, I think I'm going to love this place. Is anyone living in the house?"

Ahmed didn't answer; he had hardly heard her question, full of memories of the life he had lived here. As they entered the courtyard and dismounted, Andrea saw this was a very large compound, though she could barely make it out in the darkness–two houses, stables, and other areas.

The whole compound was redolent of wildflowers mixed with what Andrea recognized as oregano, mint, basil, and more; the aroma was intoxicating–Andrea immediately thought of what a lovely garden she could have. She turned to Ahmed. "Your mother must have loved this garden."

"Yes my love, just as your mother loves hers." The three of them explored the larger house: empty, plain–carpets and cushions would soon fix that.

"A lot of work to be done here," said Abdullah.

"We will start tomorrow," said Ahmed.

"Abdullah, where is it?"

"What?" asked Andrea.

"It was stored in the bedroom closet," Abdullah answered.

Andrea followed them as they went in search of something that must be very special. She saw them carrying out of a closet a long wooden bench. Ahmed's expression was one of joy and relief; when he saw her, he laughed.

"This is the lion bench. My father had it made especially for our family. We used to put it in the courtyard for guests. Look at the carvings."

Even in the dim light of an oil lamp, Andrea could see it was magnificent, the back depicting fierce lions with flowing manes, the sides carved into lionesses with their cubs, and of course the feet were lion feet.

"I've never seen anything like it. It's beautiful!" said Andrea.

"It signifies the Panjshir Valley's spirit–the Valley of the Five Lions. It needs a little cleaning and waxing; it's a possession our family will always cherish."

"Ahmed, what about Kabul, and what about my work at school?"

"I'm finished with Kabul. I've already resigned–we'll go back to make it all official and pack the few things we have, then this is where we'll live."

No more school, no children to teach, to sing to, to dance with, to play, to comfort–*how can I just leave them?*

Ahmed saw the look of dismay on her face; he knew how much the school meant to her. "Andrea, my sweet, in the morning you will find we have a school here and a clinic for our people. You and I will have much to do." He laughed. "You'll have a whole new career, no fighting!" He suddenly gave her a bear hug, picked her up and carried her to one of the bedrooms, full of the ever-present dust. Abdullah came in to report on general conditions in the compound.

"Nothing has been stolen or vandalized; the Russians somehow missed us, perhaps thanks to Massoud."

They said goodnight to Abdullah, wrapped themselves in a clean blanket, and, excited by the prospect of all that lay ahead, talked about their plans. A real home.

"We must rise very early, Andrea. Go to sleep," Ahmed said as she chattered about cleaning, decorating. Decorating? He put his hand over her lips. "Shhh, chatterbox, go to sleep."

She brushed his hair out of his eyes as he looked down at her; it was a simple gesture telling him all he needed to know.

Andrea scrubbed, banishing as much dust as she could, along with the ubiquitous bugs and fearsome spiders, while Ahmed and Abdullah brought in their few pieces of furniture. They wanted to make both houses clean and presentable for what now would be a true Afghan family unit–Rashid, his wife Ramina and their two boys; Soraya, her husband Abdul and their two children. Abdul's three brothers had died at the hands of the Taliban, his parents killed when their house was bombed; he missed his family, but felt fortunate to be part of this new one. Andrea and Ahmed had said their official farewells to Kabul, bringing the rest of their belongings back in an old Jeep they bought. Andrea was excited, happy, and doubtful about life in the Panjshir: a different life, a different challenge; she confessed her doubts and fears to Ahmed.

He told her, "There will be challenges, my darling, but our joys will be greater than our challenges, *'insha'allah* (God willing). This is a wilder place than Kabul," he laughed, "but I think it suits you; we'll be happy here."

"Will you protect me, Sir Galahad?" she teased.

"Of course, that is my purpose in life," he responded, smiling.

And that was pretty close to the truth. So Andrea swept and cleaned and dreamed, hoping Abdullah and Ahmed could get the generator working soon–she wanted electricity, not smoky oil lamps. Abdullah came in as she finished scrubbing.

"Don't walk over here!" she ordered. "I'm almost finished." He walked gingerly across the clean floor to the kitchen, stepping on the dry tiles, looking at Andrea kneeling on the floor, sleeves pushed up and hair tied back with a bandana. Yes, he loved her as he would a daughter; he wasn't sure how she had won him over–*oh, she has a way about her, that sly innocent wildness will never leave her.*

"You've done a good job, Andrea; everything looks very nice. This will be a home you'll love; everything will work out well, I know."

A new sense of appreciation prompted her to give him an affectionate kiss on the cheek. "You're the kindest, wisest person I know, next to my grandfather!" she exclaimed.

Abdullah smiled, happy to be the recipient of Andrea's impulsive gesture. She stopped her work, went outside into a sunny, almost warm March day and sat on the lion bench, gazing at the dancing river below, the mountains on the other shore, and laughed. *Afghanistan. I live in Afghanistan. Sometimes I can hardly believe it!*

# XVI. Transitions

I cannot let her do this, thought Ahmed. This dance, this public performance, will put her at risk for...at the least, disapproval, or–what he feared most–assassination. She just doesn't understand the danger. There are enemies who want to bring me down–Rasoul, Tabibi, Rahim, perhaps even CIA, investigating Jeff Scott's disappearance. I can't be sure... His analytical mind was paralyzed by a numbing anxiety. But the dance Andrea had choreographed after her encounter with the old Uzbek burned in her mind–she had to do it. If...if...Ahmed said yes.

"No." was his answer. She needed support, and Nuria provided it, after Andrea's detailed description of the dance to Ahmed, emphasizing the children's part in the endeavor. After all, she explained, this would be a much-needed tribute to Afghans, and the first use of the rebuilt Children's Theater.

"Ahmed, you know music and poetry is like food to Afghans," exhorted Andrea, and Nuria agreed with enthusiasm. The two of them stood before Ahmed, careful not to seem too anxious as they pointed out the benefits of their plan, cautiously sidestepping the risks.

It took Ahmed two days of making sure he could provide enough security before he agreed. Andrea's talent could not be denied–and he did love to show her off on the right occasion. Back in Kabul once more, she gave the excited children their assignments; they knew what they were doing was very important. All of the students had helped paint the backdrop in Afghan sunset colors with snow-capped mountains in the background. As they rehearsed their songs, flags were placed on the stage–Afghan and American. Before a closely monitored and guarded crowd that spilled out onto the street, boys and girls sang, Nuria directing them, to the Eastern music. I'm so proud of them, thought Andrea, as they danced perfectly and played their flutes.

The Afghans cheered and clapped with an enthusiasm and joy denied to them by the Taliban, bringing anticipation to fever pitch. Nuria and her helpers had no sophisticated sound system or Broadway orchestra in the pit, only industrial-strength speakers. They began to broadcast the CD Andrea had found, a mix of Western, Middle Eastern, and African music strongly evocative of Afghanistan. It started with a slow, seductive beat. A woman's figure appeared dressed in black, face veiled, arms crossed hugging her body, dancing to the hypnotic movement. As the music's tempo quickened, her arms unfolded, reaching out as if to beckon the onlookers, welcoming them to shelter and safety. The music's pace picked up, turning her gentle dance into a command. As she made ever faster spins, three Afghan fighters appeared holding an ancient scimitar. She seized the sword, spun it above her head; the metallic drumbeats became louder, her spins faster until she returned the sword to the soldiers. This time she was offered a Kalashnikov. The music held the watchers spellbound as the figure in black held the AK 47 above her head, spinning it from one hand to the other, brandishing it in a threat. The music reached a dramatic climax; the black clad figure ended the dance at the same time, holding up the Kalashnikov in triumph. The stage became dark; just as a roar erupted from the crowd, a flash of white came from the darkness. A flowing white *burqa* presented the Kalashnikov in a sacrificial gesture to the fighters, and the supplicating hands of a woman emerged from the *burqa*. The roar from the audience stilled to a stunned silence, then turned into applause as the children came on the stage and sang again.

Andrea did not reappear. Her passionate, soul-searching dance was not meant to elicit praise; it was her paean to Afghanistan. The American and Afghan government officials in the audience were astonished by the performance; Andrea was not aware of their presence–neither was she aware that Lauren Bannister had been watching the dance, her assignment to the states scheduled for the next day. Lauren left the theater with a great sense of relief at having escaped Andrea's fury.

Ahmed took no time to gauge the tenor of the crowd and reaction from the large number of Afghans milling about; he took Andrea from the theater and drove to the old safe house just outside Kabul, silent the whole way. Andrea waited for him to say something–did he disapprove, did he like it, hate it, what? As soon as they parked in the courtyard, he hurried her into the house and stood before her.

"Why do you do this to me? Why do you drive me crazy trying to keep you safe!"

She faced him, mouth open in dismay. "I didn't do anything to you. I danced for Afghanistan, for your country. It was my gift to you, to Afghans, to myself. I never dreamed you would hate what I did!" and tears welled up in her eyes.

"No, Andrea, you don't understand! Your dance was an amazing thing; it was beautiful, you were wonderful. I've never seen anything like it. But I wasn't sure if you would be celebrated or assassinated! And with the Americans there, well...."

Andrea threw her arms around him, irrepressible humor surfacing. "Good God," she laughed, "Do you think I've created an international incident?"

Ahmed responded with a hint of a smile, "Don't be too sure."

Andrea couldn't suppress her laughter. "I wonder what the boys in Arizona would say–I should send them a videotape!"

"You have a very strange way of putting everything in perspective. I might appreciate the humor more if you didn't drive me crazy. Speaking of protection, your official protectors, the guards I assigned to you, took part in the production that put you in danger– and without my knowledge! They'll regret..."

"No, Ahmed, no! They're innocent; they really thought they were protecting me. Please don't punish them, they're just..."

"Oh I know what they are–useless. I'm sure their idea was to 'get into show business' as you call it. Impossible, impossible. Andrea," He looked at her on the bed; her eyes were closed. Asleep. It was here in this very room that he first made love to her–a "wild creature," he had called her. He tucked the blanket close around her, walked out into the darkness, and prayed to Allah.

It was almost dawn; Ahmed said prayers, then woke Andrea, who was surprised he had not wakened her for prayers, but grateful he had given her a little extra time to sleep.

"Come, Andrea, get dressed, we are leaving."

"What's the hurry?"

"I want you away from Kabul as soon as possible."

"But I wanted to see Nuria and...."

"Not today–another time. We're going back to Panjshir, away from prying eyes and wagging tongues."

Yes, she thought, I really don't want to be questioned or interviewed. Ahmed's right. "I'm all ready, sweetie, let's go home."

Repercussions from the performance at the Children's Theater ranged from a mild scolding by Afghanistan's Pashtun president, "You must keep your wife under your thumb," followed by a grudging compliment, "she is a beautiful dancer, almost Afghan," to requests from the Kabul press corps for interviews and photographs, to a comment from Mahmood, "what a lucky man you are, Ahmed." The Americans didn't quite know what to make of it all; while it could possibly serve as a public relations coup, it also seemed to emphasize Afghanistan's determination to stay independent of foreigners. But there were no threats by Afghans, only a curiosity about this American woman who chose to make Afghanistan her home.

In the Panjshir Valley, she was "Andrea, wife of Ahmed," who rode fast and free on her Arabian, telling Ahmed, "I swear Buttercup knows Panjshiri air is superior to Kabul's!"

Ahmed would laugh at her, "I'm sure he does. Time for school, Andrea go."

Narda's school, smaller than the one in Kabul, had the usual limited resources. It was Ahmed, this time, who bought supplies. Andrea taught English, geography, and music appreciation. She knew it was not enough. Nuria had expected more from her, and she had expected more of herself. *I told Ahmed I was going to help women– as though I could change a system hundreds of years old! He took my speech for what it was, arrogance, with nothing to back it up. But I did mean it–I can't just let it go!* A whisper of a word stole into her mind–patience. Not a quality she possessed.

The phone call came on a soft spring day in April. As soon as she picked up the phone, Andrea knew. Her mother's calm, slightly hoarse voice told her, "He's gone, Andrea. I'm sorry."

Andrea took a deep breath, then answered, "I'm sorry for you, Mom; are you all right?"

"I guess, yes, I will be."

"Mom, do you want me to come? I can be there tomorrow if you need me, really."

"No, Andrea, there's nothing to be done; I'll be fine." After a moment's hesitation, she said, "I want you to know that I've decided to sell the ranch. Billy wants to buy it. Most of the money will go to the reservation, but I want to donate a good bit of it to your school."

Andrea was trying to absorb the news–Billy, owner of Paloma–well, why not?

"That's very generous of you, Mom, but where will you go? You may need that money."

"No, I have enough of my own; I've done very well with the paintings and pottery. And I'll move in with your grandfather. He can use the help; it's where I belong now…" Her voice trailed off a bit.

"It sounds as though your plans were made some time ago."

"Yes, I've been thinking about these things since your father became ill."

"Good for you. Is anyone with you?"

"Yes, Naiche, John and your grandfather, and Juanita is coming soon."

"Aunt Juanita is never there when you need her," said Andrea, then realized she herself was guilty of the same thing. "Oh, Mom, I should be there too."

"No, Andrea, don't come to Arizona. But there is something important you can do for me."

"Whatever you need."

"Your father's cremation was yesterday. We had a brief ceremony and I have his ashes. His last request was that the ashes be scattered in Ireland, in the Sperrins, and….well…."

"Oh, Mom, don't tell me he asked that I do the deed!"

"Andrea, don't talk that way."

"Sorry, but you could ship the ashes to Ireland and get one of his old buddies to throw them out there."

"Andrea, please!"

"Sorry again; but it's not fair, to me or to you...I never wanted to go back there, but...oh God, he's done it again."

"What do you mean?"

"Nothing."

"Andrea, I loved your father. I knew about him, but...well, he was always faithful to me, generous, he understood me."

Andrea had to let it go.

"You don't need to do it immediately."

"If it has to be done, I'd better not wait. I want Ahmed with me; now would be a good time for him, so...I'll call you back to confirm the arrangements. What about meeting us in Ireland? Don't you want to be there?"

Wenonah's voice was sure. "No, I don't." So here it was–she would, once again, follow her father's order. But this would be the last time.

A terrible sadness filled Andrea as she released his ashes. In a furious cloud, they stormed over the valley below, a sudden wind scattering them in every direction. With Ahmed behind her she stood silent for a long moment, then turned to face him. He took a handkerchief out of his pocket and wiped the tears from her eyes.

"Are you all right?"

"Yes, Ahmed, it's time to go."

He held her in a tight embrace–*she's too composed.*

"He loved you, Andrea–I know you must have loved him."

Yes, she had loved him without question; her volatile character matched his. She never knew the depth of his torment; he was unable to acknowledge it even to himself. But all that had passed.

"Once upon a time. When I think of what could have been...and never was–I don't want to think about that anymore."

"He taught you lessons he learned in a hard life; not all of them were wrong. You have so many wonderful qualities–you're strong, loving, generous, and," he smiled, "a little crazy. Some of that came from your father."

"Crazy? Thanks! Oh I know what you mean, Ahmed, but I paid a terrible price. I would never allow a child of mine to be raised the way

I was."

A child of mine? "Andrea, are you....?"

"No, sweetie, we'll talk about that another time."

Indeed we will, thought Ahmed.

Andrea looked out at the Sperrins once more, a lifetime of tears welling up inside her; she turned to Ahmed, and let them all go. The tears soon dried; she gave a long sigh as she held her hands over her heart. Awestruck, she cried, "I feel so light!" and threw up her arms in a gesture of victory. She cried out, "It's called freedom–and it feels so good! Seeing his puzzled expression, she said, "What?" Was the frown on his face one of concern, consternation, or disapproval? "You do think I'm crazy, don't you? Dancing on his grave!"

"No, I understand, but Andrea, don't condemn yourself for loving him. It is all right."

"What makes you think I could love such an evil man?"

"He is part of you, his blood runs in your veins."

"Well, I don't love him, I don't."

Ahmed never believed her denial.

"I will officially end this in Belfast." She was determined to do it in spite of Ahmed's telling her the death of Jeremy Monaghan had long ago been resolved and placed in the "closed" file.

Inspector O'Toole was polite but firm after listening to Andrea's "confession." After all, there was no evidence; it was only in the mind of a ten year old, probably put there by her father. Patrick McAlister was the suspect in numerous assassinations and bombings, directly or indirectly, but he was an elusive suspect. No, Jeremy's murder was chalked up as one more in a long line of Patrick's victims.

"I'm sorry to speak of your father this way, but we can close the book on him now that you've told us of his death, and I recommend that you do the same. Thank you for your information. We wish you and your husband good day and Godspeed."

The plane climbed into the sky on a beautiful clear day; Andrea watched the birthplace of her father fade from sight. I'm really free now, she thought, savoring an almost giddy sense of relief. Though it was Patrick's evil work that first enclosed her in a nightmarish cell, her own mistaken sense of guilt kept her there until the night at Paloma when she remembered what actually happened. The guilt was gone. She knew none of it was her fault, but there was always an uncertainty in her heart about Patrick–like waiting for the other shoe to drop–finally it did. With sad regret, she left a country rich in its haunting beauty and vibrant people. "I will never come back," she told Ahmed.

⁂

Narda, Panjshir Valley–Under the August sun, Andrea, Soraya, and Ramina bathed in the cold river, laughing as they compared their husbands' faults and virtues. Soraya and Ramina's children, all under six, played in the courtyard, Abdullah watching them.

Abdullah was content. He was with the family of Haroun Sharif in the home that had been a happy place until Fara and Haroun had been killed. Now Haroun's children had families of their own; he smiled at the young ones bubbling over with insatiable curiosity and energy. Even their squabbles amused him, and the warm sun lulled him into a mellow, reflective mood. Only Ahmed had no children–*when, Andrea, when?* He had worried that she might want to follow a musical career after the performance; there was certainly talk of it in Kabul, but she never expressed any desire to do so as far as he knew, and he knew their personal lives very well. Her father's death seemed to put a period on a troubled chapter in her life; here she was, bathing in the river with her sisters-in-law, happy and satisfied with being an Afghan wife! Life was good, for now.

The sisters exchanged gossipy bits of news from Narda; Andrea washed her hair with the special shampoo from a shop in Kabul. All three of them had received a bottle of the expensive stuff from Rashid as a thank you for the elaborate meal they had prepared the day before. The sisters had spent the morning cooking, yet none of them appeared before the guests–*Mujahidin* commanders–who ate the food. Afghan custom kept them in the kitchen away from the men while Abdullah served the delicacies. It was Andrea's last personal encounter with *purdah*; in the evening she told the entire family she would no longer observe that custom. Wear the veil, dress modestly, respect her husband, okay, but she could not let herself be labeled a possession to be hidden away. Her announcement was met with resigned silence and a grudging acceptance. Things were changing, even in the Panjshir, and she was the first sudden rustling of wind before the storm. Soraya and Ramina were thrust in the forefront of her independence; they professed loyalty to tradition, while secretly waiting for the wind to sweep them along a new road.

Kabul was full of women asserting their independence; Nuria was one of them. After Andrea's dance, Nuria suggested Andrea might like to become more active with the women's organizations, perhaps start a group in Narda. She could even become a professional performer, opening up opportunities for women in the theatrical world. When Andrea answered her with a firm no, Nuria was surprised.

"I thought you, of all people, would help advance women's status in Afghanistan."

"Women will advance with or without me. I'll do my own thing, and if it helps other women, fine."

"That's a change in your thinking, isn't it?"

"Not really; the changes individual women make will eventually bring change to all the women here. I don't have any interest in a career, Nuria."

"Oh, I guess your handsome, aristocratic husband is your priority."

"Hell, yes," said Andrea. She had had enough of being told what she should want or what her motives were. Though the two liked and understood one another, the conversation created a distance they could not bridge.

Andrea reached for a towel, dried her hair, adjusted her clothing, and walked up the path to the house. What a nice day. She laughed to herself, seeing Abdullah with the children, like a doting grandfather, like Jack Redbird, she thought. I wish he were here, but he'd never leave Arizona. Then she remembered her secret; Ahmed would know tonight.

# XVII. Fulfillment

The August sky that evening produced a riot of colors colliding with the white-tipped mountains.

"It looks like another planet, Ahmed, just the two of us in another world where we can do what we want."

Ahmed laughed, "You're beautiful, but you're crazy."

"Okay, so it's just an incredible sunset, but every one is a gift, isn't it?"

"I can't deny that; I wish..." He broke off, wrapping the blanket around them. "Let's go in the house; we'll have a glass of tea."

"No, not yet, sweetie. I need to tell you something."

"What is it?" he asked, expecting a problem of some sort.

"I had a clever little speech ready, but now... I can't remember it... I know you'll be glad..." She took a quick breath as Ahmed prompted her.

"What are you saying, Andrea?"

"I'm pregnant."

"Pregnant? Pregnant?" He started to laugh, then shouted, "You are pregnant–what wonderful news. My wild child pregnant!"

"Ahmed, be quiet–everyone will hear you!" But he didn't care; he picked her up and spun her around, laughing. "If they didn't hear me, we'll go tell them now!"

"No, wait till tomorrow. Let it be our secret if only for tonight." Ahmed became quiet; "yes, for tonight," and he carried her into their bedroom. Ahmed couldn't contain his excitement; even after they had settled into bed for the night, he kept talking. "You will have a beautiful baby, we'll love him and teach him, and..."

*Him? It could, after all, be a girl.* Whatever, he already loved this

232

child. Andrea had closed her eyes, starting to drift into sleep.

"Andrea, I love you, I love you."

A murmured response came from Andrea, "Me too."

She awoke to an ecstatic Ahmed's "Good morning, my beautiful mother-to-be; almost time for prayers."

For a moment, she forgot she was pregnant. At first, she had been unable to believe the doctor when he confirmed it. Slightly amused at her doubtful, dismayed expression, he told her, "You are definitely pregnant. Does that make you a bit nervous or fearful? Quite understandable. America would be a safer place to give birth, granted."

"Oh no, doctor, it's not Afghanistan that I'm nervous about, it's me. There are so many things I'm involved with, and...well, I never dreamed...a baby!" Andrea had struggled for words that might soften her first response to the news. "I know Ahmed will be thrilled. And I..."

The doctor had smiled, "You will change. Children are the greatest blessing one can have; you will know that when your baby's born." He had said it in such a matter-of-fact way that Andrea left feeling he must be right. After all, how could she be shocked? She knew when she stopped taking the pill what the results would be. So she put the doubts behind her. *Well, Laura, here I am, going to have a baby–imagine! I'll do the best I can.*

Ahmed knew her too well to believe she was happy about the pregnancy, but he knew she would love this baby. "I will be with you when the baby comes," he told her.

"Oh, that's so sweet, Ahmed, and so un-Afghan."

But he didn't care; he would do what he thought best, Afghan or not.

233

*Dear Mom,*

*How are you? Sit down; I have big news. I AM PREGNANT! Can you believe it?! I can't–it doesn't seem possible, but here I am, two months along, in a state of bewilderment and anxiety. As you can imagine, Ahmed is thrilled. So thrilled he's driving me crazy. Ramina and Soraya give me all kinds of advice–I don't know why everyone is so attentive. I think they don't believe Americans can handle it as well as Afghans. In my case maybe they're right. Babies! I just pray I'll feel like a mother– just now I don't know; I do know this is what Ahmed wants most in the world; he'll be such a good father–oh–you'll be a grandmother! I'm feeling fine. HELP!*

*Love, Andrea*

*P.S. Say hello to the boys for me–they'll get a charge from hearing this news–I can hear them now!*

Her mother promptly replied to the letter, saying she was coming and would stay for the summer if it was all right. Was there a spot for her potting? As time went by, Andrea felt the entire family was consumed with her pregnancy, always watching her.

"Ahmed," she said, "I feel like I'm losing control–my mother's going to be here for four months–four! Suddenly she wants to fuss over me, along with Soraya, Ramina and Abdullah–and you, you're the worst, my darling husband, worrying because I actually feel fine, and don't have any morning sickness. You won't let me ride Buttercup–ooh damn, I feel smothered!" she exclaimed.

No one heard her loud protest; Ahmed just hugged her. "Love me?" he asked after a few minutes.

"Endlessly," she said, grateful for the comfort of his arms.

Ahmed awoke thinking, as he did much of the time, of the life inside Andrea. His child; his son?

She opened her eyes, still half asleep, and asked, "Ahmed, why are you awake? It's not even dawn yet; is anything wrong?"

"No, just waking early." He kissed her slightly swollen belly, her still sleepy eyes, her lips. "I wonder what he or she will look like, hmm, a curly-haired redhead?" and he chuckled at the idea of an Andrea lookalike with her rebellious temperament.

"No, Ahmed. This baby is going to look exactly like you, a brown-skinned, black-haired, dark-eyed boy." It sounded like a refrain from an old spiritual.

Though Andrea still didn't feel like a mother, her pregnancy went well, until she had a sonogram at Kabul Hospital. She had gained what she felt was an extraordinary amount of weight; even the imperturbable Dr. Faheem seemed concerned. In her sixth month, Andrea was shocked when she accidentally caught a glimpse of herself in the mirror, but still she ate ravenously, promising herself she would stop tomorrow. At the hospital, Ahmed instructed the doctor not to reveal the baby's sex to himself or Andrea; all they wanted was to be sure the child was all right. The two of them nervously waited to hear the results.

When Dr. Faheem appeared, smiling, they knew it was good news, but they were unprepared to hear his triumphant statement, "No wonder you're big–you are going to have twins!"

"Oh, no!" exclaimed Andrea.

"Praise be to Allah!" said Ahmed.

Wenonah came in March, unfazed by the inoculations against disease, the still-prevailing dangers in Afghanistan, a culture foreign to her, or her scant knowledge of Dari. Those things she could handle, but it took all her strength to suppress her nebulous fears and insecurities. She was determined to banish them. She did seem to be reborn. Andrea needn't have worried about being fussed over. Her mother was quite content with the sisters, with the children, and with Abdullah. They came from the same generation, Abdullah fifty-three, Wenonah forty-eight, and shared similar interests and points of view, Wenonah remarking to Abdullah one day after a long discussion of world history, "Why, Abdullah, you're a wonderful collector of obscure information!"

"I've often thought of writing a book about tribes, and the similarities of all of us. I have read books about tribes, but they were, I felt, superficial. It would give me great pleasure to learn more about Indian life in America."

Wenonah said, "I could give you some very good books about the Apaches. But you should stop thinking and start writing."

"Ah, my writing would be looked upon as too old-fashioned, I'm afraid. Kabul University, or what's left of it, still has papers I did write; perhaps I'll compile them and add new observations." Abdullah was happy to have Wenonah as a friend; she was a lively, satisfying companion. Ahmed and Andrea were amazed at Wenonah's revitalization, and Andrea attributed the change to the death of her father. Free at last! she thought.

"Mom, you can stay as long as you want. I'll need a lot of help with twins. My God, twins, can you believe it?"

"I don't know, Andrea," sighed Wenonah, "this country is so, so......"

"Beautiful?" prompted Andrea, knowing that was not the word her mother was struggling for, in her effort to be positive.

"Yes, it's beautiful," Wenonah acknowledged, "but it's so-raw," she said slowly, hoping not to offend, but unable to contain her new transparency.

April 4: With Sima, the midwife, attending, and Dr. Faheem standing by, Andrea gave birth to twin boys who, as she predicted, looked exactly like Ahmed. Her labor lasted ten hard, painful, hours, and Ahmed stayed with her, encouraging her, patting her face with a cool cloth, and praying silently to Allah. At last it was over. A triumphant Dr. Faheem presented the babies to her. "Here you are, Andrea, two healthy boys; each weighs a little over six pounds, a good size for twins. You've done well. Praise be to Allah."

There had been a moment when the babies were not positioned well, requiring Dr. Faheem's skilled manipulation. Sima breathed a sigh of relief; rarely did she need a doctor's assistance with her deliveries, but she gave thanks to Allah that he was attending this birth. Ahmed was beside himself with relief and joy.

"I'm so proud of you, my love. They're perfect."

"They look like you–now I've got three beautiful Afghans!"

They all laughed.

"A happy day," said Wenonah. In obedience to the Qur'an, Ahmed held each child and said the first words spoken to his sons.

As Andrea took the babies in her arms, she immediately experienced the unique love of a mother for her children. It wasn't exactly a Norman Rockwell moment, but close enough for Andrea, who embraced the scene in front of her: Dr. Faheem and Sima exchanging information and opinions, Soraya, Ramina, and Wenonah at the foot of her bed chattering away in Dari and English, Ahmed repeating how proud he was of her and the babies in her arms, sleeping in the most blissful moments of their lives. She couldn't help thinking of Laura, letting the sadness wash over her. Ahmed leaned over to kiss her. "I love you," he said. "Do you want me to chase them all out?"

"In a little while."

June: The two-month-old twins were squalling, hungry again.

"Babies are very demanding," laughed Andrea. Wenonah sat across from her, feeding Sadiq a bottle while Andrea nursed Hajii.

"Yes," acknowledged Wenonah, "these are hungry little angels. You know, Sadiq looks like a little Apache."

"Don't let Ahmed hear you say that," joked Andrea.

"Oh, I know they look like Ahmed, but after all, they do have Apache blood, too."

"Umm, plus Irish."

"Don't hold that against them, Andrea," she said. They'll make good storytellers, or poets."

"Right. I can't imagine what they'll choose to do...I just hope they won't be soldiers."

"When is Ahmed coming back?"

"Tonight, I think. He hates being away from them for too long."

Hajii had gotten his fill and was asleep; Andrea burped him and put him in his cradle. "Here, Mom, I'll take him," and she gathered Sadiq in her arms, giving him a kiss.

"They're so sweet. You've been a big help to me; I'm going to miss you. Abdullah's really going to miss you!" she said, a sly smile on her face.

But Wenonah resisted all pleas to stay–Jack Redbird wanted her in Arizona. Her work in Afghanistan had fulfilled a deep longing to widen her world, and the paintings and pots inspired by Narda with their Afghan designs were unlike anything she had ever done. Wenonah invited each family in the compound to choose something, donating the rest to a shop in Kabul where the proceeds were used for refugees and widows and children.

"Next time, we could do this on a bigger scale," she told Andrea. Business will boom when the tourists come."

"Tourists? That'll be the day!"

"Yes, it will come; I feel sure."

That evening, Ahmed walked into the bedroom, coming upon a scene that stirred his heart. Andrea was holding the babies, singing a lullaby to them, "Sleep well, my babies, dream as you rock on that misty sea…" She looked up at him, smiling, "I think they're asleep for the night; I'll put them down now."

Ahmed kissed her and said, "No, let me." She handed Hajii to him, then Sadiq, after he had settled Hajii in the cradle. "My precious jewels. I love you," he said.

She smiled, her thoughts in another place. "I think of Laura a lot these days. I never thought…" she started.

"Ah, that the wild party girl in New York could imagine having a child? I think she's grown up a little!"

Andrea gave Ahmed a half-amused, half-scolding look, silently cursing the second video her mother gave her when they met in Bonn. Wenonah had meant it for Andrea as a fond remembrance of the days in New York–Laura, John, and friends celebrating a birthday–Andrea dancing to the music of a wild rock group. What Ahmed saw was a teenage American girl living a life foreign to him.

Andrea replied, "Enough to understand these are two little miracles. Ahmed, did your mother sing to you?"

"Yes, she loved music; I don't remember the lullabies."

"Are there Afghan lullabies? I mean, every culture has its lullabies."

"Just sing your American ones; it doesn't matter."

March 2004: Not quite a year old now, the boys were the joy of Andrea's life. They did indeed look exactly like Ahmed, a subject of delight for Andrea and the entire family, and she loved teasing Ahmed about it.

"They have your good looks, these little Afghans–beautiful, just like you!"

"Men are not beautiful, Andrea. I wonder if they're going to be as stubborn and disobedient as their mother!" Probably, she thought. She knew Ahmed was pleased that Hajii and Sadiq were images of him, and wasn't surprised when Ahmed told her, "Andrea, I want more children, another baby."

*Oh hell, I'm not ready; it's too soon.* "Ahmed, they aren't a year old yet..."

"There will never be a better time. Have you been taking those pills?"

"No, I was going to..."

"Please don't, my love." He said "please," a courtesy most Afghan men would not extend to a wife, but it was just a word. Andrea knew it was a command, a gentle one, but an order none the less.

"Must I obey my lord and master?" she teased.

"It's the most loving command I could ever give you. Trust me, my darling."

It was one of those moments of reality that brought her up short; this was not an easy world she had chosen. "Well, I hope it won't be twins again. I'm the one who has to do all the work–they don't call it labor for nothing, Afghan!"

Ramadan and the feast days of Eid-L-Fitr had been a trial for Andrea, coming as they had in her eighth month of pregnancy. She was finally back on track, ready to give birth any time this month. Unexpected memories of Christmas in Arizona stole into her mind, and the mild December evening beckoned her outside. She sat on the lion bench, contemplating the sun setting the snow-covered mountains on fire. All was quiet, prayers were over, Panjshiris settled down in the adobe houses, soft gleams of light could be seen here and here. It was almost a Christmas scene, this quiet December night. And not too far away was the country where Jesus was born. Lulled into a different time, she started humming "Silent Night;" her song was interrupted by a howling wolf and a flute echoing a mournful tune. Held captive by the haunting beauty of Asia, she prayed this child would be as healthy as her almost two-year-old twins, and woke from her reverie to see Ahmed coming to bring her back to the house.

"It's too cold to be sitting out here, love."

"I know. Merry Christmas, sweetie."

Laura was born on December 27th. Andrea's labor this time was short, only four hours. There was no question about what to call this baby; it had to be Laura. Though the little girl had Ahmed's eyes and black hair, her face was a blend of Andrea and Ahmed; her exotic, slightly Asian look gave a hint of the adult beauty. Sima eased the baby out of the birth canal and Soraya and Ramina cleaned the infant, presenting her to Andrea and Ahmed. The three sisters-in-law had helped one another with all their pregnancies, which resulted so far in a total of eleven children in the family compound. Rashid boasted that his family would be the largest; Ramina was pregnant with their fifth child, and she decided it would be the last. Soraya was satisfied with her four; neither of them wanted to submit any further to Afghan tradition in this aspect of their lives.

As soon as Sima pronounced the baby safe and healthy, she left to help another life into the world, this tall, strong sixty-something who had the worn, weathered look of most rural Afghan women, and the commanding presence of one who was expert at her job. Dr. Faheem was unneeded this time, thank God. If Ahmed was disappointed at the birth of a girl, that changed as soon as he held her in his arms, enchanted with her beauty and contentment.

Cold and snow seldom deterred Afghans, and this day was no exception as Rashid waited in the Jeep while Ahmed said goodbye to Andrea and the twins. In the frozen courtyard, Ahmed lifted the boys in his arms and kissed them. They gave him their usual enthusiastic wet kisses, babbling baby phrases to him and squirming and gesturing in all directions. Ahmed laughed at their happy antics; then he felt Andrea's eyes upon him, studying every move of this scene between father and sons. He looked at her–such sadness in her eyes. Time to leave. He put the twins down, reached out for her and kissed her. "Tears, Andrea? Don't cry. I've had to leave you before, why so sad?"

"I miss you already; I can't wait for you to come back. How long did you say?"

"I don't know–much depends on the weather."

"How inconsiderate of the president to summon you in this weather!"

"I must go."

"Ahmed, please stay safe."

"Of course. I love you. *Allahu Akbar.*" He kissed her once again and strode over to the Jeep. "*Natars*–don't worry–he called back, "everything will be all right." Everything will be all right–hah! That well worn Afghan phrase translated to "only God knows what the next disaster might be." Her intuition told her this wasn't an ordinary mission. But there was nothing more she could do. Andrea looked resentfully at the dense snow falling, picked up her sons, and went into the house to feed Laura.

The brothers arrived at their destination, but it was not the palace of the president. Rashid waited for Ahmed's signal, but it didn't come. What had happened? One more minute, and he would go in. Then Ahmed appeared, running to meet him.

"Ahmed, what's going on?" Rashid stared at his brother in alarm.

"Be quiet, Rashid. Let's go–now," he ordered.

They scrambled down the steep ridge so fast they were slipping over the gravel and stones; Rashid lost his balance and fell, cursing, irritated with Ahmed's lack of explanation. Once on level ground, they piled into the hidden Jeep; Rashid flashed angry eyes at Ahmed but said nothing. Ahmed drove full-speed in the direction of Dowshi. As they bounced along the rock strewn road, they made a sharp turn and just missed slamming into the back of a disabled truck. The driver and his teenage helper were on the ground, grappling with a broken axle. Ahmed and Rashid resigned themselves to helping so everyone could continue on their way; there was no room for them to pass without falling over the cliff into the river below.

"We will fix it, we will fix it!" the truck driver cried in desperation when he saw the two heavily armed *mujahidins*. From the jumble of old parts in the back of the truck, he produced a spare axle which might give them a few more miles before it gave out. In the truck, passengers were crammed against one another, immobile, waiting in typical Afghan acceptance of disaster. Ahmed and Rashid got down on the ground with the driver, all pounding the axle into place, making sure the wheels were firmly seated. Finally, both vehicles were on their way; Ahmed passed the truck when they came to a wider stretch of road. They traveled the remaining distance to Dowshi without conversation, Ahmed deep in thought and Rashid perplexed by his brother's behavior.

When Ahmed pulled up near a village *chaikhana*, he said, "Rashid, I know you don't understand, so listen, I will tell you. Today was the day Rasoul was to pay with his life for betraying me at Mazar. I saw no guards–there he was, sitting outside, no one with him. I had him in my sights, it was going to be an easy kill. But something strange happened. He tried to rise from his seat–he could barely move. I saw a sick old man whose days were almost over, such a change in a few years. Then–I hardly know how to tell you–Papa's face appeared before me. He was very sad, his lips formed the words 'You do not have to kill this man, he is too near death–do not do this.' "

Rashid gasped in shock. Ahmed had never been one to believe in visions or dreams. "Ahmed, you were imagining this, this vision. Perhaps you were seized momentarily by fear or pity." Rashid knew immediately this wasn't so, yet to believe their father appeared and spoke was incredible.

"I know how it sounds; I still can't settle this in my mind, but I know it happened. I couldn't kill Rasoul. I've been trying to understand it. Anyway, killing a dying man is not very satisfying. We always had to fight, to kill, you and I, but it's a waste of…of our abilities. Now I wonder if there is a different plan, for me at least."

"Ahmed, you are a commander…it's hard to change the course of one's life."

"Mine has already changed, the straight path has turned. I want to build, Rashid, I want to see forests again, gardens, fields one can cross without being killed or maimed by a land mine! I want my children to grow up safe, healthy, educated."

"You have a big vision, but there is still fighting to do."

"Yes, I will always carry the gun, but you are the warrior–one day you too will go a different way, perhaps."

Rashid laughed. "My brother, the politician! Remember, a politician's life can be more dangerous than a soldier's." He looked at Ahmed with a sly smile, "You will always be a *mujahidin!*" The brothers embraced one another.

"Ahmed, if Rasoul is as you say, Allah will soon take care of him one way or another."

"Yes. I think we should have a glass of tea together over the fire." They went into the *chaikhana,* an imposing pair, young, strong, handsome; *mujahidin* still, with the wary eyes of the soldier.

"Ahmed, oh Ahmed," Andrea cried as she held on to him, weaving her legs into his, insistent, begging him to make love to her.

"Andrea, it's too soon, and I'm not wearing a condom."

"I don't care, I need you now."

"But you didn't want to be pregnant again this soon."

"It doesn't matter." She had never been so demanding. It was impossible to deny her desperate need; he responded almost violently. Afterwards, she clung to him, needing his puzzled reassurances.

"Andrea, what's wrong? What are you afraid of?"

"I'm afraid of losing you. I wasn't sure if I'd ever see you again...I'm not worried about getting pregnant." She paused, then said, "I hope I am." A wave of tenderness overcame him as he remembered how hard waiting was for her; she couldn't come with him–there were children to care for at home.

"You want another baby, my darling?" he asked, surprised.

"Yes, it would be a sweet gift, Ahmed!" Tired, they settled into each other's arms for the night. Though they often laughed at themselves after making love, both had a reverence for the physical expression of it. As Ahmed told Andrea, "it's a treasure more precious than all the jewels of Afghanistan."

One more child was born to Andrea and Ahmed, probably out of the night of Ahmed's return from the aborted mission of revenge. He had rejected, that day, one of Afghanistan's firmest principles–*nang* (revenge)–and nine months later a son, Hamid, was born, a curly-haired baby with green eyes.

This time, Ahmed could tell Andrea, "He looks like my beautiful Andrea, except for his brown hair," to which she retorted, "Careful, Ahmed, there's Irish in him!"

"We'll love him whatever his ancestry," he said. She smiled at the idea that Ahmed could ever do anything but love his new son.

When Andrea complained about his long absences, Ahmed exclaimed, "Andrea, this is not the time to quit! We're eliminating more mine fields, rebuilding villages–they will even have proper sanitation systems! I am finally holding in my hand the money promised to us."

"What about the poppy fields?" she asked, knowing this was a sensitive issue.

There was an abrupt change in his demeanor. Though his anger was with himself, not her, it hurt all the same, as he answered her. "It's not money that will fix that."

The brief statement confirmed her fears. Assassination, intimidation, force–those were the words he left unspoken.

"It may take a long time, but I have plans–and I will be all right." There was nothing more she could say or do except pray for him.

Andrea's days were busy–children, household duties, school, clinic. She had become a wife and mother so quickly, she had had little time to reflect on her choices, but she seldom looked back. When her mother talked about the cousins and their families living their American lives, Andrea said, "Mom, did you think that's what I was supposed to do?"

"Oh no," said Wenonah, with a hint of resignation, "though sometimes all this seems a fantasy. Are you happy, Andrea?"

"Hmm, happy...yes, but more than that. My life is completely fulfilling; it's hard work, but I love having so much to work for. I love the garden; it's not as wonderful as yours, but I'm getting there. Strange how I feel close to God in the garden; I think I understand what it means to you. Then there are the kids–they're pure magic! Did you ever imagine me with children?"

"I imagined everything for you, Andrea," answered Wenonah.

"How about you, Mom?"

"I'm at peace, satisfied with life, especially my grandchildren."

"And Abdullah?"

Wenonah replied, "He's a dear friend, the best kind of relationship there is."

"Well, maybe, but the best part for me is...."

"Oh I know."

"Yes, of course you do," said Andrea. "When Ahmed comes home and smiles at me, I know where I belong."

Next to Ahmed and her children, music was Andrea's most consuming passion, automatic as breathing. She danced for the school children, danced for the family, danced for her sisters-in-law and danced for Ahmed, only for Ahmed, the voluptuous dance of desire. He devoured every movement and gesture, teasing her.

"Tell me what you like about me–my eyes, my smile, my arms holding you? Do you think I am handsome; do I make you feel good?"

She answered, "Yes to all of the above!" then escaped his lips and danced away. The game ended as Ahmed brought her to submission with nothing but the trace of a threat in his eyes and a smile holding the promise of ecstasy. She played the game as Ahmed wanted. He was fatuously content with the knowledge that she accepted his dominance. Aware she had the power to become a significant presence in Afghanistan, Andrea deferred to her husband out of love, and he knew it.

No matter how he resisted, America insinuated itself into his Afghan nature. On his visit to Arizona, Ahmed came to know Andrea's relatives, felt at home with her cowboys, and reached a new level of acceptance of the American forces in his country. Through contacts with some of their officers and even with a few of the media people who really knew Afghanistan, he began to appreciate the American viewpoint, and the American dilemma in dealing with the East. Even the music became familiar because of Andrea.

He overheard her one day say to Ramina and Soraya, "No more American music; your husbands don't approve-you'll get me in trouble!" and she put away the CDs.

"Too late, she's let the genie out," complained Rashid to Ahmed. "Now Ramina wants a CD player and American music!"

"Just set a few rules."

"Hah! Is that how you manage her?"

"She listens to me, no matter how independent."

"Not so independent after all," muttered Rashid.

Wenonah's visits evolved into a routine. Her winters were spent in Arizona, the summers in Afghanistan. Her Indian pots and paintings of the bazaars in Kabul sold well in the small shop on Chicken Street; the profits helped widows and orphans, giving her a satisfaction sweeter than any of her efforts in New York. Wenonah blossomed into a lively, more outgoing woman, different from the careful, quiet wife of Patrick McAlister. Her grandchildren enchanted her–such interesting combinations of Andrea and Ahmed.

The years passed so quickly–their life in the Panjshir was all Ahmed had promised. The twins were ten years old, full of adventure and daring. Laura was passionate about horses, and six-year-old Hamid, a mischief-maker, kept them all on edge. All about them was the old constant, change. The winds of the West were far-reaching; they swept in deceptive, gentle, inevitable waves over Afghanistan and beyond. Kabul became a blend of East and West; even the villages acquainted themselves with the practices and pleasures of the West. It was a tentative relationship. Afghanistan chose what it needed from the other world and discarded the rest, retaining its pragmatic style of Islam. Always fierce, always independent, it remained a dangerous land in tribal areas.

The government controlled most of Afghanistan, though the lawless Northwest Frontier of Pakistan was a continuing problem for both countries. Taliban moved freely between Pakistan and Afghanistan, stirring up trouble periodically. But the Army was becoming an effective force and the country was taking its small place in the world. Afghanistan still had goals–clean water, good roads, a modern sewage system, reforestation, elimination of land mines and poppy fields–big goals, big price tags. So much had been promised, more than had been received; the erratic progress discouraged Ahmed at the same time it encouraged him. But the center of his life was his family, the three sons his pride, and Laura his indulgence. In Laura's eight-year-old eyes, her father could do no wrong, especially when he presented her with her very own Arabian she named Nishka. When she first saw Nishka, Andrea started to cry.

"Mom, what's wrong?" asked Laura.

Ahmed knew; he put his arm around Andrea and wiped the tears. "My Buttercup."

Ahmed's reply to the administrator from Kabul was not enthusiastic. "You may ask Andrea." Andrea's talents, since the dance at the Children's Theater years ago, had been confined to home and school. Now they wanted her in Kabul again. For the tourists, thought Andrea. Tourists in Afghanistan! Her mother had predicted it, but who would have thought it possible?

When the minister of tourism explained what they wanted, she answered, "I'll think about it." A symbol of a new Afghanistan, thought Andrea; she was uncomfortable with the association, feeling she had no room to fail. One celebrity in the family was enough, and that was Ahmed, whose accomplishments went beyond *mujahidin* commander; he used his hands as well as his wealth to help rebuild his country. Afghans, skeptical about the beginnings of tourism, took so much pride in their homeland they put aside their doubts. And they needed the money.

"I guess I would be an attraction, the American wife of Ahmed," was Andrea's cynical assessment.

"Andrea, my love, no matter what the reason or what your decision is, I will honor it. You would make the museum sing–Abdur reciting his poetry to our music and your dance–all would bring in the tourists and the money. One performance. But it's your decision."

"Right." More like a command performance. Andrea smiled at her four rambunctious children. She had privately dubbed them The Motley Crew. In spite of her enthusiastic directions–"no, Hajii, smaller steps, Laura, gracefully, feel the beat, Sadiq, don't step on your brother! Oh Hamid sweetie, he didn't mean it, good, you're going to be great dancers"–there were protests ending in a sudden collapse on the floor amid much laughter. So it went–they watched their mother as she demonstrated the steps. Ahmed, unseen, stood at the doorway watching the scene, smiling, shaking his head in defeat and adoration at his wife and children.

Laura looked up, saw her father and cried, "Papa, come dance with us!" Ahmed bowed to their joyful enthusiasm and became one more dancer in the circle. One by one, the children left the floor to their parents, who danced to their private music.

Ahmed's disdain for foreigners never lessened, but he was there to welcome them. And now the Afghan dream was starting to come true, with this event in the exquisite museum that once held hundreds of precious treasures, some finally returned. The sunbeams that crept softly onto the statues and relics seemed to give them life and a voice that begged for the return of their companions. Andrea was surprised and relieved at the size of the crowd, remembering the verdict of a prominent American diplomat. "We must concentrate our efforts on countries that are important to our interests. Afghanistan is not important." *Asshole!*

"I knew they would come," said Ahmed, "not just the media people, but the true friends of Afghanistan, journalists who were with us in the old days, the ones who never forgot. Now they can see this country as it should be, as they imagined it a long time ago." He was triumphant. "Andrea, this is our moment, but it's just the beginning!" Then he whispered, "You danced beautifully, my darling, it was just right. Thank you." No criticisms, no resentment, no controversy. Best of all, no bombs, no war, just the usual skirmishes in the tribal areas– one goal fulfilled.

But another one haunted Andrea. "More years than we both have…" She decided it was time, patience be damned. The Loya Jirga would be meeting soon. Tossing scruples and caution to the winds, Andrea called Nuria whose voice on the phone was polite but cold. "Oh my God, Nuria, tell me you're not still pissed at me!"

"I'm surprised you've called me. What do you want?"

Andrea explained, charmed, cajoled and finally convinced Nuria to help her. Her friend's parting words were "be careful."

"Andrea, Andrea, what am I going to do with you?" Ahmed's response to her news concerning the Loya Jirga was not what she wanted to hear; with a well-honed sarcasm, she answered, "Oh, you could divorce me, have me stoned, put in prison!"

"Andrea, don't be ridiculous!"

"Ahmed, you speak to me as though I'm still the child I was when we met. I'm a woman with four children. I deserve your respect!"

"You have it; you know that. It's just that I sometimes see you as you were when we met and fell in love; it is with love that I speak to you."

"I'm sorry," she said, "but I wanted to let you know…"

"So now I know; there is no use worrying. Sleep well my darling." Oh how typical, she thought–don't worry. Irritated, she moved away from Ahmed.

"Don't turn away from me, Andrea."

Facing him again, she asked "Ahmed...do you believe in me?"

"Yes."

His quick answer made her uneasy but she decided to go ahead; that's the whole point, she thought–I shouldn't need to ask permission.

The Loya Jirga, the grand assembly, meeting to decide the direction of Afghanistan and the status of women. Oh God, I'm on the edge of the cliff. This is going to be harder than anything... Maybe it's not the right time... Maybe it will be bad for Ahmed.

Standing in front of two hundred formidable Afghan men and five brave women, she took a deep breath and spoke, "I am Andrea Sharif. I am here to urge you to give the matter of women's rights serious attention. I was born in America, but I'm an Afghan citizen. I have four children, one of whom is a daughter. I'm sure your daughters are precious to you. They are probably, like mine, intelligent, ambitious, talented girls who have the ability to help Afghanistan reach its full potential. Some may see their roles to be wives and mothers only. Others may want to be active in business, education, medicine, law, arts and sciences, or politics. All of them are valuable human beings who deserve the chance to work in those fields if they choose. Women are more than a means to procreate children, staying hidden behind walls serving husbands. If they wish to do that, that's fine. But they should be educated and free to choose. Countries that are prosperous are countries that welcome women's participation at every level. Those that don't are doomed to remain poor. Afghanistan needs modern health care and fresh ideas to promulgate its art, music, literature. Women are a valuable resource. Please don't dismiss them because that's how it's always been. Give them a chance. With their help, Afghanistan can be a prosperous, admired Muslim country."

There was no applause, only silence from the severe Afghan faces in front of her. No woman had ever been allowed to address men, who considered any concession to women a weakness in their rigidly masculine country. But Andrea had at last officially said what she felt to be the truth since entering Afghanistan years ago, and she had done it without Ahmed's help. Her gift to Afghanistan's women. Would it be a help, or hindrance to her cause? Nuria had used her reputation and influence to persuade the president to let her speak, putting herself in a somewhat precarious position.

"Thank you, Nuria," said Andrea.

Nuria smiled, "You told them the truth. It gives us hope. I think one day things will be different." They saw Ahmed coming toward them; he stood in front of Andrea.

"I'm proud of you, both of you." He couldn't resist a wry comment. "I hope that's your last gift to Afghan women."

"We'll see."

The news came from the Afghan Embassy in Baghdad. Mohammed Shah was dead. Ninety years old, his heart had given out; they were sending him home to be buried in his native Panjshir Valley. Ahmed was grateful that the two of them had finally forged an affectionate bond. Even Rashid, reluctant to allow himself to fall under Mohammed's spell, had given in. Before he had to leave for Iraq, the family had given their grandfather a joyous birthday party, a celebration that brought rare tears to Mohammed's eyes as he was surrounded by happy grandchildren.

He was with family for whom he had not made time. His love never nourished them, his experience never taught them, his values never enlightened them. He had left it all up to Abdullah. Mohammed, on that birthday, silently vowed he would do better by his family–but they must understand he had made money for them, and making money took time. In the ten years that followed, he could not keep the promise. But he left them wealthy.

# XVIII. Reminders

2019: More change came to the land of the Afghans in the fifteen years since the birth of the twins. Still, in places, an unruly country, it was no longer the "land of the ungovernable;" still Islamic, its politics were those of a democracy; unique unto itself, it welcomed trade, tourism and industry. The change in women's status slowly drifted over Afghanistan like a persistent breeze finding its unseen way into every hidden corner. It swelled with every bit of gossip, every new piece of information, every secret communication, every innate desire for freedom and fulfillment of a dream. Unlike wars of men, it was a natural force of stubborn persuasion.

Those were exciting years for Afghanistan—Ahmed could feel his parents' spirit inside him, leading him on a path that, once again, helped lift his country from the ashes. A younger generation rejoiced in the prosperity of the cities, the modernization of the villages, proper infrastructure and clean water. Where warlords once dictated life in the provinces, governors, mayors, citizen councils and laws—elected under a democratic process—prevailed. Andrea and Ahmed thanked Allah that their children were growing up without bombs disrupting their lives, but guns did remain in the hands of almost every male Afghan, and Andrea's children were no exception. Guns and horses were a basic part of their lives; knowing the mountains of the Hindu Kush was a vital lesson learned early in life. They were true Afghans who were well-educated, on their way to university degrees. Life was as it should be.

Ahmed's political efforts paid off almost in spite of himself. He persuaded foreign governments to give humanitarian aid and money to Afghanistan, convincing them their largesse would, in the long run, be to everyone's advantage. In the end it was economics that played the biggest part in changing Afghanistan. But Ahmed's work in eradicating the mine fields would be ongoing for years to come.

Andrea sometimes felt a perverse nostalgia for the wild days on the front. *Why would I long for those terrible times?* "Would I really want to be twenty again? No." Thoughts of her father still invaded her mind, leaving as abruptly as they came. He would love his grandchildren; *I wonder if he knows they all ride well, shoot straight, and work hard—ironic, just what he'd like, except they're Afghans.*

The compound was full of busy parents and spirited teenagers growing up to be participants in the government—builders, engineers, teachers, journalists, and in Hajii's case, officers in the Army. Hamid had his sights set on the same profession; he was eager to serve his required two-year term when he turned eighteen. Somehow he doubted his brother Hajii's commitment; Hajii was an adventurer, too free a spirit to be tied down to anything for long. Sadiq was the intellectual in the family. He knew he would become an architect after he served his time in the Army.

Hamid overheard his father say to Sadiq, "I hope you will stay in Afghanistan; work here. We need your talents."

Sadiq replied, "Yes, Papa, why would I go anywhere else?"

"Many young men go to America to make money."

"No, not me, maybe for a visit to Arizona, not to live."

Ahmed was content. His sons were doing the right things, although he wondered about Hajii—he had Andrea's willful, independent personality, perhaps a few of Patrick's genes, God help him.

Andrea waited inside the house, watching as Ahmed parked the Jeep and came to the door. Unable to contain her excitement, she opened the door and pulled him into her arms; his homecoming let her breathe easily again. As soon as Laura saw him she laughed, hugging him.

"Where are the boys?" asked Ahmed.

"At school, helping to fix the roof," Laura replied.

Seeing father and daughter together made Andrea wonder if her children knew how lucky they were to have such a father. Perhaps; most Afghan men put their families, especially children, first, but not all were as loving as Ahmed. His children admired him, loved him, respected him–they did not always obey him, but he was their example of what a man should be.

"And how is my Andrea?" he asked.

"Fine, now that you're home." He held her, anticipating making love to her when they were alone. Teaching, dancing, raising four children filled her days, but Ahmed was the center of her life.

Abdullah, nearing seventy, never ceased to be amazed they weathered so many storms in their relationship, that Andrea had become, in effect, Afghan. Their devotion to one another became stronger as time passed. Some things do work out, he thought. He was looking forward to Wenonah's arrival in a couple of months; she was his faithful supporter and critic since he had finished his writings. He pondered life's surprises as the call to prayer sounded throughout the village. Prostrating himself before Allah, he performed the ritual Muslim prayer, rising at its conclusion feeling refreshed and clean in the sight of God.

Ahmed found he learned as well as taught when he had a conference with his sons. It was his custom to meet with them when he returned from his political missions, sharing his knowledge with them; in turn, they talked about what was important to them at the time: school, careers, girls. Hajii, Sadiq, Hamid and Laura all rejected arranged marriages–how could Ahmed command them to observe a custom he himself had rejected? And this was a more liberal Afghanistan; marriages were still arranged, but it was common for young people to make such decisions for themselves.

Fourteen-year-old Laura had strong opinions about everything, especially love and marriage. "Mom, if I ever get married, I want to be in love, I want it to be romantic, the way it is for you and Papa."

Andrea smiled. "Do you know any romantic Afghans?"

"No." She laughed at the idea of a romantic Afghan. "I don't really know any Afghan boys my age, except for my cousins, and they're just a nuisance, always playing tricks on everybody."

"Hamid puts them up to it, he's full of mischief."

"Mom, what's in that box?"

Andrea stopped her cleaning and took a few minutes, thinking, before she answered. "Nothing out of the ordinary…but something very special to me."

"Tell me, tell me, oh ,Mom, show it to me."

"Well…I guess it's time." And she pulled out the long box, opened the wrappings very carefully, and held in her arms a dress, a black taffeta dress. "This is the dress your father bought for me when we were on our honeymoon-a dress from Paris."

Her eyes were far away, remembering the opera, the nightclub, Ahmed taking the dress off…Laura was speaking. "It's beautiful. It must have been very expensive; what a wonderful night you must have had in that dress."

Andrea laughed. "Yes."

"You and Papa love each other so much. That's the kind of relationship I'm going to have-no arranged marriage for me! Will you ever wear the dress again?"

"I don't know that I could still fit in it, or that I want to wear it, for that matter. But I think you should have it some day. Would you want it?"

"Yes! When I'm ready. Mom, you never told me how you met Papa."

In some surprise and dismay, Andrea realized her little girl had become a romantic teenager and a beautiful young woman. "I didn't know you were curious about it-you never asked before. I don't know if I …."

"Please, Mom. I want to hear the story."

"The story? You make it sound like a fairytale!"

"Maybe it is-so tell. Don't leave anything out!"

"Well, I'm not going to tell you all my secrets! But I'll tell you how we met." And she began. "Once upon a time in the dark of night on the Khyber Pass…"

Under the dress was something else-a book about Afghanistan, an old book written before the Taliban was in power. Andrea leafed through it, finding it uninteresting until she turned to a page of colored photographs. There she saw a picture of a group of *mujahidin* sitting outside a tent in a conference-a prominent commander of the time, and three very young soldiers with their guns. Ahmed! One of them was Ahmed, looking at his commander, gesturing, appearing to be explaining something important. He wore a turban and sported a full beard-young, innocent, transparently earnest and sincere, his dark, soulful eyes demanded attention. When she showed him the photo that night, he smiled. "How naïve I was, eighteen at the time-

I thought I was so important, always right...."

"Was that before you went to Paris?"

"Yes."

"After that you were less naïve!"

They laughed about his Paris story and remembered the night of the black taffeta dress; a sweet nostalgia warmed them as Ahmed smiled at her. In a moment of reflection, Ahmed was sobered by the thought he had taken away from Andrea one life and given her another; from the first minute of surrender to him, she stepped into a world of passionate extremes and left behind her American dream.

# XIX. Long Night's Watch

*In this darkest of nights*
*I'll share your deep silence.*
*Your tears are mine*
*Through our long, sad watch.*

Andrea was surprised one day to see Ahmed leading a stranger into the compound. As they walked toward the house, Andrea decided to greet them outside, glad she had prepared a larger than usual afternoon meal. The sun was blinding; she couldn't see who Ahmed's companion was, but he could see her.

As the harsh sunlight revealed her face, Mahmood took a long, hard look at a woman he loved. *Ah, Andrea, the one who talks to horses, mature, still beautiful, as unpretentious as ever. You were always in my dreams. Now I'm not so far from death, and I hold you in my heart.*

Andrea finally recognized him; though he had lost weight and turned into an old man, he still looked fierce, with his big black moustache and generous beard. And, she thought, he still has an eye for the ladies. She greeted him with a "*Salaam*, peace be with you. Are you well?"

"Well enough," he replied.

Ahmed knew Andrea didn't want to be alone with Mahmood, with good reason. Mahmood hungered for Andrea. Let him admire her–that is all he can do. The warlord was their guest. Rashid and Abdul's family joined Ahmed's and all shared the feast in the courtyard. As he left, Mahmood commented to Andrea and Ahmed, "We shall probably never meet again, my friends."

Andrea, who never lingered in conversation with Mahmood no matter how often they met, said softly in English, "God bless you, Mahmood." The old warlord gave her a sad smile.

"Thank you, Andrea, and you also."

That night as they made love, Andrea stroked Ahmed's battle-scarred body with a special tenderness.

Hajii and Sadiq ate a bit of their *kesmesh*-walnuts and dried fruit, washing it down with the cold river water. The twins were off on a small adventure; there was a particular cave they wanted to explore, said to hold ancient artifacts and gemstones. Their mother did not like the caves; she had taken shelter in them during the fighting with the Taliban, but she hated the claustrophobic atmosphere of caves. The twins never told her about the caverns they ventured into. They didn't go into the far reaches of the Panjshir; skilled, methodical climbers, they knew where the dangers lay. Finally, they reached the cave they had marked on their map, knowing their plotting might not be exact but sure it was close. If not, they had time to look into more possibilities. After an unsuccessful search of the cave, they went into others; no artifacts, no gemstones. All they found was old military hardware, notebooks, and binoculars.

"Oh, well," said Hajii, "there are a lot more places; we'll find treasure somewhere else. I'm going to go down a different way–this slope looks easier."

Sadiq turned to see Hajii start toward the descent; horrified, he yelled, "No, Hajii, that's mined! No, no, don't!"

Hajii had already started down when he heard Sadiq. He turned, startled, looked at Sadiq, eyes wide with fear, and tried to retrace his steps. It was too late. The look on his brother's face would haunt Sadiq the rest of his life. One moment Hajii was joking, alive, the next moment he was dead. Sadiq stood like a statue, mouth open, not believing the horror. His first impulse was to run to Hajii, but another instinct held him back–to run into a minefield would not help his brother now, to have both of them dead would be unbearable for his family.

He ran down the rough trail so fast he tumbled down the last part of it, and ran screaming toward the compound, to Abdullah, to his Uncle Abdul. Abdullah ran to him. "Talk, Sadiq, I can't understand you."

After a terrible moment, they understood, and did what needed to be done for everyone.

Under a sky of inappropriate beauty, Hajii's shrouded body was lowered into the grave, his head facing Mecca. Veiled in white, eyes blank, Andrea idly thought, my children have no grandfather; where was Hajii–oh yes, in the grave now, going to Mecca, Paradise; they pointed him there. *Hajii, Hajii, get out of there, stop joking.*

The men had bathed his body, shrouded him in white cloth, taken him to the mosque and prayed. Now he was in the grave; the lamps were lighted on the grave, prayers were being said, family was gathered. Hamid, Sadiq and Laura looked lost, stricken by their brother's death. Villagers, officials from Kabul had come, everyone was there. Wenonah, her face creased with worry and grief, stood beside Andrea, her arm around her, but Andrea pulled away; she was in her own dark world. Where was Ahmed? Over with the men.

No! no! no! she had been saying over and over since it happened– *say it enough and it'll be true;* no, Hajii couldn't be dead in that grave. Not all the prayers were in Dari, why, there was Matthew McCauley from Ireland, saying something in Gaelic! What's he doing here?

That's right, he had been working in Kabul. The Irish tenor lifted his voice in song–"Danny Boy"–Andrea become aware of what was happening. She walked over to join Matthew in the last chorus of "Danny Boy." Their voices blended, his strong, hers clear at first, wavering near the end. As she started back to join the women, Abdullah came to her side and led her to stand beside Ahmed. Ahmed looked, as he had since Hajii's death, like he was made of stone, eyes dry, anguished. He put his arm firmly around Andrea. As the grave was being covered with soil, Andrea felt a compulsion to step into it, to go with Hajii; my Afghan little boy, my Hajii.

Ahmed tightened his hold on her and whispered, "I love you." Andrea looked directly at him for the first time that day; her heartbreak was mirrored in his eyes.

The ceremony was finished. Andrea realized Ahmed was speaking to her in the gentlest of tones. "Andrea, did you see Nuria and the children from Kabul School?"

"No–oh, Ahmed, come with me."

They walked over to the children from Kabul School and Narda's school; the children were solemn, tearful. Nuria said, "We are all so sorry about Hajii–we loved him–may Allah be with him, and with you."

Andrea thanked them, giving them all hugs. "Hajii would be very glad you came."

Rashid invited all to share a meal at the compound; it was a quiet occasion. Finally all was over.

Everyone was gone; there was only family left. Andrea and Ahmed stayed in the courtyard with Sadiq, who, after holding his tears back in front of the mourners, could no longer control his sorrow. Thoughts of his twin brother and the mine exploding on that hill felt like knives piercing his heart over and over; he sobbed uncontrollably. With his grief came guilt.

He turned away from his mother, looked at his father and cried out, "I let Hajii die; I am the cause of his death, I should have stopped him, I should have stopped him, I knew he shouldn't have gone a different way…it's my fault, I am evil, I've killed my brother…may Allah punish me!" He could not stop crying.

Ahmed stood in front of him and shouted, "Sadiq, stop that this instant! Hajii's death was no fault of yours. You are not to blame. You told him not to go; he went anyway. You couldn't have stopped him. It all happened too quickly for anyone to do anything. Now stop it–stop your crying, stop your ranting. I am ordering you, now!"

Sadiq stopped. He had never seen his father in such a rage and he felt a fear of Ahmed for the first time in his life.

Ahmed looked at him darkly, then put his arms around him, "You and I will say prayers." Sadiq started to kneel, but Ahmed said, "No, not here, we will go to the mosque." He took Sadiq's hand; they left as Andrea and Abdullah watched.

"Oh, Abdullah, I've never seen Ahmed so angry. Will they be all right?"

"Sadiq needs his father now."

Andrea sat down on the lion bench and cried. Abdullah sat with her and asked, "Is there any comfort I can give you, my dear?"

Andrea welcomed his affectionate embrace, but...didn't he understand? "There is no comfort; oh, Abdullah, I know you mean well, but...Hajii was all alone...if only I could have...I didn't even get to talk to him before...I just gave them both a kiss as they were leaving...I thought they going to the clinic to help out..."

"I'm glad your mother is here."

"Yes...oh Abdullah, I can't stand it..."

"You must, for yourself, for Ahmed, for your family, all of us. Hajii would want nothing less. We will hold one another close. Life here is hard, Andrea; we must accept the will of Allah. In time you will understand."

"But this...this is...nothing can fix this, my Hajii's gone, my beautiful, strong boy–oh, God."

They sat, Abdullah holding Andrea's hand, Andrea crying quietly until she felt a small sense of peace. Abdullah's words were not comforting, but they gave her a strength she knew would be needed. It was her turn to feel the agony of so many Afghan mothers whose children had been destroyed by war.

Ahmed and Sadiq returned, tired, drained of emotion, calm. Sadiq went to his mother's side and hugged her. "Mother, I'm sorry for the things I said. I'm going to help you; I'll make Hajii proud."

"Oh, Sadiq, you're a good boy; I love you," she whispered as she held him tight.

Ahmed said, "Andrea, come in the house."

But she could not bring herself to go in yet; Hajii should be there, whispering, plotting with Sadiq their newest adventure. She would hear them and tap on their door to say, "Go to sleep, boys. You have lessons tomorrow." She sat in the dark oblivious to the icy air.

"Andrea," called Ahmed. She didn't answer; he walked out to the lion bench and found her, silent and shivering. He put his *patou* around her shoulders. "Come in, my darling. Would you like a cup of tea?"

Andrea gave a wry laugh. "I always wanted coffee; now I want tea. Yes, will you have a glass with me?"

"Of course." He kissed her; they entered the house, had their tea, and went to bed.

In the months that followed, she was driven to clean and scrub; it became a compulsion she could not stop. She took long showers, even as the hot water turned to cold, scrubbing her skin in a fury to wash away the pain.

Wenonah stayed close to her, often holding her and murmuring "Hush, baby, you'll be all right," and singing old Indian chants. And Ahmed and Andrea held one another every night without making love. Eight months–they had sex a few times, but it was tense and awkward. Though Ahmed tried to make love to her, she had no interest in anything except trying to be a good mother to her children. Sex took more effort than she could manage; life became a robotic routine of work and more work, assuming a pattern that made her too tired to do anything at day's end except sleep.

Then one morning, Ahmed heard music, singing–it was Andrea, singing; what a beautiful sound to his ears. Her music had been silent for almost a year. When Andrea found herself singing in the shower she knew something had changed. The precious water cascaded down her body, warm and cleansing, as she drifted into a favorite memory–Ahmed dancing with her, telling her he liked this music. The melody was sweet; it was country; it was Western; she saw the scene clearly, heard the song–"Lonestar." Singing the wistful words, she was surrounded by the calm joy of another time. Arizona. Sunshine and music rushed through her as she sang, and the water washed away her pain. But it was cold water now. The other world disappeared and Ahmed opened the door, turning off the water, wrapping her in towels. He wasn't angry or alarmed as she expected.

He just smiled and said, "I remember that we danced to that music at Paloma."

Andrea felt warm rivulets of desire flooding her body. Would he want her after being denied for so long? Suppose he refused her? That evening after prayers, she bathed with the lavender oil harvested from her garden. When she entered their bedroom, Ahmed was asleep. She looked at the face that always held her spellbound, then kissed him. Ahmed opened his eyes, studying her.

"Are you trying to seduce me?"

Andrea smiled. "I'm trying; will I be successful?" He answered, "Do you really want to be?"

Her guilt overcame her as she cried, "Ahmed, I'm sorry, I'm sorry. I need you."

At the same time Ahmed started making love to her, he started to cry. Tears overflowed like the river overflowing its banks, unstoppable; they fell softly onto Andrea's breasts as the two murmured a rush of phrases to one another. Words of grief, loss, and love, it was a mutual confession; trying to barricade themselves from the pain of losing Hajii had not worked. Now, Andrea's tentative overtures to Ahmed, and Ahmed's tears creeping into her pores, reminded them of the healing power of their love.

The next morning she made a Western omelet, a favorite among the few American meals she prepared, serving it with *naan* and fresh fruit. Her family rejoiced at the change in Andrea–gone was the heaviness of inconsolable grief. Coffee cup in hand, she walked into the parlor and sat on the *toshak*, gazing at the rain, just a shower really, not enough for the hungry earth, but enough to satisfy her garden. Hands wrapped around the hot cup, she became lost in the music set at a low volume on the CD player; it filled her heart with joy. The rich voice was intoxicating as ever–the music had not been played since Hajii's death. Andrea's eyes filled with tears; then she heard Ahmed's footsteps behind her. His lips as he kissed her were soft and gentle.

"Tears still?"

Eyes shining, she smiled. "Tears of happiness." Wenonah came in from the garden and saw the two of them–she knew it was time to go home to Arizona and her father.

Every member of the family would carry the pain of Hajii's death; for Andrea, there was a difference. This morning was the beginning of her acceptance of Allah's will. Holding hands, Andrea and Ahmed walked out into the garden that Wenonah had diligently cared for these past months and Andrea had avoided. The pungent scent of herbs mixed with a sweeter aroma drew her into a place she had rejected in her misery. And there it was, her garden, a sanctuary of quiet gray and green foliage, soft colors and a vivid splash of purple–the petunias Ahmed had brought her; a rare bit of rain had fallen to quench their thirst, a bright, hot sun coaxed them into bloom. She shed a few tears at having abandoned the garden, for having abandoned God when she could have found him here. But would she have welcomed him in those dark months? A long awaited peace settled itself in her soul; this is Allah's garden, this is where I am nearest to God and Hajii.

Ahmed stood looking up in the direction of the cave his sons explored in search of treasure, and let out a long sigh. "I wanted to protect them, I wanted to protect them," he said, repeating the words until she put her hand on his mouth.

"I know that, Ahmed, and you did everything right, just as you've always done–please don't punish yourself." She looked in his sad eyes, feeling the hardness of his life. "My sweet Afghan–you have nothing to feel guilty about. It's the way life is, everywhere."

"Land mines are not everywhere."

"No, but there are dangers everywhere–you know that."

"I've tried to get rid of those accursed mines; oh Andrea, sometimes I wish…"

"Shhh…everything will be all right. Hajii is with Allah. I feel it so strongly here in the garden." She pointed out the patch of purple.

"Oh, sweetie, look–your petunias are blooming, aren't they beautiful!"

Ahmed saw them and said, "Yes, I think I'll get you some blue ones, or red, or all the colors they come in."

She kissed him and said, "That would be perfect," and gave silent thanks to Allah for this healing place.

It was time to keep his promise made long ago to the doctor who cared for him at Bagram. Dr. Fitzsimmons was no longer in Afghanistan, having left for North Carolina and his private practice; a tape would be sent to him. The air base, still under American command, was part of a small, continuing U.S. presence in Afghanistan. Now the Americans made a difficult request of Ahmed.

"We would be grateful if you would permit your wife to contribute in a small way to a ceremony in honor of our servicemen and the Afghan people who gave their lives to help this country."

The request, under ordinary circumstances, would be reasonable, if unorthodox, but the timing was bad–almost a year to the day that Hajii died.

"Oh, Ahmed, I don't think I can do it."

"I know you can, " Ahmed said. "It would be appropriate."

"For Hajii?" she asked.

"Yes."

Andrea stood still, her arms at her sides, body rigid, head bowed. As the music started, she tried to sing, but no sound came. Agonized, uncertain, she looked back at Ahmed standing on the side in full Afghan dress and turban, and shook her head as if to say no, I can't do it. He had been waiting, ready to help. When he saw her falter, he walked on stage and stood behind her, arms around her, and Andrea found her voice. As long as he held her, she could do it. With hands clasped firmly over hers, he stood with her; the song was a powerful story of loss and grief for those struck down in violence and hate. The sight of the beautiful American with her Afghan husband supporting her in their own loss, singing for the American/Afghan audience a tribute to fallen comrades and loved ones, was a unique moment in this ever discordant land. It saddened, yet lifted their spirits, holding Afghan and American together in a jumbled patchwork of souls.

Hajii lived in their hearts; each sibling had special memories of their brother–Hajii's quick flash of anger, then loud laughter at the jokes played on him by Hamid, Hajii's encouragement and tough advice to Laura about breaking in Nishka. Hajii's death created a vacuum that would never be filled. He was the noisiest, most vocal of their four children, a non-stop talker; even when they prepared for prayer, his father would admonish him, "Hajii, quiet, tell me about it later!" Sadiq's sense of loss was unique. He had lost his other self; his healing would take a long time. But time and tragedy passed, life went on even as it seemed it should stop.

# XX. Only the Earth Endures

*Indians dance*
*To honor the land*
*For only the earth endures.*

Her mother's call came a few minutes after Andrea returned from school. The news about her grandfather was sad but not surprising. Jack Redbird was tired. The old Apache had outlasted most of his contemporaries, and his long, active life was ending. At ninety-eight, he was ready to meet the Great Spirit. Andrea hung up the phone, thinking about her grandfather, and about Hajii. Six years had passed since Hajii's death, a tragedy burned into her soul, gentled by time. That evening she sat on the lion bench in meditative prayer, breathing in the sweetness of the garden. Ahmed came out to sit beside her, giving her a comforting hug.

"I think it's time for a visit to the land of Cochise. We'll talk with your grandfather once more."

Ahmed allowed Laura to travel with them to Arizona after much pleading; he wanted her to stay in Afghanistan, in the hope she would accept an arranged marriage to her cousin, Sayeed. But that was not to be–Sayeed himself was not receptive to the arrangement, and Laura had other things on her mind. Her mother's stories of the ranch, the Apaches, and life in America had excited her since she was a little girl; now she was twenty years old, with an incandescent beauty and a taste for danger, and America, not Afghanistan, seemed like the perfect exotic adventure.

Jack Redbird had aged well. He looked well, certainly not like one about to die, but Andrea knew he had decided to do just that. When he saw Laura, he smiled.

"You are like your mother, a wild one. Do you talk to horses?"

"Yes, grandfather, I talk to my Ali all the time; I tell him my secrets."

"Ahhh...will you stay here in Arizona?"

"I hope to." At the look on her father's face, she added, "at least for a while." Wenonah took her granddaughter outside, allowing Andrea and Ahmed some time with Jack. Their conversation was warm and lively, comforting and sad.

"Your daughter is maybe a little too much like you, Andrea. Ahmed, you are worried she may want to stay here; I think you will have to let her go, but she'll come back to you."

"Grandfather, you're so wise, it's not time..."

Jack Redbird moved back and forth slowly in his old rocking chair. "You know better, Andrea, and so does your husband. I'm pleased to see the two of you; Andrea made the right decision."

There was a twinkle in his eye as he told her, "Don't forget Wovoka's command, 'All Indians must dance, everywhere, keep on dancing,' Indians weren't smart enough in Geronimo's time; now they're making money, still not too smart!" He laughed, and grew meditative. "Maybe some day, Indian president!" and he laughed again, much amused by such an image. Now he was tired; Ahmed saw it was time to leave. Andrea kissed her grandfather.

"'Til we meet again."

"Yes," he said, falling asleep.

Wrapped in a blanket, his body was placed in a sacred burial ground in the White Mountains. They sprinkled ashes and pollen in a circle around his grave so he might have a safe journey to heaven. Wenonah rejoiced for her father and wept for herself, knowing how much she would miss his commonsense wisdom, his humor, his comfort when she felt sad. But she had her granddaughter with her until they made the journey back to Afghanistan; Laura's first wish was to see the ranch where her mother grew up. Andrea decided not to go with them to Paloma. Ahmed understood her decision, though he found it difficult to explain to Laura.

Wenonah simply told Laura, "Your mother promised to do a few things for me here at the house. She'll go back to Paloma some day."

True or not, Laura accepted Wenonah's explanation, and Ahmed, Wenonah, and Laura made the trip to Paloma.

Andrea called out as they were leaving, "Say hello to the boys for me, and to Maria!" She went back into the house, breathing in Jack Redbird's aura, admiring her mother's Apache artifacts. Playing a Santana CD, she walked into the garden and started to dance. *I need a glass of wine; I saw some in the fridge.* Ah, yes. California red wine. She took it out into the garden, setting it on the table while she danced. Wild music, wild dance. I'll always need a wild place, she thought, and a wild man–she started laughing at herself. *Oh you're silly, Andrea, you're getting too old for…no, I'm not, I'm just right, I'm okay. God, how I love my Ahmed and I love this land.* She raised her glass; this one's for you, grandfather. *I'll dance forever, into Paradise.*

Ahmed returned the next night, without Wenonah and Laura. Andrea was surprised he had agreed that Laura could stay in Arizona until his mother-in-law brought her back to Afghanistan.

"I don't know what Laura will do next," he complained.

"Come to bed, Ahmed, don't worry about it." He felt her restlessness during the night. Was she cold?

"What is it, my love?"

"Dream," she mumbled.

He whispered into her ear, "What wild tale is your imagination weaving now?"

She sat up, awake. "A beautiful vision." Ahmed surrendered to the night–his wife's sensuality made magic real. Kissing her, he asked, "What is your vision?"

"Umm, mountains, volcanoes, palm trees, sandy beaches, sky-blue water in gentle waves, tropical colors drifting into one another. I feel warm sunshine, I hear music–Caribbean, African…"

"Then that's where we'll go; we'll play on your sandy beach, dance to the music, and make love." She responded to his caresses, laughing at the fantasy.

"Perfect."

They said goodbye to Wenonah and Laura–"Obey your grandmother, and help her with the work in the house and garden; remember, you cannot spend all your time riding horses or talking to those cowboys; they have their work to do. Be very kind to your grandmother, don't wait for her to ask you to do something. You must go ahead and do the things you know need to be done."

"Oh, Papa, I know that. Don't worry about me, I'll be good," she said, laughing at her father.

"And we'll see you in July!" Her careless answer to his speech was not reassuring. When he turned and saw Andrea smiling at him, he felt foolish to be lecturing a daughter he knew was nothing but kind and good-hearted.

"Well, she is a little impulsive."

"Oh I know, sweetie, but she'll be all right."

She touched his arm in a comforting gesture. They knew their daughter would soon go her own way.

# XXI. Buttercup Days

Back to Afghanistan, back home. They were greeted by Abdullah and Hamid, who explained Sadiq was not able to leave his post at Kandahar.

"I can't understand why he wants a career in the military after so much..."

Hamid stopped, afraid he had said the wrong thing to his mother. But Andrea understood; she knew Sadiq had soldiering in his blood. She had once told Abdullah, half joking, "My poor kids–they inherited some pretty violent genes."

"No, Andrea," he replied, "they're intelligent; they know how to make good choices."

Hamid would soon be getting his degree; an architect! A happy pride crept through her as she looked at her curly haired, green-eyed son. He was a strong, handsome man. Oh, God, she thought, he must be attractive to many women. I hope he picks the right one. She forgot she had not been the "right" one, according to Afghan standards.

Chicken Street in Kabul–Andrea and Abdullah approached the carpet seller's stall. Just as she turned to ask a question, a shot exploded. She saw Abdullah fall, saw the tall man behind him look into her eyes, and knew the enemy. "Only one man knows Abdullah and he's not here..." The sentence uttered so long ago penetrated her consciousness instantly. His surprise at seeing her gun raised to kill caused a second's hesitation on his part, a second too late.

"You son of a bitch," she shouted, stepped forward, aimed at his chest and fired, killing him on the spot. Bedlam followed. Andrea heard loud shouts, frantic voices, one of which was her own. She seemed to be two people, one an observer, the other a hysterical woman calling out, "Help me, help me get him to the hospital!"

As the crowd closed around Abdullah and herself, she heard a calm, firm voice saying, "Do not move him; an ambulance is on its way." She looked up and saw a young bearded Afghan with a medical bag–a doctor?

"I am Dr. Hussein, please give me room." His eyes went to Andrea's gun. "You'd better put that away." She was unaware it was still in her hand; what did it matter? But she returned it to the holster, and looked at him with glazed, shocked eyes.

"Please don't let him die. Oh, God, Abdullah, can you hear me? I'm praying for you, and a doctor is caring for you. Hold on, Abdullah, you'll be in the hospital soon."

Dr. Hussein said, "He's asking for Ahmed."

"Oh, my God–Ahmed–I've got to call him."

Before she could make the call, Ahmed was there; as soon as he heard about the shooting, he raced to the scene at breakneck speed. The ambulance was there, police were trying to keep an angry throng of men away from the dead assassin, and Andrea was by Abdullah's side.

She burst into tears when she saw him; he ran to her, asking, "What happened? Abdullah, I'm here, you'll be all right."

The young doctor said, "Please meet us at the hospital." Andrea and Ahmed saw the dead man being taken away by police as they started on their way to the hospital, Andrea crying uncontrollably.

"I'm sorry, Ahmed, I'll…be all right…oh God, please let Abdullah live…oh God… "

"You've nothing to be sorry for, Andrea. Any responsibility is mine. Abdullah will be all right; I'm sure of it."

Abdullah lived. The doctors removed the bullet from his back, a difficult operation because of the risk of damage to the spinal cord. The waiting was long and tense; after an hour or so, Andrea could hardly stand the strain of it. At last the doctor appeared with good news–Abdullah had survived the surgery and would make a slow recovery. The tension lifted, but Andrea's question had to be answered.

"Who was that man? Was he the one you referred to as the one who knew Abdullah?"

"You remembered that?"

"Yes, it stuck in my mind; I always thought it was strange."

"The man you shot was Alamdar. His brother, Abdul, was the one who assassinated my parents."

"And Abdullah–he killed Abdul?"

"Yes, he avenged my parents' deaths; neither Rashid nor I did what Abdullah was able to do."

"Both of you were too young! Alamdar was trying to avenge his brother's death by killing Abdullah?–oh Ahmed, this revenge thing, it's…" He stopped her.

"I renounced it years ago, but it remains part of…" he gestured to indicate a hopelessness that left him unwilling to speak of the often deadly principle.

"And I continued it, killing that man…but…"

"You had no choice; he would have killed you."

"He was about to kill me, I saw it in his eyes."

"Yes."

It seemed the primitive cycle of violence would never spare Afghanistan, or mankind. I never wanted to be part of it, Andrea told herself; all I wanted was to dance–and sing. Oh really, laughed the voice inside–you didn't love the feeling of triumph when the gunfire missed you, the thrill of victory when you killed, the excitement of risking life and limb climbing impossible mountains–or the thing most dangerous of all, loving and living with a man who could control you, in a country of barely civilized tribes. All right, all right, she yelled silently to the impish voice, maybe I should just thank Patrick for his training and be done with it.

When Ahmed saw Abdullah after the surgery, he said, "Abdullah, forgive me, forgive me."

Weak and tired, Abdullah replied, "There is nothing to forgive."

"I didn't keep him close, I should have tracked him more carefully."

"And I grew careless. It's over, Ahmed, praise be to Allah. Now let me see Andrea." Andrea came to Abdullah's bedside and kissed him.

"I'm so glad…you're going to be fine…"

"Thank you, Andrea, for all you did. Are you all right, my dear?"

"Yes."

Voice growing faint, he fell into a much needed sleep. The inquiry was a formality; those who witnessed the event were clear in their stories of what happened. Wenonah and Laura would arrive in a couple of days; Wenonah would take good care of her friend.

Through the years, Andrea had inspired a myriad of emotions in Afghans–awe, admiration, respect, love, suspicion, fear. To many of them, she was too American; to Americans, she was too Afghan–trapped in the no man's land of the mixed breed. On a certain slope near a certain cave, be it Afghanistan or Arizona, she still heard the flutes that Wenonah claimed never to have heard, but Wenonah felt blessed; she had her daughter back, a daughter who passed on to her children tales of the Apaches, who kept in her Afghan home, in a place of honor, a painting of her grandfather on his favorite horse, in full Apache ceremonial dress. Life was good. If only Hajii…it was not to be.

Ahmed walked with his arm around Andrea through the peach orchard, inhaling the spicy scent of ripened peaches; they luxuriated in the warmth of the summer sun. Safe and peaceful. Andrea stopped, lifting her lips to his. Ahmed kissed her.

"My darling, what's making you so happy today?"

"Oh, sunshine after a rain shower, that little grove of young oaks across the river, the taste of a ripe peach, lunch with our friend Raheem, and…let's see, oh yes, a kiss from my sweet Afghan!"

He gazed at his wife's beautiful face, older now than nineteen, just as appealing as the child she was.

He smiled, "It's good to be in love at nineteen, yes? Even better when you are approaching fifty; I love you more each passing year!"

"You're making me old before my time, but I agree!" She gave him a familiar sly smile. "At least I know how to make love as skillfully as your Parisian teacher!"

They laughed together at the memories. As they walked on, Ahmed felt a sharp sadness, a momentary tightening of his chest, a faint pain in his head–Hajii. The first to be born–the first to die. But Allah has blessed us; so many lost everything. He saw Andrea, so young, so wild and obstinate, and smiled at the memory of her at nineteen, with Buttercup.

"Andrea, why would a cowgirl from Arizona name a horse Buttercup?"

What made him think of that? She frowned, hesitating to answer, then replied, "He was named for the poem my father used to read to me when I was six years old–Buttercup Days."

"Ah, now I understand."

Three weeks later on a hilltop in the Panjshir Valley, Hamid was about to warn the pretty girl sitting near him when the Afghan wind abruptly sent an angry cloud of its fury into her eyes and nose, choking her.

Hamid ordered, "Put your scarf over your face!" The American exchange student stood paralyzed by the swirling wind and dust. "Here, I'll help you." Hamid covered her face up to the eyes with her scarf.

She struggled to hide her fear of this wild place, forcing herself to be calm; finally the wind subsided, and she looked up at Hamid, asking, "What is this crazy game called?"

His gaze was riveting; green eyes boring into hers, he growled, "*Buzkashi!*"

## The Reluctant Prophet

In a dream she said to him,
We've bridged our own divide
But how can all of us reach the highest mountain
And overcome the chaos of our time?

Why my dear Roxana, he answered,
By the divine grace that forces all
To climb one painful step after another
Until we reach the summit.

Such a long time, sighed Roxana.

## The End